A Good Year for the Roses

A NOVEL

Gil McNeil

HYPERION

NEW YORK

Hyperion
Hachette Book Group
237 Park Avenue
New York, NY 10017

www.HachetteBookGroup.com

Printed in the United States of America

RRD-C

First Edition: July 2014
10 9 8 7 6 5 4 3 2 1

Hyperion is a division of Hachette Book Group, Inc.

Library of Congress Cataloging-in-Publication Data

McNeil, Gil, 1959-
A good year for the roses : a novel / Gil McNeil.
pages cm
ISBN 978-1-4013-4191-6 (pbk.) — ISBN 978-1-4013-3070-5 (ebook)
I. Title.
PR6113.C58G77 2014
823'.92—dc23

2013047427

For Joe

Contents

A Good Year for the Roses

CHAPTER ONE

In the Bleak Midwinter

October

Alba Roses

An ancient variety which dates back to Greek and Roman times, these are the toughest of all the Old Roses. With elegant grey-green foliage, the flowers have a delicate tissue-paper quality in a range of soft pinks and whites, and a purity and clarity of fragrance, often with hints of citrus. Notable examples include Maiden's Blush, a gentle marshmallow-pink rose with a refined sweet scent; Belle Amour, a strong coral pink with a rich myrrh fragrance; and the creamy white Jacobite Rose, with a lingering sweet-citrus scent, which was also known as the White Rose of York during the Wars of the Roses.

It's Thursday morning and I'm trying to make packed lunches for the boys as quietly as possible so nobody wakes up before I've had my second cup of tea. Both Ben and Alfie are still young enough to surface early, but there could be a brass band going at full pelt in the living room and Dan would stay asleep. At thirteen he's definitely doing the teening thing now, and he'd be completely nocturnal if left to his own devices. It's absolutely bloody typical of the wonderful world of motherhood—you spend the first ten years trying to get the little sods to sleep, and the next ten trying to wake them up. The only guaranteed way to rouse him nowadays is flicking water on him—although only when his brothers aren't watching, since I go for light droplets from the toothbrush mug in the bathroom, whereas Ben would opt for the shower on full jet, if he could work out a way to get it to reach that far. I caught him trying to bring the hosepipe in from the garden last week, and Alfie thinks his plastic pirate chest would be the perfect water carrier, and it's huge. Mind you, there might come a morning when a giant pirate chest full of cold water is exactly what I need, so I'm not ruling it out.

I'm enjoying picturing the total immersion of my firstborn, when the phone rings. Great. Bang goes my attempt at a quiet half hour.

"Oh good, you're up."

"Morning Mum."

"Are you about to set off?"

"Not yet. I've got to get the boys to school first."

"Yes, but you know how upset your father gets."

Bloody hell, she's ringing me at seven a.m. to remind me that Dad likes people to be punctual.

"I'll be there as soon as I can Mum."

"Don't forget to bring something smart for the funeral will you?"

"I've got my black trouser suit."

"You used to have some lovely black skirts when you worked at the hotel."

"That was nearly twenty years ago Mum, when I was a student. And Dad hated them because they were too short."

"I know, but—"

"I know he's on a one-man mission against trouser suits Mum but I'm a big girl now, I can wear what I like."

She sighs, and I feel guilty, like I always do. She'll be sitting in her dressing gown in the kitchen, looking tired. Family gatherings always reduce her to a nervous wreck long before anyone arrives.

"The only suit I've got with a skirt is navy blue Mum, and that doesn't seem right for a funeral. And I can't afford to buy something new just because Dad thinks I can't wear trousers for formal occasions. And by the way, if he goes into a trouser tirade later on, you could always remind him they're good enough for Princess Anne. She was on the news last night, on an official visit somewhere, with no horses in sight, and she was still wearing trousers, so that's got to count as a formal occasion, what with her being royalty and everything, don't you think?"

Dad has always had a soft spot for Princess Anne and her I-may-be-a-Royal-but-I-can-still-swear-at-photographers approach to regal life. Actually, if I could channel my inner Princess Anne, I'm sure my life would be vastly improved—and I could get my horse to kick people if they were being annoying, so it would be win-win all the way. But the last time I was on a horse, I fell off, so maybe not.

"I'm sure it'll be fine Mum."

"Well, I just hope you're warm enough. It's been bitter here the last few days. Georgina bought a lovely new suit with a matching coat, and it's got a sort of quilted lining. She says she can lend you something if you like. Wasn't that kind?"

Charming. Lend your rejects to the newly divorced sister-in-law. Particularly ones with quilted linings. How selfless.

"Thanks Mum, but tell her I don't need to borrow anything, would you, or she'll try to give me stuff I don't want, like last time."

"You'll see her yourself, at supper tonight."

"Okay."

Bugger. I'd forgotten Roger and Georgina would be around this evening. So not only do I have to sit through supper with my annoying brother and his stupid wife, but I have to thank her for offering to lend me items from her wardrobe which I wouldn't be seen dead in, not least because they're bound to be at least three sizes too small. What a huge treat.

"I thought I'd make a shepherd's pie, and Georgina's making a pudding."

"Great."

So that'll be two raspberries each and a teaspoonful of sorbet. Georgina's always on a diet, since her only real passion in life is buying clothes in smaller and smaller sizes. She's got more outfits than anyone else I know apart from Lola. But Lola's my best friend, and she buys the kind of things you instantly covet, whereas Georgina prefers fussy little suits with shiny buttons and hideous sparkly evening wear. She keeps all her shoes in special boxes with photos on the front so she never has to search for a cerise satin sandal or a navy court shoe. It's like an alternate universe: Barbie meets Imelda Marcos, but with a posh accent. Most mornings I'm lucky if I can find two shoes that match. I did the school run last week wearing one black loafer and one navy. I had to stay in the car and then belt home to change, so nobody would think I was having some kind of post-divorce breakdown. And Georgina always has immaculate makeup, even at breakfast. She's like one of those women who squirt unsolicited perfume at you in department stores—always a shade too orange—with slightly manic smiles plastered on their faces. Sometimes I wonder if she's secretly signed up to a postmodern version of *The Stepford Wives*. She'll probably be getting a hostess trolley next.

Mum is running me through the list of ingredients for her shepherd's pie, as if I'm the kind of nutter who really wants to debate whether King Edwards or Maris Pipers are the perfect potatoes for mash at ten past seven in the bloody morning.

"Are they bringing Henry and Alicia with them tomorrow?"

Georgina isn't a hands-on mother, and Roger's hopeless too, so it's quite hard to warm to their kids. They've both been packed off to the local prep school practically since they could walk, so they're that lethal combination of snooty and spoilt and not very bright, which private schools seem to specialise in. Good table manners, but such a strong sense of entitlement, you almost want to slap them just to see the look on their faces.

"No, they'll be at school, and Roger says their education has to come first. I do worry about Roger you know—he works so hard."

He bloody doesn't, he spends most of his time playing golf in between annoying all the staff at the hotel, who get on far better when he's not around. The hotel's been in the family for three generations now, and was a much happier place when Granddad was in charge, by all accounts. Even Dad was less useless and bossy than Roger, who likes to patrol round in the evenings, steadily getting drunker and drunker and playing the genial host, and then falling asleep in the office behind Reception. In fact he passes out so regularly that the staff have taken to calling him "Roger and Out."

"Is he still finding time to play lots of golf?"

"Yes, but don't forget he's on the committee this year, so he has to be there as much as he can, and your father thinks he's got a good chance of becoming captain next year."

God, he'll be even more unbearable if he becomes captain.

I bet he'll get a special jacket, and wear it all the time. He'll probably get a second one to sleep in. Dad will be thrilled though—he's been trying to get Roger to the dizzy heights of captaincy for years.

"That's great Mum. Look, I better go so I'm ready to leave on time."

"Well drive safely love, and we'll expect you around lunchtime shall we?"

"Teatime Mum. I told you yesterday, there's no way I can get from South London to Devon in three hours, not unless I hire a helicopter, and we know what happened last time—he ended up covered in mud."

"That wasn't Roger's fault Molly, you know that."

"I'll see you later Mum."

It bloody well was his fault. He was determined we needed a helicopter landing spot at the hotel, to attract a better class of clientele. Even though the hotel's managed to survive perfectly well without guests arriving by air, apart from the RAF pilot who parachuted onto the roof of the kitchen during the War—we've still got his photograph up behind the bar. Granddad invited his squadron to dinner and there's a picture of them all raising a glass. Apparently they drank the bar dry that night, and one of the waitresses went missing for three days. But when Dad took over he went for a bit less of the jolly host approach than Granddad. And now Roger's in charge, he's determined to go upmarket, or what he thinks is upmarket, which seems to mean hiking up the pricings, painting everything taupe, and serving amuse-bouche before dinner. Nobody ever arrives by helicopter, apart from wedding parties with more money than sense. Last autumn a groom opted for the airborne option, and Roger insisted on giving himself a central Air Command role, putting on the orange jacket ready to supervise the landing, but then he stood in the wrong place, and nearly got blown off the cliffs by the downdraft. He ended up facedown in the rough grass by the tennis courts, covered in mud and leaves. The staff were so pleased they practically put the Jubilee bunting back up in Reception.

I finish making sandwiches and try not to think about how much I'm dreading today. Apart from driving all the way to Devon and listening to Roger bang on about becoming captain while I try to resist the temptation to stab him with my fork, it's the funeral tomorrow. Helena's funeral. And Helena and Bertie are the only two people in my whole family I actually like, apart from Mum, and she's definitely getting worse. She's spent so long pandering to Dad, she's a nervous wreck. She practically quivers when he goes into one of his rants now. You're longing for her to show some glimmer of disapproval, but she never does—unlike Helena, who never stood for any nonsense. Bertie can be pretty stalwart too, and since he's Mum's older brother, Dad's usually a bit muted when he's around. But Helena was the one who was in charge of everything, she used to take Mum out for a tour round the garden if Dad was in one of his moods. She even walked out of a family lunch once, when he was banging on about something—I can't remember what. She simply stood up and said he was giving her a headache and she'd rather be out in the garden than listen to him being so boorish. He went bright red, and nobody spoke on the drive home. It was brilliant.

I so wanted to be like Helena when I grew up I even practised doing my hair in a bun, like she did. She was so wonderful, and now I'm going to her funeral. The perfect end to a perfect year, and it'll be Christmas next and I haven't got a single present yet.

I only just managed to pull off Ben's birthday last week after a frantic last-minute present-buying frenzy, where I spent far too much money. But eleven is a tricky age for birthdays—young enough to still want balloons and cake, but old enough to want something more grown-up than party games. We had a cinema-and-pizza party in the end: fifteen eleven-year-olds in the dark, with popcorn and ice cream. God knows what I was thinking, but I pity the poor people who got our seats for the next screening. And now we've bypassed the mellow fruitfulness of autumn and gone straight into freezing October fog and belting rain. All the shops are full of tinsel, and if I don't sort something out in the next few weeks when the sale of this house goes through, Mary and Joseph won't be the only ones looking at stables as a possible venue for Christmas lunch. And to top it all I've got the funeral of the person I liked most in my entire family. And I'm not allowed to wear trousers. Dear God.

"Mum?"

Bugger. Alfie's up.

"Yes love?"

"Can I have bacon?"

"No, it's a school morning Alfie. It's cereal today."

"I need bacon, I really do."

He's still half-asleep, with his hair sticking up in tufts and his pyjamas on inside out.

"What happened to your PJs love?"

"They were itchy, so I turned them round. That was very clever, wasn't it Mum?"

"Yes love. Do you want apple juice or milk?"

Please let him not start wearing all his clothes inside out. School mornings are tricky enough already.

"Orange."

"Orange what?"

He grins.

"Juice."

"Alfie."

"Please. Orange juice, please."

"That's better. I might make toast and honey?"

He claps, which makes me smile. It's always nice to get a round of applause first thing in the morning.

"Can I have cartoons?"

"Yes, but only for half an hour, and very quietly."

He skips off into the living room. It really doesn't take much to make your morning perfect when you're six. Despite all sorts of dramas going on around you, if there's still toast and honey, and clandestine cartoons, everything is right with the world. Perhaps I should try to channel my inner six-year-old rather than my Princess Anne—I've got a much better chance of pulling that off, although I'm not sure kids do that well with Peter Pan parents busy trying to pretend they're not grown-ups. It's hard enough to navigate adolescence without your parents sharing your tastes in music and wearing the same clothes, and they've got enough to cope with after the divorce.

After the initial shock and humiliation of discovering Pete had been having an affair, it's the only thing I really mind about: how the boys will feel about it all. So far it's been fine—more than fine, if I'm honest. It feels like there's much more room for everyone without Pete sitting at the head of the table dominating everything, giving us all lectures about the importance of good table manners, while our food went cold. Making everything about Him, and banging on about the proper way to behave. Things are so much calmer now, we've recalibrated our family life over the past year, and it's definitely an improvement, a real improvement. Which does beg the question what on earth was I doing treading water in a marriage that hadn't been working for ages, when everyone seems so much happier now that the divorce is over and our new family life is starting to emerge.

So that's one more thing to feel guilty about. If I'd been devastated or heartbroken, it would have been more in keeping somehow. I'd be the ubiquitous Good Wife dealt a cruel blow. But instead there was a quiet kind of relief about it all. And spending so many years just ticking along is definitely not what I was hoping for when I was twenty-three and getting married and the future seemed so shiny and full of promise. I can't work out when I turned into the maternal version of a tugboat, chugging along towing my flotilla of boys, carefully navigating around any potential tricky bits. But it does dent your confidence, realising you've chugged yourself right into dry dock. I was so busy keeping everything calm and quiet I hadn't spotted the captain was about to jump ship. I can't help thinking that with such a lack of skill at forecasting when something is about to go totally tits-up, I shouldn't really be left in charge of the average domestic appliance, let alone three growing boys. Someone with a clipboard will probably press the doorbell one morning soon and say "Seriously? Don't you think we should start you off with something a bit simpler, like a rabbit, and see how you get on?" So I'd better make sure I salvage something positive from the wreckage. A whole new family life, with more fun and less chugging along. Although possibly not today, what with the funeral and everything.

I take Alfie his toast, and receive another round of applause. I'm really going to miss this house, even though while I was using all my free time to redecorate, Pete was using his to have an affair with his school secretary. I'd just finished the dining room when he announced he wanted a divorce so he could marry Janice, with her high heels and little angora cardigans. Perky and petite. She collects glass animals—and other people's husbands, apparently. Still, she who laughs last laughs the longest.

Looking back, I can't quite pinpoint when Pete changed from the young radical who wanted to change the world into Peter, the headmaster of the kind of private school where the parents pay a small fortune in fees precisely to ensure that the world doesn't change at all, thank you very much. When I dropped the boys off in the park for their Sunday afternoon paternal moment last week, he was wearing a new jogging outfit, with Janice in a matching one, with a tiny pink vest. For a moment I hardly recognised him, he looked so different. I can't imagine any circumstances where we'd have gone jogging together. And not only because I often run into kids from my school when I'm out, and if they saw one of their teachers in a special jogging outfit, they'd just run along behind you, making comments. It gave me quite a jolt, realising just how much he'd changed. Jogging along, with a special new watch to measure his pulse, busy fretting about what canapés to serve to the parents at Musical Evenings, while I'm teaching at the local secondary school and trying to find new ways to engage the interest of fourteen-year-olds who couldn't really give a fuck about the causes of the First World War, although they can get you a new laptop at a bargain price whenever you want one. Still, it's not all bad; at least I don't have to take up jogging.

If I can just shake off the panic attacks and transform myself into a capable grown-up and find us somewhere to live, we'll be sorted. Houses I can afford with my half of the sale of this place are as rare as hen's teeth round here, and I don't want to move too far because Dan's just got into the only good local secondary school, where you don't have to pay or go to church for years to guarantee a place. It's remarkable how many local parents discover a previously hidden faith when their children are around eight, but as soon as they're eleven and safely in their secondary school of choice, they stop attending every Sunday. Perhaps if the Church would admit that half their regular congregations are only there for a good school place, or to arrange a wedding, they might spend a bit less time obsessing about women vicars and gay bishops and a bit more time trying to work out why most of the general population seem to regard their local Vicar as about as vital to modern life as a chocolate teapot. I'm almost tempted to write a letter to the Archbishop. But then again, I might need to start turning up every Sunday too if I can't find us a decent house nearby, so possibly not.

I could try asking Dad for a loan, which will make today even more of a treat. He gave Roger and Georgina a "loan" for thousands for their hideous new conservatory, full of horrible teak furniture and triffid-like foliage, and the biggest television I've ever clapped eyes on. But Roger is the firstborn, and the golden boy. And I'm . . . well, I'm not the golden girl, that's for sure. Not even bronze, especially if I'm wearing trousers. Talk about a Mission Impossible. And even if he does agree, I'll have to pay him back, so it won't exactly solve the problem, but it might be the only option unless we want to live in a caravan in someone's garden, maybe the grounds of Pete's school. I'm sure the Board of Governors would love that. I might suggest it next time I see him. I bet his pulse would go up a bit at the prospect of his ex-wife and three sons in a trailer by the tennis courts. His special new watch will probably go into meltdown.

I'm debating having another cup of tea versus waking up Dan and Ben, when the phone rings again. Mum probably wants to check what colour shoes I'm wearing. I must stop this, or I'll morph back into my teenage self, choosing outfits on the basis of what was likely to most annoy Dad. The pink-and-orange sari was a definite winner—it's a shame I don't still have it, or I could wear it for supper tonight. I'd probably get frostbite, but it would be worth it.

"Hi Mum."

"Sorry, darling. Just me. Is there fog in Devon? It's terrible in town. I can hardly see the end of my road."

Lola. Brilliant. A cup of tea and Lola, the perfect way to jump-start a tricky day.

"No, but they're forecasting freezing rain."

"What a treat."

"Mum's already been on the phone getting agitated, and it's going to take me hours to get there."

"And the wanker formerly known as your husband is having the boys tonight right?"

"Yes, in theory. Although I bet he leaves it all to Janice."

"And how is the lovely Janice?"

"Busy buying new dresses with matching jackets so she can look like a proper headmaster's wife. The ankle chain has gone, and so has her perky smile. But living with Pete will do that for you. Actually, I'm starting to feel a bit sorry for her."

"Sometimes I worry about you Molly Taylor, I really do. How can you possibly feel sorry for the woman who nicked your husband? I mean, granted you were thrilled someone was finally taking him off your hands, but seriously..."

"Not thrilled exactly Lola."

"Admit it darling."

"Well how tragic does that make me? We're all so much happier, it's like the whole house suddenly got lighter, especially at meals, without him lecturing us all like he was addressing a school assembly and leaning back in his chair and saying 'That was very nice, Molly,' like he was being polite to the domestic help. It used to make me want to pour custard over his head."

She laughs.

"Like there's ever any custard left at the end of meals at your house. And anyway, if you'd left him years ago you wouldn't have had Alfie, and he's my absolute best boy in the whole world."

Lola is fond of Dan and Ben, but she adores Alfie, and it's a mutual adoration which shows no signs of waning. He trots round after her looking devoted, and she buys him presents and takes him out for treats on his own, without his big brothers.

"How is my gorgeous boy?"

"Watching cartoons. Dan and Ben are still asleep, so he's king of the castle for a bit longer. Why are you up so early?"

"Aren't you impressed? It's my Pre–Festive Season Assault."

"On?"

"My tragic fucking life. I'll be in elasticated trousers by Christmas if I don't get a grip."

"They're comfy."

"'Comfy' is not the right look for killer agents darling. I saw Nigel Jones last night at a party, tottering around on six-inch heels in a black-leather miniskirt, trying to nick half my clients."

"You'd think he'd know better."

"She. Nigella. She calls herself Nigel so people won't think she's going to make them a tray of cupcakes and lick the spoon in a lascivious manner."

"Seems fair enough to me."

"Not if she's after my clients it bloody isn't."

"I can't see any of them having the nerve to leave you Lola, not really."

"You'd be surprised darling. They're like toddlers—leave them alone for a moment and they wander off in search of something new and shiny."

"Or paint the television screen bright green with finger paints."

"You're never going to get over that, are you? I was only on the phone for five minutes. Seriously. And it washed off, didn't it?"

"Eventually, yes."

"Well then, get over it. Alfie's a creative spirit—I've told you, that's why we get on so well. You need to encourage him. I've been thinking, maybe we should enroll him in art classes. I bet they do some great ones at the Tate."

"Do they have televisions you can paint?"

"Leave it to me. I'll get someone in the office to research where the best places are. Then we can go shopping afterwards. He's such a sweetie to take shopping."

"Not in the local supermarket he's not. He was having races up and down the aisles with Dan last time I took them. I nearly got thrown out."

"Sounds like fun. Anyway, back to special me. I've got so many events coming up it's enough to make a girl weep. I'll be so tinselled out by the time we get to Christmas I might have to shoot someone. Probably my mother. And that fucker Clive is in meltdown. He's way over budget on his latest shoot, and I'm supposed to magic up some more finance, even though they're practically sending him cash by the lorry load as it is. Nathan from the studio's ringing me every day whining about money. Talking of whining, how's Pete doing with the child support?"

"Late again, and he likes to be called Peter now. It's more fitting for a headmaster, apparently."

"I wish you'd let me hire a hit man."

"Can I get back to you on that?"

"Not if you're still planning on giving him half the money from the sale of the house, no you can't."

"It's what we agreed in the divorce. Apparently Janice needs to make lots of alterations to the Headmaster's House, to bring it up to her exacting standards."

"Can't be that exacting darling, given her taste in men. You should tell him he's got a free house with his job, so he can fuck right off. I still don't get why you have to sell."

"Because we agreed a fifty-fifty split and I can't afford to buy him out, but also because I think it will be good for us. If I can find somewhere I can afford, it'll be a new start. I've applied to go full-time at school, but all the budgets are being cut. Going part-time when I had Alfie was a big mistake you know."

"Yes darling, but you were knee-deep in small boys, so you didn't really have a choice did you?"

"I suppose not, but I can't afford anywhere round here on a part-time salary, especially anywhere with four bedrooms. Even three is out of my price range. I may have to sleep in the kitchen."

"What, like Cinderella? Please. Can't the boys share?"

"Are you mad? Nobody can share with Alfie, not unless they like sleeping covered in bits of Lego. And Ben can't share with Dan, they'd kill each other. Even Ben has his limits. No, I'd rather sleep under the sink in the scullery than have the three of them going tonto every half an hour, trust me. They were all so sweet when they were babies. I don't know what happened, apart from a maelstrom of testosterone and a divorce in the family. God knows how I'm going to get through the next few years. Maybe I should just leave them in the dark to sweeten up a bit, like rhubarb."

"Don't talk to me about bloody rhubarb. I don't know which bright spark decided it should become so trendy, but if I get one more pudding with a surprise rhubarb element, there's going to be trouble. And get a grip darling—you don't want to turn into one of those old bat mothers who bang on about how sweet you used to be while you're desperately trying to learn how to be a champion shagger."

"And how is your mother?"

"Driving me crazy, planning Christmas lunch and trying to set me up with one of her friends' reject sons, Jeffrey. He's an accountant."

"Handy for the business."

"Not my top criterion when interviewing new candidates for the Dance of Delight."

We're both giggling now. Lola discovered the delightful dancing euphemism in some Pre-Raphaelite poem she was studying when we were both at university and it still reduces us to giggles twenty years later.

"Anyway I've met him. Dance of Death, more like. Which reminds me—oh, sorry. That wasn't very subtle. Are you sure you're okay about today? You don't want me to drive down with you?"

"It'll be fine. And anyway, I'm dreading it enough already without having you and my father in the same room."

"Old bastard."

"Charlotte Linford, what would your mother say?"

"I don't give a fuck what she'd say. He is."

"I know."

"I'll come if it will help darling, I'll even try not to have a pop at your dad. I loved Helena. It'll be a tough day, funerals always are."

"I know. I just hope Bertie is okay."

"Well give him a big hug from me. That's what we want, you know, a couple of Berties."

"Oh yes, that's just what I need—a barking-mad pensioner to replace my ex-husband. How perfect."

"Someone to spend the next forty years with, who doesn't cling or watch your every move, or bore you to tears and then sneak off to shag someone else."

"It sounds great, but I draw the line at my very own Bertie. He's always been a few sandwiches short of a picnic. Actually, never mind the sandwiches—he's missing the whole hamper. And the thermos flask."

"Yes, but he's lovely barking. He doesn't wander around with no trousers on or anything."

"True."

"Is he bringing the parrot to the funeral?"

"Betty? I bloody hope not. She bit Dad on the ear last time they met."

"He should definitely bring her then. Put the 'fun' back into 'funeral,' that's what I say. When are they reading the will? That's another moment where a parrot could come in handy—cut the tension while everyone waits to hear who gets what. I bet Roger's already got someone on it, working out how he can get his hands on all that money."

"He'll have a hard job, since there is no money. The house will go to Bertie, and he's as fit as a fiddle. Barking mad of course, but fit, so Roger will just have to wait."

"She was rather wonderful, old Helena, wasn't she? I always loved that house. Georgian gorgeousness with hints of ancient manor house, a timeless classic, been in the same family for generations and all that bollocks. Ooh, if Bertie can hang on for a couple of years, I might make enough money to buy it. And then we can all live in it and grow sheep. You can learn to spin and weave artisan garments, or make some special kind of designer cheese. It'll be fabulous."

"Sounds great. Will you be weaving too? Or churning?"

"I'll come down for rural retreats. We can keep the parrot in case your dad pops round."

"Excellent."

"Tell Bertie I'll come down to see him very soon, as long as he promises to make me one of his gin slings. Call me later darling, and wrap up warm. I'm off for a swim, and then I've got an hour with my sadist trainer. Christ, who'd live my life?"

I would, it would be wonderful for a day every now and again: waking up child-free, where my biggest decision was where to have dinner and what to wear. Not how to jazz up mince or make packed lunches for three boys who keep changing their minds about who will or will not eat cheese.

"Mum?"

"Morning, love."

"Where's my PE kit?"

"I've got no idea. Is Dan up yet?"

"I don't want cheese in my sandwich. I hate it."

"Ham?"

"I'll just have bread, unless there's chicken?"

"Of course there is Ben—I got up at five a.m. to roast one specially."

"Excellent news Mother. I'll have chicken too, thanks."

"Morning, Dan. Ham or cheese, or you can make your own packed lunch, how about that?"

"Cheese is fine, I suppose."

"Thank you. That'll be three pounds ninety-nine, sir."

"You're so hilarious Mum. I've got a cramp from laughing so much. I may need tablets."

"If you find any, give me a couple. You can have a fruity vitamin if you like."

They both grin. There's a limit to how much healthy food one woman can force into three growing boys without paratroopers on standby, so I give them multivitamins every few days to top things up. It makes me feel like a proper mum, and they like them, even if they pretend they don't. I hand Ben the packet.

"I'll have one Mum, if you promise I'll grow up big and strong."

Dan snorts.

"You'll need more than a multivit for that. You'll need a total body transplant, O puny one."

They start shoving each other as Alfie races in to join the fun.

"There's toast and honey for anyone not pushing their brother. Alfie's already had his."

"Yes, but I need some more, I really do. And Mum, Dan is pushing Ben and that's not allowed, is it? Tell him Mum."

Dan glares at Alfie.

"Good morning Annie Rose, and how are we today? Wearing our PJs inside out, I see. You total knob."

Alfie hates being called Annie Rose. He's not that keen on being called a total knob either, obviously, but at least it's vaguely masculine, whereas "Annie Rose" is guaranteed to cause drama. It seemed like such a good idea when he was born, letting his brothers choose his name, and the Alfie books were some of their top bedtime reads, particularly the one where Alfie's new baby sister, Annie Rose, arrives. Let the big brothers name the baby, and peace will reign triumphant throughout the land, was what I was hoping for. Little did I know they'd be calling him Annie Rose at crucial moments and totally screwing up my day on a regular basis.

"Dan, stop it."

"What?"

"Dan. Please."

"Mum, Dan said 'knob' and that's very rude, isn't it?"

"Yes, and you can stop it too Alfie. Just ignore him. Ben, do you want toast? I'll make you some more too Alfie, if you stop whining. Dan, when you can be civil, you can join us. Otherwise..."

"You're not going to make me sit on the naughty-step, are you? A nice little time-out, so I can think about not being a naughty boy? One minute for each year of my age. Excellent. That's thirteen minutes of peace. I might have a little nap."

Sometimes I really wish I believed in smacking children.

"I wouldn't dream of suggesting you need to think about anything Dan. You're always so kind and encouraging to your little brother, who looks up to you so much and only wants to be just like you. Always helpful to your mum, particularly when she's got a hell of a day in front of her. Do you want me to help you polish your halo?"

He hesitates.

"Let's start again, shall we? Good morning Dan, I hope you slept well, and if you could try to avoid upsetting everyone within two minutes of coming downstairs, I'd be very grateful. I can make you something to eat, or you can strop off upstairs and come back down when you're ready to be nicer. My guess is a few years should do the trick. It's up to you. Toast? Which is what you're going to be if you carry on being annoying."

He grins.

"Please."

"Anything you'd like to say to your baby brother?"

"Sorry Alf."

"I'm not a baby Mum. You've got to stop saying that. I'm in Year One at school now, not silly Reception."

Dan nods.

"You tell her Alf. You've got to stand up for yourself in this family."

Alfie heads back towards his cartoons, skipping.

"Only five more minutes Alfie. Big boys don't watch too many cartoons."

Ben shakes his head.

"You walked right into that one Alf."

I'm pretty sure I hear Dan mutter "total knob" under his breath, but I'm ignoring it, and Alfie doesn't seem to have heard. Ben winks at me.

"Can I have three slices of toast and honey? I'm starving. And are you sure you don't know where my PE kit is?"

By the time I'm in the car and on my way to Devon, I'm exhausted and I've got the beginnings of a headache. Dan made a last-minute appeal against Pete looking after them tonight, and lobbied to be left in charge for the evening, like I'm completely insane. He'd even recruited Alfie to his cause by promising pizza and ice cream for supper. And then the car wouldn't start and we were nearly late for school. So that's another thing to add to my list of Things I Will Spend Money On If I Win the Lottery: a car that will start first time on cold mornings. And if I do ever win, I'm going to buy Pete's school, and then sack him. I've spent many a happy half hour having that particular daydream. Perhaps I should start buying a ticket, just in case.

It feels weird driving home without the boys; I think the last time must have been when I was at university. But then I met Pete in my second year and we started alternating between his parents' and mine, before his dad died and his mum moved to live with her sister in Australia. She sends the boys birthday cards, but she's not exactly a hands-on grandmother. She wasn't much of a hands-on mother either, from what I can gather, so maybe that's why Pete's such an idiot. I think the general consensus tends to be that it's always the mother's fault, which doesn't bode well for my relationships with my future daughters-in-law, or "partners," or whatever they go in for. I really don't care what they do as long as I'm not still doing all their laundry. But I predict a few tricky conversations when some poor woman asks me exactly what I was doing letting Dan get away with leaving things in little heaps everywhere and then expecting someone else to pick them up. Actually, the idea of some poor woman trying to tame Dan has cheered me right up. I stop for a quick coffee and entertain myself by imagining a grown-up Dan with his very own toddler. My first grandchild, who if there is any justice in the world will be just like Dan was. In other words, a complete nightmare. I'll buy lots of sweets and unsuitable toys, and then bugger off home when things get too lively. It's going to be brilliant.

My options for celebrating my child-free status are pretty limited on the A303, which is thankfully empty of the summer miles of queuing traffic, so I content myself with singing along to the music, a forbidden activity with the boys on board. It feels like I've gone back in time, except I'm more smartly dressed. In fact I'm wearing exactly the kind of navy-blue trousers I swore I'd never wear, with a navy-and-cream silk shirt and a cream cardigan. Come to think of it, I look like I work in a bank; all I need is a bloody name tag. Bollocks. But Mum will be pleased that I'm not wearing one of what Dad likes to call my hippy outfits—basically anything that doesn't come with a matching jacket. Although in his parallel universe women only wear trousers for gardening or golfing, or on a cruise. None of which are on my list for today, at least I bloody hope not.

I'm quite enjoying being on my own for a change, singing along without anyone making sarcastic comments. I'm sure I can find a new house for us, somehow. Somewhere which is ours, with no echoes of Pete. We got a good price for the old one, so that will help; the estate agent was very complimentary about my decorative finish. Apparently some post-divorce properties are in a shocking state, with ex-wives trying out new paint effects from the Lying Cheating Bastard range, where you paint rude words in big red letters on the living room walls. I was almost tempted, just to see Pete's face. But I want to move, and not just for a new start. Our road has got posher over the years, and although I'm on nodding terms with everyone, it's never been more than that. Pete was always better at bonding with them than me, and at least when we move I won't be surrounded by people calling their children Inigo and putting in loft conversions for the au pair. The women treat me like divorce might somehow be contagious, and the men seem nervous I might ask them to do a spot of DIY, but mainly I'm persona non grata because I teach at exactly the kind of school they're all determined to avoid for their children. Last term we even had a stabbing, with a teacher moments away from death, according to the local paper. Actually, it was Mr. Hutchins, the kind of faded and furious teacher who quite a few of us would like to poke with something sharp. He bullies and shouts at the kids, and he wasn't stabbed, he just tripped and landed on Dean Carter, who was busy brandishing his compass in an attempt to protect himself from Darren Knutley, who was in one of his Moods, and is known as Nutter to staff and pupils alike. So essentially Mr. Hutchins managed to stab himself in the leg with a piece of his own mathematics equipment and was back at school the next day, much to his annoyance. But that didn't stop the local paper from describing it as a stabbing, so a few more anxious middle-class parents enrolled their kids in expensive private schools, or started going to church every Sunday so they could get them into snooty St. Edmunds. And our deputy head took the rest of the term off with stress-related headaches, stupid woman.

Once I'm driving through familiar villages near to home I know exactly when I'll catch my first glimpse of the sea, but it still gives me a thrill. It's somehow comforting driving through landscapes that I know so well, beautiful even in winter, with fields of pale stubble and the hedgerows full of berries. Maybe I should have brought the boys. They love it down here, and we don't come as often as I'd like. Neither Dad nor Roger go in for offering family rates in the hotel, and renting anywhere round here in peak season costs a fortune. We had a few long weekends this summer, including one when Dad was away on a golf trip so Mum was relaxed. We went on a damp boat trip and Alfie saw a seal. I must fix up another weekend soon, maybe at half term. The hotel's always half-empty at this time of year, despite Roger's Winter Saver promotions and glossy brochures about the new spa—which is basically the old hairdressing salon with some new towels.

Crossing the river on the old bridge at Launton just before the village, I can't help wishing Mum and Dad still lived in our old house, where there was room for all of us to stay. Mum loved the garden, but they moved into one of the new bungalows on the golf course a few years ago; it's handy for Dad, but a lot less handy for Mum, who doesn't actually play golf. You can't sit in the garden if anyone is on the fifteenth, unless you want golf balls whizzing past your ear while you're sipping your tea, so she concentrates all her efforts on the tubs and window boxes at the front now, and mows the back lawn at dusk, when the golfers are in the clubhouse boasting about their new cars. God, I'd forgotten how much I love Aretha Franklin. I'm in the perfect mood to get a little bit of R.E.S.P.E.C.T as I arrive, which is a good job because Dad's standing checking his watch as I park, and Mum's looking anxious.

"It's nearly half past four."

"Hello Dad, there was traffic on the M-25. Shall I bring my bag in Mum, or am I staying at the hotel?"

Please can it be the hotel. I'm not really in the mood for dodging golf balls.

"We thought you'd prefer to be with us, but we're having dinner at the hotel later with Roger and Georgina. They're organising something special. I'd already made my shepherd's pie, but Roger insisted. I hope you've brought something nice to wear?"

God I wish I still had that sari.

It's pouring with rain on the morning of the funeral, and supper at the hotel last night was so annoying I ended up drinking too much. I wake up feeling like someone has repeatedly banged me on the head during the night, which is ironic given how much I wanted to do exactly that to Roger, who was in full flow, while Georgina simpered in head-to-toe sparkling chiffon and spent hours telling me about all her new outfits for the various social events which are meant to culminate in Roger's coronation as captain of the golf club. Sally was on Reception when we arrived, and winked at me, which was encouraging. We were good friends at school, and worked together in the holidays, making beds and serving cream teas while we practised our flirting skills with the summer waiters. She's head of housekeeping now and manages to ignore Roger most of the time, but it can't be easy.

Old Mr. Parsons was head waiter in the dining room, wearing the same shiny suit he's worn for years. Roger likes him because he thinks all the staff should be as obsequious as possible, especially to him. What he doesn't know is that they all make fun of him behind his back, even Mr. Parsons, who winked at me during one of the particularly boring golfing monologues.

Christ, this is going to be a long day.

"Are you ready dear?"

"Nearly."

"Your father wants to leave soon."

"Okay."

Dad's pretty thin-lipped about my black suit, but contents himself with a glare before he stamps off to the car and starts tooting the horn because Mum takes more than five seconds to find her gloves.

"Sorry dear, I couldn't find them, but they were in my bag all the time. I hope this rain stops."

She looks anxious.

"I'm sure it will Mum. And the rain won't matter, not really."

Dad tuts.

"Won't matter? Of course it will matter. There will be important people at this funeral, unless Bertie has forgotten to invite them. I gave him a list, important county people."

"People who knew Helena?"

"Of course, some of them, but you know what she was like, downright rude most of the time."

"So you've come up with your own guest list for Helena's funeral?"

He ignores this, and starts telling Mum off for not remembering to bring a spare umbrella so he can offer to lend it to anyone important—local business and golf club people who he wants to impress. The backdrop of Harrington Hall is impressive, in a dilapidated, faded, aristocratic kind of way, and the local snooters have always been keen to include it on their endless circuit of lunch and dinner parties. But Helena was never interested in playing Lady of the Manor. She wouldn't let the village Horticultural Society include it in the Village Garden Safari, where all the locals troop round each other's gardens and raise money for the village hall. Even though the society was set up by a Harrington, her great-grandmother, I think, Helena was adamant. She used to say she didn't want a load of ghastly types milling about snipping cuttings from her best plants when her back was turned. She'd be thrilled to know Dad's invited them all to her funeral.

It's a shock seeing all the black cars lined up on the drive as we park by the stables. The house looks much bigger than I remember, cold and grey and forlorn without Helena standing at the front door smiling. And then I see the hearse and the coffin, covered in roses. It's almost a physical jolt, like I've somehow managed to give myself an electric shock. She'd have loved all the roses, in all her favourite colours, pinks and lilacs and creams and pale yellows. "No common red ones"—I can almost hear her saying it—"red roses are for supermarkets and romantics, and I'm neither of those things, my dear." I bet Celia arranged them; she and Helena spent years working together in the garden. Friends since they were at school, you'd often find them pottering about in the garden in the kind of silence only true friends ever manage. And now she's gone, the last of the Harringtons. Bloody hell, I'm nearly in tears and I haven't even got out of the car.

Bertie emerges from the house, looking older and smaller than when I saw him in the summer. There's no sign of the parrot, thank God. Although actually I think Lola might be right: the only way I'm going to get through today is if Betty puts in an appearance and sorts out Dad. Roger too, hopefully. Bertie is smiling, but pale.

"Everyone's gathering inside, do come in."

"Hello Bertie."

I kiss him on the cheek and he hugs me.

"Hello my dear. Thank you for coming. Been counting on you to come and save me from all these ghastly people. Don't know who half of them are. Appalling man just started talking to me about chickens."

"Chickens?"

"Apparently Helena sold him some a few years ago. God knows why he wanted to tell me all about it."

"Where's Betty?"

"In the library. Do you think I should bring her out to greet people?"

There's a faint smile.

"Maybe later?"

"Good plan my dear. Excellent. Right, let's get started then. Need a drink first, steady the buffs. Care to join me?"

"Yes please."

"Ivy is handing round glasses of sherry in the library. Henry, Marjorie, do go and find her, oh and Henry, I did get your note but the invitations were all arranged by Helena. She'd written a list—demon for lists. Strict orders not to add any more names. She said she didn't want a circus."

Good for Helena. Dad looks pretty narked.

"I thought a few of the more important people in the area would like to pay their respects."

Bertie gives Dad a surprisingly firm look.

"Have a snoop around, more like. As I say, Helena's instructions were crystal clear. Do go through. Ivy will take care of you. She's been such a brick, I must say, both her and Dennis. Don't know what we'd do without them." He hesitates, clearly remembering there is no "we" anymore. I put my hand on his shoulder.

"Come and say hello to Betty with me Molly, and have a snifter."

Dad hesitates, but clearly doesn't feel up to running the parrot gauntlet, so he heads towards the drawing room, where people are standing in quiet groups, sipping glasses of sherry.

"Look at them all, don't look like a lively bunch do they? That might be the filthy sherry though. Follow me my dear, and let's get you a decent drink. I've got a bottle of sloe gin open—great stuff on a cold day."

"Lovely."

"Here's Molly come to see us Betty. Say hello."

Thankfully Betty contents herself with walking up and down her perch and fluffing up her feathers. But she does fix me with a very beady look, so I'm taking no chances while Bertie pours us both a glass of gin.

"Where are your manners? Say hello Molly, stupid bird."

Betty squawks and then starts repeating, "Hello Dolly. Stupid bird," over and over again and then suddenly launches into "Polly Put the Kettle On" and makes piercing whistling noises, just like a bloody kettle. I'd forgotten about that—she did it last time I visited too, in the summer, and the boys thought it was hilarious.

"I don't know why I keep her—be much more useful as a feather duster. Did you hear that Betty? Shut up, or you'll be dusting the furniture."

"Polly put the kettle on."

"I should put another log on the fire—cold day. Sit down my dear. Daft bird, be quiet. Helena couldn't stand her you know."

"I know Bertie."

"But she'd give her a bit of apple sometimes when she thought I wasn't looking, so I think she was secretly fond. Hid it well, but fond nonetheless. Everyone thinks I named her after Her Majesty, but it was Betty Grable I had in mind—million-dollar legs and all that. Always had a soft spot for Betty Grable. Helena was very like her, in her day—complete stunner. Not that Her Majesty's legs are anything to be ashamed of, of course. Met her on board *Britannia* once—nice girl. That Philip's a decent chap too—knows how to have a laugh. Anyway, where was I? Oh yes, Betty Grable. Helena had the same effect, a real bobby dazzler, used to take my breath away. I shall miss her, don't mind admitting that. I liked seeing her about the place in that dreadful old hat she used to wear. I wonder where it's gone?"

Oh God. He suddenly looks confused and very old, as if he might start searching for Helena's old gardening hat.

"I'm sure it will be somewhere Bertie. And of course you'll miss her—we all will."

I give him a hug, and he holds my hand, tightly, for a moment.

"Terrible day."

"Dreadful."

"Drink up my dear. Here, let me top you up. And then I suppose we should go."

We sit by the fire for a few minutes, sipping Helena's sloe gin, which is delicious, but very strong. I think I may have sipped too quickly though, because I'm not sure I can still feel my feet. Oh God.

"Polly put the kettle on."

"Is she going to do that all day do you think Uncle Bertie?"

He smiles.

"Probably my dear."

"Fair enough."

Betty squawks and hops along her perch.

"Bugger off."

Bertie ignores her.

"One last top-up? Need to fortify ourselves."

"I'm fine, thanks."

Betty squawks and flaps her wings.

"Bugger Bugger Bugger."

My feelings exactly.

The funeral is as terrible as I knew it would be, and beautiful at the same time. The village church is packed, and full of flowers, and the vicar seems genuinely moved and talks about Helena with real affection. And then we're standing by the grave and throwing in handfuls of earth in the freezing rain, and I'm holding Bertie's arm as people start to move away and stand waiting by the cars. Dad and Roger are both rather pointedly looking at their watches, and Georgina looks half-frozen, so maybe her quilted coat isn't quite as quilted as she'd hoped. I definitely can't feel my feet now, and it's absolutely pouring.

"Shall we go back to the cars now Bertie? You're getting soaked."

"Not quite yet my dear. Just give me a moment."

"Of course. I'll wait for you by the path. Here, you keep the umbrella."

"Thank you my dear."

He takes something out of his pocket and drops it into the grave. It looks like some dried flowers, but I don't want to stare. And then he stands, in the rain, for what seems like ages.

Sally comes over and gives me a long hug, and we stand sheltering under her umbrella, watching Bertie.

"Poor old thing."

"Thanks for coming today Sal."

"Ring me next time you're down and we'll have a proper catch-up?"

"Yes please."

We hug again and turn to look at Bertie, standing completely still by the grave.

"Should you go over, do you think?"

"I'm giving him a bit longer. It's the wrong way round, you know. It's so unfair. Helena would have been fine without Bertie—well, not fine—she loved him very much, even though she pretended she didn't, but she'd have managed, spent even more time in the garden, and got on with it. But I'm worried about Bertie, I really am."

"But Ivy will still be around, won't she?"

"Oh yes, and Dennis—at least I think they will. Ivy practically runs the house—she has done for years. She'll keep an eye on him, and Dennis will keep the garden going, so he won't be on his own. But still. I thought I'd have a quiet word with Ivy later, and ask her to promise to call me if she's worried about anything. Do you think she'd mind?"

She pats my arm.

"I think that's a lovely idea, and she'll appreciate it. She was in the hairdresser's last week and she was saying how she was looking forward to seeing you."

"Did she? Well that's a relief, I always feel like she disapproves of me."

"That's just her way; she's always been very protective of both of them. She got really upset in church, did you see?"

"Yes. Dennis has taken her back to the house."

"It'll have hit her hard too. She worshipped Helena."

"I think we all did. I wanted to be just like her when I was a grown-up."

"How's it going so far?"

"I haven't started yet."

"Me neither."

We both smile.

"I'll call you. Chin up love."

"Thanks Sal."

I'm about to go back to Bertie, when he turns and walks slowly towards me.

"Found it, in the end. Her wedding bouquet. Took me ages, but I knew she'd kept it. Found the box in the attic. She kept all sorts of stuff up there, complete hoarder, always was. I remembered the flowers, roses of course, but some other things too—forget what they were now, remember the smell though—beautiful, although not half as beautiful as she was, on the day. Thought I might keel over when I saw her walking up the aisle. Couldn't believe she'd go through with it with a wastrel like me. Now then, this is important my dear, so do pay attention. I've kept a few of the flowers back at the house, from the bouquet. They're in my wardrobe, on the top shelf, with my medals. And I want to be buried with them. Not the medals—don't give a bugger about them—but the flowers.

Could you do that for me, do you think my dear? When the time comes?"

"Of course I will, but let's not talk about it today."

"Yes, but do you promise?"

"Of course I do."

He pats my hand.

Oh God, I'm crying all over again now.

I walk him back to the cars, and he insists I get in the lead funeral car with him. Roger and Mum and Dad were with him on the way to the church, so I should probably get back into one of the other cars. Georgina has already got into the second car, along with the Vicar and his wife. Mum and Dad are standing waiting, and Dad is looking impatient, but Bertie won't let go of my hand, and it's really belting down now, and the wind is picking up.

"In you get, there's a good girl. Getting a bit breezy. Seems strange to be going home without her."

He gets his handkerchief out of his pocket. It's one of Helena's, with an *H* embroidered on it, which almost sets me off again.

He squeezes my hand.

"No shame in tears on a day like this my dear, be a bit hard if nobody gave a bugger. And she was very fond of you, very fond. Always said what a good girl you are. If we'd had a daughter, we'd have both been very proud if she'd turned out like you. Very proud."

This nearly finishes me off entirely. Oh God, I'm being so useless. He coughs again and wipes his eyes.

"Oh Bertie, I'm so sorry."

"Very fond. In you get."

Dad gives me a furious look. I've usurped Roger, who is also looking pretty thunderous and seems to be hesitating by the car door now.

Mum is looking flustered, as usual.

"Oh dear, where will Roger sit?"

Bertie smiles.

"In one of the other cars I should imagine, unless he wants to run along behind us. Do him good. Could do with losing a bit of weight. That'll be the booze though."

Dad is even more furious now as we get into the car, and Mum tries to smooth things over, as usual.

"I thought the service was lovely."

"Yes, not a bad chap that vicar. Most of them are such dead-legs, but he wasn't half bad. Bit young for a vicar I thought, but then everyone seems young when you get to my age. How's that girl you used to bring down with you, Lily?"

"Lola? She's fine, Uncle Bertie. She sends her love."

"Does she? Well that's a spot of good news on a dark day. Lively sort of girl, I always thought. Bit of a goer."

Dad looks at the driver.

"For heaven's sake, this is hardly the time for that kind of talk."

Mum starts to fuss with her handbag, which is always a sign of distress, but Bertie fixes Dad with a rather beady look.

"Nothing wrong in being a bit of a goer Henry. All the best girls have a bit of spark to them—know how to have a good time. Quite right too. Give her my best Molly, and tell her she's very kind to remember an old man."

"I will, and she says she'd love to come down with us, next time we visit, as long as you make her one of your gin slings."

"That's the spirit. See what I mean Henry? Girl knows a good drink when she's had one. Not like the half measures you serve at the hotel. A proper drink. That's what people want."

Dad is going red now, which is never a good sign, and Mum seems to have entered herself into some sort of *Guinness Book of World Records* attempt to see how many times one woman can open and close her handbag for no apparent reason.

"For God's sake, stop fussing with that bag Marjorie."

"Sorry, I was just checking I'd got my keys. Did I tell you, Molly, I went out last week and forgot your father had borrowed my set, and he was playing golf so I couldn't interrupt him? I had to wait for nearly three hours in the car until he got home. Lucky I had my library book in my bag."

"I have told you, Marjorie, all you need is a spare set hanging in the garage. Put a label on them—problem sorted. Even you should be able to manage that."

Mum looks close to tears. Actually, bugger this.

"That's a great idea Dad, and then any passing burglar can just help themselves to all the keys and drive off with anything they fancy. They'll probably leave you a thank-you note, commending you on your excellent organizational skills."

Bertie snorts and Dad glares at me.

"Obviously she wouldn't write 'house keys' on the label Molly. Do use your brain. She'd use a code word."

Mum looks panicked at the thought of having to think up a code word and then remember it.

"I bet that would fox them Dad. They'd never think of trying the keys just to see if they happened to fit the front door. Actually, Mum, I've got a much better idea. I'll get you one of those key rings with an alarm for Christmas, and then if Dad nicks your house keys again, you can just press the button and they'll start beeping. I bet he can't play golf if his pocket is beeping. It's probably against the rules. That'd soon bring him home and then maybe he'd stop taking your keys in the first place."

Bertie laughs.

"Like your thinking Molly. Helena got me something similar, made a frightful noise. Luckily Betty soon took care of it. She's excellent at dismantling electronic devices. Have to hide the control box for the telly, she's had her way with so many of them. Good strong beak, and she's very determined. Bear it in mind Henry. I'd be happy to offer her services for a small fee."

He winks at me.

"Nearly home, my dear. Nearly home."

The house seems even colder and darker when we get back, and the wind from the sea is battering rain against the windows. Bertie was adamant he didn't want the usual gathering after the funeral, so it's just the family for lunch, soup, and sandwiches, and one of Ivy's lovely walnut cakes, which almost sets me off again. We always had walnut cake when we visited as children, and Helena used to cut me a slice which had two walnuts, whereas Roger only got one. She did it every time, and every time she used to smile. Christ, I've got to try to get a grip, and be helpful and cheering instead of sodden. Maybe that gin earlier wasn't such a good idea after all. Maybe that's why they call it mothers' ruin, I'm a complete wreck.

"Shall I serve the coffee in the drawing room, Mr. Bertie?"

"Please, Ivy."

"And Mr. Crouch has arrived. Dennis is helping him get everything ready."

"Right you are."

She nods, and then turns and gives me a small nod too. I try to smile. She's looking tired; it's been a long day for her. For all of us.

Bertie stands up.

"If everyone would like to move into the drawing room, the legal chap has arrived. Thought we'd get the will done and dusted—Helena's idea, got it all planned, as usual."

Roger looks pleased, now we're finally getting to the bit that interests him. Bertie hasn't had any claim to Harrington up to now—some complicated family will protected the Harrington line—but he'll definitely own it now. And I'm pretty sure Roger and Dad are hoping they can persuade Bertie to sell it to them at a knockdown price, and then they'll redevelop, or turn it into holiday flats. God knows what scheme they're hatching, but I bet Bertie will be the loser. I think they may be underestimating him, though. He's always loved it here, and Harrington Hall has been in Helena's family for generations. She was the last of a long line of Harringtons after her brother died in the War. So I can't see him selling it, I really can't. And I'm determined to stand up for him, even if it does infuriate Dad.

I help Ivy collect up the plates, but Bertie follows me into the kitchen.

"Can't begin without you my dear. You too, Ivy. We've got our instructions. And Molly, I just want to say that Helena and I spoke about this and we agreed, so come along, there's a good girl. Let's get this over with, and then we can get a bit of peace and quiet."

Oh God, I bet he's talking about the necklace. Georgina will be furious; she's had her eye on it for years. Helena used to say it was the only decent item of jewellery she owned, inherited from her mother: rose-cut diamonds and beautiful emeralds. She used to show it to me as a treat when I was little, taking it out of the faded white-leather box to show me the silver frame and the tiny screwdriver in a velvet pouch at the bottom of the box so you could screw the necklace onto a frame and turn it into a tiara. She'd brush my hair and put it on for me, and I'd sit very still, feeling like a Princess while she told me about her mother wearing it for grand parties, and the long silk dresses and the house full of music and candles. God knows where I'll ever wear it, but I'm pleased Helena wanted me to have it.

Ivy pats my arm.

"Right you are Mr. Bertie. We'll just bring the trays in with the coffee."

She hands me a tray loaded with cups and saucers.

"Be careful with those Miss Molly. Antique they are, Royal Worcester, and they're a devil to wash—the handles are right fiddly—but I thought they'd be fitting for today. Only they need to be back in the china cupboard safe and sound afterwards."

"They're lovely Ivy."

Actually they're rather hideous: all gold handles and lustrous fruit.

"I'll get the milk and follow you in. In for a bit of a surprise, some of them, and a good thing too. And that's all I'm saying."

Excellent. I just hope nobody breaks any of these bloody cups, or Ivy is bound to blame me.

"Good afternoon, I'll just switch this on and we can begin."

Mr. Crouch is fiddling with cables and an ancient video recorder, which he's connecting to an equally ancient television. The screen flickers and suddenly there's Helena sitting on the sofa, and then the screen goes black again.

Christ, I nearly dropped the sodding tray. I'm handing round cups while he continues to jiggle cables, and Ivy pours the coffee.

"I think we can proceed now, if everyone is ready?"

I sit down as everyone looks at the screen, and it flickers again and then Helena reappears, sitting on the sofa where Mum and

Dad are sitting now. She's wearing one of her best summer frocks, the ones she used to wear for tea on Sundays, not her usual outfit of baggy cotton trousers and an old gardening jacket with pockets stuffed full of string and her favourite secateurs. Oh God, I'm close to tears again and we haven't even started.

"Is this thing working?" Helena looks at someone, presumably Mr. Crouch. "Good, because I can't spend all day doing this, I've got things to do in the garden. I'll get straight to the point, shall I? I think that's best. Before I start, I want to make it clear that I've discussed this with Bertie, and he's in complete agreement, although whether he'll remember everything we've discussed is another matter entirely. So I'm using this video contraption so you can hear it from the horse's mouth, so to speak. Mr. Crouch has put everything in writing, so there can be no confusion. First things first: the Hall. I'm leaving it to Molly, in its entirety. Yes, Molly, you my dear. You'll have Harrington Hall and the land, what there is left of it, on the condition that you don't sell until Bertie is six feet under. Or he goes completely round the twist, in which case you can stick him in a home and sell up, with my blessing, only do choose somewhere decent to park him; some of them are quite dreadful. Wouldn't put a dog in them, but I know I can count on you to make the right choice if he does go completely round the bend. Although how you'll know is beyond me, what with that bloody parrot and his patrolling the cove at all times of the day and night. But if there ever comes a day when he can't remember his own name, then pop him somewhere safe. Otherwise he has a home at the Hall. And Molly, I'm sorry, my dear, but he is going to be a great trial to you, as he has been to me." She pauses and her face softens. "I know you'll watch over him. Keep him fed and watered, and stop him getting up to too much mischief. And good luck to you because he'll run you ragged if you let him."

She pauses again, and looks over her spectacles, as if she's in the room and wants to see my face. I'm so shocked I don't know what to do. Bertie winks at me. Crikey. I feel like I might faint, actually keel over at the shock of it all. Thank God I'm not holding my antique coffee cup, because that would definitely be in pieces by now. Bloody hell.

Mum is opening and closing her handbag again and looking almost as shocked as I am.

"I do hope this doesn't make things too difficult for you Marjorie, but I'm also leaving the necklace to Molly, so she can sell it. I could never bring myself to do it, sentimental nonsense, but Molly, you're to sell it. I'm sure you're going to need the money. You'll want to make improvements—God knows some of them are long overdue. The heating bills alone are enough to make you weep. But I have faith in you. I'm sure you'll make a go of it. I do know that the expectation was that Bertie would inherit the Hall, and as his sister your mother would lend a hand. But I also know if I leave things to Bertie, that ghastly man will get it."

Helena often referred to Dad as "that ghastly man."

"And I'm sorry to say it Marjorie, but the idea of Henry and Roger getting their hands on the Hall, particularly my garden, is just too appalling. Not an ounce of soul amongst them. No sense of history. Only small fly in the ointment was that idiot husband of Molly's, but now she's got shot of him, it's all fallen into place rather perfectly. And if I may say so, Molly, God knows why you ever married him in the first place. Never right for you, pompous bore. Thought it was odd you saddled yourself with such a dead-leg. Do try not to do it again, my dear. How your mother has put up with your father all these years I'll never know. Be better for everyone if she pushed him off a cliff. Metaphorically speaking, of course. And yes, I do know I'm being frightfully rude, but if you can't be rude when you're dead, then when can you? I'm rather enjoying it. Tricky moment being told the curtains were about to close, of course. Always thought I'd be the last to go, but it comes to us all, and at least I've had a bit of warning, so I've been able to put things in order. Now I've got used to the idea, it's all been rather liberating. I shall miss my garden of course, but it can't be helped."

Oh God, we didn't know she knew she was ill, that somehow makes it all worse. We all thought it was a heart attack, out of the blue. Dennis found her, in the garden, and that seemed so perfect in a way. But she must have known for ages.

Roger is sitting with his mouth slightly open, and Dad is clearly beyond annoyed now and has gone into a sort of apoplectic fury.

"I'm not sitting here listening to this rubbish. Switch it off and read the bloody thing. There must be a way we can challenge this. It's ridiculous, leaving valuable property to Molly, quite ridiculous. It should be part of the family holdings. That was always the understanding. She must have gone soft in the head."

Mr. Crouch presses the pause button.

"My instructions are quite clear. Copies of the will are to be circulated only once you have viewed the recording. And if I say so myself, I think you'll find there are no grounds for any challenges."

He gives Dad a rather steely look.

"For God's sake, get on with it then."

Mr. Crouch presses the button again.

"I'm counting on you, Molly, not to let your father take over. You've always been rather brave about that, and Bertie will help you. He's always been rather good at standing up to bullies—they didn't make him an Admiral for nothing, although he might need a boat to do it on, but I'm sure that can be arranged. But don't let him try to move that ridiculous cannon. It took four men and a huge lorry to get the blasted thing here in the first place. God knows what would happen if he tried to get it onto a boat. Right, well, I can't sit here all day, I've got cuttings which need planting out. All the detail is in the papers, and I warn you, Henry, I've already had one of those ruinously expensive firms in London check it over, and everything is completely watertight. Oh, yes, one other thing. I've given Ivy and Dennis their cottage, signed it over rent-free for as long as they need it, complete treasures both of them. It comes back to the estate only when they no longer need it. Ivy will show you the ropes, Molly, but don't let her boss you around too much. Carry on with the bed-and-breakfast if you like—it brings in a bit of money, keeps the place ticking over, and Ivy takes care of most of that side of things for me. Just be firm with the guests—ignore them as much as possible is my advice—but Ivy will show you what's required. And Dennis will keep the garden in shape. Although don't let him do the planting—he puts everything in straight lines. Dreadful, you want groupings, not a parade ground. Leave that to Celia. She'll keep an eye on things for me and she's familiar with my garden notebooks. I've left her a few things, including my secateurs—she's always trying to walk off with them—so I'm sure she'll continue to lend a hand. But you have free reign in the Hall Molly, so do what you like my dear. And the best of luck—you're certainly going to need it. Right, I think that's everything. Switch this thing off. I need to get changed, can't plant out dressed like this."

The screen goes blank and there's a silence.

"Good God."

For once in his life Roger has said exactly the right thing.

* * *

There's another awkward silence as Mr. Crouch gives everyone copies of the will. Dad's so furious he's not speaking at all now, and Roger gets up and walks out, with Georgina running along behind him. He drives off so fast he sprays gravel all over Dad's car. Bloody hell. Mr. Crouch says he'll call me to discuss a few details when I've had time to gather my thoughts, and Mum tries a faint wave as she gets into the car, and Dad drives off, looking thunderous. Ivy is standing in the doorway with her arms folded, and mutters something which sounds like "Good riddance," before turning to go back towards the kitchen.

"Thanks Ivy, for everything today."

"You're welcome Miss Molly."

"Please Ivy, just Molly."

"We'll see. Will you do it then?"

"What?"

"Take on Mr. Bertie. Your aunt was counting on you. Will you move down here, then? He's a full-time job in himself, wandering about in all weather and losing track of time, and there's the B-and-B guests to see to as well. Not that we get many, except in the summer, but there's a lot to do."

"I don't know Ivy, I haven't had a chance to take it all in yet, but I promise I'll think about it."

"Well, you can count on me and Dennis, that's all I'm saying."

"I know that Ivy. And thank you."

She nods.

"Well, those cups won't wash themselves. She was always on at me to put them in the dishwasher, but you don't put good china like that in the dishwasher, not if you want it to last."

"I'll just go and say good-bye to Bertie."

"He's in the library, talking to that silly bird."

She raises her eyebrows.

Bertie is sitting by the fire, looking half-asleep.

"I'll be off now, Bertie, but I'll call you later."

"Right you are my dear. All a bit of a surprise, I shouldn't wonder, but we'll muddle along."

"Of course we will. I just need to think through all the details, work out what's best for everyone, but I'll come back down, maybe at the weekend, and we can talk then?"

"No point talking to me about details. Always left that to Helena. I'm sure whatever you decide will be best. I think I'll go for a walk, haven't been down to the cove yet today, where's my coat? I looked for it earlier on, but I couldn't find it."

Ivy will have hidden it. It's nearly dark now, and freezing cold, and she won't want him clambering down to the cove in this weather.

"I don't know Uncle Bertie, I haven't seen it. I'll call you when I get home, shall I?"

"Yes dear, you do that. Although I may be out on patrol."

"Bye Betty."

"Bugger off. Stupid bird."

Quite.

Thankfully the effects of the gin have worn off by the time I'm driving home, and I drank loads of black coffee at Mum's before I left. Dad is still not speaking to me, and Mum was pretty silent too, like I've done something wrong somehow. I'm beyond exhausted, and everything is so confusing I don't know what to think. It's all very well for Helena to decide I'll move to Devon, but what about the boys and what's best for them? And if I don't move us all to the Hall, then what happens, apart from Roger and Dad opening the champagne while they try to work out how quickly they can persuade Bertie to sell it to them. I can't let that happen. It's not fair. And moving could be a whole new start for us, and it's a pretty good answer to where on earth we're going to live when the sale of the house goes through. At least there are enough bedrooms, and I've always wanted the boys to have more space to grow up in, more of a country childhood and less urban angst. But they might hate it. And what will we live on? Helena only ran the B&B so she could buy new plants; it's hardly going to support three growing boys. I could sign up to do supply teaching locally, but filling in for teachers who are off sick is hideous, and anyway I can't leave Ivy in sole charge of Uncle Bertie and the boys, let alone that bloody parrot. She's good, but she's not bloody superwoman. Oh God.

I stop for more coffee in a motorway service station, and do what I always do when I'm about to go into complete meltdown. Thank God for mobile phones.

"Lola?"

"Hello darling, how was it—totally grim?"

"Yes, terrible. The church was good though. Full of flowers and people who really cared about her. They read the will—actually Helena did, on a video."

"Spooky. Although I quite like the idea, get the last laugh and all that."

"She certainly did that."

"Ooh, what did she do, did she leave you the necklace? I bet she did, how brilliant."

"Not exactly."

"You sound a bit shaky darling. It can't be that bad. What did she leave you? Something to remember her by, I bet. She adored you, anyone could see that."

"Bertie."

"Sorry?"

"She left me Uncle Bertie."

I'm crying again now.

"Darling, please stop, it'll be fine, although fuck knows where you'll put him. Well, that settles it: you'll have to buy a bigger house now. Did you get the diamonds too? They'll be worth a fair bit, so that should help, and I can lend you some money, you know I've already offered."

"No, I'm not explaining it properly. She left me the Hall too. Uncle Bertie and Harrington Hall, and the land, all of it. You know you were saying earlier about weaving, or making cheese? Could you run me through how that would work? Because, to be honest, I haven't got a clue."

"Fucking hell."

"You can say that again."

"The whole house? Christ, it must be worth a fortune. I bet your dad is furious."

"Incandescent."

"Well, thank God for Helena. It's about time you got a lucky break. I always knew she was a star, I just didn't know how much, ooh, and I've just thought of something else completely brilliant."

"What's that?"

"Just imagine Pete's face when he hears."

"I hadn't thought of that."

"He'll be livid. He ditches you and the boys and rebrands himself as a pillar of the establishment with his new Stepford wife, and hey presto, you become Lady of the Manor and inherit a minor stately home. It's almost too perfect."

"It's hardly stately, Lola. It's practically falling down. It's freezing cold in winter, and every time it rains you have to put saucepans under the leaks in the attic. I doubt the B-and-B makes enough to feed Bertie, let alone support me and the boys."

"My heart bleeds, darling—your very own beach, and the meadow and the woods, and a beautiful house and Helena's garden, and all you have to do is grill a bit of bacon."

"I think it might take more than that Lola, and none of it is mine, not really, I just have custody of it."

"If she's left it to you, then it's yours darling, and that woman will be around won't she, the housekeeper woman?"

"Ivy? Yes, thank God, and Dennis. But that's another thing: Ivy likes doing things her way. She won't want anything changed."

"Well, she'll have to get over it then won't she, since you're the new Lady of the House."

"Please stop it Lola, you're really not helping. And what about the boys, what on earth do I tell them?"

"Didn't you say you wished you could move out of town?"

"Yes, but not to the middle of nowhere by the sea, right next to my bloody parents."

"Tell me again how your dad took the good news, on a scale of one to ten?"

"Three hundred and fifty-six."

"Excellent. Just goes to show, be careful what you wish for."

"You're telling me, except it never even occurred to me to wish for it, or anything like it, and—"

"And nothing, darling. Just go with it. Life has finally given you a lucky break, so just go with it. It could be a whole new adventure, just what you need. And you can book me a room as your first official guest."

"I'll think about it."

"You will not, you'll bloody do it, if I have to drive you down there and lock you in the cellar. It's going to be fantastic. Actually, is there a cellar?"

"Yes, by the pantry. Don't you remember, Roger hid down there that time we all got drunk and played Hide and Seek, and we pretended we couldn't find him."

"Oh yes. Right, well, I'm writing a list."

Christ. Once Lola writes one of her lists, there's no escape.

"I can write my own lists, thanks very much."

"You can, if you like, but I've already started mine. You need decent bed linen for the bed-and-breakfast. None of that polyester rubbish. And proper products for the bathrooms. Luckily I'm a bit of an expert on luxury cosmetics—I knew it would come in handy one day. You need organic soap, and beautiful candles."

"Stop it, right now, or I'm going to go into hysterics."

"Fine, you go into hysterics, and I'll finish my list. I'll email it to you when you get home. Call me later darling."

"I hate you, Lola. I really do."

"Book me in, darling, your first guest."

Bloody hell. As if I haven't got enough to worry about now I've got Lola, the world's most demanding guest, booked into a B&B I didn't even know I was running until about five hours ago.

"Call me later, when you're home. And Molly?"

"Yes?"

"I like my orange juice freshly squeezed, none of those ghastly cartons, and, actually, shall I get my PA to fax you a list?"

"Lola, this is so not helping."

"Deep breaths darling."

"I'm already hyperventilating, so I'm not sure that's such a good idea."

"Shallow breaths then. Have you got a paper bag?"

"Not on me, no. Would my handbag do?"

"Not really, you might inhale something unexpected."

"That would just finish off the day perfectly."

"Well try to breathe slowly darling, and think about something calming. I know, imagine Pete's face when he hears the good news."

"Actually, that is helping, a bit."

"I'd love to be there when he finds out. Make sure you tell him in person, so you can see how he looks. It'll be worth it, trust me."

I'm smiling as I walk back to the car. Admittedly it's the kind of smiling which can easily turn into sobbing hysterics. But it's a start.

CHAPTER TWO

Jingle Bells

December

Bourbon Roses

Originating from an island in the Indian Ocean, these roses are prized for their combination of beauty and scent. With ruffled silky petals and fragrances with undertones of peach melon and jasmine, they are often grown as climbing roses on arches and pergolas. Notable examples include Queen Victoria, a sweetly scented lilac-pink rose with hints of honeysuckle; Boule de Neige, with milky-white curled petals; Madame Isaac Pereire, a deep pink with a strong raspberry scent; and Souvenir de Malmaison, a blush-pink fragrant rose with hints of nectarine, cinnamon, and nutmeg.

It's Friday morning and I'm in the kitchen trying not to have a complete meltdown; I may need to set myself up with some sort of emergency drip. Perhaps if I lie on the floor with a bottle of gin set on a slow trickle. If only I'd nicked a bottle of Helena's sloe gin, I'm sure that would do the trick. I've lost my main list, so I'm writing an emergency backup one now, and if I could find any gin, I'd definitely give the drip thing a go, or pour myself a stiffener, as Uncle Bertie would say. It's Moving Day today, and the boys are due back with Pete in a couple of hours, and there's still loads to do.

I've spent the last six weeks driving up and down to Devon, sorting out papers with Mr. Crouch whilst simultaneously keeping an eye on Uncle Bertie and trying to give Ivy a hand, which hasn't been easy, because she's been on a manic cleaning mission ever since the funeral. I'm sure it's some sort of displacement activity, but she's been washing and polishing like a woman demented. I've resigned from school and term finished last week, thank God. I've found new schools for the boys, and had a series of increasingly tense conversations with Dad and Roger, who seem to think if they just go on about it long enough, I'll sign everything over to them. I had to get Mr. Crouch to ring up Dad in the end, to explain that I can't sign anything over to anyone except Bertie, so Dad's not speaking to me at all now, except via Mum, which, all in all, is probably a good thing. I'm hoping I've made the right decision, for all of us, but it still feels like a bolt from the blue has thrown everything up in the air, just like I felt during the divorce, bobbling along and then suddenly you're hit by lightning that you didn't see coming, and you've no idea what just happened but you're left feeling a bit crisp around the edges. I'm not that good at change. I need everything to settle down, just for a while, so I can get my breath back, and then I'll be fine. Although obviously not today, not with everything being in boxes.

"This is going to Devon, right love?"

Mick, our head moving man, is holding up a plastic laundry basket.

"Yes please. I thought I'd put labels on everything, sorry."

I've been sticking on labels for days, but Mick keeps finding things I've missed. Perhaps I should just stick a label on my forehead and go and sit in the back of the van. God knows if we'll need an old plastic basket which only has one handle, but I've got a horrible feeling that what with the B&B laundry on top of the usual endless loads generated by the boys, I'm going to need as many laundry baskets as I can lay my hands on. Right. Time for a cup of tea, I think, since I can't find the gin. And try to avoid remembering that it's Christmas next week and I haven't really started on Operation Tinsel yet.

"I'm putting the kettle on, Mick."

"Lovely, two sugars, and then you'll want to pack the last bits in them boxes, unless you're leaving them here."

Maybe everyone could just head off to Devon and I can have a nice little lie-down, just for a while, in a completely empty quiet house. How lovely. But the final completion on the contracts went through about an hour ago, and the new people are moving in this afternoon, so they might be a tad surprised to find me fast asleep in the middle of their new living room, like a rather grubby Goldilocks, without the porridge. I feel like I've been covered in a thin layer of grime and dust for weeks now, what with emptying out cupboards and trying to clean and pack up here, combined with Ivy washing everything that doesn't move at the Hall like some mad Spring Clean on fast forward. She even gave Betty a bath the other day, which was rather brave of her. Apparently parrots are meant to like a bit of light sprinkle with warm water, but this was more of a total plunge into hot soapy water in a washing-up bowl. The language was quite spectacular, particularly from Betty, and it turns out there's nothing quite so bedraggled and tragic-looking as a sopping-wet parrot in a sulk. By the time she'd finished, Ivy was soaked from head to foot, and so was Bertie. Thankfully

I only had observer status, so I could lurk in the back of scullery trying not to laugh. God help me if parrot-washing duties are handed on to me at any point in the near future, but I'll definitely be borrowing Dan's snorkel.

"What about this bag? In the car or the van, love?"

"In the car please, Mick. It's stuff we'll need tonight. Or some of it, there should be another bag somewhere, a blue one."

"Right you are. First van's nearly full, good job we started yesterday, always more to go than you think."

They're loading everything into three small vans, because their usual lorry would never fit down the drive to the Hall, not without some drastic pruning to most of the trees and shrubs. And pruning over half a mile of rhododendrons was never going to be top of my list today, if I could bloody find it. Although I still think I deserve a gold star for anticipating the lorry would get stuck before we arrived and had to park it by the stables and form a human removal chain to get everything into the house. We're bringing most of our furniture; there's a room next to the kitchen which I want to turn into a family room. It'll be perfect for after-school telly and homework and a playroom for Alfie. Helena used it as an office, so there's only a rickety old desk in there now, and a couple of chairs piled up with old seed packets and gardening magazines. Although now I've seen everything being loaded up, I can't imagine how it's all going to fit in, and I'm not sure how much we'll be able to get up the stairs into the attic, so we might need to use the old stables too, and none of them have what you'd call a complete roof. Either that or we can have a bonfire. Our stuff is mostly what I think the furniture trade would refer to as "old tat."

I've just boiled the kettle when Pete arrives. He's not meant to be here for another hour yet and I'd hoped to have everything ready to go before they came back. The boys go straight out into the garden to play football, even though it's cold and they'll get muddy, which isn't exactly what I had in mind for our journey to Devon. Damn.

"Coffee?"

"Black, please. I decided to bring them back a bit earlier. Janice and I are going shopping later on. I hope that's okay?"

What am I supposed to say, "No, it's not, go away and bring them back later like we agreed?" Despite being surrounded by boxes and removal men, clearly what is most convenient to him is all that matters, as bloody usual. He's doing it on purpose, I know he is.

"It's fine. Biscuit?"

"No thanks. Janice and I are on a diet."

Oh please.

"Won't that make Christmas rather difficult?"

"We're poaching a salmon. There's no need to overindulge, if you don't want to. Which reminds me, could you make sure there's something light for lunch on Boxing Day when I come to see the boys."

"Sure, or feel free to bring your own salmon."

He raises his eyebrows and gives me his soon-to-be-patented The Headmaster Is Not Amused look. God, he's annoying.

"Will you be staying for lunch then? I thought you said you wanted to pick them up and head back."

"I'm not sure; I might just visit for the day. Janice will be at her mother's, and I think the boys might find it strange staying with me when Janice is away."

And he'd find it strange having to do all the cooking and keep them entertained, which is what he actually means. The boys weren't keen on the idea to be honest, he's only managed to have them stay a handful of times over the last year. They don't really enjoy it, so we usually stick to Sunday afternoons. So I'll try to rise above it. Again.

"Mum, can we have hot blackcurrant?"

"No Ben, all the bottles have been packed and they're in the van. But you can have tea, or hot milk. I've got loads of milk left."

I bought extra, for the removal men, and then forgot to cancel the milkman's delivery. So milk is one thing I'm not short of.

"Can we have hot chocolate then?"

"Sure, if you can find it, maybe in that box over there?"

He starts rootling through the box by the kitchen cupboard.

"Ta-da."

"Okay, find me a saucepan, and then give me five minutes."

"Thanks Mum."

Pete is not looking happy.

"Do you want some hot chocolate?"

"Hardly. I did just say we're on a diet."

"Oh yes, sorry."

"I know we discussed this, but I still think you should have mentioned it, I want to make that clear."

"Mentioned what?"

"That you were about to inherit such a large house, and all that land."

"All that land? It's only twenty-two acres Pete. Helena sold the rest of it over the years, you know that."

"Yes, but the house, the stables, everything, by rights you should have declared it."

"Declared what, when?"

"That you were due to inherit such a valuable property, during the divorce. Why did you never mention it before? Janice and I have been discussing it, and we think it should have been included."

I might seriously need to find that gin if he carries on like this.

"It was as much a surprise to me as it was to you. A nicer one for me, of course."

I can't resist saying this.

"And what about the cottage?"

Bloody hell, he'll be asking me for a list of the furniture next.

"Yes Pete, the house, the land, the stables, the cottage, although Ivy and Dennis are living in it and they get to stay for as long as they want, but the old gatehouse, or what's left of it, the gardens, the meadow, the cove, Bertie, the parrot, everything, God help me. I could get Mr. Crouch to send you a complete inventory if you need it? Only you'll have to pay him for it, he bills by the hour."

"That won't be necessary, thank you. But you might have spoken to me, before you decided. After all, I am their father. But I suppose my views don't count at all."

God, if I keep trying to rise above all this bollocks, I'll be bloody levitating.

"Not really Pete. Not now we're divorced."

"There's no need to be bitter Molly, it's very unattractive."

"I'm not bitter, far from it. Maybe everything is starting to come up roses after all, particularly given Helena's famous rose gardens. And this is just what we need, a whole new start. I talked about it with the boys, you know that, and they're excited, well apart from Dan, and the local schools are good—you've read those inspection reports I showed you—and they'll have so much more space."

"Yes. All twenty-two acres of it."

Time for one of Lola's lines I think. They always hit the spot.

"It's kind of you Pete, but don't worry, you can have the boys to stay whenever you like. We can fix up a couple of weeks in the summer holidays too?"

The sad thing is I know he'll say no to this, or he'll make arrangements and then cancel. He's done that for the last two Sundays, so I can't see him managing a whole fortnight in a hurry.

"Let's see, shall we. I am particularly busy at the moment. I still think you should consider selling—it must be worth a fortune—surely that would be the best thing to do? I'd be more than happy to help. It would be important to find the right kind of agent, it's such a unique place."

He tries a smile.

God, he's so transparent it's almost shocking.

"And then if I sold up, you could stop paying maintenance for the boys, is that the idea?"

"Not at all, and I wouldn't be so hasty you know Molly. It might be worth considering."

"It won't, because it's not an option, the terms of the will make that clear. And anyway, I would never do that to Bertie. I'll run the bed-and-breakfast, and I might sign up with an agency for teaching work, once we get settled. I'll need to find a way to make a living, just like I do now."

His smile has vanished, and he looks cross again.

"If you time it right Pete, it's only a six-hour drive—five, if you're lucky—and I know it's a long way, but you'll be welcome to come down and stay anytime you like. You'll find our B-and-B rates are very reasonable."

He looks horrified.

"I'm joking Pete."

Actually I'm not. I'm not having him coming down for weekends and expecting me to run around serving him breakfast. I wouldn't put it past him to try to bring bloody Janice, and there's no way on earth I'm serving both of them breakfast in their new matching bloody tracksuits.

"There are loads of places to stay nearby. I'm sure we can work something out so everyone is happy."

I've been half hoping he'll say he minds about the boys being so much farther away. Even though it would have made everything more difficult, I'd have understood if he'd not been keen on that. But over the past few weeks it's been pretty clear that hasn't really bothered him at all. Which is so sad and disappointing, I don't really want to think about it.

"You could always sell some of the land, I suppose?"

Christ. He's really starting to annoy me now.

"No I can't, not without Bertie's agreement, and anyway, I don't want to. I want to try to make a go of it. Money will be tight, but I'm going to give it my best shot—and by the way, this month's money is late again. So can you sort it please? I did think about breaking the terms of the will, dumping Bertie at the hotel with Roger, and leaving the boys with you for a few months while I floated round the world on a luxury cruise, but I decided against it."

"Don't be ridiculous."

"I quite like the idea of a cruise. I think it would be very restful."

"Apart from anything else, you don't know the first thing about running a bed-and-breakfast, so I can't see how that's going to work. It would have been far better to sell now and save all this upheaval."

"Pete, I practically grew up in the hotel, and I worked there every holiday for years. I should be able to cope with a few B-and-B guests."

Actually I'm pretty nervous about this aspect of our new life, but I'm not letting him know that.

"Yes, but..."

"Please stop being so negative, Pete. It's a great failing of yours, you know, and it's very bad karma."

This is another of Lola's suggestions for ways to annoy him, and it seems to be doing the trick.

"Now, are you sure you don't want some hot chocolate? I've got loads of milk. Call the boys in, would you? Theirs is ready, and we really need to get a move on."

"I'll just say good-bye and then I must be going, I've got a great deal to do today."

"Right."

Christ. Still, no use crying over spilt milk, as they say. Which is a good job, because I manage to pour a fair bit over the kitchen counter while I make the hot chocolate. Right. Find my list. One last check in all the rooms. And good-bye Pete. And good riddance, as Lola would say if she were here. God, I wish she were here. I might need an emergency backup call before we set off. Either that or find that bloody gin. Just a sip would help—I don't want to get arrested for drunk driving. Or I could drink the whole bottle and give one of the removal men my car keys. I think I'll make do with hot chocolate for now, and see how it goes.

By the time we're finally in the car, heading to Devon, I've found my list and everything is relatively peaceful.

"How much longer Mum?"

"Quite a while yet Alfie. Listen to your tape love, and then we'll stop for some food in a bit."

Dan sighs.

"I suppose that'll be pasties all round then."

"Pasties are a speciality of Cornwall, you idiot. They were

invented for miners so they could hold the pastry when their hands were dirty and just eat the filling."

"Thank you, Wikiben. Mum, you've got to stop him using the computer all the time. He's turning into a total nerd."

"Shut up Dan, and that's great Ben, did you find out anything about Devon?"

"It's famous for clotted cream."

Dan sighs again.

"That's so much better."

"Dan, stop it, please. Nobody is going to force-feed you clotted cream."

"Good, because I've already told you I don't want to live in bloody Devon."

"No, but you don't want to live in London either. You don't want to do anything except moan as far as I can work out. And please stop being so rude. We've already talked about that today. Just give Devon a try, that's all I'm asking. We were always going to have to move when we sold the house, you know that, love. Be fair."

"Alright, alright. I said I'd give it a go and I will. But you owe me one Mum, big-time."

"Fair enough."

"Can I have a motorbike when I'm sixteen?"

"No. But if you don't like your new school, you can go to Hogwarts."

He grins.

"Okay."

He spent ages trying to convince me that Hogwarts really existed after we read the books. He was sure if he could persuade me to enroll him, he could be the next Harry.

"I'm putting an owl on my list for Father Christmas. Just so you know."

"Thanks for the heads-up, Dan. But Father Christmas doesn't do pets, you know that."

Thank God I had the sense to invent this Santa Claus disclaimer, or I'd be living in a bloody menagerie by now.

"He might, in Devon."

"I wouldn't hold your breath, love."

We stop at a café recommended by the movers, where they can get sausage, eggs, and chips and huge mugs of tea for less than the price of a packet of coffee and a muffin in a motorway service station. There are lorry drivers from every nation sitting side by side, eating and looking tired. But the food is delicious, and we're clearly a bit of a novelty, because the woman behind the counter gives the boys a free doughnut each. Alfie gets sugar everywhere and makes me promise we will come here every single time we go in the car, which might make the school run a bit tricky, but I play along for the sake of in-car harmony, and eventually he falls asleep, still covered in sugar.

"Can we turn the music up a bit?"

Ben clearly wants to enjoy his turn in the front seat.

"No, Alfie's just got to sleep—please let's leave him that way. He was up really early this morning and it's going to be a long day."

"Good job he's asleep. I wish I was too, listening to Ben's crap music."

"Dan, when it's your turn in the front, you get to choose, okay? Or else I'll choose for the both of you."

"Great, so that'll be 'The Wheels on the Stupid Bus,' totally awesome way to arrive in the Land of Clotted Cream."

Ben sighs.

"Shut up Dan, or she'll throw apple juice at you. Again."

"I didn't throw it; it just squirted out of the carton. And don't say 'she.'"

"Shut up Dan, or Mum will throw apple juice all over you again."

His blue T-shirt is now covered with dried brown spatters. But the look on his face when it happened was almost worth the laundry nightmare I will no doubt be having when I try to restore the T-shirt to its former glory. Because of course it's one of his best ones. Of course it is.

"I don't know why you made such a fuss, Dan. It looks just like that one you tried to con me into buying you when we got your new jeans."

They both tut. United tutting. Great. This is going very well so far. Dan mutters "completely bloody hopeless" under his breath.

"Mummy, Dan said 'bloody,' and that's a rude word isn't it? Can I say it, because if he can say it, I should be able to—that's fair, isn't it? It's important to be fair you know Mummy. Can I have some juice?"

Ben and Dan both sigh.

"Mum?"

"Yes, Dan?"

"I think the Kid has woken up."

"Yes, thanks Dan, I'd spotted that."

"Just like to keep you informed. Shall we dope him up again? Where's the Calpol?"

I know without turning round that Alfie is now sitting up a little bit straighter in his seat, eyes widening at the prospect of his brother doping him up.

"Stop teasing him, Dan, and pass him a drink. There's a carton of juice in the bag, and be careful with the straw."

"Are we nearly there yet?"

"Not yet love."

"I'm hungry."

"There's fruit in the bag."

"I don't want fruit. And I don't want Calpol."

"I know, love. Dan was only joking. You only have Calpol when you're feeling ill, you know that."

"I know. And I don't want it. I want vodka."

"I have taught you well, O little one. Go forth and share thy wisdom."

"Don't do your Darth Vader voice Dan, you know it scares him. Can anyone still see the removal vans?"

Bugger. A series of roundabouts seem to have separated us from the vans.

"Great, so not so much of a convoy after all then Mum, given it's just us."

"Thanks Ben. I had worked that out for myself. Ring them would you Dan, and check they're still on the right road."

"Heading back to London, if they've got any sense."

Alfie starts to sing.

"Put a sock in it, would you?"

Alfie carries on, and there's a muffled sound, and then a shriek from Alfie.

"Mum, Dan put his sock in my mouth. Right in my mouth."

"Dan, stop it."

Dan has been taking his socks off ever since he was old enough to be wearing them. I used to spend ages retracing my steps around shops looking for tiny baby socks, which he'd pop onto the nearest shelf while I was trying to read the ingredients on the jars of baby food. Although why I bothered, God alone knows. He seemed so fragile, and giving him organic carrots seemed so important then, but now he's nearly six foot tall, with enough testosterone to power an entire flotilla of teenage landing craft, it doesn't seem to matter quite so much.

One minute you're pureeing veg, and the next you're into the sex-and-drugs-and-rock-and-roll chats, and trying to make sure you eat at least one meal together every day. Or most days, when nobody has stormed off upstairs in a sulk.

I really want to make sure we carry on with our family routines at the Hall, even if we have to adapt them to include Bertie and a mad parrot. Family mealtimes are the only way to really keep track of what they're up to, and I need all the help I can get. When they were babies, it was all so much easier. It didn't seem like it at the time, but it was. Dan was only two when Ben was born, and then Ben never slept, literally never for more than about fifteen minutes at a time for the first few months. He had terrible colic, and then eczema, and then just as he started to grow out of it and they were both at school, Alfie arrived. If I didn't know better, I'd think Alfie was nothing to do with Pete at all. We all have brown hair and dark-green eyes—in my case, hazel—but Alfie's my blond and blue-eyed boy. Pete's brother Sam is the same, so that's the genetic clue which averted a steward's enquiry. Although Sam took one look at his family and promptly buggered off and joined a band. He's quite a famous music producer now, so we only see him once in a blue moon. I must remember to send him our new address. He can come down for the weekend; at least we've got the room now. Unless we're packed to the rafters with all our tatty furniture of course. Oh God, I'm dreading all the unpacking.

"Mum?"

"Yes Alfie?"

"It's not fair I can't sit in the front."

I'm going to ignore this.

"Mum?"

"Yes Alfie?"

"It's very rude to ignore people."

Ben sighs.

"Give it a rest, would you? She heard you, we all did. Since we're not allowed to have my music on loud enough to drown out whining brothers, we haven't really got a choice."

"I can't drive with loud music Ben, it's dangerous, and we'd all be deaf by the time we got to Devon."

"That might work actually; I wonder how you say 'Annie Rose' in sign language."

Alfie reacts instantly to the dreaded Annie Rose name and an apple comes sailing over the top of Ben's seat and lands on the dashboard.

"Alfie, that's very dangerous. Don't ever throw things in the car. Ben, don't you dare throw that back, and Dan, stop teasing him. Honestly Alfie, only babies throw food."

He'll hate being called a baby, but I can't drive all the way to Devon dodging fruit.

If we were richer, we'd be in one of those huge cars with DVD players for every passenger seat, but we're not, so they're stuck in a small family hatchback with not much in the way of in-car entertainment, unless you like dodging fruit. Although to be honest I'm not sure a childhood where you're never bored for more than five minutes is ideal preparation for life. I'm pretty sure a bit of being bored and just having to get on with it is probably better for you than being treated like a VIP who has to be constantly entertained. What happens when you start your first job and nobody has thought of how you can be entertained during a boring morning? It must be such a shock.

"Ben."

"Yes?"

"Thanks for not retaliating."

"That's okay Mum, he can't help being such a total wanker."

Alfie's screeching now.

"Be quiet Alfie, right now, or there'll be no cartoons at all tonight."

Actually there may be no cartoons even if he does stop yelling as God knows what channels the telly gets, but I'm not telling anyone that until after we've arrived.

"And Ben, if you can't say anything nice, then don't say anything at all."

When they were born, I had visions of being the kind of mother who inspires creativity, whilst simultaneously making perfect scones and soothing furrowed brows with a cool hand and a peaceful manner. Little did I know that what I really needed was a mixture of the kind of nerves of steel more usually associated with fighter pilots. Judging the perfect time to deploy your countermeasures is pretty vital too: use your ammunition too early and you miss your target; too late, and it can hurtle straight back at you. You need to keep your eyes on the horizon whilst simultaneously scanning your instrument panel to see where the red lights are flickering, before the engine bursts into flames and you have to press your emergency ejector seat, only to discover you've left your parachute at home underneath a pile of coats in the hall. I've always thought family cars should have ejector seats. Never mind the DVD players, I'm sure a button that propels your nearest and dearest into a nearby field would be a guaranteed winner in the family-vehicle market.

Alfie is still yelling, and Dan and Ben are now joining him.

"The next person who yells or says anything rude about their brother loses all their pocket money this week."

This is risky because Ben sometimes does a quick calculation and decides that five pounds is a price he's willing to pay to repeatedly call his brother a wanker, but I know he's saving up for a computer game, so I'm in with a chance.

"There might be extra pocket money for anyone who is being extra nice though."

"Mum."

"Yes, Ben."

"I thought you said bribery was a bad thing."

"For the police, yes, and for banks. Not for mothers."

"But when the police stopped us that time..."

I once got stopped for speeding, and they've never forgotten it. Forty-three miles per hour in a thirty-miles-per-hour zone, hardly likely to get me featured on the next *Police Camera Terrifying Drivers* television special. But still exciting when you're small and there are blue lights flashing.

"I was trying to get home before Alfie woke up and needed feeding."

"Yes, and then you handed him to that policeman."

"Well what was I supposed to do, leave all three of you in the car on your own, sobbing?"

"I wasn't sobbing, and neither was Dan."

"You soon would have been if I'd left you locked in a car with a screaming baby."

"He let you off though, didn't he? And that's bribery, using a baby to bribe the police. I bet that's against the Highway Code Mum."

"No it isn't Dan, the Highway Code was written by men, so there's no mention of babies."

Actually the police let me off with a warning and they both saluted as they drove past. The older one told me he had two girls under four at home and sometimes did extra shifts just to get a bit of peace and quiet.

"Babies can't drive, so why do they need to be in the Highway Code? That's just stupid."

"No it's not Ben. Babies should at least get a mention, since they're a major driving hazard. You could have special passes for your windscreen if your baby is about to wake up, or your toddler is about to wee all over the backseat, so you're allowed to use the bus lane and get home in half the time. Never mind buses and taxis, anyone trying to get home before their toddler goes into meltdown should definitely get priority."

All three of them tut. Time to change the subject.

"I know, let's play a game. I Spy?"

"I spy with my little eye something beginning with *W*."

"Dan, it better not be anything that rhymes with 'banker.'"

"Give me a minute, I'll think of another one."

Bertie is standing at the door when we arrive, with Betty perched on his shoulder.

"Hello my dears. Welcome all. Brought enough vans with you? Come in and have a sharpener. Need a decent drink on a busy day."

"Thanks Bertie. A cup of tea would be lovely."

"Need more than tea, small glass of something warming?"

The removal men are all nodding.

"Let's start with tea please, Uncle Bertie. Hello Betty."

"Bugger off."

Dennis appears with Tess, his sheepdog, who starts barking

and running round in circles, trying to herd us into the house. The boys are thrilled, particularly Ben, who's always wanted a dog. So now we've got a parrot doing high-pitched whistling and telling the dog to bugger off, and a hysterical sheepdog alongside three boys letting off steam after being stuck in the car for hours. Perfect.

The next couple of hours pass by in a blur of boxes and removal men asking where to put things whilst simultaneously trying to give Betty a very wide berth—apart from Mick, who seems to have taken a bit of a shine to her. Bertie has thankfully stopped trying to give everyone a drink, although I have a sneaking suspicion Mick has already enjoyed a glass or two of something on the quiet. Not that anything is exactly quiet, particularly with Betty around, entertaining us all with her full repertoire, including a very realistic impression of the telephone ringing, so I have to keep rushing to answer it only to find it's not actually ringing. Mick seems to find this particularly amusing.

"Nice place this is, love, and that parrot's a bit of a card, isn't she? I should think you'll do alright here—good B-and-Bs are hard to come by, me and the lads have stayed in some shockers. The parrot will be a nice feature, make people remember you."

"That's one way of looking at it, I suppose."

"That Ivy was saying your aunt only went in for it as a sideline."

Mick has also spent a fair amount of time in the kitchen, helping Ivy unpack boxes.

"Yes, the garden was her pride and joy."

I'm half tempted to wander out there myself; at least I'd get a bit of peace.

"You can see that love, even this time of year, laid out lovely it is. Take a bit of looking after I shouldn't wonder, a great big place like this."

I think that may be the understatement of the century. A late-Georgian manor house, with more egg-and-dart cornicing and fluted columns than you can shake a stick at, even just doing a quick Hoover round takes hours, never mind all the polishing. There's even a ha-ha, which Alfie has already fallen into twice playing football; the new definition of "goal" now appears to be if your brother drops out of sight into the four-foot ditch at the end of the lawn. I think "a bit of looking after" won't even begin to cover it.

"Right, well, this won't get that last van unpacked."

We're walking across the hall towards the front door when all the lights go out.

Bloody hell.

"That'll be the fuse box love. Too many lights on, I shouldn't wonder. Where is it?"

"I've got no idea."

Ivy appears, thank God, followed by Bertie, carrying a ship's lantern.

"Always comes in handy, this."

"Don't you worry, Miss Molly. Dennis is down the cellar and he'll fix it in no time, happens all the time."

Bugger, so that's something else to add to the list: sort out the electrics and the fuse box, so we don't have to keep trooping down to the cellar in pitch-darkness. And get Dennis to show me what to do if it happens when they're not here.

"Mum?"

"Yes, Dan."

"It's going really well so far, isn't it? When are we having supper?"

* * *

By the time the removal men leave, all our furniture appears to have been swallowed up by the house. I still can't quite believe it, there seemed so many boxes, but they've all fitted in somehow. I spent ages planning who would have each room with Ivy before we arrived, so the boys could feel at home with familiar things. Dan was keen on having a room in the attic, but I'll need to sort out the heating and the roof before he can escape to a different floor from the rest of us. There are eight bedrooms, and the staircase divides halfway up. There's a door on the upstairs landing dividing the two halves with four bedrooms in each, which is a particular blessing since it means we'll be separate from the guests. Bertie has a huge room to the right, with a dressing room and his own bathroom, and then there are three B-and-B bedrooms: two doubles and a single. One of the doubles has a sea view and an en suite, and the other one looks over the front of the house and shares a Jack and Jill bathroom with the single, although why they're called "Jack and Jill" I have no idea, particularly if you're a complete stranger to the Jack or Jill who comes wandering in while you're in the bath. The rooms are large and rather grand, if a bit faded, and all the windows have shutters, and there are working fireplaces in each room, with lovely old tiles and antique grates. There's so much potential to make something glorious, if you had endless money, but even without any money I'm still going to aim for glorious. It might just take a bit longer.

The other four bedrooms to the left of the stairs are similar. Actually there are five if you count my dressing room, which used to be Helena's, but I'm trying not to think about that. We've moved the beds around, and put a couple of old mattresses up in the attic, and I've spotted an old brass bedstead up there which I've got my eye on, but we'll see. I've got a huge bathroom too, with an enormous cast-iron bath, and then there's a family bathroom for the boys to share, thankfully without doors opening into anyone's bedroom. There's a walk-in linen cupboard too, by the stairs to the attic, and I've already had quite a few peaceful moments in there amongst all the piles of linen and dried lavender; it will be a perfect bolt hole when it all gets too much. I can pretend I'm counting sheets when I'm on the verge of hysterics—although if today is anything to go by, I'll be spending a fair bit of time in there, so I might see if I can fit a chair in. It can be my very own version of a meditation zone, but without the annoying music or beanbags. But first I better start on supper and baths, particularly for people who have fallen into the ha-ha playing football.

By nine Ben and Alfie are upstairs and officially in bed, but are probably unpacking toys and reuniting themselves with long-forgotten treasures. Dan is having his precious extra half hour watching telly. Ivy's booked the telly man to come tomorrow to sort out the satellite, so for now they've had to content themselves with just four channels, which hasn't gone down well. I'd like to sort out televisions for the guest rooms too eventually—I'll add it to the list. But the new family room has worked out, and all our stuff doesn't look as tatty as I feared. I did wonder if the mix of cheap and cheerful Ikea in amongst all this Georgian glory might look a bit pathetic, but it's fine, probably because we're in the servants' quarters, right by the kitchen and the scullery, with the old chipped sink and the washing machines, so there's a bit less in the way of ornate cornicing. The walls could do with painting, and the fireplace has a battered old electric fire, which I'll definitely move before anyone tries to turn it on and burn the house down. But so far so good.

Ivy's in the kitchen.

"Shall we have a drink Ivy?"

"I was just putting the kettle on."

"Lovely."

"I could fancy a drink too Mum. Have we got any lager?"

"Don't be cheeky, Dan."

Ivy smiles.

"Get away with you, and here, take these up, there's a dear. Put one in each of your beds, take the chill off."

Dan trots off clutching three hot-water bottles.

"Thanks so much Ivy, for everything today. I don't know how I would have managed without you and Dennis."

"I'll just rinse these things, and then I'll be back up in the morning, around seven suit you?"

Bloody hell, that's early.

"I think we'll have a lazy start tomorrow."

She sniffs.

"I don't hold with stopping in bed. I like to be up and about."

"Right."

"And Mr. Bertie has his breakfast at half past seven."

"Okay."

"I wasn't sure what the boys like, so I got some extra bacon, and eggs? I haven't got any mushrooms, though, I didn't like the look of them in the farm shop."

"Bacon will be lovely, Ivy, only you don't have to cook for us. We've already talked about that. If you just carry on looking after Bertie, that would be great, but we'll be fine."

"Let's see how we get on."

This is what Ivy says when she's about to completely ignore you.

"I'll cook breakfast for the boys, and then we'll make our plans for the day—how does that sound?"

She nods, and there's a ringing noise.

"What's that? Is it Betty?"

I'm definitely going to get a new phone system, with cordless phones I can carry with me, preferably with parrot-proof ring tones.

Ivy gets up and walks towards the door.

"It's one of the room bells upstairs. I expect it will be one of the boys."

We both look up at the board on the wall, and sure enough the Bedroom 3 bell is flashing, and making a piercing ringing noise.

Christ.

"I didn't know they still worked."

"Oh yes, although that silly bird can do them too, so you're never sure."

"Great. Can't we disconnect it or something? The bells, not the bird. Although on second thoughts."

She giggles, not something I've seen her ever do before.

"Shall I go up then, see what they want?"

"Definitely not Ivy. You go home, and we'll see you tomorrow. Leave it to me."

"Well, if you're sure."

"Absolutely."

The bell rings again.

"Alfie, you're not to do that. Ever again."

"But I need a drink of water and I didn't know where you were."

"I was down with Ivy, and that's not the point."

"Yes, but I called you and you didn't come, so I had to press it. Dan told me to."

"Well I'll talk to him about that, but if you need me, come and find me."

"It's dark."

"No it isn't. The light's on in the hall, and downstairs, and this is our house now, Alfie, just like our old house. What did you do if you wanted me at our old house?"

"I came and found you."

"Yes. So that's what you do here. But not just to pretend you need a drink."

"I do, I really do."

"Just this once then, but not every night, Alfie. And if you need a wee in the night, you know where the bathroom is, don't you?"

"Oh yes, I've already done a wee."

"I know, but if you need another one?"

"I'm not a baby Mum."

"Sorry."

"And Mum?"

"Yes love?"

"Can I have a snack, because I'm starving?"

"No. You can't. And if you keep on, you won't get a glass of water either."

He sighs.

Christ, I'm going to have to watch it or all three of them will be ringing for room service. I might as well start learning to bloody curtsy.

I'm filling a glass with water in the kitchen, when Dan appears.

"Hi Mum, are you getting him his drink, then?"

"Yes, and thanks for telling him to ring the bell, that was so helpful. Next time just come and find me, would you?"

"In this great big old place? No thanks; it's probably haunted."

"Of course it isn't."

He grins.

"I thought the bell would be handy. Save him whining at me and Ben."

"Sure. But it'll cost you. How about one pound every time he uses it? I can take it from your pocket money. Unless you want to be the person who answers it every time he rings?"

"That's so not fair."

"No, and neither is me becoming a housemaid racing round answering bloody bells. It's bad enough with that stupid parrot. So think about it."

The bell rings again.

"That'll be your brother—shall I go, or will you?"

"I hate this house."

"No you don't. And tomorrow we can talk about how you want your room done. We can choose some paint if you like, and get you a proper desk."

"And I can have my own computer, in my room?"

"Yup."

I've been pretty strict about TVs and computers in bedrooms, but he'll need a computer for his homework and I want to be encouraging.

"You can have a laptop, but it needs to be back downstairs on the kitchen table by ten thirty every night."

"Ten thirty?"

"That's the deal Dan, otherwise you'll be up all night watching God knows what, keeping us all awake."

"I can wear earphones."

"That's not my point, and you know it. Ten thirty or no laptop. And I'll be checking. Take it or leave it."

"And the others can't touch it. It's just mine?"

"Yes, love."

He hesitates.

"Okay. Thanks Mum."

The bell rings again.

"You better go love, or you won't get a tip."

"Don't worry Mum, I'll be giving him a tip of my own."

"Yes, but don't frighten him Dan. Remember, he's a lot littler than you."

He grins.

"And then we can get your laptop, tomorrow maybe."

He gives me a hug.

"I'll be up in a minute. Night, love."

"Night Mum. I think it might be alright here, you know."

"That's good. So do I."

I finally get to bed at two a.m., after making the mistake of opening just one more box and unpacking clothes. I'm so tired I walk into the bathroom door, and now it feels like I've broken my toe. It's cold, and hearing the sea is oddly familiar, like when I was little and we were in the staff flat at the hotel, so I'm half expecting Mum to come in and ask me why my light is on, or to make me a milky drink. Actually a hot drink might be a good idea, but I can't face hobbling down to the kitchen and I'm a bit nervous of that bloody AGA cooker. I know they're very fashionable now, but I'm bound to lift the wrong lid and then it will be stone-cold by morning and I know they're a total bugger to turn back on. We had one years ago before Mum got her new kitchen, and after watching her spend a fair bit of time crouching down peering into it, twiddling dials to get the stupid thing hot enough to actually cook things, I'm pretty keen to avoid Ivy coming in tomorrow morning to find me doing the same.

And it's not just the stupid AGA. God knows what I was thinking moving us down here. I'm never going to be able to pull this off. At least in London I had a job, and a grown-up life, of sorts. Now I seem to have turned myself into a glorified housekeeper, and not a very good one if I can't even face making a milky drink, and seeing Pete earlier didn't help either.

I'm sure he wasn't such a total arse when I married him, but maybe he was and I just couldn't see it. Or I was so keen to get away from here, I ignored it. And now I've come back to where I started, with three boys and no money to speak of, and I know you're not meant to look a gift horse in the mouth, but it's hard remembering to be grateful when the horse arrives at full gallop and tramples you into the mud, and I've got a feeling our new country life is going to involve a fair bit of mud. And I'm running a B&B, and catering to the great British public, who everyone knows are completely bonkers. I'll spend years dealing with people whining on about how they want their bacon and why can't I stop it raining, in between trying to stop Bertie causing a major coast-guard incident by firing his cannon at the wrong moment, and simultaneously fending off a mad parrot who keeps telling me to bugger off.

Christ, what have I done? If my toe didn't hurt so much, I'd run away, right now, in my PJs. There must be somewhere a woman on the edge can go until she can pull herself together. Or there bloody well should be. They have rescue homes for cats and dogs who've got a bit frayed round the edges; there must be something for women who've Had Enough. Actually maybe that could be my theme for the B&B, I can still go for the nautical stripes and pale seaside tones I was imagining, but I can specialise in providing an escape for women in urgent need of a break. No husbands, partners, or kids. Just a few days peace and quiet, with nobody asking you a single question apart from what would you like for breakfast. It wouldn't need to be fancy, just warm and quiet like one of those convalescent homes they set up in grand country houses during the Second World War, where people who'd survived the Blitz could sit in a wicker chair and try to stop shaking. Pack up your troubles in your old kit bag and smile, smile, smile. I'm humming to myself now, which is helping, a bit. So that's a start. But still. Bloody hell.

"Mum?"

"Yes Alfie?"

"I can't get to sleep, and my duvet's gone all faffled."

"I know just how it feels."

"Yes, but can I be in your bed, just for tonight. Please Mum."

"Just for tonight."

He wriggles about a bit, and I keep a firm grip on the duvet, or he'll roll himself up in it like a sausage roll, and I'll end up frozen stiff.

"Mum?"

"No."

"I didn't even get to say my thing."

"It's very late Alfie. Either go to sleep or go back to your own bed. You can save any questions for morning, that's the deal. Okay?"

"Okay."

"Night love."

"Night Mum. But if I get my own parrot, it can sleep in my room with me, can't it Mum?"

Bloody hell, another parrot? I don't bloody think so.

"Nobody is getting a parrot Alfie. Betty wouldn't like it, and neither would I. Now go to sleep, or go back to your own bed. I'm counting to ten."

"I'm asleep now, nearly. Count slowly."

* * *

Alfie is up at the crack of dawn the next morning, as usual, and I briefly surface, but he seems quite happy pottering about unpacking boxes of toys, so I treat myself to a lie-in, and then wake up at eight, to silence. The boys must be downstairs already, and I'm dithering about whether to get dressed before I go down. It feels wrong to be going downstairs in my dressing gown, a bit like that dream where you're doing an assembly with the whole school and it's all going fine until you look down and realise you're not wearing any trousers. But we live here now, and I've got to get over the idea that Helena will wander in from the garden at any moment and give me one of her Looks. I just wish I had smarter PJs on though. I think I may need to invest in what I think the fashion police call leisure wear: velour tracksuits in pastel shades, that kind of thing, so I can get dressed quickly in the mornings, although if we ever get any bookings for the B&B, my wearing a velour tracksuit will probably be the least of my worries.

Ivy's serving breakfast to the boys in the kitchen when I get downstairs, wearing a floral apron and humming to herself. Damn. I'll have to make sure I get up earlier from now on. Not that it isn't lovely of course, but I don't want them thinking everything has changed, and apart from that they'll be ordering light snacks and running her off her feet.

"Thanks, Ivy, we usually just have cereal, so this is a real treat."

"Shall I put some more toast on?"

"Please. And then Dan, when you've finished, you clear the table. And Ben, we'll go up and make the beds. Alfie, you come too. And then we'll get more of the unpacking done."

"I can manage, Miss Molly. You just go ahead."

Damn, she's back to her "Miss Molly" routine. I thought we'd had a breakthrough on that front yesterday.

"I know you can, but you really don't have to, Ivy, because Dan is going to help you. Aren't you, Dan?"

He nods, thank God. This would not be a good time for one of his "Why do I have to do it?" routines.

"I thought we'd head into Ilfracombe later for some Christmas shopping, or maybe Barnstaple? Come with us if you'd like to, Ivy?"

"Ooh, that would be lovely, only could it be this afternoon? I thought I'd make a chicken pie for lunch and I've still got the veg to do. There'll be more than enough to go round, so there's no need to worry about lunch, dear."

Good, we're back to "dear." Maybe we're just going to have one "Miss Molly" each day. I can probably live with that.

"Perfect, and Ben's great at peeling veg, aren't you, Ben?"

He nods, whilst trying to shoot me dagger looks at the same time.

"That'll be champion then. Nice to have a bit of help. After your breakfast you can nip out and see what Dennis has got in the garden, there's a good boy, only don't let him tread mud across my scullery floor—he's a devil for keeping his boots on when he brings the veg in. Do you like turnips? Mr. Bertie is quite partial to mashed turnip with a bit of white pepper."

Ben is clearly surprised to find himself talking about vegetables quite so early in the morning, but he rallies and soon they're discussing cabbage and sprouts, which Dan seems to be finding highly amusing as he starts to clear the table.

"Do you like turnips too, Daniel? I like to see boys eating up their veg."

"Er, kind of."

She pats his hand.

Bless.

My Christmas shopping list gets longer over the next few days, but at least we finally unpack all the boxes and I'm starting to feel like we actually live here now. The boys aren't spending all their time glued to the television, partly because the satellite still isn't sorted, but also because they've taken to roaming around with Bertie, patrolling the cove and exploring the old stables and generally becoming much more pink-cheeked and tired in the evenings than they used to in London, which is brilliant, and just what I was hoping for. Even if there is far more mud involved than I ever thought possible.

Tess has been a huge hit too, and seems delighted with the three new family members who will throw things for her. She's taken to leaving a pile of sticks by the back door, ready for action. And Betty hasn't taken a nip out of anyone yet, so we're doing pretty well on the animal front—apart from the stupid chickens, who go into a major squawking and flapping meltdown whenever I open the door to the henhouse to feed them. In fact they go all beady-eyed and psychotic-looking whenever any of us even approaches the vicinity of the bloody henhouse. I'm seriously hoping they're going to calm down soon and get over it, or I might rethink the poultry thing and go in for something more relaxing. Like buying our eggs at the farmers' market and letting someone else handle the squawking and flapping.

I'm in the garden with Dennis. He loves the roses, but the

beautiful old walled kitchen garden has always been his exclusive domain, and he's very proud of it. Lots of the beds are empty at this time of year, but there are carrots and Brussels sprouts, and kale and cabbage, and he's just shown me the leeks and celery and something called winter spinach, which looks exactly the same as ordinary spinach to me, but with thicker leaves.

"What are these pots for Dennis?"

"They're forcing-pots, for the rhubarb. Cost you a fortune nowadays. These ones are antiques, been here as long as I can remember, but they do the trick. You put a layer of straw over the crowns, and then the pots bring them on a few weeks early. Mr. Bertie is partial to a bit of rhubarb."

"Right."

Ivy comes out to find us with a coat on over her apron.

"Are you two ready yet, because I've got ever such a lot to do you know?"

"Sorry Ivy, we're just coming."

Ivy's decided we should tour the house, with Dennis showing me all the jobs that need doing so I can write things down, which in theory is an excellent idea, but I'd much rather stay outside and look at the veg—it's so much more peaceful. My To Do list is already more of a booklet than a list. Actually, maybe we should take some brandy; I think that's meant to be the thing for shock.

As we walk through the dining room, Dennis points out where the radiator burst a couple of years ago.

"Should replace them all by rights, and those shutters need taking down and oiling, but they do keep the heat in, I'll say that for them Miss."

"Okay, Mister."

He smiles.

"What did you call Helena?"

"'Lady H'?"

"You did not."

"Sometimes I did, or 'Madam.' Sometimes a few other things, behind her back." He smiles. "She could be difficult, you know, when she didn't get her own way."

Ivy smiles.

"We will try Miss Molly—oh, I've done it again. It's hard though, after all these years."

"I know Ivy. It's mainly in front of the boys. You can call me whatever you like when they're not around."

"They're lovely boys, all three of them. Your Alfie's a bright spark and no mistake, and that bird has taken to him, never seen anything like it."

"I know. He's on about wanting a parrot of his own now, but I really don't think we want two."

Dennis smiles.

"Don't you worry. I can always get my air rifle down from our loft."

Ivy tuts.

"You're not to let those boys see that Dennis, I've told you."

"Yes Dennis, I have enough trouble getting them into bed as it is. I wouldn't stand a chance if they knew where you kept a rifle."

"It only fires pellets, just give you a sting. But point taken."

We're all smiling as we walk upstairs.

"Thought we'd start up in the attics and work our way down?"

"Good idea."

"Watch yourself Miss. There's dust everywhere."

I think my Just Call Me Molly campaign is going to take a while. I don't want to make them uncomfortable, but what with the bloody parrot "Hello Dollying" me all the time, I'm starting to feel like I'm in a weird episode of *Upstairs Downstairs* and I'm the famous Music Hall act who's visiting for the weekend. Good Golly, Miss Molly, with a song for every occasion.

"She would never let me clean up here, so it needs a good tidy-up."

"I'm putting it on the list Ivy."

"Cobwebs as big as your hat. And those trunks need a good clear-out too."

Dennis is clearly not impressed.

"Never mind about a bit of dust, woman, it's the roof she wants to worry about, not you and your dusting."

We start at the end of the corridor, going into a series of small bedrooms with tiny windows under the eaves of the roof, with old latches firmly stuck shut, and old bed frames stacked up against the walls, including the brass one I've got my eye on for my room, if we ever make it that far down my list. There's plaster coming off the walls in places, and a smell of damp.

"That guttering needs sorting, but that's easily fixed, and we'll need a few new tiles for the roof."

"I'm writing it down."

"I'm not too sure about the wiring up here, what with the rain getting in."

We all look at the assortment of old bowls and a tin bath in one corner of the room, and the old brown Bakelite light switches.

"I bring a torch up here when the weather's bad, just in case. Those switches are ancient, and you don't want to touch any live wires by mistake, do you?"

"Not really, no. Do you know a good electrician, just so we can make sure it's not dangerous while I work out a proper plan of what I can afford to do first?"

"I can ring old Ted. He won't charge you a fortune. He's a good man."

"Thanks Dennis."

"He could have a look at the gatehouse too, if you'd like?"

"That would be great. How long has it been empty now?"

"A good few years. Old Mr. Parsons used to be Head Gardener in the old days—different world back then. He'd gone by the time we arrived here, and that was over twenty years ago now. I came out of the navy at the same time as Mr. Bertie, and he offered us the job here, and we've never regretted it, have we Ivy?"

"No, we haven't. Although there's always more things that need doing than there are hours in the day."

Dennis nods.

"These big old houses need a small army of help, indoors and out. Mr. Parsons had a team of three Under Gardeners, and a lad. There are old ledgers in the library, and you can see all the names of the staff. Beautiful handwriting they had back then. Mind you, it must have been hard. He lived in the gatehouse with his family—four children I think they had—and there's no bathroom to speak of, just the old back boiler so you had to keep the fire on if you wanted hot water. I've kept an eye on it over the years: the roof wants sorting out soon, or it will be beyond saving. There were plans drawn up to renovate it a few years back, but it was too expensive."

"It would make a great holiday let, if I can afford to do it up."

Ivy nods.

"It's poor Mrs. Parsons I feel sorry for, having to do all her washing in that old copper boiler and lugging that old tin bath around. Still, it was all different years ago—you just got on with it, you had no choice. When I think of the prices they charge now, for renting out old cottages, they're asking nearly five hundred pounds a week for a poky flat overlooking the harbour in the summer. With people wandering about right outside your window eating their fish and chips. They want their heads examined."

Dennis nods.

"I'll ask Mr. Stebbings to come and have a proper look for you, shall I? We'd like the see the old place fixed up, wouldn't we Ivy?"

"We would, only would they want their breakfasts cooked, do you think, Molly?"

She pauses for us all to acknowledge she has called me "Molly."

"No, they'd be self-catering. That's one of advantages of rentals: more income and a lot less work."

"Well that's a blessing because we're busy enough with the B-and-B guests, and some of them are never happy. I had to get Dennis to have a word with one of them last year, didn't I Dennis?"

"Yes, thought he could wander down at half past eleven and click his fingers for a full cooked breakfast. I soon set him straight. Now then, the water tanks are in the next room—they got replaced about twenty years ago I think, so they should last a bit longer. If everyone runs a bath at the same time, the pipes sometimes bang. But apart from that, they should be alright."

"Are we nearly done up here, because I've got pastry to roll out, and you don't want to be worrying her sick, Dennis. Just a quick tour round is all we said, not you worrying her out of her wits."

"She'll want the full picture."

"Yes, but she'll also want her lunch, is all I'm saying."

I've noticed they do this quite often, talk about me as if I'm not there. I'm taking it as a good sign, that I feel familiar to them now—either that or it's like parents talking about a child, making sure she's not getting up to any mischief.

"This is pretty."

There's an old chest of drawers in the corner of the last bedroom, in faded pine. It's dusty, but I bet with a bit of polish it would be lovely.

Ivy nods.

"There's some nice trunks too. You should have a look through them, full of old clothes, things from years back, when they used to have grand parties here. Helena never went in for any of that. She used to say she had enough of it in the navy, what with Mr. Bertie being an Admiral and them having to go to all the big dinners in London. But her mother used to entertain."

"Yes, she used to tell me about the parties. They sounded very glamorous."

"Her grandmother danced with the Prince of Wales you know, at a ball in London. You should have a look at some of the frocks, evening things, some of them must have taken days to make, beautiful embroidery and beads. The keys are all in the jar in the pantry."

Ivy and I have been trying to gradually sort through the huge jar and reunite miscellaneous keys with various locks around the house and then write labels. Ivy very much approves of this, and has made Dennis put up a pegboard with a series of hooks so we can proudly display our new orderly system.

"I'd love to, once we find the keys."

"Some of those old clothes can be valuable, you know. Good job they've been in the trunks, stop the mice getting at them."

Dennis tuts.

"Tell me off for worrying her and then you start on about mice. Don't you worry, it's just a few field mice. They come in each winter, but I put the bait down and that soon sorts them out. And they don't tend to open trunks, not as a general rule. Now then, there's just one bathroom up here, hasn't been used for years, so I wouldn't try the taps if I were you."

"Okey doke."

Oh God. Something else for my list.

By the time we've finished the complete tour, with a break for lunch, it's starting to get dark and I definitely need a drink. With broken sash cords, sagging shutters, damp plaster, chimneys which don't draw properly in an east wind, and haven't done since the War, cracked tiles, wobbly floorboards, ancient electrics, and antique plumbing, it's a wonder the place is still standing. And that's before I get to the B&B bathrooms, with their faded floral wallpaper and stained ceilings from old leaks. They're tidy enough, but basic, so getting them looking a bit more respectable has got to be a top priority too. Helena only did B&B during the summer months, but we'll need to do better than that if we're going to make enough money to keep everything going. I can do most of the decorating myself, and Dennis knows all the local builders, so that will give me the expert guidance I'll need before I start on anything which could bring the entire ceiling down. And if I can afford to sort out the gatehouse, that will make a huge difference; it's tiny, but it could be lovely, and as a holiday let it would bring in loads more than the B&B. Helena refused to have inspectors from the guidebooks and tourist schemes visit, so it's all been very much word-of-mouth so far, with regulars rebooking and only the occasional new guest. I'm not going to rush into making any big changes straightaway, not until I've done some more research, but there's definitely lots of potential. And a huge amount to do.

But I'm still feeling a glimmer of excitement in amongst all the blind panic as I walk down to the cove to retrieve Bertie and the boys. At least Bertie isn't firing the bloody cannon today; I've already broken two cups and a plate due to unexpected cannoning. It might only fire blank powder, but it still makes a hell of a racket. He's solemnly promised to never show the boys how the stupid thing works, and Dennis keeps the powder locked safely away, so that's something. But I'd still like to find a way to push it off the clifftop.

"Mum?"

"Yes Alfie?"

"Look, I've found another pebble with a hole in it. Look, right in the middle."

"That's a good one, let's take it back up to the house and you can put it on your shelf."

Ben and Dan are collecting driftwood for the bonfire I've promised we can have for New Year's Eve, supervised by Bertie, who has firm views on the correct way to arrange a bonfire.

"Put the tarpaulin back on, there's a good chap. Got to keep it dry, storm brewing tonight, if I'm not mistaken. Hello my dear. Getting quite a collection now, and there's a few branches drying in the stables, so we can use those too, get a proper blaze going. Fancy a snifter, keep out the cold?"

He offers me his flask.

"No thanks Bertie, it's teatime, and it's getting cold. We should be getting back inside."

"Right you are. Stand to boys, we've got new orders."

We walk back up to the house, with the boys racing ahead.

"How did the tour go? Dennis show you everything, did he? Got your bearings?"

"I think so."

"One day at a time my dear, that's the ticket. Great big place like this, always something needs doing. It will drive you demented if you let it. It's survived this long, and I daresay it'll last us all out. Don't let it overwhelm you. Helena wouldn't have wanted that. Old Dennis is a good chap, but he does fuss. Gets it from Ivy. We'll muddle along somehow, won't we?"

"Of course we will."

"That's the ticket. Been meaning to say, those boys of yours are quite a tonic. Full of energy. Having a grand time building our fire—you wait and see—quite looking forward to it. Might send old Dennis off for some fireworks, make a proper occasion of it."

Great. More explosions.

It's the day after Boxing Day, and I'm sitting by the fire having a peaceful half hour. Christmas Eve was lovely, if exhausting, and Mum and Dad came to tea, which I was slightly worried about because Ivy and Mum have been competing about the perfect recipe for mince pies, so they'd both made a special batch and Mum brought some of hers, and had pulled out all the stops with puff pastry and lattice tops, with Ivy making shortcrust ones with pastry leaves on top, and it all got a bit tense, until they declared a draw, and then had a lovely time bonding over the vagaries of cooking on AGAs. Thank God Ivy made the Christmas cake months ago or they'd probably still be banging on about recipes for that too.

I finally solved the issue of what to get Ivy and Dennis for Christmas by promising to buy Ivy a new washing machine in the New Year sales—not the most thrilling of gifts, but the one they've got in their cottage could have made an interesting feature on *Antiques Roadshow* before it stopped working altogether a few months ago. She's been putting all her washing in a wheelie shopping basket and bringing it up to the house, and then trundling it back down the drive still half-damp so she can iron it. Ivy's got very definite views on ironing. She's got her eye on some terrifying-looking steam-ironing contraption for the house which apparently makes light work of sheets. She's been leaving me brochures and leaflets in strategic places, so I'm going to have to sort one of those too while I'm splashing out in the January sales. Although I might try to find one that doesn't look like you could steam-iron your own arm between two giant rollers if you weren't very careful. But the prize for the most successful present ever has to go to the ride-along lawn mower we got for Dennis; I thought he might burst into tears. I was pretty close to tears myself when I saw the price, but he's too old to be pushing the old petrol one around. It weighs a ton, and anyway it's half-broken, according to Bertie. It was Bertie who came up with the idea: one of the old codgers at the naval club was selling it, and he arranged for the delivery and everything. Dennis took it out for a few test runs in the meadow on Christmas morning and was completely thrilled. Even Bertie had a go—which, to be frank, I could have done without—with bloody Betty perched on his shoulder so he looked like a mad gardening pirate. I must remind Dennis to make sure the key is well hidden from the boys, or Alfie will be trying to go to school on it.

Pete came down yesterday, as promised, and was pretty grumpy. They're staying with Janice's mother, who lives near Salisbury, so he only had a couple of hours' drive, but I don't think he enjoyed Christmas surrounded by Janice's relatives. Not that his lunch with us was entirely successful either. Ivy insisted on doing her best "Miss Molly" routine, and was practically curtsying when she served lunch in the dining room, which she insisted on doing, using the best china, while Bertie told him all about the Battle of Jutland, for some reason best known to himself, and Betty told everyone to bugger off and gave Pete increasingly malevolent glances.

Dan is sitting by the fire reading, looking a bit smaller and younger than before Pete's visit.

"I'm sorry Dad had to leave so early yesterday, but it was nice to see him, wasn't it? Nice he drove all this way just to see you at Christmas."

"He's a total twat Mum."

"Dan!"

"Well, he is."

"Dan, that's not fair, he drove all that way, just to see the three of you. And he'd brought you all such lovely presents."

Beautifully wrapped presents in fact, carefully chosen from the list I gave him of the games and films and books that I knew they wanted. As far as I know, Pete has never organised or wrapped a present for any of the boys in his life, so I'm guessing my list was handed straight to Janice. Some things don't change.

"Chill out Mum. Seriously, it's no big deal. Can I have an orange?"

"Yes, as long as you put all the peel in the fire and don't just leave it lying on the table. And I think you're being very unfair, he loves all of you very much. And it can't have been easy coming here and putting up with Betty. But he did it, because he loves you."

There's a small smile as he reaches for his orange. I think it's vital I don't criticise Pete, a bit like a parental Maginot Line, which come to think of it was so effective the Germans just went round the back, so maybe less of the Maginot and more of the Maternal. A safety zone, so they feel there's an unbreachable border between them and chaos. There's nothing like seeing your parents have descended into one long slanging match to make kids feel like now might be a good time to go completely off the rails. I saw it so often at school, and I'm determined we maintain the united moral high ground, still minding about manners and homework, even if one of you has buggered off, and is, as Dan says, a total twat. It's the small things which add up, like school uniforms. We spent hours banging on about uniforms at my old school, but if we hadn't endlessly insisted shirts were tucked in and ties done up, some of them would have turned up in the kind of outfits more usually seen in the red-light district of Berlin. And not just the girls. Why Mrs. Trent thought *Cabaret* was a good idea for the school play is still beyond me. Gareth Finch tried to wear eyeliner pretty much permanently after his debut performance. I had to keep a packet of makeup remover pads in my desk just for him. Still, at least it increased his interest in the Weimar Republic, and he did get top marks in the exams.

"Is there any Christmas cake left Mum?"

"I think so. Bring me a slice too would you love?"

Dan's discovered a new passion for Christmas cake, once he found out Ivy puts a fair bit of brandy in it.

"A cup of tea would be nice too."

"What did your last servant die of?"

"Being cheeky."

I'm looking at the book on roses which Dennis and Ivy gave me for Christmas. I think Dennis is hoping I might discover a dormant horticultural passion, although knowing my luck it'll be a passion for parrots inherited from the Bertie end of the family gene pool. If I had a choice, I'd definitely prefer roses. The pictures are beautiful, but there does seem to be a great deal more to the wonderful world of roses than you'd ever imagine. I've already found myself accidentally triggering quite a few rounds of baffling garden chat with Dennis about Helena's hatred of modern hybrids, so I sit by the fire and try to concentrate. Maybe I should write myself notes. There are so many different varieties, all with different-shaped flowers; rosettes and quartered rosettes; rounded, flat, or cupped, all the descriptions are lovely, and I'm sure I can smell the various scents. Apricot, fading to cream, with a true rose fragrance. Tones of peach and coral, with a fruity fragrance, good repeat flowering. Ooh, I like the look of the one called Marie Louise, a gorgeous pink rose raised in Empress Josephine's gardens at Malmaison. I'm daydreaming about gathering up rose petals which fill the house with perfume as they dry, when Dan comes in with a tray.

"Ben says Alfie's fallen in the sea again collecting pebbles, so he's sopping wet, and Uncle Bertie says can you send down some dry clothes for him. Or you could just leave it, which gets my vote, because Alfie does it on purpose, you know he does. He's such a total knob."

It looks like the rose petals may have to wait.

CHAPTER THREE

If I Had a Hammer

January to March

Cabbage Roses

With loose full flowers and beautiful satin petals in tones of pink, violet, lavender, and deep purple, these roses date back to the sixteenth century and are also known as centifolia or Provence roses. Strong and hardy, they have a rich range of alluring fragrances with hints of pear and apple, peach and vanilla. Understandably popular in cottage gardens, they were widely grown, and notable varieties include Cottage Maid, *with its masses of creamy-white flowers with pink veining;* The Bishop, *with its deep-purple-and-lilac flowers which fade to violet; and* Napoleon's Hat, *a clear-bright-pink rose with a spiced, rich fragrance.*

Happy New Year darling, I've brought fizz. And presents." Lola is draped in scarves and wearing the kind of stunning white coat that no woman with children would ever dream of buying.

"How was the drive?"

"Great, once I got over the arctic landscape. I was half expecting to spot a bloody polar bear. Why is it so cold?"

"Because it's winter?"

"It's not this bad in town."

"That'll be all those central heating systems pumping out heat. We don't really go in for that down here. Well, not in this house anyway. You did bring your thermals, didn't you?"

"Yes darling, I even brought a hat, although I'm seriously hoping I won't have to sleep in it."

"I lit a fire in your bedroom earlier on, so hopefully not."

"A real fire, what a treat. Alfie, there you are, come and give your godmother a kiss. Hello, Bertie, lovely to see you."

She hands him a bottle of champagne.

"Welcome my dear, always like a girl who brings her own supplies. You're looking in the pink, I must say. Been up to all sorts, I shouldn't wonder."

"This and that, Bertie, this and that."

"That's the spirit. Surprised some chap hasn't snapped you up yet, a girl who tips up with her own champagne. Should think you've got them queuing up."

She kisses him.

"Not that I've noticed, but I like your thinking. Where's the parrot? Don't tell me you've had her stuffed and put on a shelf—I was looking forward to a bit of abuse."

"She's in the library, in disgrace. Dismantled another television control. She's a demon with them, have to get one of the boys to change the channels now, most inconvenient. Do bear it in mind my dear. Don't leave her alone with any gadgets."

"I didn't bring my TV remote with me Bertie, but thanks for the tip."

"She can make short work of those little phones you all seem to carry nowadays, especially the ones with pictures. Finds them irresistible."

"It's true Lola. We've all got used to keeping our mobiles out of sight. It's quite relaxing."

"If one of my clients goes into meltdown and can't get hold of me it won't be relaxing, thanks. Bertie, be a darling and tell her if she tries to eat my phone, I'll arrange to have her stuffed."

"I'll do my best my dear, but I can't promise anything."

Bertie pours champagne while we open Lola's beautifully wrapped parcels. Lola is brilliant at presents, and Bertie's particularly taken with his new cardigan with skull and crossbones appliquéd on both pockets.

"I thought a pirate motif was perfect for you. Molly tells me they used to call you the Red Admiral when you were in the navy Bertie. What was that all about?"

"No idea. I was never that keen on the rules and regulations and all the pomp and ceremony the top brass go in for, but I was never a Red. Knew some excellent Russians though, very good value at parties. Used to give cocktail parties on board, some of them went on for days."

"I'll drink to that."

Dan and Ben love their trendy hooded sweatshirts as well as the selection of Japanese cartoons and films from Lola's recent trip to Tokyo. She's also bought them both hats with earflaps, which

I'm slightly nervous about because I know exactly what reaction I'd get if I tried to persuade them to wear hats with earflaps. Or hats without earflaps, come to think of it. But apparently these are "awesome," and Dan wears his for the rest of the afternoon, while Alfie goes into a Lego-induced trance. I gave him the castle for Christmas, and Lola has bought every single bit of extra kit a castle could possibly require, including horses and knights and extra cannons with mini cannonballs, which he's soon firing all over the drawing room floor. She's bought so many we should be set until next Christmas, which is great, obviously, even if I do keep treading on the bloody things when I've been warming my feet by the fire. I even got one stuck inside my sock yesterday, and hobbling about trying not to swear amused the boys to no end.

We've spent ages decorating a tea set for Lola. Alfie has painted the cake plates, and Dan and Ben decorated the cups and saucers and milk jug. My pink-and-white-flowered teapot looks rather sedate in comparison, but she seems to love it, and I've filled the teapot with tiny parcels, strings of sparkly beads, and mini bottles of nail polish, as well as chocolates, so she's wearing the beads and painting her nails with silver glitter while I unwrap the beautiful cashmere twin set she's chosen for me, in just the kind of pale lilac that you never find in Marks and Spencer.

"Promise you'll only wear it with dark purple, or green."

"Of course."

"What have you got in dark purple?"

"A dressing gown and a couple of towels?"

"Just as I thought. Open that one, over there."

The second parcel contains a long velvet skirt, in a gorgeous deep blackcurrant. It's so beautiful I want to try it on straightaway. And in amongst all the tissue paper there's also a tiny dark-green woollen something. Christ, I think it's meant to be a skirt. Or maybe a big belt.

"Before you say anything, you wear it with woolly tights and boots."

"I'll look like Robin Hood."

"You will not. You'll look like a postmodern Lady of the Manor. We can go online later and I'll show you more stuff you need to buy. I'm on a mission, it's important you look right, you can't go shuffling round in those terrible jeans."

"I can. But thank you, they're all gorgeous."

"Just get a few things darling, while I'm here to help you choose."

"Maybe."

Or maybe not. Lola's idea of just a few things tends to be what most people would call a massive shopping spree. But I'll definitely need some woolly tights if I'm ever going to give the green skirt a try. "Maybe I could get some of those legging things, to wear under the skirt?"

"'Jeggings'? Please, darling. Another little joke from the wonderful world of fashion. If you're fifteen or anorexic, fine. On anyone else they look completely revolting. Trust me, woollen tights are your best bet."

Lunch is particularly successful since Lola's brought new supplies of Christmas Crackers, and hers are much posher than ours, with much better gifts inside them. Even Betty gets a cracker present: a small mirror which she sets about dismantling, in between admiring herself. Alfie is thrilled with his whistle, more's the pity. But at least we'll know where he is, anywhere in the house.

"Shall we have coffee by the fire?"

"Please, darling."

"Boys, you can watch a film, or play upstairs, but no charging around. We'll go for a walk later, so save your energy for that, okay?"

Alfie toots on his whistle, but then trots off with Bertie to annoy Betty. Excellent. Let's see how long it takes her to dismantle a whistle. Fingers crossed.

"This coffee is delicious, much better than your usual stuff. So how was Christmas, darling?"

"Fine, although I made Ivy and Dennis take Christmas Day off, which took some doing, and then I wished I hadn't because the turkey took forever to cook and we ended up having our lunch at a quarter to six."

"And what about your parents—full of festive spirit?"

"Dad's still sulking. Mum's popped in a few times though, and she's fine. And they both came round on Christmas Eve, and then we all went for sherry at the hotel before New Year, which was pretty tense with Roger being bumptious and Dad giving me the evil eye. But everyone just about managed to behave, apart from Bertie. What about you and your mum, how did that go?"

"Fine, I think, I drank so much vodka it's all a blur. Only way to handle it."

"Yes, Bertie did something similar. He had Sally in fits when we were at the hotel, telling her rude stories about his exploits in the navy, he ended up sitting in the office, with half the staff crowding in. He was a huge hit."

"I bet Roger loved that."

"Oh definitely, he was enchanted."

"Okay, I'd like the full tour now please. Pretend I'm a guest."

"You are a guest Lola."

"A B-and-B guest. Imagine I've just tipped up ready to book in."

"You're not really the B-and-B type though are you?"

"Mr. and Mrs. Normal, with matching anoraks? Don't worry, I'll summon up my inner pleb."

"Charming."

"Shut up, and get on with it. I want to see it all—the full guest experience."

"Of course. Right this way madam."

"I love the entrance by the way, huge door, proper old-fashioned bellpull and clanging bell, sets the perfect tone."

"Yes, and Betty can do a pretty good impersonation of the bell, so bear it in mind. She can do the phone too, but we've fixed that. I've got a new one and Ben and Dan have spent hours putting ringtones on for everyone."

"Clever."

"I thought so, but we've had so many debates about it, I'm not so sure now. They'd put Darth Vader on for Pete until I made them change it."

"I like their thinking. What's he got now?"

"Yoda. They put some annoying singing chicken on for my mobile, until I made them take it off, so now they've gone all James Bond. You've got 'Diamonds Are Forever,' and I've got 'Sky-fall,' which they're loving, given the subtle chicken connection."

"And exactly how does lovely Daniel 007 Craig connect to chickens?"

"Chicken Licken, the Sky Is Falling Down—they think they've been terribly clever. I'm letting them keep it for now, or God knows what I'll end up with. They'd put on 'The Sun Will Come Out Tomorrow' from *Annie* for Alfie until I deleted it."

"Has Alfie got a phone then?"

"Nope, but they couldn't resist, little swine. They keep playing all the tunes, just to be annoying. But the good news is Betty can't keep track of them—she fluffs up her feathers and goes all sulky every time the phone rings, it's great. I think that's why she's redoubling her efforts with remote controls. It's parrot payback."

We're walking across the main hall and into the entrance hall.

"When was this place built, do you know?"

"Late seventeen hundreds."

"The staircase is lovely. Is it oak?"

"I think so."

"You're hopeless darling, I want snippets. 'Hand-carved oak, using timbers from a famous ship'—ask Bertie for something suitable."

"I don't think you can just make stuff up Lola. It's just oak, made by local craftsmen, I should imagine. But I can tell you about the floor tiles—Victorian green-and-blue mosaic. I've been doing some research to see if I can replace a couple of the cracked ones. They cost a fortune."

"I bet they do, they're gorgeous. Right, so we're by the front door, off you go. 'Good afternoon, do you have a reservation?'"

"Stop it, you're making me nervous."

"Pull yourself together darling."

"'Good afternoon, madam. Why are you wearing so many scarves, have you just arrived from the North Pole?'"

"Ho ho ho, very festive I'm sure. 'I've got a booking. My bags are in the car.' Off you pop darling."

"'This is a B-and-B, madam. We don't have a porter.'"

"Very good, going for five stars, I see—be rude to your guests. If it works for Michelin-star restaurants, why not B-and-Bs? I like it. So, do I have to sign in, or what?"

"Yes, on the hall table, in this book, just your name and address. And there's a visitor's book too, in the guest sitting room. Full of nice comments because Ivy takes out the page if anyone writes anything she doesn't like."

"Do you want my credit card?"

"No, because you're not paying. And we don't take credit cards yet—it's on my To Do list. Actually it's more of a To Do booklet now."

"I bet. And I am paying; I want to be your first official guest. So shut up. Is the usual drill they pay after they've had breakfast?"

"Yes, if we're open, which we're not. Helena didn't open until Easter, so I'm sticking with that while I get things sorted. So you're not paying, and that's final."

"I can see your influence here already you know darling—the twigs and berries in that vase, the Christmas tree and all the holly and ribbons, it's all gorgeous."

"I've just tidied up a bit so far, I'd like to move some of the furniture around, but I don't want to upset Ivy, so I'm taking it slowly."

"This isn't a remake of *Rebecca*, darling, even if this place could be a mini Mandalay. There's no Mrs. Danvers lurking, waiting to set the house on fire."

"I bloody hope not."

"It could be stunning. Get a business loan, don't look at the bills, and focus your energies on making it beautiful."

"I'm sure the banks will be falling all over themselves to give me a loan with a detailed business plan like that Lola."

"With the equity you've got here, it won't matter what you say, they'll be falling all over themselves to sign you up to pay them vast amounts of interest. Bastards."

I show her the guest sitting room, to the right of the entrance hall, with the breakfast table for the B&B guests.

"It used to be the old morning room, it gets the sun first thing."

"I've always wanted a house big enough to have a morning room. Imagine sitting giving orders to your staff. Six for dinner, let's roast a brace or two of pheasant."

"You can try it if you like. Ivy and I can line up wearing our best aprons."

"I love the huge windows, floor to ceiling Georgian gorgeousness."

"They're great aren't they, and the shutters work too. I'll show you. Most of the rooms have them, and the dining room has window seats too. When I was little I used to hide in them, pull the curtain across, and make a little camp. Helena used to bring me snacks and I'd sit reading my book, it was perfect. Come on, let me show you your room."

We walk upstairs.

"I've put you in the big double."

"It's stunning darling, and thank you for the fire. Very country house."

"It's either that or freeze. I'm tempted to start redecorating in here straightaway, but I need to meet the builder first and make sure nothing crucial will collapse."

"This wallpaper is truly hideous."

"Yup, William Morris meets the nineteen-seventies. But I think I can do something with the curtains, if I de-floral everywhere else, and go with cream and pale blues?"

Lola is looking at the curtains, which are heavy paisley damask in silver and china blue. She doesn't look convinced.

"If you say so darling."

"The bathrooms are old, but at least they're white, and I can get rid of the terrible old carpets. I've already checked and the floorboards are great, so I'll sand them and give them a pale whitewash and then varnish them. With new towels and blinds I think they'll look quite good."

"Sounds great, and the proportions are brilliant with the shutters and the windows. The bones are there, and all the views are wonderful. If you turned the whole place into a country-house hotel, you could make a fortune."

"Yes, but we'd be homeless, and so would Bertie."

"Show me your room, and then the attics."

"Are you sure? It's pretty cold up there."

"I want to see it all."

"Okay, and then I've got something to show you which is going to make you very jealous."

"What? Tell me now, you know I hate surprises."

"I've got a dressing room, off my bedroom, it's huge."

"Christ, the irony, I can't bear it. You know I've always wanted a proper-sized dressing room. It'll be completely wasted on you."

"I thought I might turn it into a sewing room?"

"Are you taking up sewing then?"

"Probably not, but it sounds nice."

"Or you could just buy more clothes."

"You haven't seen the size of it yet."

"Shut up."

"Christ, it's cold up here."

"I know, there are only a couple of radiators, just to stop the pipes from freezing. God knows how the servants used to manage. There are fireplaces, but they're tiny, and I bet they weren't allowed fires unless they were at death's door."

"No wonder they got up so early in the morning, probably the only way to get warm. What's in here?"

I turn on the light to show Lola the water-tank room, and all the lights go out.

"Bloody hell, is this part of the tour darling?"

"No, it's the fuse box. It does it all the time, just hang on, I've put torches all over the place. There should be one by the stairs on top of that cupboard."

"Well hurry up. I hope this place isn't haunted by the ghost of some housemaid frozen to her washstand, because I'm not really up for any more shocks. I'm still trying to get over the idea of you having a dressing room."

"Here, I've found it. Let's go back down, and then I'll sort the fuse box. We had too many lights on—that's the usual reason it trips."

"Good. And then we can open a bottle of something, good plan?"

"Excellent plan."

I take Lola breakfast in bed in the morning, and she says she slept very well, and she doesn't appear to feel fragile at all, which is impressive. If only I could say the same. I'm outside feeding the silly chickens with the boys, and wishing everyone would be a bit quieter. Chickens always look so peaceful on television, pecking and clucking about, but these ones are almost the exact opposite of that. Given half a chance, they shoot past and escape into the orchard, flapping and squawking every time I open the bloody door to feed them. I spent nearly an hour running round last week trying to get the little sods back in for the night, admittedly with Alfie and Ben helping, which probably made things worse. And then when I finally gave up and started walking back towards the house, they all trooped back into the henhouse, almost in single file. I'm sure they were doing it deliberately to annoy me. If chickens can laugh, then the buggers were definitely laughing.

The boys are running round throwing sticks for Tess, while I try to work out how to get back out of the henhouse with having another Great Escape on my hands, when Ivy comes out, with Dennis carrying a bucket of warm water.

"They like a drop of warm water in this weather."

"They like cider vinegar too Ivy, in their water, I've been Googling them."

Ben is on a mission to help me embrace the wonderful world of poultry keeping.

"I thought Googlies were cricket dear?"

Dennis shakes his head.

"Google not 'Googlie,' you daft woman. It's the Interweb he's on about. You can look up all sorts on it."

"And if you tie vegetables on a string, they can peck them and not get bored."

God forbid we'd have bored chickens.

Ivy is impressed.

"Fancy, did you hear that, Dennis. You've got to tie some of your veg on a string. Do you think you can manage that, in between being sarky to me?"

Ben looks pleased that someone is finally taking his research seriously.

"You can hang up old CDs too—they like pecking at them. And if they eat grass you get darker yolks. And raw potato is poisonous for chickens, so you can't give them potato peelings. And they need lots of water, because eggs are seventy-five percent water."

"Well I never, there's a good boy finding out all that."

I'm still stuck inside the henhouse, trying to work out how to get out.

"Thanks Ben, you didn't happen to see any top hints on how to open the door without the stupid things all running out did you love?"

He grins.

"Not really Mum."

"They're just getting used to you, dear. It takes them a while. They'll start laying again soon and then they'll settle."

"That's good news Ivy."

Either that or I might just peel a few potatoes when nobody is looking.

"Morning everyone, what are you all doing? Do they always make that racket darling?"

Lola has emerged, draped in cashmere and looking as fresh as the proverbial daisy.

"When I'm around they do. I thought you were having a lie-in?"

"I got bored. The white ones are lovely, usually they're that horrible sludge-brown, but these look much more upmarket."

Dennis nods.

"That's Vita and Gertie—they're both Ixworths, rare breed. Them speckled black-and-white ones are Connie and Beth—they're Dorkings, nice calm hens."

He pauses to watch Beth race past me, clucking.

"Usually they're calm. The other three are Speckled Sussex—Penny, Rosie, and the Duchess. We had a flock of over thirty at one point, used to keep quite a few rare breeds, for breeding, but now we just keep a few for the eggs. Good layers, this lot are."

"All girls? Don't you need a cockerel as well?"

Our new poultry expert, Ben, steps forward.

"No Aunty Lola, chickens lay eggs all the time, you just need a cockerel if you want them to do sexing and have chicks."

From the look on her face, I'm not sure Ivy is that impressed with Ben's latest bit of research, but Dennis nods.

"That's right, and cockerels make too much of a racket to be worth the bother."

Lola is clearly trying not to laugh as I manage to exit the henhouse with a nifty move which leaves all the chickens still inside, albeit in mild hysterics. It's the first time I've actually managed this, so I'm pretty pleased with myself. It's just a shame I've left the bucket inside.

Dennis retrieves the bucket by sauntering in, picking it up, and then sauntering back out again, with no mass flappings or screechings. The buggers are definitely doing it on purpose.

"Great names darling. Did you choose them?"

I can tell she's still trying not to laugh.

"No, Helena named them after gardeners: Gertrude Jekyll, Vita Sackville-West, Penelope Hobhouse, Beth Chatto. There are loads of books in the library; they were a fascinating bunch, from what I can gather. Constance Spry pretty much invented modern flower arranging. The Duchess, after the Duchess of Devonshire, the one who's mad on chickens, she used to have flocks of them wandering round Chatsworth apparently. Helena knew her years ago; I think they came out together."

"Came out? Am I missing something here?"

"Came out as debutantes, did the Season, all that malarkey."

"It's a whole new world isn't it darling. Do they lay loads of lovely eggs then?"

"Not since we turned up, no."

"Maybe you should let them do a bit of sexing then—might perk them up."

"Thanks Lola. I'll bear it in mind."

Dennis laughs.

"They always tail off a bit in the winter. They'll start up again soon, don't you worry. Right, I'm off inside for my elevenses. Shall I put the kettle on?"

Alfie starts hopping up and down.

"I need a bacon sandwich, like Dennis, I really do. I never get bacon."

"You can have one tomorrow, if you come downstairs when I call you for breakfast, otherwise it's just cereal, I can't start making bacon now."

Ivy puts her hand on his shoulder.

"I put a bit of bacon in the warming drawer earlier in case the boys fancied some, if that's alright?"

Alfie cheers, and hugs her.

"Thank you Ivy, you're my best person in the whole world."

Dennis smiles.

"Nothing like a bacon sandwich to set you up on a cold morning, and it looks like rain later, might even be snow. Let's get back indoors before all the bacon disappears."

"That's enough of that Dennis. We don't want any snow, and there'll be nobody helping themselves to my bacon, thanks all the same. And I'll be wanting some leeks for lunch, and some rhubarb, before you come in. I thought I'd make a crumble."

I glance at Lola to see if she's recoiled in horror, but apparently her newfound aversion to all things rhubarb doesn't include crumbles.

Dennis tuts.

"You want to watch yourself Alfie, or she'll have you out digging up veg in the pouring rain too."

"You should train Tess. She's very good at digging."

"I might try that lad. Save me a lot of bother."

Dan shoves Alfie, but fairly gently, so I ignore it.

"I think we'd all rather the dog didn't dig up our lunch, thanks all the same Alf."

He's still wearing his new hat with the earflaps, which I am now coveting since it has started to get so much colder.

Perhaps a bacon sandwich might be just what we all need.

I'm sitting by the fire with Lola in the drawing room while the boys are off playing or "helping" Dennis dig up leeks.

"Right, so run me through the money darling."

"What money? Why does everyone think I've got money now?"

"Who thinks that?"

"Pete, mainly."

"Yes but I've told you, the brilliant thing about being divorced is you don't need to worry about what he thinks anymore darling. What's your budget, to transform all this?"

"Well we get just under five hundred pounds a year from renting the fields to the local farmer."

"Are you joking?"

"No, the sheep are lovely and Helena didn't want to rent to anyone else. Mr. Crouch explained it all to me, there's a proper business account and everything, and I'm the only signatory. Helena sorted it all out. She didn't put Bertie on the account, though—she said he'd be too annoying and he'd just write cheques for daft stuff."

"Good call."

"Excellent call."

"So, apart from five hundred pounds, what else?"

"The B-and-B brought in just under four thousand pounds last year, and there's money set aside in a special account for Dennis's and Ivy's wages for the next year or so. God knows where Helena got the money from, but she set it all up so I don't have to worry about that straightaway. Their cottage is rent-free, but I need to do something about how little they get paid as soon as I can. Overall the house makes a huge loss of course—it has done for years. Helena only really noticed her plants, and then whenever things got tricky, she'd sell something."

"Is there anything left to sell?"

"Not unless anyone wants to buy a parrot, not really. Helena left some money for Bertie, and he keeps trying to give me cheques, but we're fine, for now. We got a good price for our house. It would have been a lot more a couple of years ago of course, but by the time the mortgage was paid off, I ended up with over one hundred and fifty thousand pounds—one hundred and fifty-three thousand, four hundred and sixty-seven, actually—after I paid my half of the solicitor's bills."

"Christ, is that all?"

"Lola, that's a huge amount of money."

"Yes, if someone walked up to you and said, 'Here, have a bonus,' you'd be pleased, but not to live on and do up a huge place like this and take care of the boys."

"Yes, but there's the money from Pete for the boys. Even if it's usually late, it does arrive eventually, so I should be able to manage if I'm careful."

"Or I could invest."

"Yes, but we've already talked about that Lola, and I want

to try to do this by myself—well, 'by myself' thanks to Helena and Bertie. And anyway I think you'd be a very scary business partner."

"That's true. But if you get stuck, you'll let me know? I could have a word with my bank, or your bloody father could talk to the hotel's bank surely?"

"Yes, but he'd meddle and then Roger would start trying to boss me about, so I'd rather try to make it a go of it without them if I can."

"So no nest egg, fabulous house, huge potential, what's the plan? I know, turn it into a high-class brothel? Aristocratic clients only. Give them rubbish food and someone to wallop them with a riding crop and they'll feel right at home. You'll make a fortune."

"Tempting, but no. If things get too tough I can always sign up for a bit of teaching work if I have to, although by the time I've paid for child care that won't bring in much, and anyway I think I need to be full-time here if I'm going to pull this off. I've got a few ideas though. Let me show you."

"Bugger, do we have to go back outside? I've only just got those bloody Wellies off. That's how you could make your fortune darling: invent something to help weekend guests get their Wellies off."

"I have. He's called Alfie."

We troop up to the stables, with Tess barking and Alfie having an imaginary sword fight with a stick while I show Lola the beautiful wooden beams.

"Lovely darling—shame about the freezing gale blowing through all the holes in the roof though."

"Yes, but that could be fixed, and they'd make great holiday cottages. With the right plan and a few walls moved, you could turn this into two, maybe even three little terraced holiday cottages. The roof space is huge, so you could put a second floor in for a bathroom and bedrooms. Lots of places have done it and they rent them out all year round for weekend breaks, and then in the summer we can earn serious money renting them by the week. I'll need to get plans approved and talk to builders, and the bank, but while I get all that sorted, I thought I'd use some of my money to deal with the most urgent things in the house, and fix up the gatehouse, and that way I can rent that out and see how it goes. Sort of test the market. I'll still keep some money in reserve for emergencies. But it could be lovely, and it's much less dilapidated than here—well, a bit less. I'll show you, if you're up for a walk down the lane. What do you think?"

"I'm finding it a bit hard to think darling, I can't feel my fingers. I may be in the first stages of hypothermia."

"It's not that far, and the last stage of hypothermia is when you imagine you're hot and start taking all your clothes off, so as long as you don't start doing that, you'll be fine."

"Promise?"

We walk down the lane as the sun starts to go down and the stable roof turns a beautiful pinky orange.

"What does that mean then—a sunset like that? 'Red sky at night, shepherds' what?"

"'Delight. Red sky at dawn, shepherds be warned.'"

"Of what?"

"I've no idea. If you want a forecast, ask Bertie—he's got all sorts of theories about what the weather is going to do."

"Is he usually right?"

"Not often, no. Look at the stables now. If you half close your eyes, you can almost see how lovely they could be."

Lola turns to look.

"I find it works better if you shut your eyes completely darling."

Alfie starts to yell.

"It's snowing, it is, it's snowing."

And sure enough, it is. Just a few flakes. But it's definitely snow.

"Bloody hell, I've got to get back to town tomorrow, drifts or no drifts."

"There's an old tractor, I'm sure Dennis can fix it. He's been fixing it for years, and he uses it for cutting the grass in the meadow. Or he could take you on his new ride-along mower."

"To London?"

"No, to the station. You can get the train back, if it gets really bad."

"Thanks darling. But I think I'll just strip off now and lie down in the snow. Save time."

It's the last day of January tomorrow, and I'm hoping this will herald a change in the weather. We've had gales, and torrential rain, which flooded the road into the village, and what felt like weeks of snow, only a light dusting at New Year, but then three days which were so bad all the schools were shut. And last week we had a power cut, so I spent half an hour in the cellar fiddling with the fuse box until Dennis arrived, having cycled up the lane to tell me the power was off from the village all the way along the coast. So the camping torches were back on duty again, because the combination of the boys and candles is just too terrifying to contemplate, even without a resident Mrs. Danvers. We listened to the radio and I kept the fires going, which involved a fair bit of scuttling round with kindling and bags of logs, but at least it kept us from freezing, and I think the boys quite enjoyed it. The one hidden bonus to the house being so cold is the boys have taken to wearing slippers, so their socks are a lot less grubby than usual. Living in a house with flagstone floors in the kitchen seems to have converted them; Alfie's got Batman slippers with ears, and Dan and Ben are both sporting fleece-lined tartan affairs, which they pretend to loathe but wear pretty much constantly. They're all washable—I've learnt the hard way that if it won't go into the washing machine at 40 degrees, there's no point buying it when it comes to boys and clothing. Girls too, probably, but I'm guessing there's less mud and grass involved, and not so much pushing your brother into the ha-ha to score bonus points.

The last couple of days have been so stormy I've been wondering if Bertie has inadvertently shot an albatross with the bloody cannon. He's been even more Ancient Mariner than usual, muttering about the lifeboats being called out, and forecasting more bad weather. This morning he announced there were two rescues last night, but thankfully everyone got back to dry land safely, so he's firing the cannon later to celebrate. It's any excuse really; it's like living with Admiral Boom from Mary sodding Poppins. He says there's a longstanding naval tradition of firing cannons out to sea to show a lack of hostile intent, or as part of a celebration, but I think he just likes it.

"Mum?"

"Yes, find your school bag Alfie, and Ben, hurry up please."

"You know Uncle Bertie's cannon?"

"Yes Alfie, and don't just stand there, start looking properly please, and not over there, it won't be in the fridge."

"Well it has black powder, so it can't hurt people. Did you know that?"

"Yes."

Otherwise we wouldn't have moved here in the first place. I'm not completely insane.

"Well can we get him a real one, with proper cannonballs?"

Ben sighs.

"No we can't, you idiot, they're illegal. You can't fire real cannons whenever you like—you could kill people. And Mum, did you know they only do odd numbers, Bertie was telling me. If you fire an even number of shots, it means death, or something like that, that's why they do the twenty-one-gun salute for the Queen, not twenty-two. It goes down depending on how important you are."

"Well that's good news because a one-gun salute makes enough racket, twenty-one would probably make the house fall down."

Another reason to be glad we're not Royal.

"Come on, please, hurry up or we'll be late. Dan went for his bus ages ago."

There are no tractors dawdling along the lanes this morning, thank God, or stupid sheep being moved from one field to another and having mass panic attacks in front of the car, so we get to school with a few minutes to spare. Ben and Alfie have settled in really quickly. Alfie's enjoying having a big brother in the top class, and it's definitely helped that even though this is a small village school, at least half the kids weren't born round here. My old primary school is closed now and turned into houses, so everyone from Launton and the surrounding villages comes here, and it's strange seeing people I was at school with standing with their kids in the playground. Claire Denman is now Claire Prentice, and still recognisable from her seven-year-old self. But Belinda Trent has transformed herself from being shy and nervous and is now Bella who runs the local pub. Sally says she's brilliant at chucking out drunks. Her son Arthur is in Alfie's class, and along with Sally's Tom they've become a little trio, so Miss Cooper has definitely got her work cut out for her with all three of them determined to find ways to make the school day pass more quickly. Ben's Mrs. Dent gives off a much stronger vibe, but she teaches the top class, and everyone knows you've got to have your wits about you when you're teaching the oldest kids in the school, unless you want to find yourself Super Glued to your classroom chair while your class takes an extended lunch break.

Sally is standing by the fence, holding Tom's bag.

"I'm such an idiot, I promised him I'd wait until they go in, and now I'm going to be late."

I hold up my collection of book bags and lunch boxes, which makes her smile.

"Two idiots then."

"Yup, but at least the weather's better. We've got so many pots and pans and bowls up in the attic for all the leaks it's driving me crazy. It's like a very tragic episode of *Antiques Roadshow* up there, where none of it turns out to be Spode. Mr. Stebbings is due to start the building work soon though, thank God, and Bertie says the storms are over, for now, so he's doing the cannon thing later to celebrate."

"Well I hope your Alfie doesn't tell Tom, because he's desperate to see it, and I'm on until six this week, so Patrick's picking him up, if he remembers."

Sally's Patrick is setting up an organic butchery business, so he does a variety of stalls at local farmers' markets, which keeps him pretty busy.

"He only forgot that one time, didn't he?"

"Yes, but once is enough. Miss Cooper rang me at work. It was awful. You know how teachers carry on and make you feel completely crap. Oh, sorry."

"It's alright Sal. It's the first thing they teach you at college, how to look down your nose at parents."

"I bet. Oh look, there's Karen, Dylan's mum, with the new baby."

"Christ, she looks knackered."

"She was a midwife at the hospital in Barnstaple, you'd think she'd have the newborn thing sorted. Just goes to show it's different when it's your own. She's set herself up as a natural birth attendant now, whatever that means."

"Bit of raspberry leaf tea and a beanbag?"

"Pretty much. She's alright though, for a hipster. She's calling the baby Sky."

We both smile. Things have really changed round here since we were at school. Then it was mostly local families who'd lived here for generations, but now we've got more of a mixture: the locals, the rich wives, and the hipsters, as Sally likes to call them. The locals tend to work in tourism now, or catering, and are pretty dismissive of incomers, who drive up house prices and throw fits in the local shops when they can't find olives. But since most of the ways to make a living round here involve dealing with holidaymakers or new villagers, most people are pretty tolerant.

The rich wives live in the biggest houses, often newly built with mock-Georgian facades and triple garages, and spend their time organising endless rounds of lunch and dinner parties, while their husbands commute a couple of days a week or work from home. Some of the wives work, but mostly they're ladies of leisure, driving round in giant off-road vehicles, but never going off road, and sending their kids here for a couple of years to save on school fees before they pack them off to boarding schools. On the school run they're either very smart, with full makeup and matching accessories, like Georgina, or they look like they've just got off a horse, which they often have. They're not popular with the rest of the parents, because they form a definite County clique and tend to be a bit snooty and standoffish in the playground. And then we've got the hipsters: artists, surfers, or self-sufficiency fans, they move here for a more sustainable life, and do up tiny cottages, usually very slowly. They're fond of bartering, since money is short, and the men often wear sandals. We've got two aromatherapists, a crystal therapist, and a Reiki healer in the playground this morning, as well as assorted yoga teachers; we've even got one who does yoga classes while you balance on surf boards in the sea. But only in the summer, because the winter-weight wet suits restrict your movements too much, and if you fell in the sea without one the only yoga pose you could do would be Frozen Woman in a Leotard. Sally tried it once and said it was brilliant, until you fell in. We've also got a former ballet dancer with the Royal Ballet, who teaches Pilates, so all in all it's a very supple playground.

Sally's definitely a local, but I'm not sure what group I'm in, and labels are so much harder to shake off in such a small community like this, so I want to start off on the right foot. I'm not really a local, or a hipster, and I don't want to start an ex-wives category all my own, or be classified as one of the posh lot. I'm definitely not enough of a snooter to pull off the Lady of the Manor routine, even if I wanted to. It's also vital I don't start a new Parent Who Is Also a Teacher category, so I'm trying to keep a low profile on the school-activities front. I know how much moaning goes on in the average staff room about parents not pulling their weight, so I've joined the PTA, but apart from that the only way I want to find myself sorting out the school library or helping slow readers is if I'm being paid by the hour, thanks very much. I'm sure I've made enough of a contribution to the education system with all the extra hours I used to work, without starting volunteering, so I'm aiming for poacher-turned-gamekeeper, as far as school goes. Or possibly gamekeeper-turned-poacher, since gamekeepers tend to get a salary and a bit of respect, along with a gun and a special coat, and I haven't spotted any of that being on offer for the average mum.

Tom runs past us to check if Sally is still waiting, and she tries to persuade him to do his coat up. I've given up on this, partly because there seems to be some mysterious bit of genetic programming which means boys can't do their coats up unless they're up to their necks in snow, but mainly because I got fed up repeating the same phrases over and over and being completely ignored. I think one parrot in the family is more than enough.

The head, Mrs. Williams, has emerged with the bell and is surrounded by small people who would like to help ring it. She opts for a small girl with pigtails, who is tiny but still manages to make quite a racket with it until Mrs. Williams manages to retrieve it as the kids start to line up.

"That Mrs. Langdon keeps looking at us."

"Who?"

"The who drives the silver Mercedes."

"Oh, right."

She often parks it right in front of the school, on the yellow lines, which is strictly verboten, but she ignores the filthy looks from the playground. She must have nerves of steel.

"Look out, she's coming over."

"I don't think we've met, have we? Lucinda Langdon-Hill. I gather you've just moved into the Hall?"

She seems quite pushy for nine fifteen in the morning.

"Yes, that's right."

She looks at me expectantly, clearly waiting for details so she can place me in the correct clique.

"If you ever think of selling, you must let me know. Here, let me give you my card. I only handle a few of the more exclusive properties locally, very much a niche market. I've never seen inside the Hall, but I gather it's absolutely splendid. Shall I pop round?"

Bloody hell.

She hands me a card.

"Thank you, but I'm not thinking of selling, not for the foreseeable future anyway."

"Oh, right."

She looks disappointed, but rallies.

"I gather your family also owns the Sands?"

Crikey, the gossip grapevine has clearly been busy.

"Yes."

"Such wonderful views from the restaurant. We were at a wedding there a few weeks ago, terrific. You must come to one of my girls' lunches; they're such a super way to get to know people when you're new to an area."

Sally has clearly had enough of being treated like she's invisible.

"Molly grew up round here, so she already knows quite a few of us."

That will be minus ten points for me, if I'm not mistaken.

Lucinda trills out a little laugh.

"Super. Look, I must dash, but lovely to have met you properly, and I'll pop an invitation round. So much to do at the moment, but I promise I shan't forget."

She barrels across the playground towards her car as Sally makes a snorting noise.

"Sorry Moll, but I couldn't resist, she's such a cow. She's never spoken to me before, you know, not one word. I suppose you'll be dumping me now, going off with the ladies who lunch."

"Yup. Definitely. Much more my type. Super."

We both laugh as we walk back towards the gates, and Lucinda gives me a cheery wave. Oh God.

"There you go, stand by for your invite; she'll probably upgrade you to dinner."

"She can invite me all she likes Sal, I won't be going."

"No, go and then give me all the details. Please."

"In the five minutes I get in between trying to stop Bertie firing that bloody cannon and sorting out the kids and the B-and-B you mean?"

"Yes, I want details, it's bound to be horrible but none of us have ever been asked before, so you can report back."

"Like a snooter double agent? No thanks. There's no way I could pull that off, and even if I could, there's so much to do at the house, which reminds me, did you get a chance to look at those brochures on those bloody ironing things, because Ivy really wants one and she won't shut up about it."

"The tabletop ones look better than the roller ones. If you put things in a tiny bit folded, you'd steam creases in and they'd be a bugger to get out."

"Good point. Less chance of steamrollering yourself by mistake too. Great, I'll get the tabletop one then."

"I wanted to get one for the hotel a while back. That laundry is so useless, and we could do loads more in-house, but, well, I didn't get one in the end."

"In other words, Roger wouldn't let you?"

"Sorry."

"It's fine Sal. I know what he's like."

"He won't let me hire enough girls to do the rooms either."

"Or boys."

"Yes, if you can find one who can make a bed properly. We only get twenty minutes to turn a room round sometimes, and that's for everything."

"Christ, I'm sure we used to get longer than that."

"We did, but we had more staff then. You'll be fine with your B-and-B rooms, though—you can take a bit longer."

"Good job too, it takes us twenty minutes to get the Hoover upstairs, never mind finish a whole room. Ivy and Helena had their own routines, and it's an uphill battle to get Ivy to let me change anything. I'm still working on the Tupperware."

"What Tupperware?"

"She puts all the breakfast cereals for the B-and-B in horrible old Tupperware boxes, and they look awful. It's on my list, and I want to upgrade our suppliers. I thought I'd talk to Patrick about the bacon and sausages?"

"That would be great, I'll tell him, and I'll lend you the hotel card for the cash-and-carry warehouse if you like. They sell all sorts of containers and cleaning stuff, it'll save you a fortune."

"Thanks Sal. Any idea how I tell Ivy that we're going to be a Tupperware-free zone?"

"Sorry, you're on your own with that one."

Morning darling."

"Morning Lola."

"How's tricks?"

"Tricky. The builders have started work, and they're making a huge mess, which is driving Ivy mental. And old Mr. Stebbings looks like he shouldn't be going upstairs on his own, let alone up ladders and clambering around on the roof. I'm half expecting Social Services to come round and tell me off. And just getting the basics fixed and the gatehouse done is going to cost a fortune. Mr. Stebbings has sorted out all the permissions from the local council though, so that's one good thing."

"Sounds like he's a bit of a find."

"He is. It's just I'd forgotten how hideous this bit is, where everything gets worse before it gets better."

"You hope."

"Thanks Lola, that's very encouraging."

"I've sent you loads of magazines, to help inspire you."

"I got them yesterday. Sorry, I meant to ring up and thank you, they're great."

"I've put Post-it notes by the things I want you to get for my room."

"I noticed that."

Lola has taken to referring to the biggest double B&B bedroom as her room.

"Do you really want a sofa covered in vintage fabric with rabbits and cabbages?"

"Yes. I do. It's very Country House Chic."

"Country House Nutter more like, particularly at nearly fifteen quid a metre. And I'm still stuck on curtains. It seems to be trendy to have none at all, and once the shutters are sorted out and repainted they'll keep the heat in as long as people remember to close them, but I still think it will look a bit stark. I'm thinking about putting up some plain wooden rails and simple cotton curtains. Mum says she'll bring her sewing machine and we can make them."

"So you finally get to use your sewing room, which we are definitely not calling a dressing room."

"Looks like it. I've seen some great material in that shop I was telling you about, very nineteen-forties—little sailing ships and seashells, pale blue and white."

"Sounds great. It will go with my rabbits. You need a medley of motifs, or it will look too matchy, like bloody Cath Kidston. There are only so many roses you can fit into one room."

"Not down here, I think you'll find. But I'm avoiding floral—the garden can take care of that."

"What did you think of my bathroom selection—gorgeous or what?"

"Gorgeous, I'm saving them all in my bathroom file, for phase two. But for now I'm going to keep it simple, since it's all I can afford. We've already got rid of the horrible old carpets and sanded the floors, which look tons better already, and with new shower units and new towels, you won't recognise them."

"I bet I will. Having a huge rolltop bath in the bedroom is the kind of luxury people want."

"If they like parading round stark naked in front of their travelling companion, maybe, but I'm pretty sure most B-and-B guests aren't quite that liberated."

"It would give them an experience then, something to remember."

"Oh yes, the sight of Pete bobbling about first thing in the morning having a bath before I'd even got out of bed would have put me off my breakfast for sure. I'd definitely remember that. Anyway, Ivy wouldn't approve."

"Is she still doing the tutting thing?"

"A fair bit, and Mum's started popping round to help, which is nice, obviously, but somehow that means she and Ivy are sort of competing to see who can boss me about the most."

"About?"

"Pretty much everything. Yesterday it was how to get mud off Alfie's school trousers. I've hugely underestimated the amount of mud involved in our new country life."

"Tell them to bugger off."

"You tell them. Are you still coming down this weekend?"

"Yes, I need to check my room is being done properly."

"Great. You'll be in the single room, unless they've started work in there too, in which case you can have my room and I'll sleep in the..."

"Don't say it."

"Sewing room. We'll move one of the single beds in."

"Right you are darling, can't wait."

"You can try some of my bread. I've started making it again, the top of the oven is the perfect place to get dough to rise. Sally has introduced me to her friend Dave, who sells bread at the local markets and he's going to give me some of his sourdough starter."

"His what?"

"The yeast, to make sourdough bread. It's a serious business—some of it has provenance going back hundreds of years. People take their yeast on holiday with them, to keep it going."

"How charming."

"It will be, if I can serve fresh bread to guests. I'm experimenting with spelt, and wholemeal—it's quite addictive."

"Sounds like I need to get down there as soon as I can before you completely loop the loop."

After the school run, I catch up with Mr. Stebbings, and we stand looking at the ceiling cornice in the dining room.

"I'm sure I've got moulds somewhere in the workshop very similar to these. I'll bring them with me tomorrow and I can make any adjustments needed. It will look as right as the day it went up when we've finished. They knew what they were doing in them days, standards of work you don't see enough of now. It will be a pleasure to work on a ceiling like this."

"I bet some of the workers' cottages were pretty basic though?"

"That they were. Had to go cap in hand to the landlord to get anything fixed, or do it yourself. They weren't the good old days for the workingman, and that's a fact."

"Or the workingwoman, trying to do all the washing for a family with a huge pot of boiling water and an old metal washboard. Ivy was showing me the old one in the gatehouse; she can remember when they still used it. It sounds hideous."

He smiles.

"We used to stay well out of my mum's reach on a wash day, me and my brothers, or you'd get a clip round the ear before you knew where you were. She had her work cut out keeping all seven of us fit to be seen."

"I bet she did. It's bad enough with three, and they're still not always fit to be seen. Would you like a cup of tea? I was just going to make some."

"No thank you Miss. Ivy has seen us right—makes a lovely bit of cake she does."

"I'd avoid the jam tarts if I were you. Alfie was helping Ivy make them yesterday, so the pastry's a bit grubby."

"Right you are. I'll not tell Jim, though. He's got a constitution like an ox, bit of grubby pastry won't bother him."

He's chuckling as he climbs up his stepladder to get a closer look at the cornice.

Ivy's so thrilled I've finally ordered the new steam press that she hardly noticed when I said we'd have mini boxes of cereal for guests and stop using the Tupperware. So as long as I manage to avoid steam pressing my own arm and make sure nobody under sixteen ever touches the bloody thing, things are looking up. I'm trying to take advantage of my gold-star status on the domestic front by sorting through the cupboards in the scullery to find some bathroom cleaner, when Ivy comes in.

"I was just looking for some bath stuff?"

"You only have to let me know and I'll make sure it gets done."

"I know Ivy, but we've talked about this. There's four more of us now, and the boys make so much mess—we'll both need to be cleaning if we want to keep on top of it all."

I try a smile, but she's crossing her arms and looking annoyed.

"I never had any complaints in the past, and that's all I'm saying."

I think this might be a good time to stand my ground, which is tricky when I'm kneeling at her feet, but I'll give it a go.

"I'm not complaining Ivy, far from it, but I won't be out in the garden all day like Helena used to. I want to be hands-on. Hands in buckets, if needs be."

She hesitates.

"As thick as thieves they used to be, her and Dennis. Any money that came in went straight out again on that silly garden."

"I know that Ivy, and we're keeping the garden going, of course we are, but the house needs things too."

"You don't need to tell me. Times I told her."

"So how did it work then? Was there a housekeeping budget, for things like cleaning supplies?"

She tuts.

"Not that I ever saw."

"Right. So did you just settle up each time you bought new stuff then?"

She looks uncomfortable, and opens the cupboard by the door.

"There's a bottle of bleach in here, I think."

Oh God, I think I've just worked out why there's such a motley collection of cleaning things—she's been buying them all herself.

"Ivy, how much have you spent, over the years?"

"It was just a few things now and again. She had no idea what things cost, and I didn't like to say."

"Right, well that's something else that we're going to change, right now. Let's go to the cash-and-carry later on, that big one on the industrial estate, and we can stock up. And no more paying for things out of your own purse. Agreed?"

"Don't you need to be a member to go to the cash-and-carry?"

"Sally's lent me the card from the hotel. So long as I pay for all our stuff at the checkout, nobody will be any the wiser. Shall we make a list? I'd like to have things upstairs and down here too, it will save us time when we're cleaning the B-and-B rooms. Does that sound like a good idea?"

"Well, if we got a new mop, that would be handy. That old one's not much use anymore. Could we go after I've given Mr. Bertie his lunch, do you think? Would that give us enough time to be back for you to collect the boys from school? Or we could take them with us—they could push the trolley, couldn't they, they'd probably like that?"

They won't, but I can tell she doesn't want a quick five-minute dash-round.

"Good idea. We'll pick them up and then go. I'll leave a note for Dan—he'll be fine until we get back. Start writing your list Ivy."

Dear God. Without knowing it, I seem to have waved a domestic version of a fairy wand and Ivy has finally been able to unleash her heart's desire in the wonderful world of cleaning supplies. I've had to bribe Ben and Alfie with cans of Coke while we've compared brands of mop, which all look the same to me, and we've got enough brushes, sponges, and cloths to last us years. We've also got a new bucket on wheels which will transform cleaning the kitchen flagstones into a complete joy, if Ivy's demonstration is anything to go by, and more packets and bottles and cleaning supplies than I've ever seen. Ivy is so happy she's almost skipping, and by the time we get to the checkout, so are the boys, because I've had to promise extra television time to avert a postschool meltdown at my refusal to sanction mock sword fighting with washing-up brushes.

Bloody hell. I've just spent nearly two hundred and forty pounds, on absolutely nothing you can eat or wear. Poor Ivy nearly falls over when the girl tells us the total, and she's all for retracing our steps and putting things back on shelves, but I manage to get her back to the car, still in a daze, clutching a dustpan and brush, for some reason best known to herself. Ben and Alfie are keen to race the new wheelie bucket round and round the car park until I intervene.

"What's the point of it having wheels then, if you can't wheel it?"

"It's to make the cleaning easier Ben, which it won't be if you two have trundled it through the mud before we've even got it home. Get in the car please love."

"What are we having for supper?"

"Pasta bake?"

He nods, since pasta is one of his best suppers. Pasta anything actually, baked or otherwise.

"I hate pasta."

"No you don't Alfie, and get in the car please."

Ivy is studying the till receipt.

"It's right dear, and really, when you look at the prices, we've saved ever such a lot, only I never thought it would come to that much, I really didn't."

"It's fine Ivy. We needed to restock, and now we're all set. Alfie, get in the car. Now. Or there won't be time for cartoons."

Dennis is horrified when he helps us unpack, and starts muttering at Ivy, who's looking increasingly stricken.

"I'm sure we don't need half this stuff. What's this for?"

He holds up a collection of thin brushes with bristles, joined together with a plastic chain.

"It's for cleaning teapot spouts. They're very fiddly, and you can't get them properly clean with a cloth."

"Good Lord, what will they think of next?"

I'm starting to feel a bit sorry for Ivy now, and it's not like Dennis has ever needed to clean a teapot spout. It's not something I've spent a great deal of time worrying about either, but I'm sure it will come in handy.

"We need the right tools for the job Dennis, just like you do for the garden. And it's about time the house got its fair share, don't you think?"

Ivy nods.

"That's right, and don't you say another word Dennis, or you can make your own supper. She's been very kind, getting me all sorts that I've wanted for years, so don't you go spoiling it for me, do you hear?"

"I was only saying."

"Yes, well, don't. And you can get those dirty boots off my kitchen floor, thank you. Just because I've got a new bucket doesn't mean I want to be filling it up every five minutes, thank you very much. I've told you until I'm blue in the face, either take them off at the door or stop outside. Cup of tea, Miss Molly, and a slice of cake? I've got a new Victoria sponge in the tin."

"Thanks Ivy, that would be lovely, and then I better make a start on supper."

"What about you Dennis, are you stopping in, or what? And don't you think you're getting a slice of my cake, because you're not. It's for the family, not the likes of you, standing there upsetting everyone."

"No I'm not, I've got things to do in the shed, at least that way I'll get a bit of peace."

"Mum, Uncle Bertie says he's going to do the cannon in a minute, so can I help him?"

How perfect.

"You can't help Uncle Bertie Alfie, you know that. You can watch, but you can't help. Only grown-ups can do anything related to cannons. They're very dangerous."

Both Alfie and Dennis are tutting as they wander off in search of Bertie, and Ivy and I exchange a smile.

"Dennis will sort them out, don't you fret. He makes a fuss about it, but I think he enjoys it almost as much as Mr. Bertie does."

"I think they all do Ivy."

They've developed a little routine now where the boys stand at a safe distance, almost like they're standing to attention, and then cheer once the stupid thing has boomed out another plate-rattling round. The only useful thing is how much it annoys the seagulls, who tend to stay clear of the house. They're a menace in the village when people are trying to eat outside the café or the fish-and-chip shop. Actually that might be a good way to raise a bit of extra cash, particularly if we're going to be visiting the cash-and-carry on a regular basis—I could rent Bertie out as a seagull deterrent. I'm sure he'd love it.

"I've done a rhubarb crumble for your supper. Your Alfie asked me for one specially. It's in the fridge, all ready—just pop it in the top oven for twenty minutes, dear."

"Thanks Ivy. Have you made one for you and Dennis too?"

"I have, only I might not feel like cooking this evening. He might have to make do with cheese and biscuits. I haven't decided."

I'm fairly sure hell will freeze over before Ivy gives Dennis cheese and biscuits for his supper, but she's clearly still miffed with him, so you never know.

"There's soup for Mr. Bertie, the one he likes, oxtail. You go and have a sit-down and I'll bring your tea in. You've had a long day."

I think I might continue to bask in the glory of Ivy's approval for a tiny bit longer.

"Five minutes' peace before I start on supper would be a real treat, thanks. And I'll heat Bertie's soup when I make our pasta."

* * *

I end up making a proper pasta sauce for supper, mainly because there's none left in the freezer, but also because I'm hoping a session chopping and stirring might be a good antidote to our busy afternoon. The boys have all snorked back slices of cake before going back outside with Bertie and Dennis, so they'll last a bit longer before having supper on the table becomes critical. I'm chopping carrots and celery and onion, and trotting backwards and forwards to the pantry, which is probably my top alternative to the linen cupboard when I'm in need of a bit of calm pottering. There's something about all the jars of jams and pickles and bottled fruit lined up on the stone shelves, next to the big glass jars of flour and rice and all the tins and packets, and Ivy's epic collection of recycled jam jars and bottles, which gives you an instant housewifely boost. It's always cool and dark, and there are bowls and dishes and assorted saucepans and fish kettles and double boilers lined up in ranks on the bottom shelves, so if we ever find ourselves needing to cook for a banquet we'll be in with a chance. The china cupboard has the smaller bowls and plates, but there's an impressive collection of soufflé dishes and huge serving platters and tureens in the pantry, in a variety of patterns from long-lost sets: willow and Chinese, flowers and fruit with gilded edgings, alongside the blue-and-cream Cornishware I've collected over the years and all the plain white I brought with us. Somehow it all combines to look rather grand. The rest of the house might be in need of a face-lift, but the pantry is perfect just the way it is.

I'm retrieving a bay leaf from one of the jars of herbs Ivy dried last summer and making grand plans to make lots more jams this summer with the boys, when Dan comes in.

"Great, pasta again. What a treat."

"I thought you were outside with Uncle Bertie?"

"I got bored. Is it meat sauce?"

"Tomato. You can have some tuna with yours if you like. Actually, you could make yourself useful and grate the Parmesan."

"Can I use the food processor?"

"If you clean it afterwards, yes. The dishwasher's already nearly full. Otherwise use the grater."

He's grating the cheese, albeit in a rather desultory fashion, while I open a couple of cans of plum tomatoes and whizz them into a pulp with the handheld blender, when the bloody cannon suddenly booms out and I whizz tomato all over the kitchen counter and halfway up the wall.

"Mum."

"Yes Dan."

"You've got tomato all up the wall."

"Shut up and get me one of the new cloths would you, and the new bottle of cleaner, it's under the sink."

He tuts.

"If you want supper, then get a cloth. There's rhubarb crumble for pudding."

Dan loves Ivy's rhubarb crumble almost as much as Alfie does. Any crumble, come to think of it.

"With custard?"

"Possibly. But unless you want custard with a hint of tomato, get wiping."

I think I might just retreat into the pantry to find the tin of custard powder, and reboot myself back into chirpy domestic mode before Bertie Boom and the boys come back in for supper. And then I can have another look at Lola's magazines, and pretend I can afford to spend ninety-eight pounds on a roll of wallpaper.

"Mum?"

"Yes Dan."

"Can you make loads of custard? There's never enough."

"As you long as you don't want cereal for breakfast, sure."

I better make some more bread, so we've enough for toast and their packed lunches. Perhaps the magazines will have to wait.

By the time I'm finally in bed, I'm exhausted, but instead of falling asleep I end up having a series of slow-motion panic attacks. What if I can't make this work and we have to sell up? Where will we go, and how will I ever get over the shame of letting Helena down? Oh God. And what will I do if Bertie goes completely off the rails? He went out on patrol in his slippers again this evening, and came back half-frozen. Thank God Ivy had left by then, and I've washed the mud off his slippers in the scullery sink, and they're drying on top of the boiler, but there's "charmingly eccentric" and there's "completely loopy," and I'd really rather he stuck with "eccentric."

Right. I'll get up and make a pot of tea, and update my lists. That's always calming. And if that doesn't work, I'll overdose on Ivy's Victoria sponge and blame it on the boys. Bloody hell.

What's that terrible racket?"

"The builders, fixing the roof. I'm upstairs, sorting through Ben's old trousers trying to find some for Alfie. He's having another growing spurt, so he looks like he's wearing culottes."

"They're quite trendy again."

"Not for six-year-olds they're not."

"How is my lovely boy?"

"Fine, apart from the trouser thing."

"And the house?"

"We're still at the stage where you wonder if all the mess could possibly be worth it, but at least we won't get electrocuted or have the ceilings fall down on our heads."

"Has that Lucinda woman given up yet?"

"Not really. She's rung twice now, and on Monday she popped round, so I hid and Ivy got rid of her."

"That was very assertive of you darling."

"There's only so many polite reasons I can think of why I can't go to one of her horrible lunch parties, and now I've got Mum ringing me up three times a day about bloody Roger's Valentine's dinner at the hotel. It's all part of his I Will Be Captain campaign. He's inviting the current vice captain. He wants to make a big show of it. Can you think of anything more lethal?"

"You could always wear your necklace if he wants maximum showing off."

"What necklace?"

"Hello? Diamonds, emeralds, ring any bells? How many diamond necklaces have you got darling?"

"It's not really mine, not really, and Roger and Georgina are still upset about it, so it wouldn't be terribly subtle. Anyway, it's in the bank."

"It is yours, unless you sell it to buy new bathrooms, and it might be a laugh. You might meet a stranger of the tall-dark-and-handsome variety."

"I very much doubt it, not unless he's had some sort of brain injury. Why else would you be at dinner in the hotel, where everyone is in couples apart from the bloody waiters?"

"You never know darling, it might not be as bad as you think."

"It bloody will, and if I wear my black dress everyone will

think I'm a bloody waitress, and I can't wear trousers or Dad will sulk all night."

"I'll courier you a frock down if you like."

"I'd never fit any of your things. My trousers are getting shorter by the day, just like Alfie's, but in my case it's thanks to Ivy's cakes."

"I've got an Issey Miyake that might work, silk pleated dress, drapes from the neck to the floor; all you need is high heels."

"I'll look like I'm wearing a parachute."

"There is that. I only wear it if I'm in the right mood. It can be a bit barrage balloon. Ooh, I know, I've seen the perfect thing. I'll order it right away. Dark-plum wrap dress, stretchy fabric, with velvet flowers, a bit like flock wallpaper but on a frock. I was going to get it next month for your birthday."

"It will have to be very stretchy, but it sounds lovely."

"It's a wrap dress darling—it expands, so the fun never ends. You'll get an occasional glimpse of your bra, which I know will freak you out, so wear a slip if you must, but a lacy one. I want you to ping me a photo before you leave the house so I can check. Deal?"

"Deal. And thank you, millions. At least I won't look like a waitress."

"My pleasure darling. Right, I'm off to find you a pumpkin Cinderella. You shall go to the ball."

By the time I'm ready for the stupid dinner I'm seriously considering ringing up with a mystery illness, but Lola's dress arrived this morning and it's lovely, so that's helping, and Bertie is very complimentary as I'm leaving.

"Off to paint the town red my dear, that's the spirit? You look—what is it the boys say?"

Christ, I hope they haven't explained MILF to him. Dan was saying it about some actress last week, but I pretended not to hear.

"I'm not really sure Uncle Bertie."

"Sickening, that's it, you look completely sickening."

"I think it's just 'sick,' unless you think I'm coming down with something?"

"Extraordinary the way they talk nowadays. Can't imagine telling a girl she looks 'sick.' Anyway, you look very fetching, what we used to call an absolute bobby dazzler."

"Thank you."

"Don't do anything I wouldn't do my dear—should give you plenty of scope. Any chance of a spot of supper Ivy? Been out on patrol and I'm rather peckish."

"I'll bring you something in a minute Mr. Bertie, I'm just making cocoa for the boys."

"Cocoa—that rings a bell. Used to have cocoa on night watches, might fancy a mug myself."

"I'll bring you a sandwich too then, shall I? I won't be a minute. And you have a lovely time dear, you look champion."

"Thanks Ivy."

"Polly put the kettle on."

"Thanks Betty."

There's a waiter giving all the women a red rose as we go into the dining room.

Oh God.

Georgina is wearing a sequined cocktail dress, and so many sparkly bangles she jingles every time she moves. Even her eye shadow is glittery. She's on a mission to persuade me to host a lunch for her ladies' golf team, which I think is what Bertie would call the thin end of the wedge: once I agree to one lunch, she'll be pushing to use the Hall as a venue for all her lunch parties and I'd rather stick pins in my legs than become a regular feature on her calendar of snooter events. It takes me ages to convince her that I'm too busy with all the building work and redecorating. Roger is busy trying to be the host with the most with Mr. and Mrs. Vice Captain, laughing too loudly and generally being annoying. But the food is fine, thank God. Dad has a habit of sending things back and making a fuss, but the new chef is definitely an improvement. And then the bloody cabaret starts in the lounge. It's Dean and the Martins and their big-band sound, only it's slightly more of a little band since there are only two Martins. They're regulars at the hotel, and their official name is Nice 'n Easy, but all the staff call them Dean and the Martins. They make such a fuss setting up and doing sound checks they're definitely not Nice, or Easy. Dean, who is actually called Dave, has very white teeth and a gold jacket, and starts running through his Frank Sinatra/Dean Martin songbook, with Dad tapping his fork along to "Strangers in the Night." I wonder if he knows it's about exactly the kind of encounter he would thoroughly disapprove of—especially if she was wearing trousers.

We're accompanied by "Some Enchanted Evening" as we move into the lounge for coffee, and I'm trying to work out how soon I can leave, whilst simultaneously trying to surreptitiously adjust my dress, which has managed to relax itself to reveal far more lacy vest than I intended, when Roger spots someone he knows and beckons them over.

"Molly, you remember Stephen, don't you?"

Christ. It's Stephen Jackson, who I was madly in love with for about three weeks many years ago, when we were both seventeen. Thank God Sally isn't on duty tonight, or she'd be in hysterics. He used to be a Steve, with a leather jacket and carefully frayed jeans, but he seems to have moved on to being Stephen now, with smart suits and an impressive tan. And here he is, standing smiling at me. Bloody hell. Talk about a blast from the past.

"Lovely to see you again Molly. Roger told me you'd moved back recently."

Georgina has gone into full-simper mode.

"Stephen is very much a rising star locally, Molly—a very sought-after architect. He's won so many awards we've all lost count. Do join us for coffee Stephen, if your table can spare you?"

"Perhaps just for a moment. We've landed a big project, so I've brought the team out to say thank you. But coffee would be lovely."

Roger starts clicking his fingers and summoning more coffee and another chair as Stephen chats with Dad and Mr. and Mrs. Vice Captain. The raffle is being drawn, so Dean and the Martins are taking a five-minute break, and the waiters bring little plates of chocolates round. Ted Fordwich is head-waitering tonight, and gives me an encouraging wink, which reminds me just how much I'd rather be handing round plates than sitting here like a lemon, but Roger is in full genial-host mode ordering brandies and liqueurs.

"Molly, you should talk to Stephen about your plans for the Hall. Such an important house needs expert handling." He turns to Mr. Vice Captain. "Been in the family for generations, Harrington Hall, you may know it?"

Mr. Vice Captain looks suitably impressed.

Oh God, please let me get out of here without saying anything I'll regret.

"I'm not really planning anything major, not straightaway."

Roger gives me an irritated look and pretends to laugh.

"There speaks a woman who has never overseen a major refurbishment."

"I did up our last house all by myself. I spent hours up a ladder scraping off wallpaper and painting, so I do have some sense of how much work it's going to take—thanks Roger. Bertie's got some ideas too, and Dennis and Ivy, so I won't be on my own."

Actually the only idea Bertie is likely to come up with will probably involve buying bigger artillery, but never mind.

"Don't be so modest Molly. You're doing up the gatehouse too, and there's potential in the stables, huge potential. Stephen, tell her. She's got old Stebbings doing the gatehouse, and we know how long he takes to get anything done."

"I like him."

Stephen picks up his wineglass and smiles.

"Oh yes, he's decent enough, just a bit old-fashioned and slow. But look, there'll be more possibilities than you think, there always are, why don't I pop round and take a look. I'm fairly busy at the moment, but I'm sure I can make time for an old friend."

Damn. I can't help feeling I've been set up here somehow. I'm not quite sure how, but Roger looks very pleased and that's never a good sign.

"Thanks Stephen, but only if it's no trouble, I'm really not making any big decisions just yet."

"Oh look, the band's back. Shouldn't we all be dancing? Roger, surely you're going to ask your glamorous wife to dance? Molly, care to join me?"

He stands up, and holds out his hand.

Bugger.

"I'm not sure I know how to dance to 'You Make Me Feel So Young.'"

"Me neither but let's see how we go shall we?"

He walks towards the dance floor, where a variety of couples in evening dress are twirling round, including one couple who appear to be doing a tango.

"Do you tango?"

"Not that I've noticed. Do you?"

He grins.

"Not really, no. What about another cup of coffee on the terrace? It's not too windy tonight and the heaters work pretty well. How does that sound, unless you'd rather dance?"

"Coffee would be lovely."

We're both smiling now.

"Tell me about the house, but only if you'd like to. I'd hate you to think I was touting for business, despite your brother's best efforts—you know how determined he can be, it took me weeks to divert him from some of his, well, shall we say less-original ideas for the new apartments in the hotel."

"Oh, did you do those, I didn't know, they're lovely."

They are too—all pale wood and new windows and beautiful bathrooms, a bit too modern and shiny for me, but a huge improvement on the tragic old plastic and hideous carpets.

"We did, I'd have liked to demolish them and start again, but I think we managed to make a few improvements."

"Definitely."

"So are you enjoying being back home?"

"Yes, very much, it's a new start, for all of us."

"I was sorry to hear about your divorce. Been through the same thing myself—hideous, isn't it? Portia and I split up three years ago—entirely mutual decision, but still tough. Finn seems okay about it though, and that's the main thing. You've got boys too, haven't you?"

"Yes, three."

"I can barely keep up with Finn—I'd have no chance with three. He's at King's Park with your son Dan I think? He's been telling me something about a cannon?"

"That's Uncle Bertie."

"Oh right, of course. He's still as lively as ever is he?"

"Yes, but I'm trying to play down the cannon thing, or we'll have hordes of kids round every day demanding a show, and trust me, he'd oblige."

A young man approaches us, looking tentative, and Stephen gives him an irritated look.

"Sorry, it's just that we were thinking of making a move soon, if that's okay with you?"

"Just give me a minute. Sorry Molly, but look, I'll call you, and fix up a time to see the Hall properly?"

"Sure."

He hands me his mobile.

"Put your number in here—that way I won't lose it."

I key in my number, and give him his phone back.

"Lovely to see you again, Molly."

He winks as he turns to go back towards his table.

Bloody hell. Perhaps I'm not such a disaster after all, particularly when I make an effort and dress up in a Lola-approved outfit. I'm feeling rather flustered as I walk back into the lounge. Stephen Jackson, all grown up and winking at me, even if there is something a bit too slick and polished about him. Crikey. Roger and Georgina are still dancing, thank God, so if I'm quick, I can have five minutes with Mum and Dad and then leave. And that way I won't have to dance to Dean and the Martins at all. It'll be win-win, and you don't often get to say that at one of Roger's social occasions, not unless you can rent a helicopter.

"There you are dear. Your father has been waiting to dance with you."

Great.

Sally's heard all about my encounter with Stephen from the hotel grapevine, and rings for details the next morning.

"He's divorced you know."

"Yes, he did mention it."

"Did he? He must be keen then. He's got a bit of a reputation locally you know. He's always got a glamorous woman on his arm."

"That counts me out then."

"Don't be silly, you're quite a catch. He'll have heard about you getting the Hall—oh, sorry, I didn't mean it like that. You always were a catch, and you still are."

"Don't worry, Sal, I know what you mean, and he was pretty keen to come round and give me top-architect tips, that's for sure. But that might have been down to Roger—you know what he's like."

"As long as that's all he gives you. Oh God, that came out wrong too."

We're both giggling now.

"Don't worry, I haven't forgotten."

"How he dumped you for Susan Prentice? Yes, but that was years ago. And she did have the biggest chest in the school. Nobody could compete with that."

"True."

"He did have a ponytail a while back, but he's got over that now."

"Not entirely. There was something a bit ponytail about him last night, if I'm honest. Something a bit too 'Look at me.'"

"Well at least he's worth looking at—not like some of them with their sports jackets and slacks."

"Like Roger?"

"No comment. So when he rings, what will you do?"

"I think it's the house he wants to see, so he can come round for a cup of tea, and we'll see how Betty gets on with him. Anyway I haven't got time to worry about that, I've got Alfie's party to sort for next weekend. I know it made sense to invite everyone in his class since we're new here and everything, but that's twenty-five kids Sal, and all the little sods are coming."

"I did warn you. I could try to swap my shifts round if you like."

"Thanks, but I think we'll be fine, Mum's coming, and Ivy. Bertie's threatened to come too, but I'm trying to avoid that."

"He might have some good ideas—Stephen, I mean—for the house. He did those new flats by the seawall. Me and Patrick went to have a look, just to be nosy—we could never have afforded the prices they wanted."

"What were they like?"

"Very glamorous. Lights in the floors and glass staircases."

"Not really what I'm after."

"No, but they were impressive. Look, I better go. Tom and Patrick are making breakfast, so the smoke alarm will go off any minute. But good luck with the party. Let me know if you change your mind, and I'll come and help."

"Thanks Sal."

It's Saturday morning and Alfie's party day, and I'm seriously wishing I'd fobbed him off with large amounts of cash and a family tea. After days of stripping wallpaper and sanding floorboards in the guest bedrooms I feel like I'm permanently covered in dust with bits of wallpaper stuck to the soles of my feet. Mr. Stebbings has started to make real progress on the gatehouse, which is a bit terrifying because I haven't even started to think about what it should look like inside. So I'm looking at design magazines and trying not to think about how on earth I can get it all done. And Stephen rang the day after the dinner and is coming round to see the house when he's back from a conference in Madrid, and I'm trying not to think about that as well.

Mum and Ivy have launched another round of competitive baking, and are both busy cooking for Alfie's party, which is great, but I can't help wishing I could find a pause button somewhere. If I could just have a few hours to catch up, I'm sure I'd feel less like I've somehow wandered into one of those *Benny Hill* sketches where the music speeds up and everyone runs round and round waving mops and dusters—or wooden spoons in Mum's case, since she's making the birthday cake. She keeps ringing me with cake updates, so James Bond theme tunes keep ringing out at unexpected moments, along with Yoda telling me "Answer the telephone you must" whenever Pete calls. But at least he's getting better at calling the boys every few days, and he even remembered to ring this morning to talk to Alfie about his party, so that was nice, even if I'm pretty sure it was down to Janice. I know Alfie was pleased, and that's all that really matters. And Lola called yesterday from Italy, where she's sorting out some film crisis with one of her director clients whilst simultaneously having treatments in a spa hotel. Nice work if you can get it. The closest I'm likely to come to anything spa-like is the exfoliating effect produced by scrubbing off all that bloody plaster dust.

"Diamonds Are Forever" starts ringing out the minute I step into the bath. If it were anyone but Lola I'd leave it to ring.

"Hello darling. All set?"

"I think so. Hang on a minute, I was just getting into the bath."

"Getting ready for the party?"

"More like getting the paint out of my hair. I've been painting ceilings this morning, trying to keep out of Ivy's way."

"When's the architect due?"

"Tomorrow afternoon."

"Sunday afternoon? Couldn't you have picked a more useful time?"

"Useful for what?"

"You never know. A quick spot of rekindling might be fun."

"He's off to Dubai on Monday Lola, and he's coming to see the house, not to rekindle anything."

"Try not to be covered in paint when he arrives. Wear your new skirt."

"I'm wearing it today, I want to put in a good appearance for all the parents, although I'm still not sure about the wisdom of wearing a dry-clean-only velvet skirt to a children's tea party. But Ivy and Mum have appointed themselves in charge of the catering, so I'm in with a chance."

"You could always wear the green one tomorrow, with woolly tights and boots."

"I'm not sure showing him round the house dressed as Robin Hood is such a great idea. I thought jeans and a clean shirt. This isn't a date Lola."

"No, and it's not likely to be if you dress like a builder."

"Lola."

"Yes?"

"Shut up."

"Charming. I'm giving you expert tips here."

"Sorry."

"Promise me you'll wear a skirt."

"Christ, you sound just like Dad."

"Promise."

"Okay, I promise."

I'm crossing my fingers, so it doesn't count.

"And you can uncross your fingers. You promised, and it does count. And I'll ring Alfie to check."

"You will not."

"I bloody will. Have a lovely party darling, and call me tomorrow, when you've de-skirted. Unless you de-skirt with the architect, in which case call me much later. By the way, has Quentin arrived?"

"Yes, he's at the village hall, and thanks for arranging it, you really didn't need to you know."

"Since I can't be there myself I wanted a big surprise for my gorgeous boy."

I'm still not sure how thrilled Alfie is going to be with a surprise puppet show, particularly with a puppeteer called Quentin. But Lola swears he's brilliant, and I can only hope she's right, or I'm likely to have twenty-five mutinous six- and seven-year-olds on my hands, armed with cake and jelly.

"He's still insisting Bertie comes, with that stupid parrot. So I think we can pretty much guarantee they'll all be going home with some choice new phrases along with their party bags."

"Sounds good to me."

* * *

Lola is right, as usual. We played Pin the Tail on the Parrot, which was Dan's idea in the hopes that someone would get confused and try it with the real thing, and Pass the Parcel, and Musical Statues, which I know from past experience is much better than Musical Chairs, since nobody gets shoved off their chair when the music stops. But the real triumph was the puppet show, which turned out to be a wonderful mix of magicians and dragons, like a post-modern *Punch and Judy* without the rather dodgy domestic-violence subplot. Lots of bashing monsters and audience participation, and a finale involving mini explosions and indoor fireworks with copious amounts of red and purple smoke, and loud music, and then a bubble machine, which gets them all leaping up to pop the magic bubbles, because, according to Quentin, the more bubbles you pop, the more the magic rubs off on you. They're all leaping about to "Puff the Magic Dragon" as the parents start to arrive, and some of the hipster parents are humming along and looking amused as they try to round up their kids. Betty has retreated up into the rafters, and is telling everyone to bugger off, but it doesn't seem to be working, so in the end I have to ask Quentin to turn the music off or we'll never get them to leave. Dan and Ben are handing out the party bags, and everyone seems delighted.

Bertie is enchanted.

"Excellent show. Kept the ankle biters completely gripped, didn't he? Clever chap. Like to have a word with him, just what we need, a show like that, liven up our dinners at the club."

Dennis doesn't look keen.

"Are you sure that's a good idea? Some of them are on their last legs as it is."

"Just what they need to wake them up, go down a storm."

"Yes, or they'll keel over completely and then we'll have to have the ambulance back. Like we did the time you made those cocktails and told them they were fruit punch, and old Bob went all peculiar. And most of the rest of them could hardly walk, let alone drive themselves home. I was backwards and forwards in that car half the night."

"Lucky you were there Dennis. Good chap in a crisis, always said that. Don't know how we'd manage without you. Do we my dear?"

"No Uncle Bertie."

Surrounded by indoor fireworks and completely plastered is my guess, but I think I'll leave this one to Dennis.

"Thanks Dan."

"What for?"

"For helping and making his party so nice for him. What were you saying to that boy?"

"Jake? I just told him I know where he lives and if he upsets my baby brother one more time I'll upset him right back, only bigger."

"Oh Dan, he's only little."

"He's a year older than Alfie, and yes, I know, kids who bully other kids are sad and unhappy and they can't help it and violence is never the answer and blah blah blah. I've heard it all before, but he's not having a go at my brother and getting away with it. Me and Ben talked about it, and he can't do it because he's at the same school and they're not meant to put the frighteners on the little ones. So it was down to me."

"I thought Alfie didn't mind. It was only a bit of name-calling, wasn't it, nothing more than that?"

Oh God, I'm panicking now that I've managed to miss the fact that some serious bullying was going on. I'm halfway into a Motherhood Red Alert before Dan manages to convince me that Alfie's fine.

"But with kids like Jake, if they don't get a reaction, they just get worse. It'll be fine now I've had a word. Calm down."

"Are you sure?"

"Yes. He's had a go at Tom and Arthur too—it's all three of them, not just Alfie. So you're alright with it then?"

"As long as it's just talking Dan."

He grins.

"I know that Mum, but he doesn't."

Alfie spends ages making Dan a medal when we get home, which I notice he's pinned up on his noticeboard in his room when I go in to say good night.

"That's nice love."

"Yeah."

"Aren't you going to wear it?"

"And look like a total knob?"

"Dan."

"A total idiot. No thanks."

"Sweet of him though."

"He's alright. Sometimes."

That's about as good as it gets from Dan.

"Night love."

"Night Mum. And Mum?"

"Yes love?"

"When I have my birthday, promise I don't have to have puppets."

"Okay. Would you like a magic show instead? Sally knows a good magician. I think she's booking him for Tom's party."

"If he can magic up no parents, loads of booze, and fit girls, then yes, please."

"Dream on, sweetheart. And lights out soon, and your laptop needs to be downstairs."

I risk kissing the top of his head and he leans back for a moment.

"It was a good day, wasn't it Mum."

"Lovely."

"It might be alright down here, you know. I haven't decided yet, not totally, but it might."

"Diamonds Are Forever" starts ringing out across the landing.

Lola. With more skirt instructions. How perfect.

Would you like more tea Stephen?"

"No thanks, I might have a sliver more of the cake, though. Did you make it?"

"No, that's down to Ivy. She went into cake overdrive for Alfie's party. My cakes are, well, not like Ivy's. I'm getting into making bread, though, for the B-and-B."

"That's a nice touch, although as I've said, I think you can go far better than a B-and-B with a place like this."

"The gatehouse won't be B-and-B once it's finished."

"True, and he's making a good job of everything, I will say that. Mr. Stebbings has always been reliable for quality work. But you could do something exceptional with those stables. I'm sure you'd get permission to double the space at least, maybe even more, and if you put in a swimming pool and a spa, the house could be turned into luxury suites—with room for housekeeping and a kitchen, of course. You could be looking at substantial income if you did it properly."

"Which would be handy, since we'd be homeless."

He smiles, but also looks mildly irritated.

"I promised Helena that I'd keep everything going, if I can. Well, not promised, but you know what I mean. She put her trust in me."

"Sure, if that's what you want. Just don't make any final decisions. Look at all your options before you decide."

"But if I did decide to keep things simple, and do up the stables rather than anything bigger, would that be something your firm could do—as a job, I mean—because I'd definitely need help with the plans and everything."

"Of course, we'd be happy to. I tend to focus on the bigger projects, but I could put one of the associate partners on it. Bea might suit you. She does lots of renovations, and she's got a great eye. But as I say, don't decide anything yet. I'll get Bea to give you a call if you like?"

"That would be great."

I can see he's not going to give up on his idea to turn the whole place into a luxury holiday-camp/country-house hotel.

"How long are you in Dubai?"

"A week, possibly ten days. We stay in a decent hotel, so I can't complain. And then we're up for an award in Madrid, so I'll barely be home for a couple of weeks, and I hate that. I miss seeing Finn."

"Mum?"

"Yes Dan."

"Alfie's in the ditch again. Sorry, the 'ha-ha.'"

"Well get him out."

"Just thought you'd want to know."

He gives us both a rather hostile look, and stamps off.

Stephen smiles.

"I should probably be going, I've got work to finish before I leave tomorrow. Shall I say good-bye to Bertie?"

"He'll be out on patrol. He likes to keep an eye on the beach."

"What for?"

"God knows. Make sure the French aren't invading again? Who knows."

He laughs.

"You can say good-bye to Betty if you like?"

"If I want to be told to bugger off, I can always phone Finn and check on his schoolwork."

"Mum?"

"Yes Ben."

"Alfie's got a bit wet, but it wasn't his fault, not really. He was the goalie."

"Not again. You're supposed to play football somewhere else Ben, you know that."

"Yes, but it's the best flat bit."

"I'll be there in a minute. Don't let him indoors with anything muddy on, or I'll have to clean the floor again."

"Okay."

We walk across the hall, and Stephen pauses to examine the tiles again.

"I'm going to replace the cracked ones. Mr. Stebbings is getting them for me."

"Good, you want them done properly, that kind of patina is hard to replicate. But if anyone can do it, he can. And thank you, for showing me round, and for tea."

"You're welcome."

He leans forwards and kisses me on the cheek. And obviously it's not the same as the last time he kissed me, at the school disco all those years ago when I was trying to remember what Sally and I had decided was the optimum stance for kissing based on our limited but dedicated research. Obviously it's different from that, and a good thing too. But it does feel like more than just a social kiss.

"I'll call you from Dubai, and maybe we can have dinner when I'm back?"

He gets into his car and waves as he drives down the lane.

Crikey. Maybe he's just being professional, and hoping I'll decide to hand over the Hall for him to turn into a grand project. And to be honest, I'm not even sure I want to be going out to dinner, the last thing I need is anything complicated. But still, it's nice to be asked. I can't wait to tell Sally.

CHAPTER FOUR

Bringing Home the Bacon

March to April

China Roses

The arrival of roses from China introduced reliable repeat flowering for the first time. With light and sparse foliage, and delicate sweet fragrances, they are more tender than other varieties. Notable example varieties include Perle d'Or, a coral rose which fades to an apricot pink, fragranced with hints of peach; Irene Watts, a soft pink which fades to ivory; and Old Blush China, a fresh, strong pink rose scented with overtones of violets and sweet peas.

I'm halfway up a stepladder painting the newly replastered ceiling in the guest sitting room in what the paint company have decided to call "Fossil," but is actually a pale chalky cream. I've got paint up one sleeve and in my hair, but I've finally got the hang of the new roller, so it's all going rather well, when Ivy comes in, looking excited.

"Mrs. Denton's just called and they want to book in for the weekend after next, and I know we're not meant to be open until Easter, but they're a nice couple, no bother at all, so I said I'd call them back. Will we be ready, do you think?"

Bloody hell, our first guests.

"I don't know. I suppose we could be."

"Well if you're sure, I'll let them know. It is looking ever so much better in here, they'll be so impressed. Half an hour until lunch suit you?"

"I need to get this finished first Ivy."

"No you don't, you need to come down off that ladder and have your lunch. I've been telling Dennis, 'She'll work her fingers to the bone if we let her.' You've got to pace yourself. Rome wasn't built in a day you know."

"No, it was built by slaves. Who didn't stop for lunch."

She tuts, and folds her arms.

"Mr. Bertie likes eating with you. I never liked the idea of him up here in this great big place all on his own. He needs a bit of company, stop him getting up to mischief. It's made all the difference to him, you being here, having his lunch with him, a real difference."

"Thanks Ivy."

"I mean it. And you be careful on that ladder—rickety old thing. We don't want you falling off and doing yourself a mischief do we? I don't hold with women up ladders as a rule. If the good Lord had intended us to spend our time up ladders, he'd have invented men who can do the housework properly."

"Some of them can."

"Not round here they can't. Between Dennis and Mr. Bertie,

and the boys bringing in mud, and you treading bits of wallpaper and dust everywhere, it's a wonder I'm not on tablets, and that's all I'm saying. Do you want carrots with your lunch, or peas? I think I'll do both. Celia is here today doing the garden, so she'll be in for lunch, I've made a shepherd's pie—she likes that and I don't think she eats enough. Never has. She's got nobody to cook for, and I don't think she bothers."

"Right."

"Helena was the same, never learnt to cook what I'd call a proper meal. She could boil an egg or do you a bit of toast, but that was about it—no call for it when they were young, of course. Everyone had a full-time cook back then."

"Not everyone Ivy."

She smiles.

"No, that's true enough. Not everyone. Now, remember, I want you at the table when I call you. Or we'll be having words."

"Yes, Ivy. Thank you, Ivy."

I mutter "and 'three bags full' Ivy" under my breath.

"I heard that."

"You were meant to."

Right. Two weeks is the new deadline. Great. Mr. Stebbings has finished in the house and moved on to the gatehouse, but it's taking me far longer than I'd hoped to finish the painting and all the final touches. At least the guest bedrooms are almost done, and the bathrooms look nicer, even if the floors did take me ages. The sanding machine made such a noise, and then the varnish took forever to dry, but it looks so much better, I'm glad I stuck with it now—literally, in the case of the family bathroom, when I varnished myself into a corner by the sink.

Twenty minutes later I've got paint up both my sleeves, but one more coat should do it.

"Ivy says lunch is nearly ready, dear."

"Thanks, Celia."

"She's humming, so I wouldn't dally if I were you. Helena always used to say Ivy humming was an early-warning signal you ignored at your peril. Heart of gold of course."

"Yes."

"But a complete tartar if crossed. Like all good women. I think we've got shepherd's pie, quite a treat."

"That's good. Tell Ivy I'll be there in a minute, I just need to finish this last section, and then it needs to dry before I do the last coat."

Ivy and I spent ages unpacking all the new bed linen yesterday, sewing red, green, or blue thread onto all the labels in accordance with Ivy's coding system so you can spot a double flat sheet from a single without having to unfold everything. At one point I had a mini meltdown and got partially buried under a pile of sheets and blankets, which weigh a surprising amount when they fall on top of your head. But we've got neat piles of new linens in a variety of pale blues and white now, so it was worth it, and I've made up some more lavender bags, so everything smells lovely too. Mum helped me put up the new curtains in the bedrooms last week, so that's another job crossed off the list. She did most of the sewing-machine action in the end. Even making simple cotton curtains with no linings is trickier than you'd think, particularly if you manage to machine part of your skirt to them. But the wooden shutters are the real triumph, newly oiled and sanded and repainted a soft chalky cream, which reflects the light and manages to look elegant and warm at the same time. I had to try loads of shades until I found the right one, with Mr. Stebbings helping me choose between Donkey Ride and Pigeon. Donkey Ride won in the end, despite the stupid name, and Bill the window cleaner, another local pensioner with a ladder, has been very complimentary. His graphic description of what happens when old sash cords finally snap and windows descend like guillotines meant I had to divert Mr. Stebbings from his morning tea for an emergency sash-cord survey, but they're all sorted now, so I don't have to have nightmares about inadvertently guillotining hapless B&B guests. I really don't know where we'd be without all the bits and pieces Mr. Stebbings has squirreled away in his workshop. As long as Ivy keeps him supplied with tea and cake, he's always happy to fix extra things and not charge for them. He says he likes to see them put to good use, and he knew they'd come in handy one day.

"Are you coming then, or not? I'm nearly ready to serve up."

"Sorry Ivy, I'll be there in a minute, I promise."

"You better be, or I shall send Mr. Bertie in to fetch you, with Betty."

Mum?"

"Yes Alfie? Eat your supper, love."

"You know the Spring Fair. Well I'm doing singing in it, our whole class is."

"That's nice."

"Have you heard his class singing Mum?"

"Ben."

"But have you?"

"Is your class singing as well?"

"No, we're doing Francis Drake. He was born in Devon and he went round the world in *The Golden Hind*. So we're doing models and stuff."

"That sounds good."

"Yes, and he was playing bowls on Plymouth Hoe when the Spanish Armada was coming, but he said there was plenty of time to finish the game, so he did. And then they won, against the Armada I mean. I don't know if he won the bowls thing. But we're not allowed to do the fighting bit, which is rubbish. My group is doing the banner, so we don't have to dress up, but we'll be in the parade."

"That'll be good. They do a big parade every year along the seafront—the school, the lifeboats, all the local groups. It's great, if it doesn't rain."

"Let's pray for rain then."

"Thanks Dan. Clear the table if you've finished love, and put the plates in the dishwasher please."

"And Mum?"

"Yes Alfie?"

"We're going to sing pirate songs, and we've got to dress up. We're making our hats."

Bugger. Another costume for a school-related activity.

"With that mashed-paper stuff."

Dan grins.

"If you're wearing a papier-mâché hat, I'm definitely praying for rain. With a bit of luck you'll all be parading covered in bits of wet newspaper."

"Dan, aren't you meant to be clearing the table?"

"Okay, okay, don't get hysterical."

"And Mum?"

"Yes Alfie?"

"Betty can come too, because pirates have parrots, so it'll be great. Won't it Mum?"

Bloody hell.

"I'm not sure about that Alfie, I don't think Betty would like it."

"She'd love it, and I've already asked Uncle Bertie and he says she can come."

"I don't think he did Alfie."

And if he did, he can bloody well change his mind, sharpish. In an ideal world I'd rather not find myself standing watching my youngest parading around with a foul-mouthed parrot in front of the whole village. Actually, more like half the county, since people come for miles—it's one of the highlights of the local calendar, before the summer season starts and everyone is too busy. There are boat races in the bay, and lots of stalls, even if it's pouring with rain, which it often is, everyone just puts their hoods up and gets on with it, like they have done for years.

"Mum, let him take her. She'd probably bite a few people. It'd be great."

"Ben, help Dan clear the table if you've got nothing better to do than make silly comments."

"Will Uncle Roger be there Mum?"

"I expect so."

Dan is grinning again.

"Well there you go then. Betty should definitely be allowed to come with us."

By the time I'm in bed, rewriting my To Do lists whilst simultaneously mulling over my best tactics for Operation No Parrots on Parade, I'm feeling like I might be about to launch into another round of my slow-motion panic thing, which I could seriously do without. I'm mulling over an emergency slice of cake when "Diamonds Are Forever" rings out on the phone, and it turns out Lola is also having a trying time: one of her clients, who's sold his script to a big studio, is now complaining that they want so many rewrites it will be almost unrecognizable from the script they actually bought.

"Like they were ever going to say, 'Thank you so much, we won't change a word.'"

"But if they want to change it, why did they buy it?"

"Partly because I led them to believe that if they didn't, a rival studio would snap it up. But mainly because they all think they're creative geniuses, they have to meddle with everything to keep themselves and all their mates in their highly paid jobs, even though most of them have never had an original idea in their lives. Bastards."

"So you can see his point?"

"No, I bloody can't. Is the whole process fantastically annoying? Yes. Did I warn him it would be? Yes. Did he practically knock me over in his rush to sign up and get the money? Yes. Do I have all day to listen to him whining? No, I bloody do not. Christ, sometimes I wonder why I bother. I should get a proper job."

"Like?"

"Something with no whiny clients. Do they still have lighthouse keepers? I quite fancy that."

"Lola, you get withdrawal symptoms if you can't go clothes shopping every week—every day sometimes—how would that work?"

"I can use the Internet darling. Same-day delivery."

"Not in a Force-ten gale you can't. And how would it all get delivered—by helicopter? You probably wouldn't actually need any new clothes anyway, apart from waterproofs."

"Scandinavian knitwear is very in right now. I could wear lots of sweaters."

"Yes, until they got soaked, and then they'd weigh so much you wouldn't be able get back up the stairs to the turn the light on. Actually, I think the lights are all automatic now, so they don't actually have lighthouse keepers anymore."

"Bastards. Okay, I'll think of something else. How about you darling—want to run away with me?"

"Yes please. Alfie's class is singing pirate songs at the Spring Fair, and he wants to take Betty, so we'll need to find a new school—a whole new village, probably, after she's bitten someone and sworn at half the kids. Oh, and we got our first B-and-B booking today—in two weeks' time—so that's something else to worry about."

"Congratulations darling."

"If I get finished in time. I'm still up to my elbows in paint, and the bloody chimney sweep came on Monday, which wasted nearly the whole day, so that was a complete treat."

"Very Mary Poppins."

"Oh yes, it was wonderful, what with him whistling and poking brushes up chimneys, and Dennis and Mr. Stebbings scampering about checking when the brushes emerged, while Betty told everyone to bugger off, in between whistling along with the stupid sweep man. I was half expecting him to break into a chorus of 'Chim Chiminee.' Or the suffragettes to come marching past."

"I loved that film, particularly the mother—'Stand Firm, Sister Suffragettes.' She had great frocks, but she should have told George to bugger off and taken the kids on her march with her and then she wouldn't have needed a nanny, and soppy Mary could have stayed at home and talked to her umbrella. She gave me the creeps. Practically perfect in every way, I don't bloody think so."

"I liked the cook, the one who puts the saucepan on her head, or was that the Railway Children?"

"Don't get me started. That was a truly great film. So what was Bertie up to while the sweep was doing his thing? Did he fire the cannon?"

"Is the Pope Catholic? Gave the sweep a shock, he nearly got one of his poles stuck in the dining room chimney."

"Good old Bertie."

"Bonkers old Bertie more like. Celia's been telling me Helena used to threaten to push the cannon off the cliffs if he didn't stop."

"You could try that."

"Not without a handy rugby team I couldn't—it weighs a ton."

"I wonder if you can rent rugby teams by the hour. I bet you can. Perhaps I'll start a whole new roster of clients. I bet they're less whiny than creatives. Talking of which, any news from the architect?"

"No, I think he's still in Dubai."

"He'll call, when he's back."

"He might not, and that's fine Lola, I told you, he got a bit sulky when I didn't sign up to all his ideas for the house when he came round for coffee. Definite sulking."

"He'll get over it."

"Maybe, and Betty did try to bite him, but that was probably down to Bertie, I'm sure he does it on purpose. I think he may have heard him trying to persuade me to sell up and turn the house into an upmarket holiday camp."

"Which does make sense darling, if you wanted to make some proper money."

"And if I wanted to be homeless, with a mad parrot."

"Yes, but you can't blame him for coming up with grand plans—that's what architects do. He'll call, and then you can finally move on, unless you've got another likely prospect on the horizon."

"No, I haven't, and I am moving on."

"You know what I mean, a new notch on your—"

"Don't say bedpost, please. It's so *Benny Hill*."

"Saddle?"

"That's a particularly attractive image, thanks."

"Are you becoming a nun then? Nobody told me."

"No, but the last time I was on a horse I fell off. We hadn't even left the stables so I landed in a load of old straw, but even so."

We're both giggling now.

"Get back in the swing, then. Or hammock, you can't do much on a swing, although hammocks can be tricky too. We had one in that villa last year, but we kept falling out. It got quite annoying after a while."

"Have you seen him lately?"

"Neal? No, but I met his new wife, at a lunch. Stick insect. IQ of a small domestic pet."

"In other words perfect for him?"

"Ideal. God, I don't know why we bother, I really don't."

"Neither do I."

"Night darling."

"Night Lola."

I'm almost nodding off when the phone rings again, with no diamond tune. If this is another one of those calls telling me my computer needs fixing and if I would only give them my credit card details, they promise to improve my download speeds, it's going to be a very short call.

"Hi Molly. I hope it's not too late, I've rather lost track of time."

Actually half past eleven is quite late, but I sit up and try to sound like the opposite of someone who's half-asleep.

"Hello Stephen. Are you still in Dubai?"

"Yes. I thought I'd be back by now, but things have run on. How are things at the Hall?"

"Getting there. We've just got our first B-and-B booking, so I'm racing to get everything finished in time for Easter."

"I gather Bea is coming round tomorrow?"

"Yes, with Vicky, and their daughter. Vicky's in the same book group as my friend Sally. I'm hoping she'll help me with some ideas for the gatehouse. Sally says she's a designer, and if their house is anything to go by she'll have loads of great ideas."

"Yes, they're both very talented. Does Sally still work at the hotel?"

"That's right."

"I'm sure you'll like Bea. She's worked for us for about five years now, and she does some interesting work. She might even inspire you to go for a broader scheme. She's got good instincts, see what you think. And let's fix up that drink as soon as I'm back, or perhaps I could take you out to dinner?"

"That would be lovely."

"I'll call you, once I know what my diary looks like. We could try that new fish restaurant, I've heard good reports."

"Sounds lovely."

Oh God, why do I keep saying "lovely"? He probably thinks I'm a total idiot.

"Night Molly."

"Night, and thank you for calling."

Oh God. Thank you for calling. Now I sound like I work in Customer Services. What is wrong with me?

"My pleasure. I'll see you soon, and say hello to Bea for me."

Thankfully the line goes dead before I can say anything else embarrassing. I'm glad he called though. I felt like I'd failed some unwritten test when he came round for coffee. He was so impressed with the house, and the gatehouse and the stables, but definitely less impressed with my plans. I'll just have to remember to make sure Betty isn't around—either that or make her a special papier-mâché hat all of her very own.

I'm standing in the school playground with Sally, waiting for the bell to ring as Lucinda Langdon-Hill arrives and gives me a cheery wave. I'm still avoiding going to any of her snooter lunches, but either she's got skin like a rhinoceros or she's a bit thick and hasn't noticed—possibly a bit of both. She was telling me all about her business partner who does holiday rentals yesterday, and she'd be more than happy to pop a brochure round. Sally thinks it's all highly amusing.

"She's waving at you again."

"Shut up Sal."

"I will understand you know, if you feel you have to go and stand with the posh people. After all, you do live in one of our more important houses. Watch out—here comes Fliss Osborne, on her horse."

"How super."

Felicity holds the reins while her daughter Charlotte dismounts, and then clops off down the lane with the pony trotting along beside her horse, giving us all an imperious nod as she passes.

Lucinda is waving again, which makes Sally laugh.

"Blimey, there's posh for you. Wait until she hears you've got stables—she'll be trying to get you to tack up before you know it, and then you can arrive on horseback wearing a velvet riding hat just like she does."

"With Alfie? On a horse? It's bad enough with the bloody parrot."

"Good morning Mrs. Taylor."

Great. Mrs. Williams, our head, has just heard me saying "bloody" in the playground. I'll probably get some sort of black mark in the parental register.

"Good morning Mrs. Williams."

"I gather from Alfie that you used to teach, in London."

She's probably thinking that explains the bad language.

"That's right, History, at secondary school."

She's giving me a determined look, and I'm trying to return it, to signal that no, I am not available to run historical projects on Francis Drake or anybody else with assorted six-to-ten-year-olds, thank you very much.

"Alfie has been telling us all about your chickens. You have quite a little flock I hear?"

Bloody hell. I must have a word with Alfie about sharing domestic details. The nutter chickens have started laying again, but Vita and Gertie have gone broody, so I'm wearing the long sheepskin gloves I found in the boot cupboard when I feed them, as anti-pecking protection.

"Yes, that's right."

What is she after now, my taking charge of a whole school omelette?

"Miss Cooper and I thought you'd be the ideal person to take charge of the egg stall at the Spring Fair. It's very simple, and great fun. Miss Cooper can give you all the details—and I'm sure you'll help too, won't you Mrs. Elston?"

Sally is caught off guard by this.

"Er, yes, of course, only..."

"Excellent. There's Miss Cooper now. I'll give her the good news. And all the parents help of course. We wouldn't want your chickens to have to work overtime now, would we? Good morning."

Bollocks.

Sally is still looking rather stunned.

"God, she's good. What egg stall is she on about Sal?"

"I think it's the egg tombola."

"I beg your pardon?"

"Loads of eggs, all painted, and there's numbers on the bottom of some of them. So you choose your egg and if there's a number, you get a prize. And if not, well, you get to keep your egg."

"Are you serious?"

"They started it years ago—after the war I think—when boiled eggs were a big treat."

"Dear God."

"You can say that again. We'll have to make hundreds—at least a couple of hundred, I think. More if the weather forecast is good. Everyone is supposed to bring boiled eggs into school on the day before the fair, but they always forget. Brenda Thomas was up till half past three in the morning last year."

"Are you seriously telling me we've got to decorate hundreds of boiled eggs and then stand there like nutters all day, dodging bits of shell when people don't win anything and decide to have a quick snack?"

"Pretty much."

"Jesus Sal, it's like the land that time forgot."

"I know. That's why we like it, most of the time."

"Can't we just buy loads of mini chocolate eggs? I bet we could get big boxes of them at the supermarket. It can be our contribution to school funds."

"That's a brilliant idea. But people do like the decorated eggs. Mind you, they'd probably like chocolate ones even more."

"That's decided then. If they want boiled eggs, they can run the stall themselves. If we're doing it, they'll be chocolate, yes?"

"Yes, but you tell Miss Cooper."

"Thanks Sal, you're a tower of strength."

"I was late again last week, picking Tom up, she already thinks I'm crap. I can't tell her we're not doing the boiled-eggs thing too, I just can't. But I'll owe you one, I promise. And I think the chocolate ones will be really popular. You're completely brilliant."

"Sal?"

"Yes?"

"Shut up."

Thankfully Miss Cooper approves of the chocolate-egg plan; as long as she can cross something off her list, I really don't think she cares. We promise to make sure we don't buy chocolate with any trace of nuts because we've got a couple of kids in the school with serious allergies, and we're all set. But still. If anyone suggests we dress up as chickens, they can bugger right off.

I'm back at home making a quick coffee with Ivy when Mum arrives. She and Ivy have declared a temporary truce in their home-baking competition while they focus on the big Spring Clean. They both seem to be enjoying this enormously and have spent ages working out a plan of action to fit round my frantic attempts to get the last of the redecorating done so we can get everything spick-and-span and up to Ivy's usual standards. She says she usually gets a couple of girls in from village to help with the rough jobs, so I was having visions of the kind of women who can handle themselves in a fight at the pub, but they turned out to be her friends Florrie and May, who've been helping with the Spring Clean for years. Florrie is on the waiting list for a hip replacement, and May is waiting to get her cataracts done, so Ivy doesn't let her clean anything fragile, but between them they've managed far more than a team of eight people half their age. And with Mum helping too, Ivy says they'll be done in record time. All the floors are so shiny now you can find yourself doing a pretty good audition for *Dancing on Ice* if you're not concentrating. I've managed to avoid a triple toe loop in the hall so far, but the boys have been taking full advantage of the chance to slide sideways balanced on one leg, and Alfie can get right across the dining room if he's got his school socks on.

"Coffee Mum?"

"Please, and I've brought those curtains back—the old brocade ones from Ben's room. I've taken them up six inches and given them a clean. It took three cycles in my machine, but they look so much nicer now, I thought we could hang them Ivy, if you've got a minute?"

Ivy only nods, since she's got a mouthful of Bakewell tart, so I leave them planning more cleaning while I put my painting clothes back on and start pouring paint into my tray. I'm halfway back up my stepladder when the front doorbell rings.

Bugger.

A rather posh-looking woman gives me a critical look as I open the door.

"Mrs. Pargeter. I'm here to meet Millie."

"Sorry?"

She sighs and looks at me like I'm one of life's slow learners.

"I'm Mrs. Pargeter, I have an appointment with the owner. Lucinda arranged it, to discuss holiday rentals. I'm exceptionally busy today, so if you could find her, I'd be most grateful."

She clearly thinks I'm a half-witted decorator, and I'm tempted to wave my paintbrush and say everyone has gone out.

"Right, well, that's me."

"Sorry?"

"I'm Millie—I mean Molly, sorry, I'm Molly, and I don't remember arranging anything with Lucinda about holiday rentals."

She decides to ignore this inauspicious start and goes into full meet-and-greet mode.

"Well done you. So nice to see our old estates being taken care of, so important. I do represent quite a few of the more important local properties, and your lovely gatehouse will sit very nicely on the list. I've brought my camera, so I can take a few snaps now, if that works for you?"

God she's pushy, and she's looking very determinedly at the door, clearly waiting to be asked in for coffee so she can sign us up.

"We're not really ready for photographs just yet."

I wave my paintbrush, which she ignores.

"There you are Miss Molly. You're wanted on the phone."

Thank God, the cavalry has arrived in the form of Ivy, who is giving Mrs. Pargeter a very beady look.

"Oh, right, well, I should probably take that, and then get back to my painting, but lovely to have met you, Mrs. Pargeter, and do give all the details to Ivy."

Ivy takes a step forwards, and I think Mrs. Pargeter has probably met her match, so I leave them to it. Bloody hell, my Lady of the Manor routine clearly needs more work. I bet nobody ever mistook Helena for a random gardener or painter, even if she was wearing filthy old trousers and her terrible old gardening jacket.

I'm back up my ladder when Ivy comes in.

"Rude woman. Quite put out she was. I hope you don't mind my fib about the phone call, but it's the only way to get rid of people like her, and she's no better than she ought to be, and that's all I'm saying. Florrie used to clean for her mother, years ago, and I could tell you some tales."

"She's gone then?"

"Yes, left her card, which we won't be needing if I've got anything to say about it. Think they're a cut above, her mother was the same. Ran a pub before she married, and not a nice pub either. All fur coat and no knickers—both of them—always have been."

"Don't make me laugh Ivy, or I'll fall off my ladder."

"Just you be careful. I'll go and finish thosc curtains with your mum. She's made a lovely job of them, you wait and see, and then we can have a nice cup of tea."

"Great."

With a bit of luck I'll get at least an hour before they're back in the kitchen.

"Thanks, Mum, the curtains look great. Do you want another coffee before you go?"

"No thank you dear. I better be off, I've still got my shopping to do. But I did want a little word. Georgina was wondering if you'd had a chance to think about her offer?"

"What offer?"

"You know, the lunch, for all the golf club women, now the builders have finished in the house. I'm sure it would be good for business."

"How?"

"Sorry dear?"

"How would it be good for business? They don't strike me as the types with friends who'd book into a B-and-B, and the gate-house won't be ready to show anyone. So no, I don't want a load of Georgina's snobby friends having lunch here, thanks all the same. Sorry Mum, but I've already told her, so she can stop trying to get you to fix it up for her."

There's a pause.

"You're probably right."

Crikey, is Mum actually agreeing with me?

She smiles.

"You've worked so hard here, and Ivy has been singing your praises, and everything looks so much nicer, it really does dear."

"Thanks Mum."

"I'll tell Georgina no, then, shall I?"

"Please."

"I know I shouldn't say it, but she could probably do with being told no a bit more often, the fuss she makes about those clothes of hers. She was trying to persuade me to buy a new coat yesterday—there's plenty of wear left in my old one, but you should have heard her. I'd better be off, but I'll see you on Friday. Ivy and I are planning to turn out the big china cupboard and give everything a good wash. She says some of it hasn't been out for years."

"Okay Mum, and thanks."

She kisses me on the cheek as she goes out.

Crikey. It looks like Harrington may be working its magic on Mum too.

It's still chilly in the afternoons, so I light the fire in the drawing room for tea with Sally, and Bea and Vicky. We've had a quick tour round the gatehouse and the stables, and now we're back in the house, and the kids are playing upstairs, and I'm hoping they stay up there. Bea and Vicky's daughter, Daisy, is in the same class as Alfie and Tom, so she's heard about the cannon, and asked to see it. But luckily Bertie is out for the afternoon with Dennis at some navy gathering, so they settled for playing with the Lego castle.

"When you rent out the gatehouse, and the stables when they're done, will the guests have the run of the house and gardens?"

"I don't think so Sal. I thought we'd say guests can use the meadow and the path down to the cove, but keep the rest private?"

"Good idea, you don't want them in and out all the time. B-and-B is one thing, but if you're renting by the week, they could drive you mad thinking you're at their beck and call all day."

"That's what I thought, I had enough of that when we were growing up, having to be polite to the hotel guests all the time. And I don't want Bertie or the boys to feel like this isn't their home."

Vicky pours herself some more tea.

"So who's your ideal guest? It might help to work backwards from that."

"Anyone who's got a bit frayed round the edges and wants a bit of peace."

Bea smiles.

"A few days by yourself, to regroup—there's a huge market for that. We've got lots of friends in London who'd love it."

"I want everything to be simple, warm, but nothing fancy, no taps you have to wave at, but not pretend-Victorian either, all fake pine and twiddly bits."

Vicky nods.

"So no boys' toys, cupboards with no handles and tiny bins hidden inside so you have to empty them every five minutes, shiny surfaces that you have to polish with a special cloth or they show every fingerprint, that kind of thing?"

"Exactly, nothing that makes you feel like you're on display. No mirrors where you catch yourself getting out of the bath and end up depressed before you've even had your breakfast."

"Got it. One of my clients has just had us fit a new bathroom with floor-to-ceiling mirror tiles—on the ceiling too actually."

"Crikey, how does it look?"

"Hideous. His wife hates it."

"I bet she does. Well once I'm up and running with my 'Escape Your Tragic Life' holidays you can give her a brochure."

"Actually I can think of quite a few potential clients for you already. I'm working on a farmhouse renovation at the moment for a city type—weekend place—and he wants stainless steel everywhere, and marble. The kitchen will be freezing-cold in winter, although the wife is only twenty-three, so she probably doesn't do that much cooking. But she's the second wife, so it serves her right."

I'm liking Bea more and more.

"I should probably mention I'm under strict instructions from the boss to make sure you know there's potential for a much bigger scheme—and he's right, there is, loads of potential."

"I know Bea, but this is our home. Everything needs to start from that."

"I just felt I should mention it. And for what it's worth, I think you're right. This is a special place, and it would be a shame to overdevelop it. But please don't quote me on that."

"Of course not."

She smiles, and Vicky pours her some more tea.

"You could always look at 'glamping.'"

"What, that new 'glamorous camping' thing they do at Glastonbury?"

"Yes, you could get a couple of yurts or those posh tents in the field behind the stables, and that way you'd get some income this summer. Lots of people are giving it a go, and they charge way above usual rates. I'll get you some details, and I can drop them round when I bring you those brochures. It might be worth looking at."

Vicky's promised to help me with ideas for the gatehouse, and she's launching a holiday-rentals website alongside her interior design business, so she's a great source of local information. Bea is her partner in the new rentals agency, along with a friend of theirs from London, and they seem very clued up about everything.

"Thanks Vicky, that would be great."

"We're setting up the new website now. We're going for a personal word-of-mouth feel, and we'd love to sign you up. No pressure of course, but we'll be charging far less commission than the big agencies. Belinda Pargeter will be furious if you sign with us, she likes to think she gets all the choice properties round here. I bet she'll be round any minute."

"She's already been. She thought I was the painter."

I tell them about my encounter with Mrs. Pargeter and we have to bang Sally on the back because she chokes on a piece of cake.

"Afternoon everyone, sounds like you're having fun."

Great. Bertie is home early. And he's brought Betty to say hello.

"Would you like a cup of tea Uncle Bertie?"

"No thank you, never been that keen on tea."

Betty is whistling like an old-fashioned kettle now.

"Ignore her, stupid bird. Just showing off."

"This is Bea, and Vicky, and I think you know Sally, Uncle Bertie. Bea's an architect, and I'm hoping she'll help me with the stables if I can get everything lined up."

"Excellent. About time they were put to good use. Did think of building an aviary at one point."

Christ, not more parrots.

"Helena wasn't keen, soon put a stop to that. Shame, but there you are, no point trying to argue with her. Now then, who's for a proper drink? Anyone for a sherry—filthy stuff, never drink it myself—or I could make us all a cocktail?"

I'm not sure a round of Bertie's killer cocktails at half past four on a school day are such a good idea.

"Thanks Uncle Bertie, but we're fine."

"Right you are. Lovely to have met you all."

He gives Bea his best twinkle.

"Bugger off."

"Stupid bird. Be quiet."

Bea is trying not laugh.

"Does she like walnuts?"

"Adores them."

"My aunt had a parrot and she loved them too. Would you mind?"

"Not at all."

She takes one of the walnuts from the top of the cake and holds out her hand to Betty, who climbs onto the back of the chair and hops along before eating the nut.

"Well I never. Usually takes her ages before she'll do that. You're clearly made of the right stuff my dear. Sure you don't want a proper drink?"

A parrot-proof architect. This just gets better and better.

"Mum?"

"Yes Alfie?"

"Can we do the cannon, now that Uncle Bertie is back?"

Bugger.

I'm awake at half past five due to a combination of worrying about Mr. and Mrs. Denton arriving and the sodding birds kicking off their dawn chorus. If I didn't know better, I'd swear they were all massed outside my bedroom window on purpose, chirruping and chattering and making as much racket as possible. There's no way I'll get back to sleep, so I make a pot of tea and wander round checking everything. I rearrange the towels in the guest bathrooms one more time, along with the handmade soaps I bought at the farmers' market; I got the lavender, and rose, and the lemon balm for guests who'd rather not be too floral. Ivy isn't convinced about putting nice things in the bathrooms; someone helped themselves to the plug from the bath a couple of years ago and she's still not over it. In an ideal world she'd like one of those scanners they have at airports where you can see everyone in their underwear, and check what they've got in their bags. But even though I know from my days working at the hotel just how readily some members of the Great British Public abandon all decorum the minute they're paying for their room, and help themselves to anything which isn't nailed down, I'm hoping most of our guests will appreciate the nice soaps and old bottles in pretty blue glass on the newly painted windowsills. Either that, or we can look into getting Ivy that scanner.

It rained last night, but the weather is definitely getting warmer; I'd forgotten how much earlier everything arrives down here. The Lenten roses have been out for ages, in pretty combinations of purples and pinks and creams. Celia says they're called hellebores, which is a rubbish name for something so lovely. And we've had masses of snowdrops and crocuses too, alongside early narcissus and daffodils dotted about in chirpy clumps. The winter honeysuckle has been blooming since the start of the year, and the magnolia branches I've put in a big jug in the hall look great with their delicate white stars and gorgeous scent. The rhododendrons and azaleas in the lane are pretty stunning too—the yellow ones smell particularly lovely. And there are buds on the incense rose by the back door now, and Dennis says it blooms early, so hopefully we'll have roses round the door soon. That's one of the things I've noticed most about living here—all the wonderful smells: log fires and beeswax, dried lavender and salt in the air from the sea. If you could bottle it, you'd make a fortune.

Lola rings at half past seven, to wish me good luck.

"All set darling?"

"I think so. You're up early?"

"I'm off to Frankfurt, for a meeting. I'll swap if you like."

"No thanks, I'm sure it will be fine, I'm still worried about the breakfasts though. All the posh B-and-Bs do things like kippers, but Ivy's not keen on preparing smoked fish every morning."

"That's fine by me, I hate kippers."

"Yes, but I've only just managed to persuade her to stop making people order their breakfasts when they arrive."

"Like when you're in hospital and the person in your bed after you leave ends up getting what you ordered for lunch?"

"Exactly, so we're not doing that now. And we've got that organic bacon from Sally's husband, Patrick, and homemade bread, but it's not what you'd call five stars."

"Are you going for five stars then? I thought Helena refused to have the inspectors round for all the guidebooks?"

"She did, and I'm not going to either. Half of them charge you to put you in their guides, and the more you pay, the more stars you get—it's a complete con. As long as we never have more than six guests at the same time, we don't have to register with anything official, or go in for any environmental health stuff. But I'd like to get a good reputation, and have people say nice things about us."

"I'll say nice things darling, and I'll bring Tre down with me next time, and he can say nice things too."

"'Tray'? As in 'tea tray'?"

"No, As in '*très bonne*.' He teaches yoga. He's very flexible."

"He'd have to be, with a name like that."

"He's a vegan."

"Bloody hell. I better buy more cereal. Good luck explaining that to Ivy."

"I thought I'd leave that one to you."

"Thanks."

Mr. and Mrs. Denton arrive at half past four, in an ancient but highly polished Mini. It's Ivy's afternoon off, so I don't have an audience for my first arrival, although I'm half expecting her to pop in at some point to check up on me. I show them the guest sitting room and they sign the new register, and we go up to their room. They're impressed with all the changes, and I offer to make a pot of tea, even though Ivy doesn't hold with making tea for B&B guests. She's adamant "bed-and-breakfast" doesn't include afternoon tea, or morning coffee, or lunch or dinner, and I know she's right. I've got enough to do without turning myself into a full-time waitress. But for our first guests I don't think a pot of tea will open any catering floodgates.

"Thank you dear, just what I need after the journey."

"I'll bring it into the sitting room downstairs, in about ten minutes?"

I lit the fire earlier to make it more inviting, but when they arrived I noticed they both walked round the edges of the newly decorated room, as if they were on a visit to a stately home and there was an invisible rope line protecting the carpet, so I'm hoping the tea might help them relax.

When I bring the tea tray in, Mr. Denton has nipped back outside to give the car a quick once-over and wipe things with a rag.

"Just ignore him, love. He spends hours fussing with that silly car—he's had it since it was new. It's his pride and joy. He'd spent all day on it if I let him. You've certainly made some changes here haven't you? It was always comfy of course, but it's much smarter now."

"Thank you, but we just moved things around a bit, and got new covers for the sofa and armchairs."

"Well it all looks champion. We'll be off in a minute, to our daughter's, but we'll be back by ten, so we won't keep you up late."

"If there's anything else you need, just let me know."

"I will dear, and thanks for the tea. You can't beat a nice cup of tea after a journey."

"Mum?"

"Yes Alfie?"

"When are we having our supper, because I'm starving, I really am."

"Not until Dan gets home."

"I can't wait that long, I really can't."

Mrs. Denton smiles.

"You can have one of these biscuits if you like love. If it's alright with your mum?"

Before I can stop him, he's bounded across the room to retrieve a biscuit, and she asks him what school he goes to, and he's telling her all about the song his class is doing at the Spring Fair. The poor woman will be getting a solo performance if she's not careful.

"Alfie, let's leave Mrs. Denton in peace to drink her tea, shall we?"

I give him one of my Let's Do It Right Now looks, which he ignores.

"I think your cartoons will be finished soon Alfie."

He gallops back across the room, but hesitates by the door and thanks Mrs. Denton for his biscuit before heading back to the telly.

"Sorry about that. I should probably warn you, I've got three boys. The other two are a bit older though, so they won't be helping themselves to your biscuits. Well, probably not."

She smiles.

"It's nice to see youngsters here. Always thought this would be a lovely house for youngsters—we often used to say that, me and Harry did. Must make quite a change for you, were you living locally before?"

"No, in London, but I grew up round here."

"My sister lived in London for a few years, but she didn't take to it—so many people and all of them too busy. And the traffic, you've never seen anything like it. There you are Harry. Come and have your tea, and then we should be off. We need to get those presents from upstairs. They're in the blue bag."

"Right you are. I'll just wash my hands."

"Yes and don't you go dirtying the sink when she's got everything so nice. Make sure you give it a proper rinse. She won't want an oily ring left. Sorry, dear, but you've got to tell them, haven't you?"

"I think I can be trusted to leave a clean sink behind me, I've had years of training. I'll use the downstairs cloakroom if that's alright? Across the hall, isn't it?"

"Yes, just past the stairs."

I'm glad I remembered to put some of the new soap in there too, and fresh towels.

"You can always come and inspect after me, Mary, make sure I've left everything as you'd like to find it."

"Get away with you, daft as brush you are, and your tea's getting cold, so get a shift on."

"I just brought that dish back Miss Molly. I've put it in the kitchen. Lovely to see you again Mrs. Denton. How was the journey?"

As predicted, Ivy has found an excuse to nip in and check on progress.

"Not too bad this time. Much better traffic than in the summer. Isn't the old place looking grand? You've all been working hard—anyone can see that. There's more tea in the pot if you've got a minute, be nice to catch up?"

Ivy hesitates, clearly disapproving of the tea tray, but I know she won't want to miss out on a chat, so I leave them talking about curtains, and check on Alfie, who's watching cartoons but still complaining he's hungry.

"Not much longer now. Dan will be home soon."

"Can we have roast and Yorkshires, and gravy, because that's my best meal?"

"What about pasta, with lots of cheese?"

He tuts.

I'm awake again at half past five the next morning worrying about poaching eggs for' my first official B&B breakfast. Ivy's been teaching me how to make them using the special wide pan on a slow simmer, but mine don't always look as neat as hers. Thankfully neither of them asks for anything poached, and despite a minor drama with the bacon because the bloody oven is so slow, I manage to produce toast, scrambled eggs, mushrooms, bacon, and sausages which look fairly respectable, and the boys take the opportunity to put their orders in. Dan even announces he is now all for the B&B if it means there will be proper breakfasts every day, but he's less keen when I volunteer him as my new kitchen assistant and send him upstairs with Bertie's breakfast on a tray.

Investing in a new toaster was definitely one of my better ideas. Our old one stopped popping up toast ages ago, and retrieving toast with a fork whilst making breakfast for people who are paying for it is bad enough without giving yourself a new electric-shock-induced hairstyle, particularly if you're simultaneously trying to poach things.

"We'll be off now love, and thank you—we've had a lovely time, and that breakfast was top-notch. We were just saying, weren't we, Harry? You'll be putting the prices up soon, I shouldn't wonder, and you'd pay twice as much in a hotel and it wouldn't be half as nice."

"Thank you."

"Your aunt would be very proud of you. Very proud."

Oh God, I'll be in tears in a minute if she carries on. I'm so relieved. "That's enough, Mary. Can't you see you're upsetting the girl? We'll definitely be coming back later in the year, so come on, let's be off, I've promised to take my grandson fishing. Probably won't catch anything, but he doesn't seem to mind. I might take him out on one of those boats and see if we can't get a few mackerel in the summer."

"You will not, he's far too young to be off in a smelly old boat with you for hours."

"We'll see."

He winks at me.

"Say good-bye to Mr. Bertie for us."

They're still bickering about mackerel fishing as they walk towards their car, but give me a wave and a chirpy toot as they drive off.

If all our guests are as nice as this, I might be able to make this work. And they paid me in cash, which was a thrill. It might only be seventy pounds, but it's a start. And nobody wanted poached eggs, so it really couldn't have gone better. If I could go back to bed and sleep for the rest of the day, my cup would truly overflow.

"Mum?"

"Yes Ben."

"Bertie says we can have a camp on the beach and cook sausages later. Have we got any sausages left?"

"No."

"Well can you get some, because it's going to be brilliant. And can you get some vegetarian ones, because I've decided I'm not going to eat meat any more. It's just not sustainable."

Oh God. He's been talking about becoming a vegetarian for a while now, and I've been trying to ignore it.

"Right."

"I might still eat fish, but only if it's caught properly—not in those big nets that destroy the seabed. Or on the endangered-fish list, like sharks."

"Damn, bang goes my plan for shark fin soup for supper."

"I'm being serious Mum. If we carry on like this, there'll be no fish left."

"Sorry. Okay, well if you've made your mind up, then I suppose that's fair enough. It's good to have the courage of your convictions."

He nods.

"Thanks Mum. So will you tell Ivy?"

Bugger.

I'm in the scullery on Monday afternoon, sorting through the laundry, when Celia phones, sounding flustered; she got back from a weekend away this morning to discover her water tank had burst and flooded what sounds like most of her house.

"You wouldn't believe the mess, appalling. I shall have to move out, so I wondered if I might come to you as a PG? I know Helena never took in paying guests, didn't want people hanging about the place all day, B-and-B is much better, give them their breakfast and get rid of them. But I wouldn't want any fuss, and I'm perfectly capable of lending a hand, although I will admit housekeeping has never been my forte. And this place is far too big for me.

Once everything is back up to scratch, I'm thinking of selling—been meaning to for ages, but I've kept putting it off. Dusting a great big house like this—completely hopeless. By the time I finish, I've got to start all over again."

"I know what you mean."

"Precisely my point, I don't want to cause any extra work. I do hope you don't mind my asking, only I am rather stuck for the next few weeks while the worst of it gets done, so I thought if I came to you... but please say if you'd rather not."

"Of course you must come here, but you do so much work in the garden, we couldn't possibly charge you."

"Then I shan't come. The insurance company will be paying—they've charged me enough over the years, about time I got something back. And I'd much rather the Hall got the money than anywhere else, much rather. I've spotted a cottage I might buy, needs a bit of work, small but enough of a garden to be worth bothering with. Extraordinary what they're selling them for now, even those hideous new flats—they call them a retirement village—more like a series of prison blocks if you ask me. Surprised none of them are digging tunnels—geriatric gulags, that's what they are, never seen anything so revolting in all your life, load of old people stuck together moaning. I'd rather shoot myself. Now, where was I? Oh yes, thought I could have your single room. Don't mind sharing a bathroom if you've B-and-B people in the double. That way I wouldn't take up too much space. Only fly in the ointment is Jasper. I could put in him a kennel, but he'd absolutely loathe it."

"Right."

Oh God, so that's Celia and Jasper, the amazing leaping terrier. Betty will be thrilled.

"I know it's a great deal to ask, but he's perfectly house-trained,

I can promise you that. You'd hardly know he was there. Ridiculous I know, total nuisance, but I am rather fond of him."

"What about if you had the double and we could move the furniture around? There's a little table and an armchair we could move upstairs for you, and then you could have a sitting area too, and Jasper can have his basket in with you."

She goes quiet. Oh God, I think I've offended her. Maybe I should have offered to have the dog downstairs in the kitchen or something, but I'm really not keen.

"Thank you my dear, Helena was right, you're an exceptional girl. I'd like that very much. More than I can say."

Ivy is highly diverted by the news and starts making pastry.

"She'll be hungry, wet through too, I shouldn't wonder. Floods can make a terrible mess. I'll make a chicken pie—she likes them—and I'll do a little cheese-and-onion quiche for Ben, shall I?"

"That would be lovely Ivy, thanks."

"Got to make sure he keeps his strength up until he comes to his senses."

I'm not sure my budding eco-warrior is going to be changing his mind any time soon, particularly if Ivy keeps making him little quiches. Pete was predictably sarcastic when I told him, and tried to give Ben a lecture about protein, which backfired somewhat when he realised Ben has been collecting fascinating facts from the wonderful world of vegetarians for quite some time, and was able to reel off statistics about lentils and quinoa and pumpkin seeds versus pistachio nuts. Which reminds me, I must add quinoa to my next shopping list. Apparently you cook it just like rice, and it's a superfood, so we'll give it a go. I've already stocked up with cans of tuna, with the dolphin on the label so we know they weren't caught by industrial trawlers and nobody has to go on hunger strike.

"You go and tell Mr. Bertie, and then we can start making up the room. The bed will want making up, and you can put some of your nice soap in the bathroom for her—she'll like that. Is she bringing that silly dog with her then?"

"Yes, but she'll have him in her room with her."

She tuts.

Bertie is in the library, peering out to sea on his telescope.

"I did say she didn't need to pay, Bertie, but she says the insurers are footing the bill, and she won't come if we don't charge her."

"Well in that case, go ahead. Don't know what Helena would have done without her—they used to spend hours in that garden lost in their own little world. Should be amusing, she's a card."

A card-carrying nutter, more like.

He hands me a gin and tonic, with very little tonic. Here we go again. I must remember to sip, and not knock it back like I did last week with the glass he offered me before lunch, or I'll have to ask Sally to collect Alfie and Ben again.

"I've always been fond of old Celia, like to see her pottering around the place. Reminds me of Helena—always hatching some plot to annoy Dennis, moving things about and planning new borders and suchlike. Ran the poor man ragged, they did—and he does his best, can't say fairer than that. I spent a fair bit of time this morning looking for my specs, until Dennis pointed out I was wearing them. Awkward moment. Good chap. Be totally buggered without him. And Mrs. Dennis too, of course, although she leads him a merry dance with all her fussing—decent woman at heart of course."

"Of course."

"Always knew Dennis was a decent chap. We had some larks in the navy—you wouldn't think it to look at him, but he knows how to let his hair down. Mrs. Dennis less so of course, but she's a treasure in her own way. Yes, we struck lucky with both of them. But we were very lucky all round, never a cross word between us. She did have a passion for opera—terrible racket if you ask me, but Helena adored it, and do you know, the extraordinary thing is I miss it now."

"I'm sure you do."

"That's the key you know—got to have passions in life, something to believe in, not that you want to be one of those bores banging on at people telling them what to think—perish the thought—but something you care about, a reason to get up in the morning. The basics are important too of course—kindness, decency, lending a hand. Hugely underrated. Won us the war. Will win us the next one too, I shouldn't wonder. And love of course—important not to forget that. And I'm not talking about sex my dear."

I choke slightly, which makes him smile.

"The hurly-burly of the chaise longue is all very well, but it tends to fade after a few years, and the deep peace of the double bed can be overrated too, particularly if you're stuck with an idiot like your husband. Can't see how that would have been terribly nice for you my dear, if you don't mind my saying. No, I mean in the broadest sense, love your fellow man. Not that I've ever tried any of that—fair bit of it in the navy, never bothered me, each to his own. But doing right by the people around you, people you're fond of who don't set your teeth on edge. Children too, if you can manage it. We'd have liked children, Helena and I, we came close a couple of times. Thought I was going to lose her at one point, never been so frightened in all my life, but there you are, these things happen. And we muddled on, made the best of it, and I don't regret a moment. Hope she didn't."

"I'm sure she didn't Bertie."

"Must say I'm enjoying having your boys here—decent chaps. Gives you a sense of a toehold on the future. Helena said I'd enjoy it, said they'd be the perfect age for me since I'd never grown up, and she was right, as usual. For her it was her roses. She was fond of me, I know that, very fond, but it was the roses which lit up her life. For you, it's your boys."

"She loved you very much Bertie—anyone could see that."

"I miss her, every single day. Takes my breath away sometimes, when I think I see her, often in the garden, I think I catch a glimpse. But I can't complain at my age—every day is a bonus, might as well try to enjoy it. And what about you my dear. When the boys grow up and bugger off, will you stay on here do you think?"

"I love it here Bertie. Where else would I want to go?"

He smiles.

"Good for you. And if some chap comes along and sweeps you off your feet, then that's all well and good—but don't be too hasty, that's my advice. Having a home you love, somewhere for the family to come back to, very important. Might not be a sweeper of course."

"Sorry?"

"Might just be a bit of fun. Nothing wrong in that, as long as you're not hurting anybody, or likely to find yourself up on a charge. I've always been fond of a bit of gallivanting."

"I can't see me going in for gallivanting Bertie."

"Well you should—put a spring in your step."

Betty hops along the back of the sofa.

"Pretty Polly, Pretty Polly. Make mine a large one."

"Doesn't always talk rubbish you know, most of the time, but not always. Would you like a top-up?"

"No thanks Bertie, I need to get Celia's room ready and then collect the boys from school."

"Fair enough. Let me know if I can lend a hand. Leave your glass here and you can come back for the other half later on. I'm sure Celia will want to join us; she's always liked a tipple. Makes a decent martini too, although don't tell her I said that."

How's it going with Celia?"

"Fine, apart from the stupid dog yapping at the stupid parrot. She's out in the garden most of the time, and the boys like her—they're saving all their best stories from school to tell her and Bertie over supper."

"I've been thinking I might like to keep a room on permanent standby too."

"Yes, but you don't actually want to live here, do you?"

Please God she says no, I'm not sure I could cope with Lola 24/7.

"No, but I've been toying with the idea of making you an offer you can't refuse for the gatehouse. That way I'd have a place of my own in the country. Only I think I'd prefer a refuge from the madding crowd where it doesn't rain all the bloody time."

"It hasn't rained here for days."

"Probably saving it up for my next visit—talking of which let's fix up some more weekends, before you take in any more waifs and strays."

"Don't be daft, there'll always be room for you, come anytime you like. The boys can stay in the attic if push comes to shove, which it probably will. Dan's still desperate to move up there and Ben's keen too."

"Or you could create a deluxe attic suite, just for special me. I quite like that idea."

"Can I get the gatehouse finished first please, and then have a break from builders. I'm still trying to finish all the painting in the house as it is. Ivy would probably walk out if I launch into another project. Actually, I might too."

"I've been telling Tre how gorgeous it is, and by the way, he's not strictly vegan any more, just vegetarian."

"That's very good news. I don't want Ben getting any more ideas. God knows what you'd make vegans for their school packed lunch."

"I knew you'd be pleased. You'll like him. He does a couple of hours' yoga every day when he zones out completely, so we'll have plenty of time to catch up. Or we can just sit watching him, which is very relaxing too, almost as good as actually doing the bloody yoga."

"He might find zoning out a bit harder down here, what with Jasper barking and Betty telling him to bugger off."

"He'll cope darling. He grew up on a commune. His mum was a bit of a hippy—he was her third child, hence the name; there were stacks of them by the time she'd finished."

"Is there a Quattro then, or is that just Audis?"

"If there is, I'll bring him with us. Trust me, six foot three in his socks and solid muscle—what's not to like?"

"I can't think of anything offhand."

"Precisely. Talking of which, have you decided what you're wearing tonight for your dinner date with Stephen?"

"No, and I don't want to talk about it, thanks. And it's not a date, it's just supper. Bea has started work on the plans for the stables so he probably just wants to talk about the house."

"It's early days yet darling. Nothing ventured nothing gained."

"I think I like the idea of him asking me out more than I actually want to go. It's such an encouraging antidote to Pete."

"Darling."

"I know, but I feel like I'm proving a point, to myself if nobody else. I'm not sure I even like him, Stephen I mean. I've definitely gone off Pete."

"Take your velvet skirt out for the night—you never know, it might be fun. Are you meeting him there?"

"No, he's picking me up at the house."

"Nice. Do you want me to text you, around nine, so you can pretend you need to leave if it's too deadly?"

"No. It's only supper in Launton, and he's not a stranger or anything, so I should be able to cope, but thanks."

The new fish restaurant turns out be quite busy, and once I get over the novelty of being out on my own for the evening, with no small boys demanding chips, I relax and start to enjoy myself. The food is delicious, and Stephen is easy to talk to, and has lots of amusing snippets about clients and their unreasonable demands. We talk about the Spring Fair on Sunday and he promises to come and see our stall, and we move on to talking about divorce and how hideous it all is, but even this doesn't dampen my mood. He's clearly rankled that his ex-wife Portia, who is a potter, has moved her young artist boyfriend into the former marital home. Apparently he makes plates, and is only twenty-nine. I'm not sure which of these things irritates Stephen the most.

"Every time I collect Finn, there are more of his creations on show. Although I must say, I'm enjoying calling him Tony."

"Sorry?"

"He likes to be called Anthony, hates being called Tony. As if collecting my son from the house I designed and paid for isn't awkward enough, without having to look at the world's most pretentious tableware. I'm sure you know what I mean. Does your ex have a new partner?"

"Yes, a whole new wife actually, Janice, and she'd probably prefer being called Tony than half the names I've called her over the past few years."

He laughs.

"You win. A new wife definitely trumps a third-rate ceramicist, but I do feel for Finn. It's one thing having a life—obviously we all have a right to that—but I have no idea why she needed to move him into the house."

"Were they seeing each other before you split up?"

He looks rather uncomfortable.

"Sorry, you don't need to talk about it if you'd rather not."

"No, it's just, no, they weren't, there wasn't anyone else involved, not in the divorce. We'd both had our moments, nothing serious, we had an open marriage in many ways, but we drifted apart, which almost made it worse. If there'd been someone else significant, that might have been easier. Oh, sorry."

"No, I know what you mean. At least I could blame it all on Janice, which is rubbish, obviously."

He smiles.

"Tempting though?"

"Very, and she is quite annoying. But to be fair, so is Pete."

"It was all so much simpler when we were younger wasn't it?"

He's twinkling again, a smiling flirty routine, which he's been doing all evening. The waitress has been very impressed.

"Some of it, yes."

"Here's to the simple life."

He clinks his glass against mine.

"Would you like pudding?"

"Yes please."

"Good, I make it a rule never to trust a woman who pretends she doesn't want pudding—who knows what else she might be hiding?"

He turns, and the waitress materialises, in full simper mode.

"What's most delicious?"

"Well, the lemon soufflé is lovely, and the chocolate mousse. And we do homemade ice cream—that's good too."

"How about you bring us a selection and two spoons—could we do that?"

"Of course you can."

I'm feeling particularly mellow on the drive home, listening to Nina Simone and enjoying someone else driving, for a change. Pete always made me drive on the rare occasions we went out for the evening. In fact I'm so relaxed I'm nearly asleep as we drive up the lane towards the house. Bugger, I'd forgotten about the good-night thing. I can't remember how that bit goes: do I ask him in for coffee, which seems daft since we've just had coffee, or what? Oh God. He turns the engine off, and gets out. Right, I guess that's coffee then. I'm about to open my door, when he opens it, and holds out his hand to help me out of the car. Crikey.

"Thank you Molly, for a lovely evening. Rather different from the last time we were out after dark?"

"Definitely."

Actually, I think the last time we were out for the night was when he dumped me for Susan Prentice with the giant chest, but I'm guessing he means our teenage dates with bags of chips and walking along the seawall. At least I hope he does, unless he's going to drop me off and drive back to the restaurant to pick up that waitress.

"Let's do this again soon?"

He leans forwards, but instead of the usual social kiss on the cheek which I'm expecting, it turns into what we used to call "a proper kiss" when I was a teenager, which come to think of it, was the last time he kissed me. So in the space of ten seconds things seem to have changed, and my only contribution seems to be standing frozen to the spot. Bloody hell. I'm not sure I want to be doing kissing, as Alfie would say. Please God nobody is looking out of the window.

"Night Molly."

"Night."

He smiles, and gets back into the car before waving as he drives off back up the lane, while I stand like a complete idiot watching him. I should probably go in now, unless I'm going to stand here all night. Christ, I'm not sure I want to be kissing him outside my front door like a lovesick teenager. Or kissing him anywhere else. I'm not even sure I want to be kissing anyone at all. Although it is nice to be asked, not that he actually asked, and it did seem a bit rehearsed, like it's a routine he's very familiar with, but that's probably a good thing. The last thing I need is anything that gets too serious, or complicated. And it is all rather flattering. But still. Hopefully next time, if there is a next time, I won't stand frozen to the spot feeling so self-conscious. I'll kiss him back. Or sidestep the kissing thing altogether. I haven't decided. But something a bit more grown-up. Maybe. Bloody hell.

It's half past three on Sunday afternoon and Sally and I have been stuck behind our stall at the Spring Fair for what seems like hours, flogging tickets at one pound a go and doling out the little bags of sweets as prizes. We've made just over two hundred pounds so far, and we're running out of change. A few of the parents did have a brief moan about tradition when word got round about the chocolate eggs this year, but once Miss Cooper told people we were happy to include hand-decorated hard-boiled eggs too if they brought them in on Friday morning, everyone went quiet.

Pete is down for the day, with Janice, and wandering about with the kids trying to avoid spending money. Our stall is in front of the seawall, which is low enough to be a handy seat, and Sally's brought a camping stool too, and a thermos of tea, which we drank in the first half hour since unpacking all the boxes was such thirsty work. Nobody has won the star prize yet—a giant Easter egg donated by the newsagents by the pier, but we've given away quite a few bottles of bubble bath, and two of the mini boxes of Lego.

"Sal, how many more boxes of eggs have we got left now?"

"Four more under the table, and you said you'd got three more in your car, so that should last us."

"Great."

We both look at the sky. We've been hoping for rain so we can pack up early, and it's been overcast for most of the day, but so far the rain has held off.

Patrick brings Tom and Alfie back from their session on the bouncy castle.

"It was great Mum, and I want to go again and I've got enough money, but I need an extra pound, because me and Tom want to buy a raffle ticket."

"Wait until after you've done your parade love."

"No, we need it now."

Pete appears with Janice and the boys, with Ben looking anxious.

"Miss Cooper says we've all got to be in the car park in five minutes."

"Okay love. Pete, could you take Ben and Alfie to the main car park—that's where the parade starts from. And Dan, could you help get the last boxes of eggs from the car?"

Pete is clearly not keen.

"I've just bought us a coffee and a sandwich. I was hoping to sit down for a moment."

"Oh, right."

He sits on the seawall, while Janice passes him a polystyrene beaker of coffee and starts unpacking packets of sandwiches from her bag.

I notice he hasn't bought sandwiches for Sally or me, or the boys. How thoughtful.

Dan gives him a look.

"I'll go with them Mum. Do you want me to bring you back a drink or anything?"

"Thanks Dan, tea would be lovely. Are you hungry?"

He grins.

"Tell you what, bring the boxes of eggs back and then I'll give you the money to get teas and something to eat."

"You're on."

*   *   *

"Hello Molly. How's it going? Sold loads of tickets?"

It's Stephen, with his son, Finn.

"Quite a few, thanks."

"Hi Sally, nice to see you again. Finn, how many tickets shall we get, or don't you like crème eggs anymore?"

Finn gives his father one of those teenager Help, My Parent Is a Moron looks, which Stephen wisely ignores as he hands Sally a five-pound note.

"Just give us a ticket each and keep the change. Got to do our bit to help the school, haven't we?" He turns and looks at Pete and then back at me.

Bugger.

"Stephen, this is Pete, and Janice."

"Nice to meet you. Did we win the star prize Sally?"

"Sorry, no, but you get a bag of sweets."

She hands Finn one of the cellophane bags of dolly mixtures, which makes him smile.

"Cool, thanks."

"Hello darling, there you are. We've been looking for you."

A tall blond woman draped in layers of cream cotton over a denim miniskirt and black footless tights and wearing lots of silver bangles and necklaces is kissing Finn. I'm guessing this is Portia, and the bored-looking man is Anthony, in which case we've got a full house of exes. Never mind the chocolate eggs; there should probably be some sort of special prize just for that.

"Portia, this is Molly. She's just moved back here after a few years in London. She's the new owner of Harrington Hall."

"Hello, lovely to meet you. I saw your house once when I was delivering leaflets for the Art Fair, and it's beautiful."

Stephen smiles and turns to me and winks out of sight of the ex-wives and ex-husbands, which makes me smile.

"Hopefully it will be even more beautiful soon, if that's possible. We're looking at some conversion ideas aren't we, Molly? We better leave you to get on; you don't want us all standing around cluttering up your stall. Portia, I meant to say earlier, you should definitely give the new fish place a try. Molly and I had dinner there last week and we'd highly recommend it, wouldn't we Molly?"

"Er, yes, the food was lovely."

He's doing his twinkling thing again, and I think his stellar performance is definitely having an impact on Portia, who looks decidedly disgruntled.

"Isn't it just fish and chips?"

"Not at all, he had a Michelin star in London, or was it two? We thought it was very promising, and Molly persuaded me to try his homemade ice cream, which I must say was absolutely delicious." He pauses and gives me the kind of look you give someone when you're remembering a special moment, rather than a half-decent pudding. "Good to know we've got a decent local restaurant now, and about time too, but then those of us who grew up round here have always found ways to keep ourselves entertained."

Portia is giving me very flinty sideways glances now, and even though I don't actually have eyes in the back of my head, I know Pete is looking Irritated and Tense. Which is exactly what Stephen intended. Hurrah.

"Do try it. I'd book ahead though—it was pretty busy. You never know, he might be in the market for some of Tony's plates. Platters maybe. Just an idea. Come on, Finn, I'm sure there are more things you want to con me into buying. Nice to have met you Pete, and Janice. And lovely to see you again Sally, as always. And Molly, keep up the good work. Speak later darling."

He winks, this time in clear view of everyone, a proper lascivious wink. Sally is now grinning so much she has to pretend to look for something under the table. With a bit of luck Pete will now be so tense he'll have fallen backwards off the wall into the sea.

I kneel down and join Sally under the table, whispering as we rearrange the bags of sweets in the big cardboard box.

"That was great Moll. You should have seen Pete's face. And Portia didn't look happy did she? Stephen was always great at that kind of thing."

"What, flirting you mean?"

We both smile.

"I know he's a bit full of himself."

"A bit?"

"Alright a lot then. But honestly Moll, if you'd seen Pete's face, it was brilliant. Janice didn't look that thrilled either."

We're both trying not to giggle now.

Dan comes back with the boxes of eggs from the car, and has brought me and Sally a crab sandwich, and a burger for himself, and is all for going back for a second one.

"You can't still be hungry."

"Well I am."

Sally laughs.

"You wait until your Tom is Dan's age. It's no joke Sal. It's like he's got hollow legs—whatever you feed him, he's always got room for more."

"Dad, have you got any money?"

This day just keeps getting better.

Pete reluctantly hands over a fiver.

"When is this parade starting? We really need to be leaving soon."

"I'm sure they won't be much longer."

"We've brought you a drink Miss Molly. You've been on the go for hours."

Ivy gives Pete a rather fierce look, and he sits back down on the wall.

"Thanks Ivy."

She's been keeping an eye on Bertie, while Dennis and Celia are on duty on the plant stall run by the local Horticultural Society. They've spent the last few days potting things up and bickering about what to charge and whether Dennis will or will not include some of his tomato seedlings. Dennis won in the end and donated six pots, but refused to let any more go.

"The parade will be by any minute. They were all lining up when we went past. Alfie looked lovely with his pirate hat on, and his sword."

"Fat lot of good a plastic sword would be."

"Yes, we know that Mr. Bertie, but don't you go spoiling for it for him, will you?"

"Wouldn't dream of it. But if I'd known, I could have lent him one of mine. I've got a few ceremonial swords knocking around somewhere, would have been just the ticket."

Both Ivy and I decide to ignore this.

"We're off to see the lifeboat people after the parade has gone by. They've got a big stall with tables and chairs, so we might have a little sit-down. They're doing teas and coffees. Spirits too, I shouldn't wonder, knowing that lot."

"You wouldn't be fussing about a bit of strong drink if you were caught out in a Force-nine with half your rigging gone, I can tell you."

"No probably not, but then I wouldn't be, would I, Mr. Bertie, since I don't go messing about with boats in the first place."

The parade starts, led by the sea scouts and their marching band. The local fire brigade are driving their engine along very slowly, tooting and waving, with the siren on in short bursts, and all the lights flashing. But the local lifeguards definitely win the most-glamorous-group award, since most of them are bronzed surfers, and their bright-yellow truck appears to be packed full of young women wearing bikini tops and very small shorts. And then the school appears, to rousing cheers and applause from all the parents, who hold up phones and video cameras to capture the moment. Each class has made flags or banners, and the school recorder group is tootling away. Ben is holding up his *Golden Hind* banner with his friend Sam, only they keep lowering it so it hovers above the heads of the kids in front of them, who are dressed as Elizabethan sailors.

Alfie's class gets the biggest cheer since they're all dressed as pirates, including the parent helpers, who are making sure nobody ends up walking the plank into the sea or pokes anyone with their plastic swords. They're also singing "What do you do with a drunken sailor" quite loudly and generally having a wonderful time. Alfie spots us and starts waving, and we all wave back, apart from Dan, who mutters something rude under his breath.

"Dan."

"Yes?"

"Do you fancy an ice cream later on?"

He waves at Alfie and gives him the thumbs-up sign, which makes Alfie go pink and wave his sword even more enthusiastically.

"That do?"

"That will do nicely, thank you."

There are more boat races in the bay after the parade, and we've nearly sold all the eggs when everyone comes back from watching the races.

"Mum, Mum, guess what?"

Alfie's in a state of high excitement, and even Pete is looking more chirpy.

"Me and Tom won."

"Won what love?"

"The pig, the top prize in the raffle, and we won it, and we're going to share it, and when it's bigger, we can make it into bacon."

Bloody hell.

"I suppose congratulations are in order."

Pete is clearly highly amused.

"Thanks."

"We really do need to make a move now. I'll call you during the week to arrange the Easter holiday dates."

"Okay."

"Thank you so much for inviting me; it's been a lovely day."

Janice has clearly been practising this. She turns to Pete for an approving look.

"You're welcome Janice."

Actually I didn't invite her—Pete just announced she was coming—but I probably should have. It's got to be good for the boys to see everyone being civilised.

"You must come and see the house—maybe when you collect the boys for the holidays?"

"That would be lovely."

She looks pleased with this, unlike Pete, but then he rallies.

"I'm sure Alfie will be very sensible looking after his new pig, won't you, Alfie?"

"Yes Dad, of course I will."

Sally and I are packing up the stall while Patrick takes the boys for an ice cream.

"Well I think it's great, and it will be something Tom can do with Patrick."

"What, butcher his new pet? How lovely. I've already got one vegetarian, thanks, and if this turns Ben vegan and he takes Alfie and Tom with him, I'll never forgive you."

"I don't think Patrick would be that pleased either, given he's in the butchery business Moll, and honestly, they'll be fine. They'll probably be bored by then."

"There is that."

"And you've got an old pigsty at the back of the stables, haven't you?"

"The one in the orchard, without a roof—that one?"

"Yes, but Patrick could fix that, no trouble."

"Isn't he too busy, with doing the farmers' markets and everything?"

"No, and he does need to do more things with Tom, so this is perfect."

"Can't he just make things with Lego like other dads? And anyway, won't the poor thing be lonely all by itself?"

"Patrick just told me that he thinks we should get another

one—then they could have one each. Weaners don't cost much, and he knows the farmer—he'll probably do a deal with him. Makes sense really."

"On Planet Pig, maybe."

"There is that."

It finally starts to rain.

Great, how perfect. One more animal to add to the menagerie, possibly two, and now it's pouring and we've got to get everything packed up and back in the car before Alfie's pirate hat melts.

"You can say you do homegrown bacon, for your B-and-B people, and Patrick says they eat anything, and we'll help, with feeding them and everything."

"Sal."

"Yes Moll?"

"Shut up."

CHAPTER FIVE

Tea for Two Hundred

April to June

Damask Roses

Widely grown in ancient Persia and introduced into Europe in the thirteenth century, damask roses have plentiful foliage and lush clusters of highly scented flowers. Traditionally used to make perfume, their elongated leaves and abundant satiny petals guarantee them a place in all rosarian collections as examples of the true essence of roses. Famous varieties include Marie Louise with its large, intensely pink full flowers which open flat and then gradually curl; Ville de Bruxelles, a luxurious pink with a rich fragrance; and the stunning pure-white lemon-scented Madame Hardy.

It's half past four on Wednesday afternoon and it's pouring with rain. It's been raining on and off ever since the Spring Fair. In between torrential downpours, we've had steady rain interrupted by drizzle; if it carries on like this, I'd probably be better off asking Mr. Stebbings to leave the gatehouse half-finished and start building a sodding ark. The Harrington menagerie is about to expand yet again with the arrival of the piglets, so Patrick and the boys have waded out to the stables and are busy rearranging damp straw and filling up the water trough. Apparently a constant supply of water is vital, or we'll end up having to rehydrate two piglets on top of everything else, and God knows what that would involve, but I'm guessing it wouldn't be pretty.

"The pigs should be arriving soon Bertie."

"Jolly good."

Nothing ever fazes Bertie. I'm sure if I popped into the library with his afternoon cup of tea and announced the unicorns were about to arrive, he'd tell me that was jolly good too.

"Stay inside in the warm, and we'll come and get you once they're settled."

"Right you are."

In an ideal world I'd like to avoid Bertie joining the piglet meet and greet—I'm not sure how they'd react to a spot of celebratory cannon activity, and he's already got a rotten cold after getting completely plastered with the lifeboat people at their stall at the Spring Fair. The awning collapsed in the wind and the rain, so they all ended up getting soaked trying to put it back up again. By the time Dennis brought him home, they were both pale blue with cold. Ivy's still sulking with Dennis, and didn't speak to him at all on Monday, so that's been a treat on top of all the piglet prep.

Betty is giving me a particularly malevolent look, walking along the back of the sofa and bobbing her head up and down.

"Knob. Knob. Knob."

"Mum, the farmer's arrived."

"Thanks Dan. I'll be there in a minute."

"Knob."

"I wonder where Betty is picking up her new vocab Dan?"

He grins, and then looks at his feet.

"Sorry Mum."

"Is Celia out there with you?"

"Yes, and Jasper."

Great. More leaping and barking.

At the mention of Jasper, Betty puts her head down and fluffs up her feathers.

"Get to your basket."

She's taken to screeching this at random moments whenever she thinks Jasper might be in the vicinity. If only I could find my basket, I'd definitely go and sit in it, particularly as an alternative to introducing piglets to their new home. Dennis and Patrick have spent ages fixing the pigsty roof with a sheet of corrugated iron and some bricks Mr. Stebbings gave them. They've even painted the door and the gate a chirpy apple green.

"Dan?"

"Yes Mum."

"If she starts saying anything beginning with an *F*, you're grounded for a month okay?"

"Polly put the kettle on. Knob. Knob. Knob."

Bloody hell.

There's quite a crowd by the time we get to the stables. Even Ivy's put her coat and Wellies on and come out to witness the arrival. Tess is trying hard to herd everyone back out of the rain and into the stables, which would be a top plan under ordinary circumstances. But at least the flaming things can't get dehydrated on our first day as pig people given there are puddles of water everywhere. So that's a small bonus to make up for all the squelching.

You wouldn't think two eight-week-old piglets could cause so much chaos, or make so much noise, but they gallop around in circles squealing, with their ears flapping, looking very sweet, pinky white with black splodges. Until one of them manages to squeeze past Patrick when he opens the gate and it all goes a bit *101 Dalmatians*, with dogs and boys running and yelling and falling over in the mud, until Patrick finally manages to grab the piglet and reunite it with its brother.

"Let's go back inside and leave them to settle for a bit, shall we?"

Sally looks at his jeans, which are caked with mud.

"You can't go into Molly's house looking like that."

"O ye of little faith, I've got spare trousers in the car. I thought something like this might happen."

He looks at the boys, who also require urgent de-muddying assistance.

"We'll have to get them plastic trousers."

Sally tuts.

"Less of the 'we,' thanks. This pig thing was your idea, not mine, so you can sort the trousers. And get some for yourself while you're at it."

"If you find out where they sell them Patrick let me know and I'll get some for the boys."

Dan tuts.

"I'm not wearing plastic trousers like a total twat."

"Dan."

"Twit. A total twit."

"So you'll be doing all your own washing from now on, will

you? Rinsing anything muddy in the scullery sink so it doesn't clog up the machine?"

Ivy nods.

"Dennis has got waterproofs. They're handy if you're working outdoors, not that he always has the sense to wear them of course. Coming back with Mr. Bertie soaked to the skin, both of them giggling like a pair of naughty schoolboys. Haven't got the sense they were born with. So you just listen to your mother, there's a good boy. Shall I go back in and put the kettle on, then?"

"Please Ivy. Dan will help, won't you Dan?"

He tuts again.

"Mum?"

"Yes Alfie?"

"Our pigs are great, aren't they?"

"Yes love."

"If we like them we could get more, couldn't we, and then they could all have races?"

"Let's see how we get on with these two first."

We're back indoors sitting round the kitchen table drinking tea and eating slices of Ivy's lemon cake while the debate about what to call the piglets continues. Alfie's keen to name them Ben and Dan, which I've vetoed in deference to family harmony, but Ben is still busy Googling alternatives on Dan's laptop in case my veto weakens and they end up sharing their names with anything porcine.

"What about Biffer and Boffer, from *The Hobbit*? Biffer likes raspberry jam and apple tart, and plays the clarinet, and Boffer likes mince pies and cheese and also plays the clarinet."

Fingers crossed nobody gets hold of a clarinet.

"They're not dwarves, they're pigs, and me and Tom want them to have proper names. And we're going to choose them all by ourselves. They're our pigs, not yours."

"Alfie, don't be rude, Ben's only trying to help."

"What about Dumb and Dumber?"

"Mum, tell him."

"Ben, don't tease him, unless you want a piglet named after you."

Ivy pours Sally some more tea and sits down.

"I've always thought Pinky and Perky are nice names for pigs. They used to be on the television years ago, when it was still only in black-and-white. Lovely little things they were, puppets, they used to do a little dance."

Dennis makes a disapproving noise.

"They're a grand old breed, the Gloucestershire Old Spots, used to call them the 'Orchard Pig.' They don't want daft names like Pinky and Perky, stands to reason."

Ben nods.

"It says here farmers used to keep them to stop their orchards getting overgrown, and they used to say their black spots were bruises from the falling apples."

Patrick smiles.

"Once they've had a couple of days to settle I'll get the electric fence rigged up, and we'll move them round the orchard—they'll like that."

Patrick's put a lot of work into the piggy project already, sorting out all the official paperwork and the herd number. He's also worked out some complicated strip-grazing plan with Dennis, or it might be grazing strips; whatever it's called, it's supposed to mean the orchard doesn't end up looking like we're paying homage to the Battle of the Somme.

"It says here pigs love apple slices as a treat."

Dennis nods.

"Yes, but there's no need to spoil them with slices of apple—they'll have all the apples they want come autumn. You can take out the veg peelings though—they'll like that."

Ivy folds her arms.

"They'll have to share with the hens then, because we need our eggs too you know."

"The traditional day to kill your pig is Saint Martin's Day—that's the eleventh of November."

"Cool. Can we do it?"

"No Dan we can't. And we don't want to know when to kill the poor little things thanks Ben—they've only just arrived."

Alfie gives me a pitying look.

"Yes we do Mum—it's all part of the circle of life. Uncle Patrick's explained it, and you wouldn't have pigs if we didn't make them into bacon." He pauses, clearly thinking about scampering piglets. "But only when they're much bigger."

He seems fine with this, so I think it might be just me and Ben who'll be having qualms about the bacon issue.

"Yes Mum, honestly, get with the program—where do you think bacon comes from? Packets? They wouldn't be here at all if they weren't bred for bacon. That's the deal, and they'll have a good life with us."

"Yes thank you Ben, when I need you to be cheeky, I'll ask, okay?"

So that'll be just me having the qualms then.

Celia pats my arm.

"We always had a pig when I was a girl—can't remember their names though. Think we had one called Edward."

Alfie gives Celia a worried look.

"Edward's not a very good name for a pig Aunty Celia."

"Fair point, Alfie, fair point. We had one called Prudence too—named after a relative of my mother's—caused no end of ructions, so on balance, perhaps people's names are best avoided. Why don't you make a list of things you like best, that might that do the trick?"

Bertie is clearly rather taken with this idea.

"Well strong drink and strong women would definitely be at the top of my list. Can't go far wrong if you'd got ready access to both my boy, remember that, it will come in very handy one day. Not ideal for pig-naming purposes, I grant you. No, you want something more fitting. Bacon-and-Eggs seems rather harsh, but it's on the right track, I know, what about calling them Bubble and Squeak?"

The boys adore bubble and squeak, so I often cook extra potatoes and veg so there are leftovers ready to fry up the next day. Watching the vast quantities of what Alfie likes to call "squeaker," which they consumed at supper last night, has clearly made a lasting impression on Bertie, and everyone agrees these are excellent names for piglets as Tom and Alfie start skipping round the table chanting, "Bubble and Squeak, Bubble and Squeak."

"Let's go out and tell them their new names Dad."

"Can I finish my tea first?"

I think Patrick would like to stay inside in the warm for a bit longer, so Tom and Alfie stand hopping up and down beside him while he finishes his tea, which makes Sally laugh.

"You'll have to put your old jeans back on again, and get the boys changed back into theirs."

"Thanks, I'd never have thought of that."

"Maybe getting those waterproofs should be a top priority tomorrow?"

"You can go off sarcastic women you know."

"Not as quickly as you'll go off washing muddy trousers."

Happy Easter darling."

I'm in the orchard on Sunday morning with Lola, who is wearing her dark glasses despite the drizzle. She and Celia discovered a mutual passion for martinis last night and then moved on to a cocktail-making competition with Bertie, which he inevitably won, but only when all three of them were so plastered we had to practically carry Celia up the stairs. Tre doesn't drink alcohol, and appears to be in some sort of yogic trance most of the time, but he's so breathtakingly gorgeous it doesn't really matter. He just sits there looking astonishing and breathing very slowly. He smiles too, and that's about it; he's a very peaceful and relaxing guest. Even Betty seemed calmer when he was in the room.

"Did they do the Easter-egg hunt already?"

"No, I said we'd do it after lunch. Give us time to hide the eggs properly."

"Great. So you're officially open now darling, congratulations. I can't believe how much you've done in so short a time."

"Thanks Lola."

"And?"

"And nothing really, we've had a few bookings, a nice woman called Mrs. Allen who Ivy likes, she was here last year apparently. She was sweet, although she likes poached eggs, so she's never going to be top of my list. And another couple on Thursday, who were less sweet, and kept moaning."

"About what?"

"The weather mostly, but also how they liked their room better before because they preferred the old wallpaper."

"Nutters."

"Yup, but it's been fine, so far, and we've got a few more bookings in for the summer holidays, so that's good. And now that Celia is booked in for a few weeks, that really helps, and I can concentrate on the gatehouse. We've had a few setbacks there: the ceiling in the bedroom collapsed, and one of the main beams is rotten, so that will cost more than I budgeted for, but we're getting there. Thank God for Mr. Stebbings."

"So the B-and-B thing will work then, as a way to pay the bills?"

"No, absolutely no way. Not with just the B-and-B, even if I go into all the guidebooks and run ads and put the prices up as high as they can go, and get to around an eighty-percent occupancy rate—which is really going for it, since it's been more like thirty percent so far—it'll still be chicken feed, literally in our case since I've just had to buy new sacks of feed for Gertie and the girls. No, the gatehouse is definitely going to be key, and the stables."

"So will you stop doing B-and-B?"

"Probably, once everything is up and running."

"Good plan darling. You don't want to spend the rest of your life cooking bacon for strangers. Not unless they're girls the boys have brought home."

"Hopefully they'll be cooking their own breakfasts by then."

"I wouldn't count on it darling. God, this headache really isn't shifting you know. I thought the fresh air would help."

"I'm sure it will, give it time."

"Bertie was on fine form last night—he's adorable."

"He is, although he's a bit less adorable when he's setting fire to things."

"Sorry?"

"We had a bit of a moment a couple of weeks back, he fell asleep in the library and set fire to his newspaper. It fell on the hearth and he'd forgotten to put the fireguard in front of the fire properly, so the next thing we knew Betty was squawking and screeching, and he was trying to put it out by bashing it with the poker, which meant he ended up burning a hole in the rug."

"Right. So he's not turning into your very own Mrs. Danvers, then?"

"No, but I do a Mrs. Danvers patrol every night now, just to make sure all the fireguards are in the right place. I never thought I'd say this, but thank God for Betty, our very own avian smoke alarm."

"Like those canaries miners used to have to warn them about gas, but more aristocratic. Every home should have one."

"If they've got a Bertie they should. Or have a dog. Jasper does a pretty similar thing for Celia."

"Christ, is she setting fire to the place too?"

"No, but if she falls asleep on the sofa he yaps and yaps at her until she wakes up. He doesn't like people sleeping unless they're in bed. She says she'd half nodded off in the bath once, and he dived in."

"Handy."

"Very, unless he starts doing the same thing for our guests. I'd make sure the door's locked if you fancy a quick ten minutes meditation in the bath, unless you want Jasper to join you."

"Thanks for the heads-up, I'll warn Tre—he's always zoning out."

"Good idea, and if you see Bertie settling into his chair by the fire with his newspaper, make sure the fireguard is in the right place would you? I've put a new smoke alarm up just outside the door, and I've checked all the batteries in the old ones, so I'm really hoping I won't need to get one of those old-fashioned nursery fireguards, the ones like wire cages—they bolt to the wall, but they look hideous."

"Those curtain ones are nice. They have them in lots of the smart clubs in town, matt-black metal, very neat, you hardly notice them."

"Yes, I saw them when I was researching all the alternatives, but they're the most expensive ones, and you still have to actually shut the curtain."

"Oh right, yes, so not Bertie-proof then."

"Not really. I'm sure it'll be fine, he was pretty mortified about it, but we're keeping an eye on it."

"He's still adorable though."

"Oh yes, completely."

The piglets are now racing Ben and Alfie up and down their run, and it's hard to tell who is enjoying themselves the most.

"I still don't really get how you could win a pig darling."

"Neither do I Lola, but we did."

"It's like the twilight zone down here isn't it, and why are there two of them? Please tell me I'm not seeing double."

"No, there are definitely two. The boys didn't want them to be lonely."

"Do try not to adopt anything else though darling, yes? You don't want to turn into one of those nutters who breeds alpacas. If you see any donkeys wandering about looking tragic, just look the other way. Although a little donkey might be sweet—it could help carry all the food for the pigs."

"Thanks Lola, I'll bear it in mind."

"Sounds like the architect was in top form at the Fair though, where is he now?"

"Madrid, and yes, he was. Sally had to pretend to look for something under the table at one point she was enjoying it so much. She says he's got a bit of a reputation locally; apparently he and Portia both had affairs when they were married, so nobody was that surprised when they split up."

"So?"

"So nothing, I'm just saying."

"Well stop it. You're not looking for a second husband, so what do you care. When's he back from Madrid?"

"In a couple of weeks, but then he's off somewhere else I think. He rang to say he couldn't resist putting on a performance in front of Portia and he hoped I didn't mind. But there's something—I don't know—he's a bit too pleased with himself."

"I wish I'd seen Pete's face."

"Yes, that was a definite highlight. And it's nice, having someone showing an interest, but it's all—I don't know—somehow underwhelming."

"It's bound to feel strange, putting yourself back out there, like going on a refresher course. Refresh and revitalise, like a good spa treatment, but with better underwear."

"But that's exactly what I'm trying to say. It doesn't feel that refreshing, or revitalising, and I definitely don't have that kind of underwear—and before you say it, no, I'm not going shopping. It all feels like it's a foregone conclusion, like we've fast-forwarded somehow, and there's just a hint in amongst all the flirting that I should feel very lucky he's paying me so much attention. And I should be, I can see that, he's very much the eligible man about town and everything, but I don't want to spend my time doing anything I'm not one hundred percent keen on anymore. I spent far too long doing that with Pete. It's like Bertie says, I'm all for a bit of gallivanting, but if it all turns into dinners and what to wear and scoring points over the ex-wife, I think I'd rather stay in, pottering around the house and keeping the boys out of trouble, or out in the garden, it's so beautiful now. Gallivanting interspersed with pottering and getting into gardening—I think that's what I want to be doing."

"Good for you darling. So when are you going out gallivanting then?"

"God knows, probably never, but I like the sound of it."

"Just promise me you'll keep doing things which get you away from the Doctor Doolittle thing you've got going on, I do slightly worry you'll develop a passion for rare breeds. You'll turn into one of those women who are always covered in hair and dribble from some special kind of long-eared goat."

"I think that's rabbits. I don't think they do long-eared goats."

"See what I mean. Promise?"

"I promise."

"Good. So what's the plan for today then?"

"An early lunch, and then there's a car-boot sale and I thought we could do the egg hunt when we get back."

"I don't buy things from people's cars darling."

"There are stalls too, food and surfing kit, hippy clothes, that kind of thing. Or we can stay here and help the boys clean the pigsty?"

"Maybe the car-boot thing is worth a go. At least if there are hippy stalls Tre will enjoy himself."

"Does he ever speak?"

"Not really. He's very stupid darling, so I try not to encourage it. Beautiful though, yes?"

"Oh yes."

She laughs, and then winces.

"Christ, have you got any more Panadol? Those first two haven't quite hit the spot."

"Sure. And another pot of coffee?"

"Perfect."

Lola and Tre have a "siesta" before lunch, and Celia is in the garden with Ben planting out summer veg with Dennis, so I have a relaxing morning making lunch in between stopping the boys' bickering. Dan is still sulking because I wouldn't let him join in the killer-cocktails session last night, and Alfie is sulking because I've vetoed training Bubble and Squeak to come into the house and up the stairs into his bedroom.

"Dennis says we should be able to lift the second crop of new potatoes soon, and the asparagus is nearly ready."

Ben's a keen gardener now and spends ages with Dennis and Celia mucking about in the greenhouse or digging in the kitchen garden.

"That's great love."

"Shall I alert the BBC? They'll probably want to make a special Boring Gardeners programme."

"You don't have to eat any of the asparagus if it's too boring Dan. And Ben, take your socks off love, get a clean pair or you'll be traipsing mud everywhere."

"I said we'd help Dennis with the rabbits later."

The Easter Bunny doesn't really get a look-in round here, since Dennis is waging an ongoing rabbit battle. There are burrows along the cliff tops, and they keep trying to infiltrate the kitchen garden by digging tunnels under the walls, so he's mounting special patrols in the early morning and at dusk, with Tess and Jasper barking and the boys running around yelling. So far this, combined with sporadic cannon fire from Bertie, seems to be doing the trick, but Dennis is adamant they'd clear the garden of all traces of salad and veg if we let them, so constant vigilance is essential, despite the quantities of mud and soaking-wet anoraks this involves.

"That's fine love, but only if you let Alfie join in, and Tom if he's here with Patrick checking on the pigs."

"But he always ends up falling into the ditch and making a huge fuss."

Dan grins.

"That's why they call it a ha-ha. I'll give you a hand later if you like. You never know, you might be the one who ends up in the ditch."

"Hurry up and lay the table please. And Dan, go and tell Lola the shepherd's pie is nearly ready, and yes, Alfie does need to help if he wants to. Didn't Dennis say the more the merrier?"

"Yes, but he also said he'd get his friend round, the one with the night-vision thing on his gun, and you weren't too keen on that were you? Actually a machine gun would be better, you'd get loads of rabbits with one of those, and Uncle Bertie is bound to know where to get one."

"Don't be daft Dan, we just want to keep them off the veg. We don't want a rabbit apocalypse in our back garden—it would upset Alfie."

"It would not, he'd love it. Dennis was saying he's partial to a bit of rabbit pie, and Alfie said he wants to try it."

Oh God, if I'm not careful Ivy will be trying to teach me how to skin a rabbit before I know where I am. It's bad enough picking shotgun pellets out of pheasants, although admittedly the casseroles are delicious. But that's one of the things about country life which I'd forgotten: how things don't arrive in nice clean plastic packets. It's fine with veg, and the occasional pheasant. But I definitely draw the line at de-furring rabbits.

"Dennis said we'd get a few for the freezer. We're country boys now. Shoot things and eat them, all part of country life isn't it—well, apart from Benny boy."

Dan is definitely smirking now.

"Sure, if you skin them and do all the prep. It's a very messy job, but I'm sure Ivy can show you. I'm having nothing to do with anything bunny related. Now, please get the table sorted, and anyone not sitting down, with clean hands and socks and being nice to their little brother, and not talking about shooting things, won't be getting any lunch."

They both tut.

Bertie entertains us at lunch with tales of guns mounted along the cliff tops during the War, and makes the whole thing sound like it was all a tremendous adventure.

"It wasn't all fun though, was it, Uncle Bertie?"

"Sorry my dear?"

"We wouldn't want anyone to think that War was fun, would we?"

I give him what I hope is a firm look.

"Oh no, quite right, terrible business. I could tell you things to make your hair curl."

The boys all lean forwards slightly, clearly thrilled.

"Yes, but not at lunchtime. We don't want anyone having nightmares, do we?"

"No, quite, no need to dwell. Put it out of your mind, that's what we all learnt, else you couldn't go on, end up in the loony bin. Can't help remembering on dark days—lost so many decent chaps, girls too. Lots of tears in amongst all the larks, lots of tears."

He pauses, and I'm hoping he's not about to launch into another one of his naval reminiscences. Some of them are pretty devastating.

"What's on the itinerary for this afternoon? Dennis mentioned something about rabbits. Thought I might test the cannon, check everything's in working order, wake the buggers up."

Alfie sits up a bit straighter, looking delighted; not only has the cannon been mentioned but a grown-up has said "bugger" at lunch.

"We're off to a boot sale Uncle Bertie, but maybe afterwards? And I've been meaning to talk to you about the cannon, only do you think we could have a signal before you fire it? Just so we get a bit of warning. A warning whistle, something like that?"

Everyone thinks a whistle is an excellent idea, and Alfie races off to retrieve the one from his Christmas cracker, and we all have a few practice toots. Great. So now Bertie is keeper of the whistle and will blow it before he fires the stupid thing, which should mean I don't break quite so much china. If we can just get through the afternoon without anyone "accidentally" letting the pigs out, or trying to point cannons at rabbits, we should be in for a peaceful time.

"Alfie, eat the rest of your carrots love, and tell Aunty Lola about the scouts."

Alfie and Ben tell Lola all about the wonderful world of scouting and she's suitably impressed. Alfie is officially a Beaver, and Ben is a Scout, so they have different sweatshirts and badges. They've only been going for a couple of weeks, but so far they both love it, and there are plans for going camping later in the year.

"You'll have to get lots of badges Alfie, so Mummy can sew them on for you in her sewing room."

"You can glue them on now Lola, thank you, so less of the Mummy-sewing-things-on, if it's all the same to you."

"That's handy."

"Very. The only tricky bit is they go the same night as Dan has his lifeguards' thing, so I end up driving backwards and forwards all evening like a taxi service. I'm thinking of getting a light to put on the top of the car and see if I can't pick up a few fares."

"I'd be careful what light you get darling—anything vaguely red and you might find yourself getting some unusual requests."

Bertie starts chuckling, and raises his glass to Lola in appreciation.

"Yes, thank you Lola, and what other sort of lights would there be then? Do explain what you mean to Alfie."

"Ice-cream vans have lights darling, and you wouldn't want children queuing up for ice cream every time you stopped at the traffic lights would you?"

Celia's trying not to smile too now, and Dan.

"Tell Aunty Lola about your lifeguards' thing, Dan, I'm sure she'd like to hear all about it."

"It's just me, and my mate Robbie from school does it too. It's pretty cool. We do training on the beach and races and everything."

"Sounds exciting darling. Do you race in and out of the surf?"

"Sometimes."

"And he's got special red shorts and a bright-yellow sweatshirt, haven't you Danny?"

He gives Ben a threatening look.

"Yeah, but that's so people can see you on the beach, you idiot."

"They can probably see you from the other side of the bay."

"Ben, you can start clearing the table ready for pud, if you've finished."

Lola is smiling.

"Well good for you, Dan. Do lots of people go, from your school?"

"Quite a few: Robbie and Tom, and Sam Masters, and this girl I know, Freya. And a few of the sixth formers, but they don't talk to us."

Alfie puts his fork down.

"It would be better if there were no girls. But I might join, when I'm bigger."

"When you're bigger you might like girls a bit more Alfie, you never know."

"I do know Aunty Lola, and I won't."

"Apart from your Aunty Lola of course."

He gives her an adoring look.

"Of course. And we can have ice cream when we go to the boot fair, can't we, as many as we like?"

"Over to you Aunty Lola—more than one and he's definitely in your car on the way back, and that's all I'm saying on the subject."

The car-boot sale is quite a good one, and I find some more old glass bottles and bowls for the guest bedrooms, and a lovely old white enamel bread bin which will look great in the kitchen in the gatehouse. We meet Vicky and Bea and Daisy, buying material for Daisy's bedroom, and Vicky helps me choose some for curtains for the gatehouse bedroom, so that's another thing crossed off the list. I stock up on handmade soap, and Lola buys some too—rose geranium and verbena, and sage for Tre, because apparently sage is very cleansing.

We're back home having a quiet cup of tea while the boys count up their eggs after a rather frantic Easter-egg hunt where Alfie inevitably ended up falling into the ha-ha again, when Bertie and Celia wander in, looking chirpy. They've taken to going on little walks in the afternoons now, each treating the other as an elderly person in need of a slow pace and a steadying arm.

"Celia has a proposition about the garden my dear, and I must say I wasn't keen at first, but now I've got all the info I'm rather coming round to the idea. Entirely up to you of course."

He nods at Celia.

"Off you go then, ask her."

"I thought you were going to ask her."

"Was I? Oh sorry, forgot that bit. Mind like a sieve. Might be better if you ran her through the basics. Bound to make a hash of it if you leave it to me."

She looks at him in the same way I remember Helena used to, a mixture of annoyance and affection, rather similar to the way you'd greet an old family pet who's been chewing your slippers for the umpteenth time.

"It's quite simple: I'd like us to consider opening the garden for a day, as part of the National Garden Scheme. My friend Bobby is the county organiser, so she could give us all the details. They're very fussy, but I'm sure we'd be accepted, and you charge an entry fee—five pounds is the usual, and you donate it to a charity of your choice. I thought we could raise funds in memory of Helena, make a donation to a heart charity, and we could also sell teas and cakes, and pot up some seedlings and sell those to raise funds to renovate the fountain. Helena definitely had that in her sights as her next project, and it would be such a fitting tribute. And best of all, we could also invite the Rose Society people—they've been trying to present a medal in honour of all of Helena's work for years. She kept telling them she was too busy, although personally I think it was more a case of too shy."

"Too stubborn, more like—never did like a fuss."

She nods at Bertie.

"That's true enough, but this is a gold medal. They've only awarded seven so far, it's quite exceptional, so I do think she'd approve. I know she was terribly pleased when they first suggested it, even though she pretended she wasn't. So what do you think my dear? Shall we find Dennis and discuss it, because we'd obviously need to take his views into account."

"How many people would come do you think?"

"Around two hundred, at a guess, maybe more if the weather is good."

Bloody hell, two hundred people tramping round the garden and wanting tea. Dennis will go nuts, and if he doesn't, Ivy definitely will.

"Let's talk to Dennis and Ivy about it tomorrow."

Celia stands up.

"Ivy's in the kitchen right now actually, Dennis drove her up a few minutes ago, been shopping, something about wanting the big mixing bowl from the pantry. Shall I ask them to join us?"

"Great."

Bugger.

"Well I think it's a brilliant idea. Put you on the map—well, the gardening map anyway."

"Thanks Lola, and will you be down that weekend helping serve all the teas then?"

"Possibly not darling, but you could print up leaflets about the B-and-B you know, be great for business."

"Yes, brilliant, if we want all our guests wanting tours of the gardens every five minutes, it will be perfect. Anyway, it's up to Ivy and Dennis—they'll be the ones doing all the extra work."

I'm rather counting on them to be honest, but as soon as they come in I can see that Dennis is quite taken with the idea, even though he's pretending not to be.

"We'd need to keep on our toes, because they turn up with penknives and plastic bags to take cuttings and we don't want them snipping away at our best plants like vultures. I've seen them at it, when we've visited other gardens. Ivy and I often have a driveout on a Sunday, don't we Ivy?"

"Yes, and a right mess they usually make, with people wandering in and out of the house with muddy shoes."

Celia nods.

"We'd have to think about that, make sure we planned things properly. But the medal would be such a fitting tribute to Helena, and all her hard work over the years. And your hard work too Dennis—she couldn't possibly have done it without you."

"I'm not saying I'm against it, I'm just saying we'd need to be on our guard."

"Absolutely."

"I suppose we could have the tea in the stables, if it rains?"

"In those dirty old stables? If you think I'm serving tea on our best plates in those mucky old stables, you can think again, Dennis."

"Only if the weather's bad. And we'd clean them up, we'd want to do it properly."

Bertie stands up.

"Excellent, knew you'd come up with a plan to make it work. And if people can buy Ivy's cakes, we'll make an absolute fortune, that's pretty much guaranteed. I think this calls for a celebratory tipple. Anyone care to join me?"

We're starting on what I predict will be an ongoing series of mild bickers about what china to use and what people will sit on when they have their tea, when Alfie races in, panting.

"Mum, quick, a sheep has fell in the ha-ha. Come and see, it's great."

We troop down to the bottom of the garden. The farmer who rents the fields has had the sheep out with their lambs for a few weeks now, and they bounce about and climb on top of anything they can find, including their mothers if they make the mistake of lying down. They're still very small though, so I'm hoping it's a lamb, but it turns out to be a rather large and very grumpy sheep.

"How do we get it out Uncle Dennis?"

"Stop running about, for starters, we want to calm it down, or we'll never get it out. Ben, go and get some rope from the barn, there's a good lad."

Alfie is hopping up and down.

"Are you going to lasso it Uncle Dennis, like cowboys do?"

Dennis smiles.

"Might be a better idea, but I thought we'd try to rig up a halter first and try to lead her out and back into the field. She'll have a lamb in there and she'll go back in no bother once we get her pointed in the right direction. Stupid animals sheep, one of the stupidest creatures you're ever likely to meet. Always seem to be looking for a way to die; if they're not stuck somewhere, they're in the wrong field or out on the road. Like pheasants. They're another lot who haven't got much sense to them."

Actually in terms of not having much sense I think finding yourself in charge of three boys, assorted pensioners, dogs, chickens, pigs, and a parrot, alongside a B&B and two hundred people coming for tea and a poke round your garden might rank quite highly too.

I'm going to have to start a whole new list.

"And then shall we go on rabbit patrol Uncle Dennis?"

"Might as well I suppose, now we've all got our outside things on."

Double bugger.

After a busy few weeks I'm sitting in the linen cupboard on Friday afternoon with a cup of tea and a biscuit, trying to head off a full-blown panic attack. Mr. and Mrs. Collins are due to book in at lunchtime, and I can't help feeling B&B guests in the house on top of hordes of nutter rose people descending on us in the garden this weekend might just be the final straw. We've been fairly busy with B&B guests—I think "slow but steady" would be the official verdict—and we've also all been fighting off the cold Alfie brought home from school, which meant a few days which descended into a blur of hot lemon and tissues, so that didn't exactly help. I'm continuing my Mrs. Danvers anti-fire patrol, but thankfully Bertie is leaving the fireguard firmly in place now, although he did make Dan a hot lemon drink which turned out to contain copious amounts of sugar and a tiny shot of whiskey, so I had to have a firm word about that. Although to be fair, Dan did stop whining about his cold and sleep for ten hours straight, so all in all it could have been worse.

But the weather is finally getting warmer now June has arrived, and we're drying all the washing outdoors now, on the rotary washing lines at the side of the kitchen garden wall, which, as Ivy rightly says, is a long way to walk with baskets of wet washing. But there's nowhere else to put them, not without ruining the views, and now we're opening the garden for public perusal, and getting a medal from the Rose Society for Helena's roses, it's probably not the ideal time to stick a load of washing lines closer to the house. Dennis has put up a new bigger rotary line, so we've got three of them now, looking like a mini wind-turbine collection when they're not festooned with clothes and sheets. Living by the sea does mean mornings often start with a sea mist, but it's usually gone by lunchtime, and even the big double sheets dry in a couple of hours when the sun is out. And everything smells so fresh, with a vague hint of salt. I'm definitely turning into someone who cares about the right weather for drying washing.

I've also taken to wearing aprons like Ivy, although unlike her navy-blue cotton tabards, I'm wearing floral pinafores which I found on one of the hippy stalls at the boot fair. They're great over jeans and T-shirts, and even Lola pronounced them more Vintage Retro than Mrs. Mop. Not that Ivy is a Mrs. Mop of course, even if she has started taking her new bucket on wheels home with her after she caught Ben trying to use it to wheel vegetable peelings out to the chickens.

Celia and Dennis have been potting up cuttings and muttering about plant labels and signs to stop people wandering around the house for what seems like weeks now. We've had Celia's friend Bobby, the county organiser, to stay for the night, who turned out to be Lady Roberta Wootton, which sent Ivy into somewhat of a spin and meant the best china came out of the cupboard. They spent hours outside in the garden with Dennis wittering on about signage and proper plant labels, and deciding that the meadow and the path down to the cove must be included in the Open Garden because apparently Helena has done such a wonderful job of planting wildflowers and a top-notch collection of rambling roses and sea thrift in amongst the grasses and ancient hedgerows, and everyone will want to see those too. So that's meant more mowing of paths and extra signs to point people in the right direction.

Ivy has relented and agreed that people can use the downstairs cloakroom, but she's organising a timetable so that Florrie and May are on duty to make sure nobody goes through the hall door and starts helping themselves to all our ornaments—although God knows why anybody would want to. We've rented trestle tables from the village hall, and she's holding firm about not wasting our good china on a load of old gardeners who if Dennis is anything to go by, will hand back cups covered in dirty fingerprints with their handles chipped. So she's arranged to borrow the cups and saucers and cake plates from the village hall as well, and I have to go and collect them tomorrow morning because the Women's Institute are using them today. And the weather forecast is for showers on Sunday, so we've got to tidy up the stables and have bunting and extra tablecloths ready to turn the end barn into a tearoom if required. Dear God.

"There you are, I've been calling you."

"Sorry Ivy. I was just about to make up the room for Mr. and Mrs. Collins."

"Your mum's arrived, and Mr. Stebbings needs a word. I said you'd nip up to see him in a bit, and when you go shopping, could you add more baking paper to your list? If we're going to sugar more rose petals for the cakes, we need a couple more rolls of paper. Oh, and your mum and I are making a few batches of strawberry jam. The early strawberries are ready, so I'll need some more sugar. And we need some more of those paper doilies—we want the cake plates to look nice don't we?"

"Definitely. Is that last load of washing done yet?"

"Yes, just finished."

"Okay, I'll hang that out before I leave."

Bloody hell.

"Cup of tea before you go?"

"Yes please."

The traffic isn't too bad on my drive to the supermarket. Surfers have started appearing now, but still mostly at weekends, in beaten-up old cars and vans with boards strapped to the roof, along with a smattering of tourists, so the roads are pretty bad from Friday to Monday. Dan's getting into the local dialect and calling them "grockles," and he's particularly scathing about their fondness for getting into the sea when they don't know the tide times and then needing to be rescued. I haven't reminded him that he's technically half grockle himself, as I'm trying to encourage lifeguard thing—although I did take the precaution of checking before he joined, and you don't officially get to pull sodden tourists out of the waves until you've passed all loads of swimming and safety tests. The surf can get really big sometimes and I'm not quite ready to see my first-born charging in at full pelt with only bright-red shorts and a small plastic float to keep him the right side of needing CPR. I can still remember how long it took me to teach him to swim in the first place. I spent hours at the Baby Dolphin classes at the local pool, slowly letting the air out of his armbands when he wasn't looking, with him grabbing the straps of my swimsuit whenever he felt panicky so I ended up practically topless, much to the amusement of other mums with more aquatic offspring.

By the time I'm back from shopping and I've collected the boys, Mr. and Mrs. Collins arrive. They seem nice, if a little quiet and formal. Ivy says they've stayed here a couple of times and the wife is fussy, but so far she's been fine and seemed impressed with all the changes. They're here to see their son and his wife, who they don't like, and their new grandson, who's only three weeks old, so Mrs. Collins has been knitting. After a bit of encouragement she showed me photos of the baby on the new mobile phone Mr. Collins has bought especially to receive baby updates. And then she unpacked the collection of pale-blue cardigans and a beautiful shawl she's knitted, so hopefully that will improve things with the daughter-in-law, because I can't see how any new mum could resist such beautiful hand-knitted treasures. Pete's mum sent premium bonds when Dan was born and nothing at all for Ben or Alfie, so I hope she knows how lucky she is.

The boys are particularly boisterous at supper, but thankfully Mr. and Mrs. Collins are out. It does make the house feel different when we have B&B guests staying. There's a sense we're on parade, and there needs to be less shouting upstairs to hurry the boys up in the morning, which is probably a good thing, but definitely adds to my stress levels when Dan can't find his homework and is about to miss his school bus. And the boys still haven't entirely grasped the idea that just because the B&B guests are getting a cooked breakfast doesn't mean they can start putting in their orders for bacon and mushrooms. Celia is different of course, which is a good thing since she sold her house last week, to one of the builders, who's fallen love with it while he's been working on the flood damage. Celia knows his wife, who's a passionate gardener, so that pretty much clinched it. So the plan is she'll stay with us while the sale goes through and then she'll start looking for a cottage, but we don't really think of her as a guest now. There was an initial tussle with Ivy, who wanted her to sit in the guest sitting room and wait to be served like a proper B&B guest, but Bertie brokered a peace deal in the end, and now Celia gets to make her own porridge every morning, and eats with us in the kitchen. But she leaves the saucepan and wooden spoon to soak, ready for Ivy, who has her own routine for washing up the breakfast things which doesn't include Celia splashing hot soapy water and getting in her way.

By the time I've done supper and supervised homework and bath time, I'm knackered. I'm so much more tired at the end of the day now, and I wake up earlier too, especially if we've got B&B guests needing their breakfasts. So I really can't do late nights anymore. I'm lucky if I make it to ten o'clock most evenings.

"Half an hour of telly and then it's bedtime Alfie."

"It's not fair that Ben and Dan can stay up later than me Mum, it's really not."

"Or you can go to bed now, if you're going to be silly because you're too tired."

"I'm not being silly."

"That's good love. Half an hour it is then, and then I'll read you a story."

Ben winks at me.

"I might go up in half an hour too Mum. I'm really tired, I might read for a bit."

"Okay love."

"Have you put the chickens to bed yet?"

"Damn, no, I've forgotten again."

I give Dan what I hope is a persuasive look.

"What?"

"Please."

He sighs.

"Alright, but only if we can have bacon rolls for breakfast."

"Deal."

I'm making a cup of tea when Vicky calls.

"How's it going? I was at the gatehouse earlier and its really coming on isn't it. It's going to be lovely."

"Yes, Mr. Stebbings said, and yes, thanks to all your help I think it's going to look pretty good."

"Did he give you the auction brochure?"

"Yes, the chest of drawers looks great, and the oak bed."

"I thought you'd like it. Auctions are a great way to get great stuff cheap, if you can avoid all the rubbish. Put the date in your diary and we'll go together."

"I was hoping you'd say that. I've never been to an auction before. I'd be terrified I'd end up bidding for the wrong thing."

"This place is okay. Some of them can be tricky, especially when all the dealers gather outside and knock out stuff to each other so you don't get a look in. All set for the garden thing on Sunday?"

"I think so. Are you sure you and Bea are okay to help? It's very kind of you, but it will be quite a long day."

"Sure. Daisy's got a sleepover—we'll have to collect her by sixish—but we're free all day apart from that, and I've done the leaflets for the B-and-B and the gatehouse. They look great, same pictures we put on the website. Oh, and we've got another booking for the last week of August."

"That's great Vicky, thanks."

So far she's rented the gatehouse for the last two weeks of July, most of August now, and a week in September, at seven hundred fifty pounds a week which is brilliant, and far more than I thought we'd get.

"I talked to my friend Ella about the yurt thing, and they can earn you good money, but they're so snobby now you need plumbing and everything. And they like "experiences" as added extras, stuff like collecting eggs and helping feed animals. And some of them can be a total nightmare according to Ella; they try to dump their kids on you and then disappear for hours on end. So I think you'll be better off focusing on the stables as your next project. Once you get the gatehouse up and running you'll be itching to get the stables sorted out, you'll see."

"I hope so. It's a bit different renting by the week. The B-and-B guests are usually two nights at most, and most of them have been nice—apart from those sisters, and Ivy did warn me the youngest one was a bit of a nightmare."

"Was she the one who moaned that her tea was too hot?"

"Yup, and the weather wasn't right, and she wanted different pillows. Ivy was great though. She just took the pillows off the bed, went and stood in the linen cupboard and put new pillowcases on them, and then put them back on the bed. Daft woman said the next morning they were much better."

"Typical, honestly you should hear what some of them ask when they ring up about rentals. I just say we're fully booked."

"I do that too—Ivy's been training me. It's coming in very handy, particularly lately. A few of the teachers from my old school have been calling wanting free minibreaks, particularly the ones who hardly spoke to me when I worked there but now sound like they're my best friends before they steer the conversation round to the good news that they will be driving right past us and wondered if they could pop in to say hello and maybe stay a night or two?"

"Bloody cheek. I've got a cousin like that. I can't stand her and she's never liked me, but as soon as she got wind of the cottage-rentals business, she was on the phone chatting away, clearly hoping for a freebie."

"I haven't had to fend off any family, so far, thank God. Pete's brother is coming down in a few weeks' time, but he's insisting on paying, even though I won't actually let him once they're here, and anyway we like him, so it doesn't count."

"Brace yourself though, because Diana, who comes to our book group—the one who rents out the barn on their farm—well, she had a woman she used to work with in London turn up with her husband and three kids, completely out of the blue, and when she said they were booked up she said that was fine, they'd brought their tents."

"Bloody hell."

"I know. Diana's husband had to get rid of them in the end—they were driving her demented, using her kitchen and the bathroom, and sitting watching telly."

"Is this meant to be scaring me, because if it is, it's definitely worked."

She laughs.

"Sorry. Don't worry, you've got Ivy. She'd never let anyone get away with that kind of stunt."

"True."

"And you've got a secret weapon."

"Have I?"

"Yes. Betty. Actually, you could probably rent her out by the hour. Could be a whole new business. I might mention it to Diana. You could train her to bite uninvited guests; she could be a guard parrot."

"She'd love that."

Actually, she probably would.

We're all up bright and early on Sunday morning, ready for the Open Garden Day. The forecast is now predicting sun, which is encouraging. The boys have spent ages helping Dennis clean up the stables, moving the bales of straw and assorted bags of animal feed, and boxes full of assorted tat, out of the barn and into the middle stable. It's a far better storage area all round as the roof has fewer holes in it, so at least we won't have to move everything back out again. They've had a lovely time using the hosepipe to sluice down the years of grime and dust. But apart from getting soaked this also revealed a lovely old herringbone brick floor, which was an unexpected bonus. We've put the trestle table for the cake stall inside by the back wall and the one for the plant stall too, so even if it does rain, people can still have a cup of tea. Mr. Stebbings has rigged up temporary plastic sheeting over the holes in the roof, which looks less tragic than I thought since he's used thick transparent plastic sheets so they look like random skylights.

We've put a few trestle tables in the courtyard, with tablecloths made from red gingham Mum found at the market. We've even made bunting, using up all the leftover bits of curtain material along with the gingham. We'll put the little pots of rose geraniums on the tables later. Dennis has been growing them in the greenhouse, so they're in full flower; and the leaves have such a perfect sweet rose scent that I can't help touching them every time I see them.

By half past ten the house is so busy I retreat into the garden to help Celia and Dennis with the labels. Mum and Ivy have got a cake-and-scone production line going; they've been at it for days, with Florrie and May helping. So if nobody turns up, we'll have enough cakes to last us for months. Mum's been helping in the garden too—I'd forgotten how much she loves gardening—so I think she's been enjoying herself. At least I hope so, because she's been working really hard.

"All set dear? Dennis and I thought we'd practise on you, give you the tour, so to speak. Would you mind?"

"Not at all Celia, that's a great idea."

They're both carrying buckets full of bamboo canes with our homemade plant labels attached with green string. The usual white plastic plant labels look so awful, and the smart ones cost a fortune, so we've made our own. Celia has spent ages writing plant names onto thick pale-green card, using her thick black fountain pen and her best copperplate handwriting. We've covered them with the same sort of sticky-back plastic I used for school displays, although when I saw how many labels we needed I had to rope the boys in to help, so a few of them have creases in the plastic, which I'm hoping adds to the overall artisan feel.

"Is this all the labels?"

"No, there are quite a few more buckets, we'll get those later. Bring that one though dear, if you wouldn't mind. We thought we'd start with the roses, and then go back round and fill in the gaps."

"Sure."

Oh dear. I think I know what they're up to now. They're hoping if they trot me round and point out some key names, nobody will think the new chatelaine of Helena's garden is a complete idiot. Dream on, as Dan would say.

"Shall we start with the species roses?"

Dennis nods and starts searching through his buckets.

"Let's start at the front."

We walk round to the front door. There are a series of gardens surrounding three sides of the house, divided by hedges or old brick walls with gates or arches. A border runs right round the house and a flagstone path which widens to a terrace at the back, outside the French windows from the drawing room and the library. The main lawn is flanked by two long flower beds, culminating in the ha-ha, to stop sheep getting into the library.

There are more lawns at the front of the house, with a large circular bed in the middle of the gravel drive. Dennis has even mowed the grass all the way down the edges of the lane, leaving clumps of longer grass around the shrubs, and mowing paths through the trees. He's spent hours sitting on his ride-along mower over the past few weeks, having a wonderful time in between telling me what a boon it is not to have to puff up and down with the old lawnmower.

"Here you go. Stanwell Perpetual—lovely scent that one." He pushes the cane into the soil by a pretty pink rosebush in the bed in front of the guest sitting-room window. "That one's the Hedgehog rose, white with good red hips in the autumn. And then we've got Incense by the back door; and Persian Yellow takes over blooming once Incense is finished—both good perfumes."

"I think I should probably be taking notes."

They both smile.

"No need for that dear, the labels will be there to help you. This one's Empress Josephine, large double-cupped, good strong-veined pink and very old, named in memory of Josephine and her magnificent garden at Malmaison. She was known as Rose before she met Bonaparte, always keen on roses, her collection at Malmaison was enormous. Napoleon used to bring back plants for her from wherever he went—shame Helena couldn't get Bertie to do the same."

Dennis smiles.

"We had a few other things on our plates besides collecting plants."

"I'm sure, but I can't help thinking they'd have been far more useful than that silly parrot."

* * *

We walk into the central rose garden and it all starts to get really complicated as they begin to label all the Tea roses.

"This one is Lady Fitzwilliam, great-grandmother to most of the modern roses, double pink blooms and good strong scent. And there's Lady Hillingdon of course, that apricot one on the wall under your bedroom window—one of her special roses that was. I'll put the label in later."

Celia nods.

"Glorious. Semi-double, good strong scent. Damasks and Chinas now I think?"

Oh God, I think we should have made bigger labels.

Dennis puts a label by the low hedge which surrounds the seat, as Celia walks across to the seat on the opposite wall.

"Konigin von Denmark: quartered rosette with an excellent scent, good strong pink."

She puts her bucket down by a beautiful pale-apricot rose.

"Here's Gloire de Dijon—unbeatable for scent, blooms until Christmas. Have you got the label Dennis?"

"No, it must be in one of the other buckets."

I think this might be a good moment to escape before I go into rose overload.

"I think I should go and see how Mum and Ivy are doing, but thank you. Maybe we could leave the labels in for a few days and I might learn a few more names. Lunch is at twelve today remember, so we all have time to get ready afterwards.

Dennis sighs.

"Ivy's pressed my suit. She wants me looking smart."

Celia gives him a sympathetic look.

"I've got a frock to change into—ridiculous fuss really. Be

more appropriate if we wore our gardening clothes. But I suppose we'd better put on a show since the President of the Rose Society is coming. Great honour for us he's agreed to attend. I will admit I'm feeling rather nervous. I do hope we've done Helena justice."

She smiles, and Dennis puts his hand on her arm, and they both stare into the distance.

"I think we've done our best, and that's all she would have wanted."

"Yes."

"It'll be a grand day, you'll see."

"I'm sure it will, but I have been wondering: are we sure Bertie is the right person to speak? Don't you think it might be better if you did it my dear?"

"It's just to say thank you after the medal is presented, Celia. I'm sure he'll be fine. Or you could do it. Or Dennis. But definitely not me. It wouldn't be right."

They both look panicked.

I'm making another mental note to make sure Betty is definitely indoors for the speeches as I walk back to the house and they start sorting through their buckets and rearranging labels and muttering to themselves. The garden is looking stunning—even I can see that—so I'm sure everyone will be impressed, and they'll get all the praise they deserve. And if anyone says anything nasty, I can always bring Betty out, or get Bertie to fire the cannon at them, although I was hoping to keep the cannonage to a minimum today.

Oh God.

By half past two the gardens are packed—people were queuing from half past one—and there are little groups wandering round the orchard, saying hello to the pigs and admiring the fruit trees, with Alfie and Tom proudly standing by in clean Wellies to share fascinating pig facts with anyone who lingers too long. Patrick's in the orchard too, making sure nobody decides the pigs need a run round the orchard to say hello properly, and the chickens are out, keeping a beady eye on everyone or sulking inside the henhouse.

Dennis and Celia are on duty in the rose gardens, making sure no cuttings get snipped, with Mr. Stebbings roaming round on extra cuttings patrol, with his wife, who has been telling me how much he's enjoyed working at the Hall and how lovely it is we invited her to come along today. Mum and Ivy are putting the final touches to the tea stall, with Dan and Ben acting as sherpas; I've promised them twenty pounds each if they help nicely and don't take refuge in their rooms, and so far they've both been great, trotting backwards and forwards with trays and plates and Tupperware boxes. Vicky and Bea have arrived, and they're sitting with Sally by the gates down the lane selling tickets and telling people to park in the field and walk up the lane. They're taking turns wearing the fluorescent jacket Sally brought in from the hotel from the fire-drill cupboard, and doing fifteen-minute stints in the field to make sure people aren't parking like complete idiots. And Florrie and May are on duty in the house, ready to repel petty pilfering in between helping Mum and Ivy. So far, so good.

"There you are my dear. Thought I'd take a drink down to the girls on the gate, good idea? Nothing too pole-axing, thought a jug of Pimm's might be welcome?"

"I think they'd probably prefer tea Bertie—leave it to me. I'll take some down in a minute with some cake."

"Amazing so many people have turned up. Helena would have been so pleased. Bit nervous about my speech, Betty seemed impressed at the first rehearsal, but she's not always the best judge. Hope I've got the tone right. Garden's looking good though, so we shouldn't have any complaints. Think I might take a stroll down to the beach, make sure nobody is trying to arrive by boat and avoid buying a ticket. Locals can be very cunning you know."

I take tea down to the gate, and they all seem to be enjoying themselves immensely, especially since I added cakes to the tray.

"At the last count we'd sold three hundred and forty-six tickets, and that was about half an hour ago. It's amazing, isn't it?"

"It's brilliant Bea, and thanks so much for helping."

"Our pleasure, Vicky's always wanted a fluorescent jacket. She was keen on joining the police a few years ago, until I talked her out of it. She hates violence, and faints at the sight of blood, so I don't think it was ever going to be the ideal career for her."

Sally laughs.

"Probably not Bea, but she's a brilliant parking warden. Look at her making that stupid idiot in the Range Rover move his car into line with the others. And she hasn't even got a whistle. We should have a whistle by rights Moll. Some of them are so lazy you wouldn't believe where they want to park."

"I'll send one down. Anything else you need?"

"Is there more of this cake?"

"About half a ton, last time I looked."

"Great. We'll try to save some for Vicky this time."

Mr. and Mrs. Collins are having tea in the courtyard with their son and daughter-in-law, showing off the new baby while I sort out the extra cake supplies and send Dan down to the gates with a tray.

"This is our grandson, Luke, we thought we'd show him where

we've been staying. Kept them awake all last night he did, so we thought a bit of fresh air might tire him out."

The baby is wearing one of the pale-blue cardigans she knitted for him, over a tiny white sleep suit, waving his hands in that random way newborns do, staring intently at the sky.

"He's beautiful."

He starts to whimper and his mum gets up, looking exhausted, but Mrs. Collins stands up.

"You stay sitting down love. Let me walk him up and down, probably just wants settling, and you haven't finished your tea yet."

She starts pushing the shiny new pram around the courtyard and the baby instantly quietens, much to the evident relief of his mother, who looks pretty shattered.

"Shall we take him for a walk down the lane, give you a proper rest? I promise we won't go far."

She gives her mother-in-law a look of total devotion.

"Yes please."

"Come on then Bill, let's leave them to enjoy their tea in peace for a bit. Never get a moment to yourselves with a new baby. I'll push the pram on the way down, and you can push it on the way back."

I head back to the kitchen and find Ivy and Florrie, scattering sugared rose petals over three more Victoria sponges and buttering more scones. We're loading up more trays when we hear raised voices coming from the hallway. The door which leads into the rest of the house is closed and we've put a Private sign on it, but it sounds like someone doesn't think this should apply to them, so we both tiptoe towards the door to hear what's going on.

"I'm a great friend of Molly's, and she did say there would be tours of the house."

"Are you dear. Well isn't that nice, but she didn't mention anything to me about tours, so I'm sorry, you'll just have to go back outside and look round the gardens like everybody else. This is an Open Garden Day after all, not an Open House."

Good for May—she's definitely the right woman for this particular job.

"I may want to book the bed-and-breakfast rooms. We've got so many visitors this summer, but I will need to inspect them first."

"I'd talk to Miss Molly about that dear, they don't need inspecting, I can tell you that for free. She handles all the B-and-B side of things herself, with Ivy. I can give you a leaflet if you like. Ever so nice they are, got a picture of the gatehouse on too, done it up lovely they have, not quite finished yet but you can see it's going to be a real treat for whoever gets to stay in it, only I know they're getting booked up already. And they don't take just anybody of course. They've got their regulars, and friends of course, and they get priority, which is as it should be. Got to reward loyalty, haven't you dear?"

Ivy and I are holding our hands over our mouths now, trying not to giggle. It sounds very much like Lucinda Langdon-Hill to me, in which case I can't help thinking May is being pretty brave.

"Why don't you go and get yourself a nice cup of tea. Just follow the path round to the stables, get yourself a bit of cake too, give yourself a treat. And all the money goes to charity dear, so be as generous as you can afford, because every little bit helps doesn't it?"

"I do raise a great deal of money for charity May, as you well know, so I'm perfectly familiar with the importance of giving generously, thank you."

"That's good dear. Because they've worked ever so hard, all of them, so I'm glad to hear you'll be making a nice big donation. Say hello to your mum for me, when you next see her, won't you?"

There's the sound of the front door banging rather loudly, and May comes through into the kitchen passage.

"Did you hear her?"

"We did May. And you told her right enough. Bet you enjoyed that didn't you?"

"I did Ivy, I can't pretend I didn't. I used to clean for her mother. Always been a right little madam that one, her mother is the same, or used to be—gone a bit doolally lately. They've stuck her in that home out by Charing Ford, and she never goes to see her. I know that for a fact because Alison from the library goes every week to see her father-in-law—always been a miserable old sod—but they go every week just the same."

Florrie tuts.

"Terrible."

"I know, and the cheek of her. As if I was going to take her round to poke her nose into all your rooms—go through your cupboards too I shouldn't wonder, if she got half a chance. She must think I was born yesterday. Right, now what was it I wanted, oh yes, did you want to change the hand towel in the cloakroom, put a fresh one in? We've had ever so many people in, you know—a few of them hoping for a look round, but most of them have been good as gold. Only I think a fresh towel would be nice."

"I'll get you one May, and would you like a cup of tea?"

"I'd love one pet, if it's no trouble."

"Good, and you too Ivy, and Florrie, sit down for five minutes. You haven't had a break all day. Stay in here in the cool, and I'll make us all a cup of tea, how does that sound?"

May winks at Ivy.

"She's a good girl and no mistake, I can see why you're so fond of her now Ivy. I wouldn't say no to a scone as well pet, if there are any going spare. If they're one of Ivy's, that'll be a nice treat. I've always said she's got a very light hand with scones."

"Coming right up."

Apart from one awkward moment when a nice woman in a pretty straw hat asks me the name of a lovely cream rose and I can't find the sodding label, I manage a quick tour round the garden, and enjoy hearing people telling each other how lovely it is. And it really is, on a day like this, with most of the roses in bloom or in bud, it's almost overwhelming. It does seem miraculous that such small tight little buds turn into such magnificent flowers, with so many different shapes and perfumes, from delicate pale simple ones to great big blousy ones like pom-poms—I can see how you could get completely addicted.

Celia's looking slightly anxious.

"Shall we do the presentation now? The President is ready, if you could find Bertie? Oh, there he is, with Dennis and Ivy, and your mother and the boys. Excellent."

Bertie appears, looking very smart in his Navy blazer, beaming at everyone.

Oh God, I'm suddenly feeling rather nervous.

"Sally's on the cake stall for a bit, and she'll keep an eye on the plants, and Florrie's in the house with May, but I hope they hurry up, because that tea urn needs filling up."

"I'm sure they won't take long Ivy."

I think she's as nervous as I am.

A young woman in a beautiful dress with a lovely rose print claps her hands and asks everyone to be quiet, as the President would like to present an award to the creator of this beautiful garden. Then a very elderly man steps forwards, leaning on a stick and says a few words which most of us can't hear, and hands Bertie a velvet box. Then the young woman takes over again and says the award to honour Helena Harrington-Travers is a rare gold medal, that there is also a plaque for us to display in the garden, and that before we hear from Admiral Travers she would like to add her thanks to those of the president for what has been a truly memorable day. I have a second or two of blind panic wondering who on earth "Admiral Travers" is, until I work out she means Bertie.

He steps forwards and seems to hesitate for a moment, and then retrieves a piece of paper from his pocket, and his reading glasses. There's a silence as he pauses, and then looks up.

"There are so many people to thank for making today such a success, so thank you to everyone for coming, and thank you to the Rose Society for acknowledging just how special this garden is. I know they did try to present the medal to Helena herself, but she was a stubborn girl. Often find the best girls are. She was never one for ceremonies and suchlike. So thank you, on her behalf. I know she would be pleased that her garden has received such an accolade, particularly since she doesn't have to be the one to stand here and accept it." He pauses, and smiles. "The garden is open today as part of the National Garden Scheme, and we're delighted that the county organiser, Lady Wootton, has been able to join us today. Excellent idea, opening gardens to raise money for charity, so thank you for all your help Bobby—much appreciated. And last but not least, thanks must go to Celia and

Dennis, without whom we wouldn't be here today. All I can say is Helena would have been lost without you. As Ernest Dowson once said:

They are not long, the days of wine and roses:
Out of a misty dream
Our path emerges for a while, then closes.

"Poor Ernest came to a sad end, dies penniless far too young, booze got him, just shows you've got to be careful, important not to overdo it."

He pauses to smile at everyone again. Ivy and I are holding hands now, both of us willing him not to start listing his top ten cocktails.

"But for those of us who are lucky enough to make it to a grand old age, it does all turn into something of a mist on occasions like this. And yet there are moments of such perfect beauty and clarity, they quite simply they take your breath away. I've always found that this garden is a good place for that. As usual Wordsworth says it far better than I could ever manage:

The rainbow comes and goes,
And lovely is the rose,
The moon doth with delight
Look round her when the heavens are bare;
Waters on a starry night
Are beautiful and fair;
The sunshine is a glorious birth;
But yet I know, where'er I go,
That there hath pass'd away a glory from the earth.

"And that's what she was, my darling Helena—a true glory of the earth, and her roses are a fitting testament to that. So here's to Helena, and her glorious garden, and to days of wine and roses."

A few people are sniffling now, including me, and there's a small silence before people start to applaud, and Bertie goes very pink—bless him. Even the president seems moved, and shakes Bertie's hand so vigorously it looks like they both might fall down the steps, until Dennis intervenes.

Ivy pats my hand.

"Wasn't that lovely? He's as soft as butter underneath all that bluster, always has been."

"Lovely."

"Look at my Dennis—doesn't he look smart."

"He does Ivy."

"Pleased as punch he is."

"And so he should be."

"Well this won't get the tea urn filled."

"No."

"Lovely though. I'm glad I didn't miss that. I just wish she could have seen it—she'd have been tickled pink."

"Ivy, please don't, or we'll both be in floods."

"That's true enough, and Dennis would probably join us, and Miss Celia's not far off either, or Lady Bobby. Bound to be a bit emotional on a day like this I suppose."

"Yes. Oh, hang on, I think Bertie's waving at us."

"He'll want to fire that silly cannon, you mark my words. Still, on a day like today it almost seems fitting doesn't it?"

"Yes, I suppose it does Ivy."

"Be nice if they could change out of their best things first."

"I'll see what I can do Ivy, but I'm not promising."

* * *

I'm helping Mum and Ivy serve a last few cups of tea and start tidying up, when Dad arrives, looking cross. Here we go again. He's made it pretty clear he's not keen on Mum spending so much time at Harrington, but I know she enjoys it, and she's been so much happier over the past few months, I wish she'd just tell him to get over it. But then I did the same thing with Pete, going along with things to avoid a scene. I was thinking about it the other day, and even though Pete was the opposite of Dad when we first met, gradually he sort of ended up being the same. There was less shouting of course, but he was just as pompous and domineering. Although to be fair Dad hasn't had an affair with his secretary. God knows who would be mad enough to have an affair with Dad, but I bet they wouldn't even *own* a pair of trousers.

"There you are Marjorie—aren't you ready yet?"

"I did say six o'clock, didn't I? It can't be six already, surely?"

"It's a quarter past five Mum. Why are you so early Dad?"

"I've got a round of golf booked. I can't be hanging around waiting for your mother to be finished mucking about with cakes."

"I'll drive her back Dad. There's no need for you to wait if you're busy."

I still don't know why he had to book her car in for a service on Friday, when he knew she was here this weekend; it's almost like he did it on purpose. But rather miraculously Mum seems a bit irritated.

"Or you could collect me after you golf dear, and save Molly the journey. She's been working so hard today, so I think that would be best. Shall we say half past seven? Later is fine—there'll be plenty to do here with all the tidying up. I think I'd better just nip back to the house and get the last of those scones."

Crikey. Dad looks even more surprised than I am.

"But..."

"I'll see you later dear."

I'm clenching my hands to stop myself from clapping as Dad stamps off back down the lane.

"See you later Dad."

Mum winks at me.

Harrington is definitely working its magic again.

I'm collecting up teacups in the gardens when I notice Celia sitting on the seat in the rose garden talking to a young man.

"Molly, this is Edward, my nephew, or is it great-nephew? My sister's daughter's boy—ghastly snobs both of them, probably shouldn't say it, but they are. Edward, stay here and make sure Jasper doesn't escape and try to round up those chickens, or he'll get pecked again. Molly, shall we make some tea? I think Edward could do with a cup."

He stands up.

"I wouldn't want to be a bother Aunt Celia, really, I just wanted your advice. A cup of tea would be lovely, and then I'll head back to town, honestly."

He's got the kind of accent and impeccable manners you only get from years of expensive schools. He'd probably be completely relaxed in a top hat and tails.

"Of course you're not a bother my boy. What are dotty old relations for if not to offer a port in a storm?"

He smiles, and sits back down, clicking his fingers so Jasper jumps up into his lap to be stroked as we walk back to the house.

Ivy has finished stacking cups in the dishwasher and is heading back towards the stables with the tray.

"Could you hang on for a moment Ivy? I'd like your views on this too. Frightful mess."

"What's he done now? I told him not to take Betty outside, but you know what he's like, said he didn't want her to miss out on all the fun. Honestly, he's a caution, he really is."

"Nothing to do with Bertie, no, this is my nephew, Edward. Poor boy has been working in the City in some ghastly job his father lined up for him—not what he wanted to do of course, he's very musical, always has been. But everything has come to somewhat of a crisis. They offered him a promotion, but he decided he'd had enough and resigned. Apparently he had so much holiday due he left the same day—they all work ridiculous hours. He's well rid of the place if you ask me. But it caused the most almighty stink with his parents apparently. They're beyond furious, and the tricky thing is he was living in the basement of their house, he's been trying to save up and get somewhere of his own of course, but he couldn't afford it, and now they've thrown him out. I ask you, how petty can you get? So now the poor boy is homeless, with no job to speak of. Bit of a pickle all round."

Ivy is agog.

"They just threw him out on the street? Their own flesh and blood, that's terrible."

"Quite. My sister has always been the nasty type, could see it ever since she was a girl. Never happy unless she was making someone else miserable—I'm sure you know the type. And he really is talented at the musical thing, always has been, plays the piano beautifully, and the guitar. He's had bookings, in local pubs, that kind of thing, but he's never been able to devote himself to it properly. So now the poor boy needs somewhere to stay and since I'm between houses at the moment I was hoping, if you'd agree, that I could book him in for a few weeks as a PG? I'd be happy to cover the costs now the sale of the house has gone through. I do know it will make more work for both of you, but I would very much like to help him if I can?"

"Well it's not my place to say of course, but I'm sure we could sort something out, since it's an emergency. You wouldn't credit it, throwing him out onto the street like that. I never heard anything like it. If we get busy with B-and-B people at weekends we could always fix up one of the rooms in the attic at a push, couldn't we Miss Molly? Now it's not so chilly at nights, there's that mattress up there already, nearly new that is. And we've got all the lovely new sheets you bought, more than enough to make up another bed. I'll put the kettle on shall I, and then you can take this tray out, and we'll sort out a room for him?"

Celia kisses her on the cheek, which seems to take them both by surprise.

"Bless you both. It will mean so much to him, a safe haven while he gathers his thoughts. I can't thank you enough, if you're sure?"

She's looking at me now.

"Of course Celia. The only problem I can see is Dan. He's wanted to move into the attic ever since we arrived. We might need to make up two rooms Ivy, or we'll have to listen to him moaning on about it, and I did promise I'd get round to it eventually."

Ivy smiles.

"We better sort out two rooms then."

"Oh dear, I really didn't want to put you to any trouble."

"It's no trouble Celia. We've been meaning to make a start cleaning up there. I'll make up the single for now, and we'll sort out the attic during the week."

Ivy nods.

"Is he hungry do you think? I bet he is, I'll make him a sandwich. Does he like ham, or would he prefer cheese? I've got some lovely tomatoes fresh picked today. Or I could make him up a bit of a salad. I've got a ham-and-egg pie in the larder—would he like a slice of that do you think?"

I leave them discussing whether Edward does or does not like tomatoes as I head upstairs. I'd better check on the towels in the bathroom too. Bugger, this isn't exactly what I was hoping for at the end of a long day. I might have a quiet moment in the linen cupboard; actually, I might just stop in there, see how long it takes before someone comes to find me, hopefully with a large gin and tonic. I'm halfway up the stairs when the unmistakable sound of the warning whistle tells me Bertie is about to start cannoning again.

Double bugger.

CHAPTER SIX

Sex, Drugs, and Bacon Rolls

July

Gallica Roses

Thought to be the oldest of all garden roses, Gallicas form dense shrubs in strong pinks and purples, and are often used in potpourri, since their rich fragrance gets stronger as the petals are dried. Notable varieties include Rosa Mundi, with spectacular blush-pink flowers mottled with fuchsia-pink, and a spicy-rich fragrance; Empress Josephine, with tissue-paper-thin ruffled pink-veined petals; and Belle de Crécy, a pink-and-mauve rose fading to a soft violet and lavender with a rich, spicy fragrance.

It's Wednesday morning, and we're late arriving at school.

"Morning Molly, you look knackered."

"Thanks Sal. It's all Roger's fault."

"What's he done now?"

"Alfie, here, take your bag love. The bell will be going in a minute. We had the Now I Am Captain drinks at the stupid golf club last night, with so many toasts and speeches he could hardly stand up by the end."

"What a treat."

"Oh yes, it was great, with Georgina wittering on about all the amazing activities she's got lined up for Henry and Alicia during the summer holidays: she's packing them off on a sailing course, and some art thing where they're dragged round Italy looking at statues, and then a really horrible-sounding Outward Bound thing in Wales. I told her she was welcome to bring them round to meet the pigs and play with my philistine boys, but she didn't seem keen."

"Poor little things, away all term and they don't even get to be home during the school holidays."

"I know, but she might be on to something you know Sal. If we sorted something for our lot, we could sit sipping drinks and doing our nails. Just imagine."

"Sounds great to me. Patrick was talking to Tom about camping last night—I think he meant a night in our back garden, but we could probably organise something different for him if we put our minds to it."

"What, send him off with four boys and a tent on a tour of Britain's cultural hot spots? He's daft Sal, but he's not insane. No, leave it with me. I'll find something for them all to do, something cultural but cheap, just as soon as I've booked the piglets their first flying lessons."

She laughs.

"Weren't you seeing Stephen yesterday? What's Finn got lined up for the summer holidays? I bet Portia is taking him somewhere posh."

"Yes, we went to that new bar on the seafront. He didn't mention Finn, the music was a bit loud, and then we met a few people from his office, out for a drink with their girlfriends."

"It's meant to be very trendy, some of the girls from reception went last week—they got all dressed up."

"Yes, there were quite a few short dresses or tiny vests and bare midriffs. I felt about a hundred. God, this headache really isn't shifting. I think I need more tablets."

"How many have you had so far?"

"Two and a half. I'm saving the other half for when I get home."

She smiles.

"That explains why you're wearing sunglasses. I thought you were just trying to be stylish."

"As if. Oh God, look out, bandits at two o'clock, Miss Cooper is heading our way. Please don't volunteer us for anything Sal, I'm totally full on with the bloody gatehouse."

"Good morning Mrs. Taylor, lovely to see the sunshine, isn't it?"

I think she might be making a crack about my sunglasses. Perhaps she thinks I'm off for a busy day sunbathing.

"We've been hearing all about your new arrivals."

She smiles and looks encouragingly at both of us, which is a shame since I've got absolutely no idea what she's talking about, and neither does Sally, from the look on her face.

"Alfie and Tom are giving us regular updates."

Bugger. It's the sodding pigs.

"The whole class would all love to meet them, and I was wondering, we do usually have a class picnic, at the end of the term, so I thought perhaps we could combine the two? It would be such a treat for the children in the last week of term."

"A picnic, with the pigs?"

She trills out a little laugh.

"Well, perhaps not *with* the pigs, but I'm sure we could find a nice shady spot in a field?"

Bloody hell. If I'm not very quick off the mark here, I'm going to find myself with thirty-two of the little sods swarming all over the place.

I take my glasses off and step forwards.

"I'm so sorry Miss Cooper, I'll make sure to send in treats for the picnic of course, but I can't possibly host it. We've got guests booked in—summer is our busiest time of year, I'm sure you understand. It's one of the things I really miss about teaching actually, apart from the kids of course, the six-week school holidays." I pause. The reference to the long summer holidays will definitely annoy her, just like it used to annoy me when I was teaching, but I don't really care. "If you think they'd really enjoy meeting the pigs though, I'm sure we can arrange for Patrick to bring them in for a visit—couldn't we Sally?"

"Oh yes, of course, he can borrow a trailer from Dave—he farms sheep on Exmoor."

Miss Cooper looks horrified.

"I must be off, so busy, but let us know. Sally, do you want a lift to work?"

"That would be great."

We sit in the car trying to stop laughing.

"I'm fine walking to the hotel Moll."

"I know, but I'm going that way."

"She's got a bloody cheek you know. She never asks any of the county set to do stuff like that, they never lift a finger."

"I think she's got us down as complete idiots after we did the egg stall."

"I think you might have just got us off the idiot list Moll."

"Well I bloody hope so."

I start driving along the coast road to the hotel.

"How was Stephen then—still on top form?"

"Yes and very tanned. He says he spends all the time working but he still manages to get a very impressive tan. He's off again tomorrow for work, so it was just a quick drink. He had some work to finish, and I had to get back for the boys."

"So no snogging?"

"Not in the middle of the wine bar, no. It was a drink Sal, not *Nine and a Half Weeks*."

"I love Mickey Rourke, especially before his face went all weird."

"I know you do."

"I tried that fridge thing once, with Patrick—you know, in the film, where he feeds her food and it drips everywhere?"

"How could I ever forget?"

"He didn't really get it, so we ended up making a sandwich."

"Bless."

We're both giggling again.

"This really isn't helping my hangover Sal. I think I'd better have some more coffee before I start on the gatehouse. We've got to be ready by the weekend so Lola can be our first trial guest, see if we've missed anything. And we've got B-and-B people in tomorrow, and another two next week, so it's a bit full on. And then next Friday the first proper guests are booked in the gatehouse for a week, which is rather scary."

"You'll be fine. I can always come over if you need a hand."

I turn into the hotel car park and wave at two of the chambermaids, who are standing behind the bins having a clandestine cigarette.

"They should both be upstairs cleaning."

"I don't think they expected you to arrive by car, give them a break."

"Oh sure, I'll give them a break. They can have a nice long one if they don't buck their ideas up. They're always disappearing when you want them. I think I'll split them up, put them on different floors. Thanks Moll. Morning Tiffany, Chantelle—all the rooms on your floor finished, are they?"

Vicky is waiting at the gatehouse when I get back, and she's making a pot of coffee, thank God.

"I've brought croissants too; I thought we might need a bit of a boost. Is the water hot?"

"It should be, I set the boiler to twice a day."

"We've only got downstairs to clean and we'll be done."

She hands me a mug of coffee.

"Apart from all the unpacking and tweaking."

"Yes, but that's the fun part. And I prefer to call it 'dressing,' thanks. I 'dress' rooms, I don't 'tweak' them."

"Sorry."

She grins.

"Here."

She hands me a croissant.

"Thanks Vicky, this is just what I need."

"Don't let me forget to take more pictures. I need them for the website. I uploaded the upstairs ones last night—do you want to see?"

"Yes please."

She opens her laptop and starts clicking away.

"Oh Vicky, they look great."

"All part of the service, madam. Right, what's first?"

"Just let me finish this and I'll start on giving the kitchen a proper clean."

"I'll do that."

"No, you do the dressing thing, I've brought the books, they're in the car. I got some for babies too—I asked the boys if they'd let me have some of their old ones, I only wanted a few of their old picture books—they never look at them—but they were so outraged they spent ages sorting through all their books, so I didn't sneak any out. They found all sorts of things they'd forgotten, so all three of them ended up reading, for nearly two hours—it was great. I nearly rang *The Guinness Book of Records.*"

She smiles.

"Daisy does that too. If her room gets too crazy, Bea gets a cardboard box and says we need to take a few bits to charity and she tidies up at the speed of light."

"Top tip—I must try that."

She brings the books in from the car.

"Oh, I love this one, I remember reading it to Daisy. These are great, Molly. We might get a few people bringing babies, they'll love this, I've put a No Children Over Two restriction on for bookings, and they can see there's only one bedroom, so that should take care of anyone wanting to bring bigger kids."

"I keep wondering if we should have put in for planning permission and put an extension on for the bathroom, gone for two bedrooms. But it would have taken ages and blown my budget completely."

"No, it works perfectly as it is. The proportions are right, and Bea says they're getting a lot more picky about people sticking extensions on lovely old buildings like this. Anyway, when you do the stables, you'll have two-bedroom rentals to add to your portfolio, won't you?"

"That sounds good. A portfolio."

"I'm learning the agency lingo. Shall I unpack the rest of the china too?"

"Great, and I'll find the rubber gloves and give the kitchen cupboards a good clean, before Ivy sees them."

We both smile.

It's been great seeing everything starting to come together over the past couple of weeks. The wood floors look transformed, newly sanded and stained, and we've put sisal matting down in the kitchen and underneath the dining table, and a thick wool rug in front of the new log-burning stove. The combination of blues and greens downstairs makes everything look fresh and elegant, acid greens and cornflower blues, with cushions and throws on the slate tweed sofa and armchair. Vicky has worked wonders finding things which look expensive, mixing in cheaper fabrics for cushions and the blinds, and the polka-dot curtains we made for the kitchen. All my boot-fair finds of old blue-and-white china will look great on the dresser, and I've put a large blue glass jug filled with dried alliums from the garden on the windowsill by the front door. The glass sparkles in the sunlight, and the soft, chalky paint on the walls and duck-egg blue in the kitchen somehow brings everything together, even if it did take four coats.

Upstairs we've gone for toasted-almond-and-cream paintwork in the bedroom and a soft pinky cream in the bathroom, with wallpaper Vicky found of March hares leaping, in a pretty pale butterscotch and white. It cost a fortune, but we've only done the end-gable wall, and it makes the whole room look like something you'd see in a magazine feature on luxury bathrooms. There's a plain white freestanding bath in front of the window, which is so big Mr. Stebbings had to take the window frame out to get it in, and a separate shower, and a comfy slipper chair covered in some special soft-white Italian rubber, which Vicky got at a huge discount from one of her trendy suppliers. Even after the discount she negotiated, it still cost a fortune, but with the wallpaper, it makes the room look designerly without being clinical. And I've bought thick white towels and bathmats, and cotton bed linen in creams and caramels, with butterscotch-and-cream check linen curtains with thick linings for guests who don't want to wake up at dawn.

I'm cleaning the kitchen windows when Mum arrives.

"I thought you might like a sandwich. I've brought one for Vicky too. Doesn't it all look lovely?"

"Thanks, Mum. She's just left, she'll be back tomorrow, but I think we're getting there."

"Ivy's been telling me all about the rabbit wallpaper in the bathroom. Can I go up and have a look?"

"Sure, and it's hares, Mum, not rabbits. Go up and see, and I'll put the kettle on."

We sit at the dining table.

"Thanks, Mum, this is great. I didn't know I'd got so hungry."

I've eaten Vicky's sandwich as well as my own.

"It was Ivy who made them. She was making lunch and she was all for sending Dennis down to fetch you both, so I said I'd bring them down. You've worked wonders here, you really have. I quite fancy the idea of booking in for a few nights. Although what your father would say heaven alone knows. What's this?"

She picks up the blue suede folder Vicky left on the dresser.

"We're making up a book for guests, leaflets on local things to do, bus timetables, tide times. Vicky's putting the final touches to the how-to notes tonight: how to switch the boiler on, what day the bins are collected, what day we'll change the linen—that kind of thing."

"This jug is pretty. Is this one you found at one of your markets?"

"Yes, it was only a couple of quid. I thought I'd fill it with roses, if Dennis will let me have any."

We both smile.

"I've been in the garden with him and Celia this morning, starting lifting up paving stones to see if they can work out what's happened to the pipes for the fountain. Did you know she's Flora?"

"Who is?"

"The statue. It's the goddess Flora, and the water she pours from her jug represents Spring, or it will do if they can ever get it working. Edward was helping them. He's such a nice man, isn't he? He was doing most of the lifting until the man arrived to tune the piano."

"Good. I was hoping I'd miss that."

"You should have heard them, he ended up playing tunes with Bertie and Betty while the piano tuner had a cup of tea—they had us all in stitches. I didn't know he could play so well. Terrible about his parents isn't it, sound like nasty sort of people to me. Celia says they're so cross they're not speaking to her either now. I think she's quite enjoying that, though."

"Yes, I think she is."

"She was telling me all about her new cottage, and how Mr. Stebbings will be doing it, before he starts on your stables."

"That's right, if I can get the plans approved and all the paperwork sorted with the bank."

"Celia was saying her new cottage is up on the hillside, behind the harbour."

"Yes, in the lanes, right up at the top."

"She said the garden needs a complete overhaul. It's steep and terraced, but it's got out of control, so she's thinking of alpines, only she doesn't know much about them. She said Helena told her I had a lovely rockery at the old house, so she was hoping I'd give her some tips. Wasn't that nice?"

"Well you did Mum. The whole garden was lovely."

"I've said I'll be happy to help, but I'll want to make sure I have time to help out here too. I enjoy it and I don't care what your father says. I like feeling useful, and it's not him stuck indoors all day, is it? It won't hurt him to have a sandwich for lunch occasionally. I always leave everything ready for him in the fridge, and I always make a proper cooked meal in the evenings."

"I know you do Mum, and you are useful, very useful. But you can come and just sit in the garden and read a book you know. Harrington is a part of you too."

She seems very pleased with this, and gives me a hug.

"Look at the time—I better get to the shops. I want to get some pork chops for supper. But make sure you have an early night tonight—you don't want to get exhausted before the first guests arrive."

I think that ship may already have set sail some time ago, but never mind.

"Thanks Mum."

I'm rather impressed she's decided Dad can cope with the occasional sandwich for lunch. I just hope she sticks to it. We've spent years avoiding him getting into a temper, and mealtimes were always particularly bad, with her looking nervous and fussing. It's no wonder I love picnics so much—they were the only time we didn't have to worry about Dad getting into a strop. We'd sit on the picnic blanket in the garden, or on the beach, with nobody yelling about sitting up straight or not eating too quickly. Actually maybe we can have a picnic at the weekend, if the weather holds, although possibly not within sight of the pigs, not unless we want to share all of our food.

We're in the garden after school, and I'm enjoying a quick ten minutes of deadheading roses while Ben picks peppers and tomatoes for supper. It's surprisingly relaxing wandering around with a basket snipping off fading flowers and taking the petals indoors to dry. I'll cut the lavender soon and dry that as well. On days like this I could seriously get into this gardening lark.

"Mind you don't go cutting any of those for your vases."

"Without permission Dennis, would I dare? Ben's in the kitchen garden picking tomatoes for tea, I hope that's okay?"

"I've just seen him. He's got all the makings of a proper little gardener, that one—reminds me of our Michael at that age."

"He really enjoys it. I was just going to take these in and make some tea. Would you like a cup?"

"No, I'm keeping out of Ivy's way. She's in a mood today, always the same the day after our Michael phones."

"You must both miss him. How long has he been in Australia now?"

"Nearly ten years. The littlest one was born out there. She's moved her mother out there now, my daughter-in-law, she lives in a bungalow near them. Wouldn't fancy that if I was him, your mother-in-law moving all that way to keep an eye on you. Ivy's mother was bad enough, when we were first married, always popping round to poke her nose in, but you move round a lot with the navy, and that soon got rid of her. Still, he's got himself a good job and a big house with a pool and all sorts, so he made the right decision."

"It's such a long way though. Have you ever thought of going over to see them all?"

Please God he doesn't say, "Yes, we're going next week," or I will be well and truly buggered as Uncle Bertie would say.

"Not really. His wife, Christine, well she's a nice enough girl, but she and Ivy fell out over the wedding. Ivy was only trying to help, but Christine and her mother wanted everything done their way, and then, well, it just carried on that way when Joshua was born. Which I suppose is to be expected—a girl wants her mother at a time like that. I know that. But Ivy felt shut out. We didn't have the space for them to stay with us, and money was a bit tight, and one thing led to another and they stopped coming. And then they told us they were emigrating, and that was that. She and Ivy are too alike—that's the trouble. They both said things they shouldn't have said, silly little things. I bet if you asked them, neither of them could remember it now, but one thing led to another, and they ended up not speaking. Still don't. He rings us every few weeks, and we speak to the boys, but she never comes on the line."

"What a shame."

"It is. And Ivy minds, I know she does. She won't say, but I can tell."

"Can't we do something?"

He smiles.

"I've been thinking about that. There's no point trying to get Ivy to back down, got to go round sideways if you want her to change her mind—after being married to her so long, I've learnt that if I've learnt nothing else. But it'll be our golden wedding the year after next, so I thought I'd see if he'd come over for that. What do you think?"

"I think that's a brilliant idea, but why wait? Why don't we have a party for her birthday and invite them over for that. Actually, when is her birthday?"

"The end of September, but she doesn't like a fuss. Well, she says she doesn't, but I'd never hear the end of it if I forgot."

"Do you think they'd be able to come?"

"Our Michael's like me—anything to keep the peace, but I know it bothers him, so I know he'll try his best. And Ivy would be tickled pink. But I think we should keep it quiet, or she'll fret about it, and you know how she gets when she's got a bee in her bonnet. And I'd want to ask Mr. Bertie—he's very good at keeping secrets, and he knows her very well, I'd want to have his opinion. I wouldn't feel right not discussing it with him."

"Of course, and if he thinks it's a good idea, they can stay in the house. I can reserve the B-and-B rooms and she won't suspect a thing. I'll make up a name, and it will be my treat Dennis—the party and everything. If they can get cheap flights, then I'd really like to cover everything else. I've been wanting to find a way to thank you both."

He smiles.

"Let's see what Mr. Bertie thinks, but I think you might be on to something. And you're right, no point in waiting. Been long overdue as it is."

He's whistling as he walks towards the orchard, unlike Ivy who is banging saucepans around and muttering when I get back into the house.

"Is Mr. Bertie still out there? Silly man won't sit still for more than five minutes before he's off making mischief somewhere."

"I'm not sure Ivy. I haven't seen him."

"I've made you an apple pie for supper; it's in the bottom oven keeping warm."

"Thanks Ivy."

"Mr. Edward asked for it special, poor thing. He says he's always been partial to apple pie. I don't think anyone has fed him properly for years."

"Probably not. It's lucky he's here now so you can rescue him before he gets rickets."

She hesitates, and then smiles.

"I like to see people eating up."

"That's good, because we all love your food."

"Apart from Mr. Bertie—he only picked at his lunch today, he's always been a fusspot. And I know he's never been that keen on liver and onions, but it builds you up. I've got some for our dinner tonight, with a bit of bacon. No doubt Dennis will twist his face as well, but it's good for you, so he'll just have to lump it."

"Right."

Bloody hell. I seriously hope she likes the surprise party, if Bertie gives it the green light, or I think we might all find ourselves eating quite a bit of liver. Yuck.

"Mum, what's for supper?"

I'm half tempted to say "liver and onions," just to see Dan's face.

"Tuna quiche and salad, and Ivy's made an apple pie for pud."

"Great. Shall I lay the table?"

"Yes please love, although it'll be a while yet."

"Okay, I'll do my homework first, and then I'll set the table."

"Thanks love."

"It's fine, Mum, I know how hard you've been working."

He trots off upstairs, and Ivy and I exchange glances.

"Either he's starving, he's broken something, or he wants something. Fingers crossed it's food he wants."

She nods.

I'm making a salad with the tomatoes Ben picked, and I can't resist eating a couple while I'm chopping. They taste so different from shop-bought ones, it's the same with the lettuce and the cucumber—straight from the garden, they taste so much fresher. And the really brilliant bit is I don't have to be the person who grubs about in the mud growing them. Dan is still being hyperhelpful, and is now offering to shut the chickens up for the night later on, if I could just let him know when I'd like him to do it.

"Okay, I give up, what have you broken?"

"I don't know what you mean, can't I just be helpful without getting the third degree?"

"Okay, sorry, so what do you want?"

"Nothing."

"Really?"

He grins.

"Well, it's just this party I'd like to go to, but we can talk about it later—it's no big deal."

"Nice try love. What party?"

"Robbie's mum has already said he can go. It's on Saturday night, in a couple of weeks, on the beach. One of the lifeguards, Jack, he's eighteen, and he's invited everyone from the club, and loads of his mates too, for a beach party, with a barbecue. It's going to be epic."

"Eighteen is a lot older than fourteen love."

"Yes, but I'm nearly fifteen."

"Not until next month you're not, and you know what I mean. I'm guessing people will be drinking, and doing all sorts of other things too probably."

"Oh God, this isn't going to be another one of your sex-and-drugs chats is it? Please, they're so embarrassing."

"Not as embarrassing as finding yourself with a toddler before you're old enough to vote, trust me."

"Please don't go into one Mum. I know the drill."

He adopts a rather tragic pose.

"'Make sure it's someone special, make sure you're careful, watch out for scary diseases, and watch out for naughty men who try to get you into their cars,' blah blah blah. I promise, okay? If the glorious day ever comes, I promise I'll be careful."

"Good. And I'm not sure anyone would try to get you into their car Dan, not unless they were completely insane."

He grins.

"Anyway I wouldn't start looping out about it Mum, I haven't even persuaded her to talk to me yet."

"Who?"

"Freya?"

So it's still Freya then, oh dear. Even as his mother, and hugely biased, I can see she might be a tiny bit out of his league: tall, blond, and looking every inch the poster girl for the joys of surfing, she's also clever and in the same top classes at school as Dan.

"Don't you ever talk in History or English? She's in your group for those isn't she?"

"Yes, and sometimes we do, but not out of school."

"Girls like clever boys love, if they're clever too. Just try to relax and be yourself."

"Like I'm going to be able to pull that off. Last time I tried to talk to her, my voice went all weird."

"Focus on school, where she can see you shine."

"There's only three weeks left before the holidays, and anyway, I think 'shine' might be pushing it a bit Mum."

"Not if you do your homework. Won't you have a holiday project, for English?"

"Yes, Mr. Ellingham has already told us, but its crap, he wants us to write about our summer. Honestly. Couldn't he have thought of something more boring?"

"What books are on your course list for next year?"

"Pride and stupid Prejudice, and I've seen the film, and I don't get why that wanker Darcy doesn't just get on with it."

"Probably the same reason you don't declare your intentions to Freya."

"I would if I had a great big house like he does."

"But he does, and she turns him down."

"Yes, but that was his own fault, for being such an arse."

"Maybe you could write about different kinds of prejudice, things you've seen over the summer."

"What prejudice? It's pretty cool down here Mum."

"Everyone is prejudiced against the tourists though, aren't they?"

"Yes, but they deserve it. Although Mr. Ellingham did say we could make stuff up too, so you can write about the summer you wished you had, and compare it to the one you actually got, so maybe I could do some *Pride and Prejudice* stuff in that. Cool. Thanks Mum."

I think Mr. Ellingham is being rather brave asking teenage boys to write about the kind of summer they wished they'd had. I'm guessing girls in bikinis may feature in quite a few of the essays which get handed in.

"Just make sure you write something he can read out to the class, something that shows what a creative genius you are."

He grins.

"And I'd like to read it, when you're done."

He tuts.

"So can I go then, to the party?"

"I suppose so, if you promise to be sensible. I'll come and pick you up, at eleven?"

"It won't even be properly started by then Mum. And you can't come and get me—everyone will get cabs."

"Midnight and I'll come and collect you. You haven't got money for cabs, and neither have I. And I won't sleep until you're home safe. So take it or leave it."

He tuts again, but he's smiling as he goes upstairs.

I've just settled Alfie into bed when Stephen calls.

"Hi Molly. Bea tells me the gatehouse is nearly finished."

"Yes, it's looking great, mostly due to Bea and Vicky—they've been brilliant. You must come and see. How is . . . where are you again?"

"Barcelona, and it's good, thanks. The job's going well, and I'm thinking about opening a European office. We're up for a couple of big projects, and if we get them—which I'm reliably informed we will—then the new office will be part of the deal."

"How exciting."

"Yes, it is rather. I'll still be based at home of course—got to keep the core business ticking over. Anyway, enough business. I'm calling to invite you to a ball."

"Sorry?"

"White ties, tiaras, that sort of thing. Lucinda Langdon-Hill is on the committee. She's been badgering me about tickets, they do it every year, and it's usually pretty good. Chance to wear a long frock and glam up for the evening. They do all rather go to town with their outfits."

Oh God.

"I haven't actually got a long frock Stephen. I haven't got many short ones either to be honest. But thank you, for the invitation."

"Good excuse to go shopping."

"It doesn't really sound like my sort of thing but . . ."

"It raises lots of funds for charity. Last time it was retired racehorses I think, and the local Tory party."

"All causes dear to my heart."

He laughs.

"There is that."

"I've only just managed to persuade Lucinda that I don't want to be on her Ladies Who Lunch list. I don't want to start her off all over again. I'm sorry, but thank you for asking me."

"Well, if you're sure, I suppose I can see if Bea is free that night—it will be very useful for work."

Poor Bea.

"That's a good idea."

"I'll fix up another dinner when I'm back?"

Oh dear, I'm not sure I've handled this very well. But seriously, a long frock and a load of hideous county types. I'd rather stick pins in my legs.

"That would be lovely."

"Night Molly."

"Night Stephen, and thanks for calling."

Oh God, I've done it again. Thanks for calling. Christ. I know he's smiling now—I can almost hear it.

"My pleasure."

It's Saturday afternoon and we've got a full house. Lola and Tre arrived late last night, and Sam and his wife Angie have just arrived, with their kids, Silas and Ruby. I'd forgotten how much I like Pete's brother, and Angie arrived with two bags full of the kind of treats you don't often buy for yourself: posh pasta, jars of artichokes and peppers, a huge chunk of Parmesan, all sorts of delights from a smart Italian deli, as well as a fabulous collection of chocolates and a big box of Turkish Delight. So she's a strong contender for Star Guest of the Year. They're out in the orchard while the kids have a run around and meet the pigs, and I'm in the kitchen with Lola, making coffee.

"So you really liked it then—no snags at all?"

"It's great, comfy, but gorgeous too, and the bathroom's perfect. Very designerly. Talking of which, what's the latest from the architect?"

"He's away again; we're having dinner when he's back, at least I think we are, if he's got over me refusing to go to the local Tory ball with him. As if."

"So you'll be selling the house and giving all the money to poor people will you?"

"No, but that doesn't mean I want to go to a ball with the kind of local snooters who think poor people are scum."

"You could have worn your necklace."

"Oh well that's different then. If I can wear an emerald necklace which isn't really mine and I get to show off, I'm definitely going. What was I thinking?"

She shakes her head.

"Alright Comrade, but if I find you a champagne socialist ball to go to in town, then will you wear your emeralds? I know property is theft, but until the glorious revolution Helena left them to you, so they're yours. And I want to see you wearing them."

"Sure. At least the other guests wouldn't make you want to shoot yourself, or them. They still go hunting round here you know. Some of them make Attila the Hun look like a wet liberal."

"Leave it with me. Actually, have we got any champagne? We could have a practice run."

"Not that I know of, but ask Bertie—he's in charge of booze supplies, and he's got all sorts stashed away in that cellar. Let's take the coffees out."

Lola is watching Eddie, who has turned out to be a very handy pig rustler and is busy getting Squeak back the right side of the electric fence after another dash for freedom before he knows what's happening and starts to eat Eddie's Wellies.

"You didn't mention he was so gorgeous, he could get gigs as a model if the music thing doesn't pan out."

"Who, Squeak?"

"No you idiot, your young Mr. Edward. The upper-class Burberry look is very in right now. Very postmodern *Brideshead Revisited* meets *Downton Abbey*, and all that bollocks. Does he have a tweed suit?"

"I haven't asked him."

"I was watching *Cool Hand Luke* the other day, and there's a touch of the young Paul Newman about him you know. He was gorgeous, a nice man too apparently, which is rare. He could be devastating in white tie and tails."

"Are we still talking about Paul Newman?"

"You should hold a posh dinner party, make everyone dress up. You'll see what I mean. He'll look stunning. And he keeps looking at you, I've seen him."

"He does not."

"He does, when he thinks you won't notice. If you got a move on you could have a very diverting summer darling. Try a little flirting to start things off, bring him out of his shell."

"He's already out of his shell Lola. He's thrown everything up in the air, stood up to his parents, which according to Celia takes some doing, and now he's trying to work out what he wants to do next. The last thing he needs is a middle-aged woman trying to flirt with him. And anyway, I've no idea how to do flirting, I'm out of practice, and you were always the expert, even when we were at university, you were the one who could flirt better than anyone else I know."

"First of all you are not middle-aged. Because if you are, then I am, and that's completely ridiculous."

"I'm forty next year Lola, almost old enough to be his mother."

"Forty is the new thirty, and no way is that middle-aged. And unless you had him when you were twelve, you're not old enough to be his mother, so stop it right now. Just stick on something tight with a few buttons undone and see what happens."

"Does the phrase 'mutton dressed as lamb' ring any bells?"

"No, but 'lamb dressed as mutton' does. Honestly darling, what about that green skirt I gave you at Christmas? I bet you haven't even worn it once."

"The one I'm meant to wear with black woolly tights and boots, so I look like I'm channeling Robin Hood? Anyway it's way too hot for summer—I'd be boiling hot."

She laughs.

"Oh alright, but wear a dress tonight for the beach party, promise?"

"No, I'm wearing jeans, and so will you unless you want a sandy bottom."

"I give up."

"Good."

"It's a crying shame though."

"Maybe, but at least this way nobody will end up actually crying."

The pigs are playing football with the kids, with the new toy Ben found for them on the Web: a ball with holes in it—you fill it with pellets of food, which fall out of the holes whenever the ball rolls. They spend hours pushing the ball around with their snouts, running as fast as they can, with accompanying squeaking and grunting every time pellet of food falls out.

Sam is very impressed.

"I didn't know pigs played football."

"They do down here."

He laughs.

"Are they always that muddy?"

"No, but the mud helps stop them getting too sunburnt, so the boys dug a wallow for them. It was either that or keep covering them in sunscreen."

"Seriously?"

"I'm afraid so."

He grins.

"It's a whole new world, isn't it love?"

"Tell me about it. Have you met the chickens yet?"

* * *

Angie and Cool Hand Eddie help me to make a quick supper of spaghetti and salad, and then we head down to the beach. I surreptitiously try to see if I can pick up any signs of longing looks, but I can't, and anyway it's making me go all self-conscious. It's bound to be Lola imagining things, just like she did when I started going out with Pete and she set me up on a blind date with Luke Harris, who she claimed was keen on me, only it turned out he was madly in love with Lola and spent the whole night talking about her and asking me for top tips to get her attention.

The boys have been planning a campfire for days, collecting twigs and persuading Eddie to saw up some of the branches and a couple of big logs from the wood store drying in the stables. We've got hot dogs and veggie burgers, and marshmallows to toast on sticks, and we've taken folding chairs down for any grown-ups that aren't keen on sitting on the sand. Celia and Bertie are helping them avoid setting fire to their sticks, or each other, while Sam helps me carry extra rugs down, and a bag full of towels and spare tops.

"Are we going swimming then?"

"Not in theory, no, but someone is bound to fancy a paddle and end up falling flat on their face. My money's on Alfie."

"I think my Silas might give you a run for your money on that one. Fancy a quick wager: a fiver for the first person whose kid ends up soaked?"

"You're on."

"I can't believe how big the three of them are now. The country life definitely agrees with them, looks like it agrees with all of you, you look ten years younger darling, you really do. Unlike

Pete—who looks older every time I see him. I met him for a drink a few weeks ago, god, he can be boring. He's seriously pissed off you've got this place isn't he?"

"Yes."

We both smile.

"So I wanted to say, well, I'm sorry my brother is such a total arse, and if you ever need anything, just call, okay? Me and Ange talked about it, and I promised I'd mention it. Not that it looks like you'll need any help. You're making a real go of it here—anyone can see that—but if you ever do, family comes first and all that bollocks, yes?"

"Thanks Sam."

"I mean it. I don't want you thinking all the men in our family are tossers."

"I hope not, or I'm in big trouble when my three are grown up."

"Good point. Right. Okay, just wanted to say, you know, well done, and sorry about my idiot brother. Do you think there'll be any marshmallows left by the time we get back down there?"

"Not a chance. But I hid two more packets, in the bag with the towels."

"Good thinking. Come on, I'll race you."

Alfie is already soaked by the time we get down to the beach, and is now standing wrapped in a rug while Dan tries to dry his T-shirt by holding it very close to the fire.

"Did we say a fiver?"

Sam sighs.

"You can go right off people you know Molly, right off."

"Alfie, come here, I've got dry things in the bag, but you're not to go in the sea again, promise? Dan, thanks love. Just give it to me. He can put it back on if he's going for another paddle, and it'll be wet again in no time."

"I love it here Molly, it's brilliant. Is it always like this?"

"Not in the middle of winter, no Angie."

She smiles.

"But no regrets, about leaving London?"

"No, we all love it here now."

Lola raises her glass.

"I'll drink to that. What about you Eddie, anything you miss? Were you one of those City boys who spend all day on the phone yelling 'Buy six million at forty-three and sell at seventy'?"

"Good God no, nothing so exciting. I worked at one of the big law firms, in the property division. I had no idea what was going on half the time, I was in Wills and Estates before that, and that was even worse."

"I had no idea you could draft wills Edward."

"Please don't tell me you haven't got a will Aunt Celia."

"Of course I have my boy. Helena introduced me to her chap, sorted it all for me in no time."

"Well, thank heavens for that. You wouldn't believe the number of times people ended up asking me to write their will at one of Mother's hideous dinner parties, or to look at one they wanted to challenge—it was appalling."

Lola laughs.

"Like when you're a doctor and people tell you all their symptoms over supper?"

"Something like that, yes."

"I wonder if people do that to Mr. Crouch. I must ask him when I see him next week."

"Mr. Crouch?"

"Helena's solicitor—well mine now too, I suppose. He made me update mine when I inherited Harrington. Oh, I've just thought, I could ask him if he has any part-time work available if you like, I'm sure they could always use a whizz kid from London, if you're interested?"

"Less of the whizz I'm afraid. I was completely out of my depth most of the time, and the rest of time, well, you know those films where people turn to stone, or ice, and you see them slowly freezing up, from their fingertips, stuck in the same position for years? Well, it was just like that. I could literally feel myself calcifying."

Bertie raises his glass.

"Good for you my boy. Here's to melting hearts of stone."

We all raise our glasses.

"Mum, Ben has knocked my marshmallow off my stick on purpose. Again."

"I'm sure he didn't Alfie."

"Mine's fell off too."

Silas holds up a rather charred-looking stick.

"Here, let me help you. The trick is avoiding getting too close to the flames."

Bertie puts another marshmallow on his stick and pats Alfie on top of his head.

"Anyone for a cocktail, liven things up? We could send one of the ankle biters up for supplies. Oh, thank you Eddie, good man. Just bring a selection down, and I'll see what I can come up with."

* * *

Thankfully I remembered I was making breakfast for everyone last night, so I refrained from cocktailing, and manage to make endless bacon rolls for everyone this morning without requiring the assistance of painkillers. I've got the bacon-roll production-line routine down to a fine art now. It's the breakfast of choice for Dan and Alfie, with Ben opting for a fried egg roll instead, now I've finally managed to convince them they're not allowed to order a Full English just because we've got B&B guests. And Mr. Stebbings and his workforce were very partial to a midmorning bacon roll too. So if the holiday-rental idea doesn't work, I could always buy a van and drive round selling bacon rolls.

Lola and Tre still haven't emerged, so the rest of us sit reading the Sunday papers in the library, while I work out how long the leg of lamb will take to cook. Sam seems fairly perky too, but I think he's pretty used to the morning after the night before.

Eddie brings in some more coffee, and hands Sam a cup.

"I hear you want to run away to the circus. Let's hear what you've got then?"

"Oh God, right now?"

"Yup, unless you've got something better to do?"

"No, of course, it's just, well, I didn't want to presume, or be pushy or anything, so I haven't prepared anything."

"Well that's your first mistake mate, you need to get over that if you want to survive in the music business. Be as pushy as you can, whenever you can. Ange my darling, can you make sure the kids don't barge in. And Molly and Celia, if could you give us ten minutes—if that's alright with you Bertie?"

"Thrown out of my own library, thin end of the wedge if you ask me."

He pauses, and pats Eddie on the shoulder.

"Best of luck my boy."

Eddie sits down at the piano, looking white-faced and nervous.

"Could you possibly take Betty with you? She does tend to join in."

We stand outside the door, while Eddie sings two songs I've never heard before. Celia is holding my hand, quite tightly actually.

Suddenly the door opens.

"What are you all doing standing here whispering? He's not half bad, is he? Right, are we having a walk before lunch, or what?"

He turns to Eddie, who is still sitting at the piano, looking rather shocked.

"I'll make a few calls. I'm not promising anything, but you should definitely try to get a few gigs in local pubs, that kind of thing, and keep writing—that last one was pretty decent."

"Thank you, so much. I can't tell you what it means to me to have someone tell you you're not completely hopeless."

"I've been telling you that for ages Edward."

"Yes, sorry Aunt Celia."

"Anyone for a sharpener before lunch? About that time I think. Might fire the cannon later. Young Edward can be my second in command—Dennis has showed him the ropes, round off the weekend nicely."

Oh God.

"Polly put the kettle on."

"Thank you Betty, I was just about to. And Bertie, could we

leave the cannon until after lunch? I'm not sure Lola and Tre are up yet."

"Fair enough."

"Knob."

"I've no idea why she keeps saying that."

Sam is trying not to laugh.

Oh God.

Hi Molly. Sorry it's late, but I wanted to let you know straightaway."

"It's fine Vicky—I was just watching telly. Let me know what?"

"We've got another booking, for October, so that's all of August, three weeks in September, two in October, and one in November, and they booked at the four-hundred-fifty-pounds-a-week rate, so I think we should leave the autumn rates as they are."

"That's brilliant Vicky, completely brilliant."

"I thought you'd be pleased. Did Lucas and Jenny arrive okay?"

"Yup, and they loved the grocery basket. And the baby's really sweet—just four months old, I think they said. I even got a quick cuddle while they unpacked the car—I'd forgotten how much kit babies need. Lucas is a graphic designer, isn't he?"

"Yes, I don't know either of them that well. Jenny knows my friend Carla. I think I met them once at a party."

"Well, your word-of-mouth campaign is definitely working. And you could see he was impressed, particularly with the bathroom."

"Well that's good because I've been thinking that we could

really go to town on the bathrooms in the stables—they'll be bigger, for a start."

"I've been thinking the same. I've started collecting pictures. I've seen a fabulous copper bath. It costs a fortune, but it looks amazing."

"Ooh, I love them. Have you decided about Christmas yet? It's fine to close until January, you know. Lots of places do."

"I think we'll close over Christmas, and that way we can all have a proper break, but let's leave it open for New Year and see if we get any bookings."

"Great. I thought I'd call by tomorrow and say hello. Check they've got everything they need."

"Come up for a coffee afterwards, and tell me what they say."

It's Sunday morning, and I've just taken some fresh eggs down to Lucas and Jenny in the gatehouse. They seem to be loving it, and are already talking about booking another week next spring. I must remind Vicky to add a playpen to the baby kit we're going to offer as an added extra for bookings. With a decent travel cot and a highchair, and a few other bits of essential kit, like a steriliser, it will save people lugging all their stuff with them. We've tried the idea out on Jenny and she thinks people would be more than happy to pay a bit extra. So everything is going really well, apart from Dan's party last night.

He's sitting at the kitchen table, looking very pale. He could barely walk straight when I picked him up, and I had to stop the car for him to be sick, so I'm still half-furious with him, and half-relieved I insisted on picking him up. God knows how drunk he would have got if he'd stayed out much later.

"You're very quiet this morning Danny boy."

"I think he might have his first hangover Bertie."

"Poor chap. Shall I make him one of my special pick-you-ups?"

"Don't you dare. He's not old enough for any of that nonsense, and when he is, if he wants to go out and get into a total state, he needs to know how rubbish you feel the next day."

Bertie chuckles and wanders off.

"Dan."

"Mum please, I know. I feel totally crap. Please don't give me a lecture. I promise I won't do it again. I was only drinking cider, and that was fine, but then, well, some people had other stuff."

"Right. And they held you down and forced you to drink it, did they?"

"Mum. Please."

He really does look like he's suffering.

"Dry toast, and a glass of water?"

"Yes please. And can I have some headache tablets, please?"

"I'll get you some paracetemol."

I leave him sitting huddled and looking tragic, sipping water, while Ben and Alfie rather uncharacteristically manage a quiet breakfast, giving him the occasional sympathetic looks before heading outside to annoy the chickens.

"Thanks Mum."

"What for?"

"For coming to get me, and for not going on about it."

"I'm not done yet love. I'm just waiting until you feel a bit better."

He tries to smile, but can't quite manage it.

"Seriously Dan."

"I know, and I won't be doing it again, don't worry Mum. I mean, I will be drinking, obviously, but not like that. Some of them could hardly walk, you know."

"Were there drugs?"

"God, Mum."

"Dan."

"No."

"Dan."

"A few of them were smoking stuff. That's all."

"Right."

"Not me, so don't go into one, you've gone about it enough. I know it can be dodgy, and anyway I'm in training, I can't start getting stoned out of my head if I want to make the squad. Okay?"

"Okay. But this is serious Dan. And I'll know."

"From your bat-mother radar?"

"Yup. Or you'll tell me, because you'll feel even more crap than you do now."

"I don't think that's possible Mum."

"It is. Trust me. Particularly if one of you ends up drowning or chucking themselves off a cliff because they're out of their head on God knows what and think they can fly."

There was a story in the papers a few weeks ago which I made sure I showed to him.

"All sorts of terrible things can happen."

"I know. Clare Harris ended up snogging Tom Ledley, and she hates him."

He reaches over and holds my hand.

"I'm not a total twat Mum."

"You were doing a good impression last night."

"I know, buts it's hard, people were smoking and stuff and they all looked pretty chilled."

"Did they? Well, that's the tricky bit, isn't it love, like Russian roulette: five times you're fine and looking chilled, and then the sixth time it scrambles your brain and you end up thinking you're Batman."

He grins.

"I know. Although they were all so pissed, I don't see how any-one could have made it onto anything high enough to jump off."

"Was Freya there?"

"Yes. She sat with us for a bit—me and Robbie—and then she was dancing. She's a really good dancer, but then she had to go because her dad turned up really early—can you believe it?"

"And did she drink too much as well?"

"No, she was pretty cool actually. She was even cool with her dad."

I like the sound of this girl more and more.

"Me and Robbie talked about it, and I'm going to play the long game—get fitter and get on the squad, and then I'll make my move. Robbie's going to do the same, with Emma, only he'll have to be quick, because she was dancing with Mark Dawkins and he's a total shagger, and he's nearly eighteen. We're going to sign up for training after school in the gym, running and stuff, and then get the late bus."

"That sounds like a good idea."

"We can only hope. That's right Mum, isn't it—you've got to have hope?"

"Yes love. And I hope you learnt something else last night too. It's a good job Freya didn't see you in such a state. Was Finn okay?"

"You can't ask me that Mum. You'll only tell his dad."

"I won't, I promise."

"He was fine."

"But?"

"He was showing off a bit. I didn't see that much of him actually. He was off with his friends, all the rich kids—they were the ones who were smoking and everything. They've got the money for it."

"Oh, right. Well, that's a shame."

"He's a bit of a wanker actually Mum."

"Oh right. And what does nearly throwing up in my car make you, a living saint?"

"I said I was sorry Mum—please."

"Okay, subject closed. Go back and have a bit more sleep. You'll feel better later. But that had better be the first and last time I ever see you like that, Dan, understand? Otherwise you and I will be having some very serious talks."

"Will you tell Dad? I could really do without a lecture from him too. Not that I care what he thinks, but you know what he's like."

"You do care what he thinks, and yes, I do know what he's like. So no, I won't. I trust you. God knows why, but I still do. But you really frightened me Dan. Don't ever do it again."

"I won't Mum, I promise."

"And when you're feeling better, I'll have a list of jobs for you to do."

"Okay."

"Really boring jobs."

"Okay. And thanks Mum. You're pretty cool, you know that?"

"But not chilled."

He smiles, and then winces.

"No, not chilled."

"Well that's a relief."

Dan sleeps for most of the day, and Ben and Alfie are busy in the orchard. Apparently we are now building a tree house, so Bertie sits shouting instructions from his chair in the shade of one of the pear trees, while Eddie does the heavy lifting whilst simultaneously trying to avoid bowling over small boys or piglets with the planks. They're all scampering about in utter bliss, and the chickens are enjoying all the activity too, so there's a fair bit of fluffing of feathers and little dashes across the orchard to check they're not missing anything. Gertie's already taken to perching on the ladder, so perhaps they think it's a new henhouse.

I'm having dinner with Stephen later in a smart restaurant in Ilfracombe, so I wash my hair and try to make myself look respectable in the navy silk dress I bought for Open Garden Day. I'm wearing the navy high heels Lola made me buy for a wedding a few years ago, as well as the pretty silk scarf with the pink-and-orange roses pattern; if I could find the hat she also made me buy, I'd probably look like I was off to another wedding rather than going out for dinner, but never mind.

Celia and Eddie are in charge of bedtime, so I'm reminding them that Alfie needs to be in bed by eight, when Stephen arrives, wearing white linen trousers with a cream linen jacket, which makes me feel rather overdressed.

"Good evening everyone. Ready to go Molly? I've booked us a table outside and they don't tend to hold them for long, they're getting so popular now."

"Sure, I'll just get my bag."

Bertie gives him a rather pointed look.

"Evening, Bertie."

"Been playing cricket?"

"Er, no, I've been working. Lovely evening, isn't it?"

"Not sure about that. Storm brewing if I'm not mistaken. Molly my dear, you look lovely. Hope you have an enjoyable evening. Right, I'm off on patrol."

We walk towards the car.

"What's he patrolling?"

"The beach. In case of invasion."

"By who?"

"The French, the Russians, who knows, could be anyone. He's particularly on the alert for weekend sailors at the moment after that one ran aground up the coast in that great big yacht."

He smiles.

"Right."

"You can mock, but if any idiot yacht owners who can't sail their boats end up on our beach, they better be ready for Bertie to fire a warning shot or two."

"Surely he wouldn't?"

"If one of us doesn't get there quick enough he would. Dennis had to stop him firing at someone who'd stopped for a picnic a few years ago, or so he says. I think he was just going to give them a bit of a fright."

"I should hope so. He could get arrested."

"Not for firing blank powder he can't. Dennis has looked into it."

The restaurant is crowded, but the view over the beach is terrific, and it's rather glamorous sitting under umbrellas with the lights twinkling and the outdoor heaters on low.

"Do you fancy fruits de mer, they do a sharing plate, looks rather good?"

I'm not a huge fan of shellfish, but he seems very keen.

"Lovely."

The wine arrives, and the shellfish, and I eat a prawn and a little bit of the crab, and manage to avoid anything which looks like it might still be able to swim if you threw it back into the sea. Stephen doesn't seem to notice and is busy slurping away at oysters and winkling out cockles with a special fork with a prong.

"This is delicious, I must bring Finn here, he loves this kind of thing. I was meant to see him this morning, but Portia called to cancel. He was still in bed feeling a bit under the weather after the party I think. Probably just as well—we've got so much work on at the moment, the extra time was extremely useful."

"I'm not surprised. Dan was in a terrible state when I picked him up."

"Not very cool, having your mum collect you, is it? Finn insists I give him the money for cabs. He's made that perfectly clear. Parents not required. I remember being the same at his age. They've got to learn, make their own mistakes."

"I've never really got that, the leaving-them-to-make-their-own-mistakes thing. It's not like you just sit there while they crawl towards the fire when they're babies, and it just gets more dangerous as they get older."

"Well, no, obviously. But they need their freedom."

"Of course, but within limits, don't you think? They still need you keeping an eye on things. It's all so much more complicated for them than it was for us."

He spears another cockle.

"We're not that ancient Molly. Some things don't change."

"No, but the pace of everything has. And the drugs are different now—so much stronger than when we used to sit on the beach having the occasional puff and pretending to be stoned."

He's looking rather irritated now.

"Finn needs to go his own way, same as I did at his age."

Please let him not say he wants to be more like a friend than a dad.

"They cover all that kind of stuff at his school. He seems pretty clued up."

"One of the things the drugs team used to say when they came into our school when I was teaching was if they have too much cash, it makes them a target. They can't get into too much trouble if all they can afford is a bottle of cider. It might be worth talking to him about it."

"I see myself as more of a friend; I'm not really up for being the heavy-handed father."

"Right."

"You don't approve? Being a dad is different to being a mum Molly. Mothers are just so much better at that kind of thing."

"That's usually because they have to be."

"Most men aren't cut out for that level of detail. We're more big-picture, women are just better at micromanagement."

"I hope you're joking?"

"Look, I seem to have pressed a feminist button here by mistake. Can we rewind?"

He smiles, and suddenly I'm feeling seriously annoyed, and not just about the feminist-button thing. Although if I had one, I'd be pressing it for sure, and if there was any justice, it would be an ejector seat, and it wouldn't be a button, it would be something bigger, like a giant lever.

He pours more wine into my glass.

"Let's change the subject. Bea tells me the gatehouse is working out very well, and you're ready to put the plans in for the stables? Still sure you want to keep things small?"

Right. That's it. Here goes.

"I did want to talk to you about that, only I've been having second thoughts, and maybe you and Roger are right, perhaps I should be looking at a bigger development. Build something bigger, and make some proper money."

He can't hide his delight.

"Well good for you. I was sure you'd see sense eventually, and I'd be happy to invest, I really would and I'm sure Roger would too."

"Do you really think so?"

"He mentioned something about it, a few months ago, in passing, and I'm sure if we came up with the right plans, he'd be interested. He's keen on expanding, I know that."

Damn, I knew it. I'm trying to remain calm.

"Is he?"

"Oh definitely, it has so much potential. It could be part of the marketing for the hotel, widen the offer to include apartments and cottages, with the Hall as the hub, with the front office and housekeeping and a few apartments. You could move somewhere new—there's some land coming up along the coast. I've been tipped off about it by a contact at the council, and it would be perfect for you."

"Right."

He's more animated than I've ever seen him.

"I'm so glad you've thought this through Molly. So glad."

He takes hold of my hand. Bloody hell.

"So what happens to Bertie?"

"Sorry?"

"Where would Bertie live?"

"I think a project like this could transform things for all of you. We can find him somewhere safe, where he's looked after as things start to deteriorate—and they will, you know."

"Enough. I've heard enough, thanks."

"Sorry?"

"There is no project Stephen."

"But..."

"I wanted to see how you'd react. It was a feminist trick question. You pressed a bigger button than you thought. I've already told you what my plans are, but clearly you weren't listening."

"But I thought..."

"Yes, I can see what you thought, you and Roger. Make a fuss of her, and she'll go along with whatever grand scheme the two of you have been hatching to make yourselves even more money—was that the plan?"

"Don't be silly. We've only spoken once or twice about it, nothing more. I think I may have given you the wrong impression. I only offered to invest as a sign of confidence. I thought you'd find it encouraging."

"Well I don't. And the Hall is not being turned into a hub. Not while I'm in charge."

He looks furious now.

"If you can't see beyond the parochial, there's really no point in talking about this. You need real vision to make the most of potential like that."

"I can see way beyond it, thanks. Way past the let's-make-a-few-quid-and-bugger-everyone-else. Dig up the rose garden and stick Bertie in a home. Do you think they'd let him take Betty? No? I thought not. To be honest, I think it's your vision which is parochial."

Actually I'm not entirely sure what "parochial" means, but I'm guessing it's the kind of snooty thing architects say when you ask for something child-friendly and warm and they give you acres of steel and glass and no bloody bannisters on the stairs.

"In what way? Do enlighten me. Jesus, I doubt you even know what it means."

He's looking furious now.

Good.

"Oh I think I do Stephen. I just have to look at you and Roger and I get a pretty big clue. I'm keeping faith with what Helena wanted, and keeping my family safe and happy. Not lying on a beach somewhere stoned out of their heads on God knows what while I ponce about being visionary. Otherwise what's the bloody point? Thank you for dinner, but I think it's time I left now. I wouldn't want to take up any more of your visionary time—it's making me feel rather nauseous. But do enjoy your cockles."

I stand up, and there's an awkward moment when I notice people are staring, including the waiter, and I'm shaking as I walk into the restaurant and back out into the street, literally shaking as I walk towards the taxi rank. Bloody hell, I keep thinking of other things I wished I'd said on the taxi ride home, but at least I said something. I didn't just sit there. God, I wish I'd thrown my wine all over his white linen trousers—if we'd been drinking red, that would have been even better. I should have asked for a glass of red wine with my prawns. Bloody cheek. What a total knob, as Dan would say.

I'm exhausted by the time I get home and the adrenaline starts to ebb. Celia and Eddie are sitting at the kitchen table, drinking tea.

"The boys were so amusing tonight, we've just sat down. Bertie is pretending not to be asleep in the library, but you won't get any sense out of him, so I wouldn't bother dear. Did you have a nice evening? You're home earlier than I expected. Oh my dear, whatever's the matter?"

Much to my horror I've started to cry, and the more I try to stop it, the worse it gets.

"Eddie, get the brandy."

"No, really, I'm fine."

Celia puts her arm around my shoulder.

"Sit down and tell me, or don't, up to you, but you need a drink."

"There's nothing to tell really."

"I see. Well, good riddance then."

"Sorry?"

"Pour her a proper drink Edward. She doesn't want a sip, she wants a proper drink. He was nowhere near good enough for you, far too pleased with himself, fussy about his clothes too, and I never trust a chap who fusses about his clothes, very bad sign."

"Right."

Eddie hands me a tumbler with a very large brandy.

"For what it's worth, I thought he was a bit of a wanker too."

"So did I. It's not that. I'm just furious, that's all. I'm not heart-broken. And I'm starving. I hardly got to eat anything before I walked out."

"Oh, well, good."

"Give me some credit."

Celia chuckles.

"Sorry my dear. Drink up."

"I don't really like brandy Celia. What I'd really like is a cup of tea and a sandwich."

She takes the glass and knocks it back.

"Follow me, I'll put the kettle on. Oh I say, I'd forgotten how good a really decent brandy can be. That's one thing you can always rely on Bertie for—he keeps a jolly decent cellar. Always has."

Ivy has clearly been updated by Celia by the time I get back from dropping Ben and Alfie at school the next morning.

"Sit down and take the weight off your feet dear. I gather we won't be seeing any more of Mr. Jackson then?"

"I don't think so."

"Well good, because I never liked him. I didn't like to say, but he's not half as clever as he likes to think he is, with his fancy car and his special trousers. And he never visits his mum, I can tell you that."

"I don't think I could have put it better myself, Ivy."

"Oh there you are Mr. Edward. Do you want a bacon sandwich, only I'm about to start on lunch and I can't be doing with late breakfasts when I'm doing lunch."

"Yes please Ivy."

"Go and wash your hands then."

He winks at me as he heads into the scullery.

"Will Dennis be coming in?"

"I think so. He's just putting some oil on the lawn mower."

"Fuss he makes about that thing. Surprised he hasn't got a blanket for it when he puts it away at night."

Eddie and I exchange smiles. Dennis does have an old tarpaulin he drapes over the mower. He claims it stops the damp sea air getting in, but I don't think we'll tell Ivy that.

"Cup of tea Miss Molly?"

"Thanks Ivy."

Bugger. It's the last day of the summer term tomorrow and I've forgotten to buy treats for the class picnics for Ben and Alfie, so I'm up until half past eleven making fairy cakes and Rice Krispie cakes, and getting melted chocolate all over the kitchen counter. By the time I've tidied up and I'm heading upstairs, it's nearly midnight, and I'm wide awake. I've got a tray with tea and a fairy cake, and a glass of water for the morning, and my To Do list so I can have a peaceful half hour scribbling and if that doesn't do the trick, I'll read. I'm having another go with the roses book which Ivy and Dennis got me for Christmas, and it's starting to make a bit more sense. I'm halfway up the stairs when I notice I've left the light on in the pantry. Bugger. And then everything goes into slow motion as I turn, do some weird thing to my ankle, and the tray goes flying as I start to fall backwards.

Fuck. This isn't going to be good.

Double Fuck.

"Molly, can you hear me? Oh God, Eddie, phone for an ambulance. Molly, wake up my darling girl, wake up. Should I slap her, do you think?"

"Don't be ridiculous Bertie. She's unconscious, not hysterical."

"Brandy, that's what we need. Go and get some brandy Celia."

"She doesn't like brandy. Let's wait for the ambulance, poor girl, she's cut her arm, quite badly by the looks of it. It must have been the glass. Bring a towel Edward, quickly, don't just stand there."

"Molly, can you hear me? Please wake up my darling girl."

"Bertie, I, fucking hell that hurts."

"Don't try to sit up my darling, just stay where you are. I've got you, and we're all here. You're safe now, and the ambulance is on its way."

CHAPTER SEVEN

The Long Hot Summer (on Crutches)

August

Moss Roses

Dating back to the 1700s, these roses have a mossy growth on their buds and stems which enhances the fragrance of the petals with resinous undertones of moss, pine, and balsam. Notable varieties include Madame Alboni, with large violet-pink curling petals which pale with age; Rene d'Anjou, with its copper-tinted leaves, soft pink flowers, and a memorable sweet fragrance; and William Lobb, a dark-purple rose which fades to a picturesque lavender with a deep rose scent.

It's nearly six o'clock in the morning by the time we get back from the hospital. Bertie and Celia came with me, and sat holding my hand, while Eddie stayed with the boys. The ambulance didn't have the siren on when it arrived, so the boys didn't wake up, thank God, and by the looks of it, they're still asleep. But Ivy and Dennis must have spotted all the commotion, since they're both standing by the front door, looking worried.

Ivy walks towards the car, which Celia has parked as close to the house as she can get without actually driving up the front steps.

"Well I never. Just look at the state of you."

She bursts into tears and lifts her pinny up to dab at her face.

"Oh Ivy, it's not that bad."

"Just ignore me. It's the shock of seeing you all bandaged up, and what on earth you were doing making cakes in the middle of the night is anybody's guess. Couldn't it have waited until the morning?"

"They're for the boys, for their class picnics today at school."

"Well that's as may be, but now look at you, and I'd have made them, you know that. What on earth your mother's going to say I can't imagine, but I hope you'll tell her I would have made them for you, you only had to ask. The Lord knows how we're going to get you upstairs."

Dennis tuts.

"Leave the poor girl alone and let's get her indoors and sat on the sofa, and then we can come up with a proper plan. Here, take my arm love, and me and Eddie will help you in."

"I've got crutches; I just need to work out how to get out of the car. Getting in was tricky enough."

"You take your time. Eddie, you stay here, and everyone else can go indoors and give her a bit of peace. You too, Mr. Bertie. You look completely done in."

"Not one of my better evenings I'll agree, but all's well that ends well. Brave girl, hardly a peep out of her when they did the stitches. Had to have a great big injection too. Wish I hadn't watched now, but someone needed to keep an eye on them. Come on Ivy, people will be wanting a bit of breakfast and a cup of something hot, I shouldn't wonder."

She nods and takes Bertie's arm.

"You come with me Mr. Bertie, and tell me all about it. Must have been a terrible shock for you."

"Yes, it was, but at least I managed not to burst into tears. And stop patting my arm woman, I'm not the invalid."

Celia smiles and heads after them.

"Edward, do be careful, don't rush her."

Dennis tuts.

"Thought we'd never get rid of them all fussing about. Right, ready to try to stand now love? I'll stand here and Eddie will be the other side of the door, so you just shuffle along and we'll lift you out of the car—how does that sound?"

I shuffle, and put my feet on the floor, or rather one foot and one plaster cast.

"I've hurt my shoulder too Dennis. Pulled a ligament or something they think, so I'm not sure trying to lift me is such a good idea."

"Oh, well that makes things a bit trickier. Let's think a minute."

"Oh for heaven's sake, you're getting cold. Just stay still."

Eddie opens the car door, and before I know it, he's lifting me out of the car.

"Eddie, please, I'm just—"

"Do be quiet. And try not to move, or I'll drop you, and then we'll have to go back to the hospital."

Crikey.

Dennis runs ahead and opens the front door as wide as it will go, and the double doors to the drawing room, and Eddie deposits me on the sofa.

Bertie is clearly impressed.

"Well done my boy. Excellent."

"Yes, thank you Eddie."

He's blushing now.

"Yes, well done Edward. Molly, should we call your mother now, do you think?"

"Let's leave it a bit longer Celia. It's still very early, and she'll only fuss."

Bertie puts his hand on my shoulder very gently.

"Fair enough, although a word to the wise: I'd stand by for a fair bit of fussing over the next few weeks if I were you. Might as well resign yourself to it and enjoy it. Don't see you've got much choice. Only problem I can see is how long it will take Ivy and your mother to come to blows over who's in charge. You won't get a look in, Celia. And neither will you, my dear."

"Oh God."

"I'd take a few more of your pills if I were you, and brace yourself."

Oh God.

Darling, I've brought treats. How are you?"

"I'm fine Lola, until the drugs wear off. The ankle's not too bad. They said it's only a hairline fracture."

"How long will you be in plaster?"

"Four weeks, they think, but that's not the tricky bit. I've got seven stitches in my right arm and I've wrenched my left shoulder, so I can't even get my PJs on by myself. Mum and Ivy are taking it in turns to dress me."

"Your mum told me about that, so I've brought you some white cotton nightdresses, with buttons all the way down the front—very Victorian chambermaid."

"They sound perfect, thank you Lola."

"My pleasure darling. How did you manage to get a black eye?"

"God knows, but Mum and Ivy might be getting one too if they don't calm down—they're driving me crazy."

"I've brought vodka. I thought we could have it with lots of ice. Ice is meant to be good for swollen things, isn't it?"

"Not usually in vodka. I'd give it a go, only I'm not meant to drink with the tablets they gave me."

"Now that is truly tragic."

"Tell me about it. They won't even let me get out of bed."

"Who won't?"

"Take a wild guess."

"Oh dear, you know I love you darling, but I'm not taking on your mum and Ivy, or Celia. They've sort of morphed into some sort of Molly Protection League. I practically had to get written permission before I was allowed to visit."

"I know. I'm going to have to put my foot down."

"Presumably not the one that's in plaster?"

"Very amusing, I'm sure. They won't even let Bertie in unaccompanied, in case he leads me astray. Although God knows how he'd manage that, since I can't actually use my crutches until my arms are a bit better."

"Maybe you could lie on the floor and roll along."

"Rolling downstairs is how I got myself into this mess in the first place, thanks very much."

"We could sit you on a tray."

"Sure. You first."

"Sounds like Eddie's been handy, though?"

"He's been great, he carried me downstairs on Monday so I could have tea with the boys. Although he won't be able to do it for much longer if Ivy keeps feeding me up—his knees were buckling already. The boys have been sweet too, but now they're bored with it. Although they do like Ivy and Mum making their packed lunches for school—they get a lot more sausage rolls and jam tarts than when I make them."

There's a knock on the door, and Eddie comes in.

"They've sent me up with some tea and toasted cheese."

"Oh God, not another snack."

He grins.

"I'll eat it if you like."

"Please."

He puts the tray down on the bedside table and picks up a square of toasted cheese, before offering the plate to Lola.

"No thank you darling."

"Anything else you need?"

Lola gives him one of her best smiles.

"Nothing springs to mind, but I'll let you know."

"I'm going shopping with Dennis later on. Ivy's given us another one of her lists. Anything you need Molly?"

"Not unless Tesco have starting selling big bottles of Valium?"

"Christ, what have you done to him? He's gone all tanned demi-god, and those eyes, they seem even more blue than the last time I saw him."

"I haven't done anything to him. He's been working outside, that's all, helping Dennis and building a tree house with the boys."

"Well country living clearly agrees with him. Now you've got shot of the idiot architect, maybe you should consider something a bit closer to home?"

"Please. All I want at the moment is to be able to lift both my arms up, and get dressed by myself, if that's not too much to ask."

"I bet all the local girls are flocking."

"Pretty much. He's got a gig at the local pub now, and Bella says they're practically queuing up. Her son Arthur is in Alfie's class—she was telling me and Sally all about it. Apparently he's oblivious, which only makes them keener. One turned up here a few days ago with a CD for him—it was really sweet."

"Yes, I get that with Tre and some of his yoga girls—he's fairly oblivious too. Talking of gorgeous but oblivious, he sent some special arnica ointment for you. It's good for bringing out bruises apparently."

"I'm having enough trouble coping with the bruises I've got, I'm not sure I want any more bringing out—but tell him thanks, would you?"

"Sure. So are we breaking you out of here, or what?"

"Yes please, only can we give my tablets time to kick in? I only just took them."

"Of course. Does it hurt much darling?"

"A bit. Quite a lot actually, but for God's sake don't tell Mum or Ivy."

"We can always get Eddie to carry you down, show me his knee-buckling routine."

"No, I can do it, I'm sure I can. I'll go downstairs on my bottom, and the rest should be fine."

There's another knock on the door, and this time it's Celia.

"Just checking if you need anything? Ivy says lunch will be

ready in an hour. She's making a rice pudding, because you need the extra calcium. We've been doing some research, and broccoli is very good for healing bones too. Ben's been showing me how to look things up on the Interweb. Lots of Vitamin C—or was it K?—anyway, very good for you. So make sure you eat it all up. Do you like blancmange dear?"

"I'm not sure I've ever had it."

"Right. We'll stick to rice puddings then."

"Thanks Celia." She closes the door very quietly, like a sudden noise might startle me.

Lola smiles. "Christ, I see what you mean."

"I'm bracing myself for calf's-foot jelly."

Over the next few days I finally manage to find a position I can sleep in for more than half an hour without something starting to throb, and I've also realised that taking the painkillers the hospital gave me every four hours like they told me to is definitely the best way to get through the day. So I'm in a gentle semifogged state most of the time, which turns out to be rather nice. I'm not sure I'm very good at letting people take care of me. It's not something I'm used to, but I'm trying to go with the flow and be more grateful, and it is very touching how kind everyone is being. Vicky is taking care of the gatehouse and Mum's helping Ivy with the B&B guests, not that we've got that many due with Celia and Eddie booked in until next month. And thank God they are—they've both been such a help, particularly Eddie, who seems to have the great knack of noticing when something needs doing and just getting on with it with no fuss. The boys adore him, and he spends hours racing round with them keeping them busy. Mr. and Mrs. Collins are back next week for a few days, and a nice couple Ivy says come every year to go walking are due at the weekend. She says they're no trouble unless it rains, when they tend to come back soaking wet with muddy walking boots. So fingers crossed the weather holds.

Being out of action has given me lots of time to think, and I'm struck by how much safer I feel here, much more than I did with Pete. It feels like we're part of something, and if it really does take a village to raise a child, then I've definitely got at least a hamlet's worth of people surrounding us here, far more than we ever had when I was doing the Mr.-and-Mrs. thing with Pete, ticking all the boxes for a proper family life before we realised it wasn't quite what we thought it would be. A bit like those wedding cakes they used to have in the War made out of cardboard, so you got the proper three-tier wedding cake for your photographs, and then lifted the cardboard cover off to reveal a small fruit cake underneath, which was often a bit on the dry side, as eggs and butter were still rationed.

I'm starting to get the hang of using the crutches, and I'm sitting at the kitchen table reading the paper when Dan rushes in, looking excited.

"Come and see what we've done Mum. It was Eddie's idea, but we've all done it. You'll love it, honestly you will."

Dennis and Eddie have tracked down a minitrailer, which attaches to the back of the ride-along lawnmower, and filled it with cushions and blankets so they can take me out into the orchard.

"See you won't need to walk Mum. Anywhere you want to go, you can just get in and we'll take you."

"That's great."

Ivy is not impressed.

"Mind you don't tip her out Dennis."

"Thank you, I'd never have thought of that. Honestly, what do you take me for?"

"You can see our tree house Mum. It's nearly finished now—isn't it great?"

Alfie runs along beside me with Tom, both begging for a ride when I've been settled in my chair.

"Yes love, it is."

And it is. Even the chickens seem impressed and are clucking around by the ladder keeping an eye on the proceedings while the pigs race up and down in the hope we've brought food.

"I told you she'd love it. So can we go surfing now?"

"I'm not sure the mower can get all the way to the big beach Dan, sorry."

"No Mum, we thought you could be here with Alfie and Tom, and then Eddie can take me and Ben surfing, if that's okay?"

"I suppose so, only . . ."

"Great, she says we can go Ben. Eddie, can we go today?"

"I didn't say today Dan, I was thinking maybe tomorrow?"

"Can't we go for an hour this afternoon, please? I told Robbie I might see him."

"Oh, right, well, I suppose if it was just for an hour."

"Great, I'll text him."

He races back to the house to find his phone.

"Eddie."

"Yes Molly?"

"You're a total pushover—you know that, don't you?"

"On the subject of being pushed over, there is one other thing I should probably mention. We've invented a new game, a version of Simon Says, but you get squirted with the hosepipe if you forget what Simon said. It's been so hot, and they love it—the pigs love it too. The chickens aren't that keen, so they tend to take refuge in the tree house, but I'm not sure you'd make it up the ladder."

"If you squirt me with the hosepipe, I'm telling Ivy, and Celia."

"Yes, I thought you might say that."

"How have you got a hosepipe all the way out here anyway?"

"We bought an extension—well, two actually—to reach the tap in the stables."

"Right, and whose bright idea was that then?"

"Patrick's, to keep the pigs cool, but then it sort of escalated from there."

"I see."

"So if they ask you to play Simon Says, just say no, okay? I think that's probably rather crucial."

"I think I can do better than that. Boys, can I have a word please. Alfie, stop running for a minute."

"What Mum? I'm busy, and we're going to do the hosepiper in a minute, and it's great Mum, it really is."

"No we're not Alfie—that's what I wanted to talk to you about. You too Ben. When I'm in the orchard, we can't have the hosepipe on, okay? My plaster will get wet and then I'll have to go back to the hospital, and I'll get very annoyed. And then I'll come home and cut the hosepipe into small pieces and you'll be annoyed. Is that clear?"

"But..."

"I mean it Alfie."

There's the sound of united tutting.

"Eddie invented the game, so you only play it with him, okay?"

Eddie mutters something under his breath.

"Eddie?"

"Yes Molly?"

"Let's not invent any more games involving hosepipers."

"Good plan. I had to get changed twice yesterday, and Ivy told me off for making extra washing, even though I've told her I'm happy to do my own."

"But she's told you not to touch the washing machine because it's very temperamental?"

"How did you know?"

"She's said the same thing to me when we first got here. She still restacks the dishwasher when she thinks I'm not looking."

He grins.

"Oh good, I thought it was just me."

"No, it's mostly you Eddie. Wait until I tell her and Celia you've invented a game which involves soaking people with hosepipes."

Ben gives me a shocked look.

"You can't do that Mum, they'll go nuts."

"Well I better not ever get wet then—promise?"

"We promise Mum."

"Good. Now help me get up love, I haven't said hello to Bubble and Squeak for ages. Are they still playing football?"

"Yes, they love it. They're rubbish in goal though."

The weather gets hotter, and the roads are so packed with caravans and cars with surfboards balanced on top that instead of taking ten minutes to drop Ben and Alfie off for their scouts' summer picnic it takes Dennis nearly an hour. The village shops are opening at half past eight now so the locals can get their shopping done before the holidaymakers wake up and the traffic grinds to a halt. Alfie swears he's seen a grass snake, or possibly a python, on the path down to the cove, and the days pass by in a blur of sunscreen and sleeping in the afternoons, while I try to help out as much as I can by finding jobs I can do sitting down. Everyone is still being brilliant at helping out, and Sally's even insisting on doing half an hour's ironing every time she collects Tom, even though I've told her he's no trouble and having him here means Alfie has someone to play with so he doesn't traipse after Dan and Ben whining. I know how tricky it is for her and Patrick combining working full-time with the summer holidays, but she's adamant. In fact the only person who isn't going out of their way to be helpful is Pete. He's due to collect the boys for a four-day holiday just before they go back to school, but now he's making a major song and dance about my not being able to drive them up as planned.

"My foot might still be in plaster, and even if it's not, I'm not sure I'll be able to cope with a long drive. I'm sorry Pete."

"It's very inconvenient. Couldn't someone else do it?"

"I must remember next time I fall down the stairs that it will be very inconvenient for you."

"Your moving down there wasn't my decision Molly."

"And your moving in with Janice wasn't mine, so I think we're quits on that front, don't you?"

There's a silence. I'm usually more tolerant of his fussing, but on balance I think it's about time that changed.

"I'm exhausted Molly. Last term was so busy—you have no idea of the pressure I'm under as head. I think I'm developing an ulcer."

"For God's sake, you're having your sons to stay for four days, out of a six-week holiday—stop being such a total arse about it."

I can't quite believe I've said this out loud. There's a rather shocked silence. Bugger.

"I'm sorry, but the boys are really looking forward to it Pete. It would be nice if you were too."

"I am, of course I am, but I hope they're not going to be fussy about food, because I simply won't have the patience."

"Feed them pasta and pizza and they'll be fine—or don't, it's up to you. But if you shout at Alfie and try to make him eat things he doesn't want, I'd watch out for Dan and Ben—they're very protective about him on stuff like that. And this is meant to be a treat for them, a few days with their dad. You won't get many more chances, so I wouldn't waste them if I were you."

"And what precisely do you mean by that?"

"Just that they're getting older—they can decide for themselves who they want to visit, and if you carry on like this, they won't want to come at all, which would be a real shame, especially for you."

I don't tell him I've already had to persuade them that four days will go by in no time, and that it'll be great. Dan is still adamant he'd rather stay at home, so I'm really hoping Pete does some fun things with them, or Dan will call and demand to come home. Mum's already on standby, just in case.

"Janice has planned a few little outings for them."

"That's nice. But it's you they want to spend time with Pete."

This isn't strictly true either, but I'm trying to be encouraging, for the boys' sake.

"I'm sure we'll manage. But do try to make sure you pack some proper clothes for them—we may have lunch with Janice's mother on the way back, and I'd like them to look smart."

That sounds like a real treat.

"Sure."

Dear God.

* * *

I'm limping around the kitchen making tea and trying to calm down when Celia comes in.

"Let me do that dear. Edward has just called and he says he thinks it went okay, whatever that means."

Sam has arranged for a couple of auditions for Eddie, so he's gone to London for a few days.

"He also said he should be back by Thursday."

"That's good. I know he didn't want to miss his gig at the pub—he's building up quite a following now."

She smiles.

"I hope something comes of this. He was so nervous before he left, I hope he did himself justice. He's seeing his parents for supper this evening, and I've told him there's a room for him at the cottage for as long as he needs it. We should be able to move in by the middle of September, if Mr. Stebbings doesn't encounter any more major problems. He's solved that problem with the drain, and the new boiler is in now, and the new doors."

"That's good, but there's no rush Celia, you know that. We love having you here."

"I'm not sure I'd have ever plucked up the courage to sell the house if I hadn't been here you know my dear. I can't wait to get started on that garden, years of neglect, but I think we can make something of it. I'll still be here three afternoons a week though. Wouldn't want to let things slide—there's always so much to do. But coming here, and being made to feel so welcome, well, it's been a lifesaver. It has for Edward too, given him time to think."

"Yes, Harrington does that. It's a very special place."

"It's not just Harrington my dear; it's your influence, in so many little ways that add up to something quite remarkable.

Helena never really had the knack. She was my oldest friend, so I can say it. She was inspirational in the garden, but the house was never her forte."

"What a lovely thing to say."

"Credit where credit is due. I mean it my dear. Quite remarkable. Now, I did want to have a word about the nursery catalogues. We do need to make some decisions about the new white border, and the planting around the fountain needs updating now it's working again."

"Yes, I saw all the catalogues with the Post-it notes."

"Handy things, aren't they? Hadn't come across them before. Just stick them on, and you can peel them off if you change your mind—excellent."

"I'll look at them properly later, I promise."

"Good, can't stand still in a garden, things need to evolve, keeps the spirit of the place alive."

"Right."

"Would you like a biscuit? I think Ivy has some in the tin. She'll be back soon with the shopping, but I think there are some digestives. Can't beat a digestive, in my opinion."

By week three of hobbling about on crutches I'm feeling far less tragic. The local doctor took the stitches out on Wednesday, and there's only a tiny scar on my arm, so I can have a shower now as long as I remember to carefully wrap my cast in clingfilm and the variety of carrier bags Mum has been collecting for me. We're planning a camp on the beach tonight as a birthday celebration for Dan, who's announced he only wants money for his birthday this year, so he can buy a new surfboard. He's really getting into surfing now—he and Robbie would spend every waking moment on the beach if they could. Eddie's shuttling them backwards and forwards, and regaling us with tales of how packed the beach is now. He found himself paddling out with a merchant banker yesterday who was completely hopeless, and he was very gratified to be mistaken for a local when he and Dan helped him retrieve his board.

The sea is as flat as a pancake today, so they're all down at the cove making preparations for the camp. There's an air show along the coast later on, so we'll watch the planes flying in, and Dennis has finally persuaded Bertie not to fire any cannon salutes, just in case they're mistaken for some sort of insurgent incident. Mum's busy making sausage rolls with Ivy; they've managed to avoid falling out so far, mainly because Mum cleverly defers to Ivy over anything domestic. They've definitely become friends over the past few months, and Mum seems happier than I've seen her in ages.

"Anyone want tea?"

"You sit down, I'll make it. I was just about to put the kettle on."

"I can make a cup of tea Ivy."

"Has she always been this stubborn Marjorie?"

"Yes, ever since she was a little girl."

They both smile.

I think I'll ignore them.

"What's for lunch, we're starving Mum."

"Omelettes and salads?"

"Yuck."

"Don't say 'yuck,' Alfie, it's not very nice."

"Sorry Granny, but they are."

"I might put a bit of bacon in yours, if you're a good boy and lay the table."

"And ice cream?"

Dan tuts.

"In your omelette? Good choice Annie—whole meal in one."

"Dan, don't start. Help him lay the table, and it's omelettes and salads, and anyone who doesn't fancy that can wait until supper, okay? What time is Robbie arriving?"

"Around three. His mum's bringing Ella too—she lives near them."

"Oh, right."

Ella is Ben's new best friend from school. They're both vegetarians and into saving the planet. They text each other constantly, and he went to her birthday party last week.

Alfie turns to look at Ben.

"Is Ella your girlfriend, Ben?"

We all lean forwards slightly, and Ivy and Mum stop nattering.

"No, Alf. We've talked about it, but we've decided we're fine as we are for now. We might change our minds when we get our hormones, but for now we're just best friends."

Oh God.

There's a silence, and then Dan nods.

"That's pretty cool, Benny boy. Nice to know my brother isn't a total"—he looks at me and pauses—"a total idiot."

"Thanks. How's it going with Freya?"

"It's not, yet. But we're only on phase one of the plan, so it's early days."

"Oh, right."

They wander off muttering and I'm left standing in the kitchen, rooted to the spot. I think I may have caught a rather encouraging glimpse into the future, where they spend less time shoving each other and more time being supportive, but "hormones"? Dear God, he can't be old enough to be thinking about hormones. Mum and Ivy are both smiling.

"The things they come out with sometimes."

"I know Ivy."

"He's a lovely boy. All three of them are."

Mum nods and opens the fridge.

"We haven't got much bacon left. Shall I do cheese ones instead?"

"Sure Mum, and then we can see quite how lovely Dan and Alfie can be when you try to fob them off with cheese."

"There's more bacon in the freezer Marjorie. You can use up all the packet and I'll defrost some more later."

"Problem solved, hurrah."

"Go and sit down dear. We don't want you getting in the way when we've got hot pans on. I'll bring the tea in when it's brewed."

Mum winks at me.

I'm definitely going to ignore them.

The beach party is a big success, and Dennis drives me down to the beach very slowly in the trailer, as the path is quite steep, which does leave me slightly worried we won't get back up again, but thankfully he manages it. The kids have a lovely time watching all the planes, and then we light the fire and they toast pretty much everything they can fit on a stick, including their sausage rolls. Eddie sings songs and plays his guitar, and Ben and Ella sit chatting and seem very nonhormonal, while Dan and Robbie continue with their fitness campaign and run up and down the path, pursued by Tess and Jasper. Dad is late arriving, and then gets grumpy because Mum's got rather giggly after having one of Bertie's fruit cocktails, which don't actually contain any fruit. She says he can leave if he'd like to, but she's stopping for a bit longer, which makes him even grumpier, but we all pretend not to notice.

I'm emptying the dishwasher after lunch the next day, while Ivy makes a cake for tea and watches me with pursed lips because she wants me to sit down.

"I'll finish that. You go and have a little rest."

"I'm fine Ivy."

"You need to be resting."

"No I don't. I need this bloody plaster off so I can get back to normal. I can't keep hobbling about on these bloody crutches, I've got things I need to be getting on with."

I turn to make sure she can see I'm not in the mood for another lecture, and manage to drop the glass I'm holding.

"Oh for fuck's sake."

"There's no need for language."

"Yes there bloody is."

She smiles.

"Go and have a sit-down and let me sort this out. Your Lola will be here later, won't she?"

"Yes. And I'm sorry Ivy."

"Don't you worry. I might use a few bad words myself if I'd had to put up with what you've been through these past few weeks. But you need to rest more, or it won't heal properly and then where will we be?"

"Using more bad language probably. I'll be in the drawing room if anyone wants me."

"Right you are dear."

* * *

Bugger. Now I feel like a toddler who has got overtired and thrown a strop. So that's great. And it's hot, and my ankle is throbbing. I can't keep finding things which I can do sitting down, although I did enjoy helping Mum and Ivy make strawberry jam. We made some blackcurrant too, and lining up the jars in the pantry felt like we'd really accomplished something. We've made some small jars too, for the welcome baskets for the gatehouse and they've been really popular so far, but I can't make jam every day. I sit down and start making a list of all the things I want to be getting on with when I'm finally back on my feet, and the next thing I know Lola is waking me up and it's nearly six o'clock. She looks cool and elegant in a pretty sundress, which makes me feel even hotter and more lumpy.

"Sorry, I must have lost track of time. How was the journey?"

Lola has recently dumped Tre. She seems fine about it, but I've been making an extra fuss of her, just to be sure. She's got her sights set on Frank now, who owns a restaurant in London with Michelin stars and is opening up a boutique hotel just outside of Bath. She was there last night for the grand opening.

"Great. The hotel is fabulous, the party was very deluxe, and I had the air-conditioning on full blast all the way here, so it was like being in a fridge."

"Can we go and sit in your car then please? I'm so fed up of being hot."

"Sure. I wouldn't mind a drink first though."

"Sorry, of course."

"Are you alright darling?"

"No, I am not. I'm fed up with this bloody ankle, and being too hot, and well, everything."

"Right."

"It's not funny. I can't even drive, so I'm stuck here being not able to do stuff. I should be writing the business plan for the loan, and hassling the bank. We need to get the stables up and running—it's the only way we're going to be able to afford to stay here. But these bloody painkillers mean that every time I sit down, I fall asleep. And I've tried not taking them, but, well, it still hurts a fair bit. I even swore at Ivy earlier on."

"Did you darling? I bet that went down well. Never mind, you can swear at me all you like. It's completely fucking bollocks isn't it?"

"Yes. It's double fucking bollocks."

"Better?"

"A bit."

"Good, can I have my drink now? And then let's do something fun. I know, let's get those trunks down, from the attic, and dress up for dinner."

"What?"

"Didn't you say you were going to sort them out?"

"Yes, but not now, it's too hot up there, the rooms have tiny windows so they get very stuffy."

"Leave it to me darling. You sit there and practice your swearing, I'll be back in a moment."

A highly amusing half hour follows with a combination of Dennis, Eddie, Lola, and Dan carrying the three massive trunks down the stairs, with Celia, Bertie, and Betty giving them encouraging advice, and Ivy tutting in the background. There are a couple more trunks still up there, and some random boxes, but last time I looked they seemed to be full of old lampshades, or old bits of lethal-looking electrical equipment, including an old fan heater and what looked like an antique pair of curling tongs. I'll have a proper sort-out at some point, and work out a safe place to keep the small white suitcase of baby things too—tiny night-dresses wrapped in tissue paper which look like they've never been worn, and a shawl. Somehow it doesn't seem right to disturb them.

We finally finish sorting through the heap of mystery keys still unaccounted for in the jar, and manage to unlock the trunks, at which point Lola goes into a frenzy, and before we know it there are clothes festooned everywhere and she's holding things up and twirling round, while Bertie and Celia look at an old photograph album with Ivy and try to identify people. There are a couple of great black-and-white photographs of the house, which I'll get framed, and one of what we think is a very young Helena, digging in the kitchen garden.

"Ooh, look, an evening bag—how gorgeous."

Lola parades round wearing her newly acquired feathered boa and an eau-de-nil silk evening dress with no back, and shows everyone the cream silk bag. She's already tried on a midnight-blue beaded silk 1920s cocktail dress, and a 1950s floral tea dress, and will definitely be taking them both home.

"This is gorgeous too, but you'd need serious corsetry going on to get into it."

She holds up a silver sheath dress, with embroidery along the hemline.

"Definitely one for the vintage pile."

Lola is selecting things to take to her friend Magda, who runs a posh vintage shop, and pays serious money for authentic stuff apparently.

"Shall I take the gloves too?"

"Sure. I can't see when I'm ever going to wear elbow-length white satin gloves if I'm honest."

"True, and they're tiny. Didn't debutantes wear long white gloves when they were presented at court?"

"I think so."

"Ooh, Eddie, another dinner jacket."

"Oh God."

Lola gives him a dazzling smile.

"Try it on please darling—this one might fit you better."

It does.

"You look very smart Eddie. You should definitely keep it."

He grins.

"Thanks Molly, if you're sure? My old one has gone shiny, so that would be great. I'll just go and try the trousers."

Lola smiles.

"Off you pop then darling, but come straight back so we can see the full outfit."

"Lola, leave him alone."

"I told you he'd look devastating in evening dress."

"Yes. But stop making him dress up."

"We're all dressing up tonight, and he's loving all the attention."

"He is not."

"It'll be good practise for him, for when he's a famous rock star."

"Ta-da."

"Very nice darling. Give us a twirl."

Eddie ignores Lola.

"And I found this."

He hands me a white silk handkerchief, wrapped round something small.

"What is it?"

"I'll give you a clue: it's not another trunk."

"Bloody hell."

It's a pair of what look like emerald earrings.

"You can say that again darling—they're stunning. Do they match the famous necklace? Which I've never actually seen, I might add."

"I think so."

Celia and Ivy agree that they do look like the long-lost earrings which match the necklace, and we spend a happy twenty minutes making up increasingly wild and romantic stories about how they came to be in the inside pocket of the dinner jacket, before agreeing that it was probably a drunken moment at the end of a long night.

"I'm always doing the same thing—not with jewels of course, but putting something somewhere safe and then completely forgetting where."

Lola smiles.

"Me too Bertie, although I still think it was a lover's tryst. He left his dinner jacket and she promised not to wear the earrings again until the day he returned and they danced the night away. But he never came back. Maybe it was during the War. Or at one of those 1920s weekend parties—they could get pretty wild, you know. Talking of which, don't you think we should celebrate their safe return with one of your delicious cocktails?

"I thought you'd never ask. Might fire the cannon later too."

Great. I think it might be time for a couple more of my tablets.

Everyone is feeling rather fragile the next morning, and Lola has to head back to London early, so I stand at the door to see her off.

"Last night was fun, wasn't it darling? And Eddie can definitely play that piano. Wasn't Alfie sweet, dancing the night away?"

We both smile.

"I had such a lovely time, as usual, and I've got gorgeous new frocks too—top result. I'll call you when I've seen Magda. But are you sure, about the earrings?"

"Yes, we need the money, and Helena did say I should sell the necklace. I'll get it out of the bank. Dennis says he'll drive me in next week, and then Eddie will bring them to you in town when he has his meeting, and you can show them to your auction person."

"You're probably right darling. I'll ask around but I'm pretty sure Pippa is the woman to talk to for this kind of thing. They'll probably be worth much more now you've got a matching set."

"Whatever they're worth will mean I can borrow less from the bank, so it's all good."

"Yes, but—"

"Lola."

"Yes, okay. I wish we'd found more treasures though."

"What did you have in mind, an Elizabethan costume with a bejewelled ruff?"

She laughs.

"Something like that."

"I think that only happens in films Lola. This was never that kind of house. It was all making do and mending in those days, posh clothes were expensive. When they'd finished with them, they gave them to the poor, or to the servants to cut down and make into something else. I'm surprised we found so much, to be honest. I thought it would be a load of old tat."

"Well you were wrong darling, and I was right. As usual."

She starts to drive down the lane, as Bertie comes out and waves.

"Came to say good-bye earlier, and I felt quite a pang. I'm very fond of that girl."

"Me too Bertie."

"Glad she got rid of the tray chap. Not strong enough to handle a girl like her."

"I was just going to make some more coffee. Would you like one?"

"Yes please my dear. Need a hand?"

"No thanks Bertie, I'm fine. I'm feeling much better today actually."

It's the last week of the school holidays and the boys are getting bored. They always go a tad *Lord of the Flies* towards the end of the summer break, and this year is no exception. Alfie and Tom fill balloons with water and drop them on Ben and Dan to pay them back for taking the ladder away while they were up in the tree house. And Dan puts mashed potato in Ben's Wellies for some reason best known to himself, so Ben retaliates by drawing thick black eyebrows and a twirly moustache on Dan while he's asleep, which only comes off with a great deal of soap and scrubbing. In the end I have to go into a major meltdown and send everyone to their rooms, to avoid anyone else ending up with a plaster cast when I've only just got mine off. I'm still on crutches, but the hospital said everything has healed very well and I should be back on my feet properly in a couple of weeks. They've given me more painkillers, but I'm rationing myself now, so things aren't quite so foggy.

Pete collects the boys on Friday, and the house seems very quiet without them, but it sounds like they're having fun and that's the main thing. By all accounts pizza and ice cream are featuring heavily on the menu, and he took them to a local swimming pool yesterday, so I think our little chat may have hit a nerve, thank God. The heat wave is continuing, so I have an early supper with Bertie and Celia on Sunday evening, sitting out on the terrace to make the most of the sea breeze. Eddie's out surfing, but bounds back at around eight, looking thrilled.

"You'll never guess what: Sam just called and he's got a booking for me. I'll be part of a lineup at a few festivals and a big event in London. I have to leave tomorrow, isn't that amazing?"

"That's brilliant Eddie."

"Well done my boy."

"Oh Edward, I'm so pleased for you."

Bertie opens a bottle of champagne, and we toast the thrilling news. My ankle was aching earlier and I took two of my tablets, so I'm not sure I should be drinking champagne, but one glass can't hurt.

"To Eddie."

Celia and I raise our glasses as Bertie stands up.

"To new beginnings."

He raises his glass.

"And melting hearts of stone."

It turns out my tablets and a glass or two of champagne mix rather well, and instead of conking out I'm still wide awake as it starts to get dark. I wander out to talk to Bubble and Squeak and lock the chickens up for the night, which is easier said than done, when they've got the tree house as an alternative roost.

"Dennis says it's fine to leave them up there, just take the ladder away."

"Oh, right, thanks."

"I still can't really believe it."

"It's brilliant news Eddie."

"Your ankle seems better tonight."

"Yes, I think it is. It's so great not having that bloody cast on. Actually, what I'd really like is a swim."

The idea of having a swim is so heavenly I can hardly wait. Maybe I should have been having a couple of drinks every night.

"In the sea? Isn't it a bit late?"

"It's not even ten yet, and it's so hot, I'll never sleep. I think I could walk down, slowly, only don't tell Bertie, or Celia—they'll only fuss. The hospital said swimming was fine now the cast is off—I only have to use the crutches for walking."

"I think we can do better than that. Stay there."

He reappears with the wheelbarrow.

"Dennis doesn't like anyone else driving the mower. If we put some cushions in, and towels, I'll wheel you down."

"Brilliant. Could you get my swimsuit too when you get the towels? It's in the top drawer of my chest of drawers—it's navy blue."

"God knows how I'm going to get you back up. You weigh more than I thought."

"How charming."

"Sorry, I didn't mean it like that. Oh God."

"I'm deeply offended."

"What I meant to say is people weigh more than you'd think, if you're pushing them in wheelbarrows, and uphill is going to be tricky, especially in the dark. I'd hate to tip you out."

"That wouldn't be ideal."

He grins.

"I don't suppose you fancy sleeping down here, do you?"

"Sure. I took a couple of my tablets earlier, and then I forgot and had some more champagne, so I really don't care."

"Oh God, you're not going to pass out are you? Are you sure you should be swimming?"

"Yes, I am."

"Hang on and I'll come in with you."

"I can swim, Eddie."

"I know, but just in case."

"Just in case what? I'm not going out far. I'm not even going to swim, just float about."

"Sounds good to me."

The sea is wonderful. It's warm after so many days of sunshine, and perfectly flat. The tide's coming in, so I'm drifting back towards the shore, and there's a full moon.

"This was a great idea."

"I know."

He splashes me.

"I'm floating here, thank you, trying to zone out, so no splashing."

"Sorry."

And then suddenly he kisses me.

"Oh God, I'm so sorry."

"Stop saying 'sorry,' Eddie."

"Sorry."

He kisses me again.

"I've been wanting to do that for weeks."

Bloody hell.

"Ever since I got here really."

"Eddie, do you think anyone can see us?"

"I bloody hope not."

"So do I."

"Your carriage awaits madam, or rather your barrow."

"I'm sure I can walk back up, if we walk slowly."

He smiles.

"Let's see how we go. Back up to the house and a nice hot bath, wash all the salt off?"

"You read my mind."

"See if you can read mine."

At some point during the night we agree not to talk.

"If we start saying anything out loud, the spell will be broken and it will all get overwhelming, with aunts and uncles and boys, so let's just, well, not talk?"

He smiles, and kisses my foot.

"Not talking sounds good to me."

"I should probably head off to my room soon."

"Sure. Not yet though."

"No, not yet."

* * *

When I go downstairs for breakfast, he's already sitting at the table. I feel like I'm in some sort of dream and any minute I'll wake up.

"I'm all packed. Aunt Celia woke me at eight, with a coffee."

"That was kind of her."

"Delightful, particularly since I slept so well. Tea?"

"Yes please."

"This is just like when I was first sent off to school. It's all rather terrifying. I'm not even sure where the first gig is. But I'll be back, as soon as I can."

"Okay."

"I won't come back and find someone else is playing the piano, will I?"

"Not unless Alfie turns out to be musical, no. I'm pretty sure you're safe with Dan and Ben."

"Edward, I've put your bag in your car, and Ivy and Dennis have come to say good-bye."

"Thanks, Aunt Celia. Right, I better be off then."

We walk across the hall and he kisses me on the cheek, and then he kisses Ivy and Celia and shakes hands with Bertie and Dennis.

"Thank you, again. For everything."

He turns to me.

"This has been a wonderful summer."

Oh God, he's so young.

"Say good-bye to the boys for me, and Bubble and Squeak, and the hens, particularly Gertie."

He gets into the car and we all stand waving as he drives down the lane.

* * *

Bloody hell. I'm not sure I can even begin to work out what I feel about all of this. I'll call Lola later, but first I think I need to get some sleep. Ivy and Dennis head towards the kitchen with Celia as I follow Bertie into the library.

"I think I might go up for a nap, Bertie. Have you had breakfast?"

"Yes, I had mine earlier, with Celia. Did you have a nice swim?"

"Sorry?"

Oh God.

"Helena and I used to go down for a late swim quite often, when we were younger. Sea's warm enough this time of year. Wouldn't try it any later in the year if I were you, not unless you want to get frostbite. Celia was asleep, but I was watching a late film, heard you coming back up to the house. Kept a low profile, thought it was best."

"Right."

"Do you fancy a drop of something to soften the departure and speed him on his way?"

"Yes please."

"Good for you. Definite sparkle in your eyes this morning. Told you a bit of gallivanting would do you good. I'll just go and get some ice."

"Polly put the kettle on."

"Bertie will be back in a minute Betty. Be quiet."

"Bugger. Bugger. Bugger."

My feelings exactly.

CHAPTER EIGHT

A Good Year for the Roses

September to December

Tea Roses

Arriving on the tea clippers bound for Europe in the late 1800s with their highly prized cargos of tea, many of these roses have scents which are reminiscent of fresh tea leaves, or have hints of fruit, pepper, and cloves. With elegant buds and pointed reddish leaves, they need shelter and gentle pruning. Notable varieties include Gloire de Dijon, a buff-pink-apricot rose with a luscious tea fragrance with undertones of fruit; Devoniensis, bred in Devonshire and also known as "The Magnolia Rose," a sumptuous cream with a heady scent; and Lady Hillingdon, an elegant old rose with apricot buds which open to a soft, creamy butterscotch, scented with overtones of Darjeeling tea.

It's the middle of September, and the boys are back at school. Ben has started at secondary and gets the bus in with Dan now. He seems to have settled in well, no doubt helped by the fact that Ella is in the same class as him for most subjects, apart from music. She plays the piano and the flute, and Ben doesn't play anything at all, although he did go through a thankfully brief phase of wanting to learn to play the trumpet. I think Dan's quite enjoying having Ben with him. They often eat lunch together, from what I can gather, and Alfie doesn't seem to have minded Ben's departure. I think he likes not being the little brother, at least at school, and he's been having a great time working on his new project on Betty. He was trying to measure her yesterday, but she kept trying to eat his ruler, so in the end Bertie made her lie down while Alfie drew round her. She's still sulking about that. Ben has been helping him, and we now know she's a Yellow-headed Amazon, and the really bad news is they can live to be eighty. Bertie thinks he's had her for about twenty years, so we could still have sixty years to go, which is quite a long time to be told to bugger off every day.

I'm sitting on the sofa in the drawing room, writing my shopping list for tomorrow. It's nearly bath time, and Alfie will want another chapter of *Stig of the Dump*. Dan's doing his homework, and Ben's watching telly while I try to visualise what's in the fridge, a bit like that annoying game where you have to memorise all the objects on a tray and then some sod covers them with a tea towel and it turns out you can only remember four things. I better go and look properly.

"Diamonds Are Forever" trills out as I walk into the kitchen.

"How's it going darling?"

"Fine, thanks. How about you, did you see Frank?"

Lola's been having a few teething troubles with Frank, who doesn't appear to have grasped quite how much attention she requires.

"He's off the list. Too full of himself, and constantly asking me to book things for him, or get presents for people, like I was his bloody PA. Seriously darling, do I look like someone's happy helper, ready to rush round doing all the boring stuff so they don't have to?"

"Not really, no."

"Exactly. So I told him, if I wanted a job as an executive secretary, I'd have learnt fucking shorthand. How about you?"

"I don't do shorthand either."

"Heard from the Man Who Wouldn't Be King?"

This is Lola's new nickname for Eddie, after Edward VIII, for some reason best known to herself. She's also taken to calling me Wallis, presumably as a tribute to Wallis Simpson, although it's also possible she's thinking of *Wallace and Gromit*. Either way, I'm ignoring it.

"He's not enjoying Germany."

Eddie's developed a little routine over the past few weeks, where he sends me texts or random pictures of things which have amused him.

"And?"

"He sent me a picture of the supper they were given yesterday, with five different kinds of sausage. I must tell Ben never to go to Germany without backup food supplies."

"I didn't know you were looking for a pen pal Wallis."

"I like the sound of that."

"Or you could go for Friends with Benefits?"

"Definitely friends, at least I hope so. I've got no idea about the benefits—we'll have to wait and see when he's back in the country. But I'm fine with that. And whatever happens, I'm way too busy to sit around obsessing about it. I've got to finish the business plan—I'm having meetings with Bea and Mr. Stebbings, where they talk about bricks and drainage and timetables and I write things down."

"Sounds fascinating."

"In a weird way it is. And we've got Ivy's surprise birthday party next week. I've spoken to Michael on the phone now, and he sounded really excited. And then I talked to Christine, who burst into tears when I told her how much we were all looking forward to meeting her, so I'm taking that as a good sign. Mum and Celia are busy working out what food to make, and Mum's ordered a special birthday cake from the posh patisserie in Barnstaple. So I think we'll manage, and Ivy will finally get to meet her youngest grandson."

"She'll love it."

"I just hope we can keep it a secret that long. Mum and Celia are talking in code now—you'd think they were on a Special Forces mission. I've got no idea what they're going on about half the time, but I think quiche and sausage rolls might be on the menu."

"Will Bertie be making a special cocktail to commemorate the occasion?"

"I bloody hope not. The poor things won't stand a chance on top of jet lag."

By four o'clock on the day of Ivy's party the tension is starting to get to me. Celia came up with the brilliant idea of telling Ivy we've got a journalist coming to write an article about the garden, with a photographer, and Lady Bobby might be popping in for tea. So we've been cleaning and polishing all week to get the house ready, and Ivy's had her hair done and is wearing her best frock, ready for the photographs.

"It's such a shame we've got guests arriving—we could do without having to fuss round B-and-B people today. Do you think they'll want to take any photos in here Miss Molly?"

"In the kitchen? I don't think so."

"Good, because we'll want to make Lady Bobby a cup of tea and suchlike, won't we, so the kitchen will be messy."

"It's spotless Ivy."

"I made a batch of my scones earlier and we can have some of the new jam."

"Lovely."

We can add the scones to the cakes and buns and sandwiches and quiches and God knows what else Mum and Celia have got in the Tupperware boxes in their cars, waiting to be unveiled once the mystery guests arrive.

Celia comes into the kitchen, looking flushed.

"There's a car driving up the lane."

Oh God, here we go.

"It's probably the B-and-B guests Ivy. Come and help me settle them in would you?"

She drops her tea towel and heads towards the door.

"Yes, and we better be quick about it. I hope they won't want a cup of tea. I know you like to offer, but I can't be doing with it today. Not when Lady Bobby could arrive any minute."

We walk across the hall and open the front door just as the taxi stops, and the front passenger door opens. A man gets out who looks just like a younger version of Dennis, and Ivy suddenly goes very still.

"Hello Mum. Happy Birthday."

She makes a choking noise, and grips my arm as he bounds

towards us and throws his arms around her. She's still holding my arm very tightly, so he ends up sort of hugging both of us, and we all end up in tears—gentle, happy tears mostly, with a touch of proper sobbing in Ivy's case. Dennis appears from the side of the house, with Bertie and Celia and Mum, and stands dabbing his eyes with his handkerchief, with everyone else doing a fair bit of dabbing too. And then Michael stands back and Christine walks towards them and joins them in the group hug, as two rather tired-looking little boys emerge from the taxi and stand waiting to meet their gran.

Oh God. We'll all be in proper sobbing floods if this carries on much longer.

"Let's get everyone inside, shall we?"

A frantic half hour follows as we set the table in the dining room and blow up balloons. Alfie has insisted we can't have a proper birthday party without balloons, so we leave Ivy and Dennis to have a quiet moment to say hello properly, and Alfie makes friends with Joshua and Jason, with the balloons helping them get over their initial shyness. And then we all sit down and make a start on the birthday feast. Although Mum and Celia have made so many delicious things it's hard to know where to start. At one point Alfie has so much piled on his plate he starts using his empty juice glass as an extra receptacle for cheese straws.

I'm stacking plates in the dishwasher and making another pot of tea when Ivy comes into the kitchen.

"There you are. I wondered where you'd got to."

"I thought I'd get these plates out of the way."

"I wanted to say thank you."

"It was Dennis who thought of it Ivy."

"That's as may be, but you made it happen—everyone knows that. And, well, I feel so happy. I can't remember when I've ever been happier."

"So you forgive us, for the white lie about the journalist and Lady Bobby?"

"Oh yes, and that was very clever of all of you, making sure I'd had my hair done and the house was nice and tidy. You want to look your best on a day like this, don't you?"

"You certainly do."

She smiles.

"Did you see the presents they got me, and the lovely album with all the photos?"

"I did Ivy."

"And aren't the boys lovely?"

"They are."

"Our Joshua is getting so big, and he's got lovely table manners, did you see?"

"Yes, he could definitely teach Alfie a thing or two on that front."

Michael appears, looking even more like Dennis now that he's relaxed.

"Mum, the boys would like a walk, and Dad says he'll show us round, but Christine says we can't go without you."

"Off you go Ivy."

She turns to follow him, and smiles at me, and whispers "Thank you, from the bottom of my heart."

So that's me standing crying again. She's so thrilled, she doesn't even stop to rearrange the plates I've put in the dishwasher. I don't think I'll ever forget her face when she first saw him getting out of that taxi. God forbid I'm ever in the same position and haven't seen one of my boys for years. But if I ever am,

I know I'll look exactly the same when I finally get to hold him again.

"Mum, Uncle Bertie says he can't find his whistle."

"Thanks Alfie. I'll be there in a minute."

I'm guessing another round of cannoning is on the horizon. Excellent.

So how's the prodigal visit going darling?"

"Great, thanks. They're only here for a few days, Michael couldn't get more time off work, but they've invited Dennis and Ivy over for a few weeks at Christmas. Actually they spent ages online yesterday looking at flights, and they've booked them: the day after Boxing Day, for two weeks, God help me."

"And Ivy's still getting on with the daughter-in-law?"

"Yes, so miracles can happen."

"I know, and I've got more good news: Pippa finally got the report back from her experts, and she reckons an estimate of forty thousand pounds would be the right reserve to put on the necklace."

"Bloody hell Lola, that's amazing."

"I know. I wrote it all down. Apparently it's Belle Époque: rose-cut diamonds with faceted and cabochon emeralds, whatever that means. And they're of a particularly fine quality, and were probably a wedding set. I can check with another auction house just to make sure, but I know she's pretty good and she definitely wouldn't cheat you."

"I'm sure she wouldn't."

"Some of them tip off their contacts and sell stuff at a reduced price. Or they put things in the wrong sale so the price is lower. It all makes a big difference. But her idiot husband has written a screenplay and I've said I'll take a look at it, if she gets a top price, so I'm pretty sure she'll do her absolute best for you."

"Thanks Lola."

"No problem, as long as you promise to buy at least one nice thing with the money."

"A new boiler for the house would be great."

"You're absolutely hopeless."

"You won't be saying that when you don't have to wear your woolly hat next time you visit us in the middle of winter."

"True. But think of something else as well. Something fun. Any more texts?"

"Yes, he's in Switzerland now, at some festival. He's been recording cuckoo clocks and sending me little clips."

"How delightful."

"The boys are loving them."

"So everything's coming up roses then?"

"Seems like it. And thanks Lola. If they actually sell for that kind of money, it will be amazing."

"There are forms you have to fill in. I'll get her to send them to you. Speak later darling."

Ivy's understandably subdued after Michael and Christine and the boys leave, but she's got her visit to look forward to, so she throws herself into a round of what she calls a proper tidy-up and everyone else calls an almost forensic level of deep cleaning. Dennis is keeping well out of the way, and we're in the kitchen planning another trip to the cash-and-carry warehouse for more supplies, when Mum arrives, carrying her big green suitcase.

"What's in there Mum?"

"Just a few of my things."

"Are you having a clear-out?"

"You could say that. Yes, I suppose I am, and about time too because I've had enough, I really have. He made such a fuss about me making the food for Ivy's party, and well, let's just say it was the straw that broke the camel's back. We had a big row about it, and well, I've left him."

"Sorry?"

"Your father, I've packed my bag, and here I am. I thought I'd stay here for a few days, if that's alright with you, while I work out what to do. I realise you won't want me here forever—of course you won't—only I wasn't sure where else to go. I thought I could have one of the attic rooms. I know you've got B-and-B people booked in at the weekend, but I couldn't think where else to go."

She starts to cry.

Oh God.

"What's happened Mum?"

"I've finally come to my senses, that's what's happened."

"Oh Mum."

"You put the kettle on Miss Molly, and I'll take your mum upstairs. We'll put you in the front double, Marjorie—that'll be nice and quiet. You come with me dear, and we'll get you settled. Here, let me take your bag."

Bloody hell.

Over endless cups of tea and nearly a whole box of tissues it emerges that Mum wants to buy a cottage, like Celia's, so she can have a garden, and she's fed up living right by that silly golf club, and if Dad won't move, then she's moving by herself, and it's not as if money is an issue, not that she ever sees any of it. And I should ask Roger about the shares in the hotel, because she's sure he and Dad are up to something, and we've got shares too, in her name and mine, but we never see a penny, and it's about time she stood up for herself, so that's what she's going to do. Only she thinks she might have a little sleep first, because she's suddenly feeling very tired. And do I realise what she's had to put up with over the years, because most of the people at the golf club aren't very nice, you know. I give her two of my painkillers in the end, as it's the only way I can get her to calm down.

When she wakes up, she goes out in the garden, and won't speak to Dad when he calls. I remember wishing for somewhere safe to go, somewhere quiet and peaceful, when we were living in London and I was trying to work out what to do, and rather brilliantly it looks like Harrington is turning into exactly that kind of place. First Celia and now Mum have chosen us as their safe haven, so we must be doing something right. Actually, Harrington has turned out to be a pretty safe haven for me and the boys too, come to think of it. Some mornings when I wake up, I still can't quite believe we really live here. But I can't keep telling Dad she doesn't want to talk to him, so I finally get her to agree to meet him on neutral territory, which turns out to be an emergency lunch at Roger and Georgina's house tomorrow, which isn't that neutral, but never mind.

Dad is sitting in the conservatory when we arrive, and appears to have shrunk since I last saw him. He's very quiet, and I'm almost tempted to give him a hug, but I'm not sure if he'd like it, and I don't get the chance anyway, since Roger firmly sits Mum and me on the other side of the conservatory. He sits down next to Dad, and glares at me.

"Did you put her up to this?"

Mum stiffens.

"Don't be silly Roger, of course she didn't. I can make my own mind up about things."

"Well I think it's outrageous. Poor Dad has been very upset."

"I think this is between Mum and Dad, Roger, don't you? Why don't we leave them to talk?"

"When I want advice from you Molly, I'll ask for it."

"Would anyone like a sherry?"

Georgina brings in a tray with glasses and a bowl of olives, and hands each of us all a small glass of sherry. We sit sipping in silence.

God, this is awkward.

"I gather you're going ahead with the stables Molly, although why on earth you won't let us help is beyond me."

I can't quite believe this. Mum has left Dad, and all Roger wants to talk about is the bloody hotel.

"Help with what?"

He can't contain himself, and stands up.

"You know perfectly well. I happen to know Stephen tried to talk to you about it."

"You mean the plan to turn Harrington into a hub for the hotel?"

"Yes, and it's a very good idea too. There's huge potential, and we need to expand. You may not have noticed, but some of us are actually trying to run a business, a family business."

"You might be. I'm running a family, and a business."

"Quite right, Molly. And Roger, sit down and do be quiet dear. But on the subject of business, do Molly and I still have shares in the hotel Roger, because if we do, we'd like to know how many."

Roger chokes slightly, and Dad sits up a bit straighter and glares at me. Some things don't change.

"Yes, and I'd like to know when the dividends are paid."

"We don't pay dividends. We've been investing in the refurbishments, to attract new investors."

"Oh, right. Well maybe Mum and I should sell our shares to the new investors."

"Don't be ridiculous."

"I'm not, I can get Mr. Crouch to look at the paperwork. You remember Mr. Crouch, don't you Roger? You met him after Helena's funeral. He handles all the paperwork for Harrington. He's been checking the paperwork for the bank loan for me, and he was asking me if I have any shares."

"Well tell him to mind his own business. This is a private family matter."

"But I thought you were just complaining I wasn't being businesslike. You can't have it both ways Roger. And if there are going to be any dividend payments this year, I hope you'll remember to include me and Mum this time? It's not like we want to build swimming pools or anything, but every little helps, doesn't it?"

I'm looking at the swimming pool in the back garden as I say this, and he goes even paler, so I'm guessing Mum is right, and there have been a few dividends paid out over the past years. Just not to her, or me. How absolutely bloody typical. I'm really starting to lose my temper now.

"Anything else about the business you want to talk about Roger?"

He looks uncomfortable.

"I thought not. Right, well let's go and help Georgina with lunch, and leave Mum and Dad to talk. Dad, Mum wants to buy a cottage and have a garden. You know how much she loves gardening, almost as much as you love golf, and she's never been happy in the bungalow. So if I were you, I'd get talking to an estate agent, because she's made her mind up, Dad, she really has. And a cottage doesn't seem too much to ask, does it? Not if you want someone there every night to make your supper."

Mum pats my hand.

"She's right, Henry. So it's no use you trying to tell me I'm being silly, because my mind's made up."

I beat a hasty retreat, with Georgina, who's looking rather shocked.

"Well good for Marjorie, that's what I say."

"Georgina!"

"Oh do shut up Roger. Molly, would you like another sherry?"

"Yes please Georgina."

This is getting better and better.

Mum and Dad drive me home after a strangely quiet lunch, with everyone being rather formal. Dad isn't saying much, but I think he's finally worked out Mum means it.

"I'll see you tomorrow afternoon Molly dear, I want to get back home and make sure things are nice and tidy before we get the estate agents in. I wish I'd washed the net curtains in the bathroom now. I was going to do them last week. I might give them a quick rinse-through tonight, come to think of it."

They both get out of the car to see me in, more out of habit than anything else, since they both stay standing by the car.

"Bye Mum, see you tomorrow. Bye Dad."

I kiss him on the cheek, which I don't usually do, and he seems rather pleased as Ivy appears at the door, with her arms crossed.

"Did you have a nice lunch Miss Molly?"

"Yes, thank you Ivy."

"Everything alright Marjorie?"

"Yes, thank you Ivy."

"Good."

She gives Dad a rather curt nod, and goes back into the house.

Crikey. I'd almost forgotten how scary she can be.

"Cup of tea dear?"

"Yes please Ivy."

"Did she tell him then?"

"She did Ivy."

"Good. She's a lovely woman, and it's high time she had things a bit more her own way."

"Definitely."

"I bet your brother is none too pleased."

We both smile.

It's the last week of October, and I'm putting the finishing touches to the plans and schedules and costs with Bea and Mr. Stebbings for the stables. And the gatehouse is booked right up to Christmas, so I'm spending a fair amount of my time cleaning and changing sheets. But at least we're moving in the right direction.

We're having tea on Sunday afternoon, still celebrating our success at the Village Horticultural Show yesterday, when Dennis won a gold medal for his onions, and a silver for his leeks. Ivy won gold for a jar of her pickles, and Ben won Best Autumn Tray of Vegetables. Dennis is particularly thrilled, since he beat one of his oldest rivals. The only slight cloud on the horizon is the departure of the pigs. Patrick's booked them into the local abattoir next week, and I've been dreading it, although nobody else seems to be that bothered. Typically contrary, Ben has now decided he might eat meat again, but only if it comes from a local sustainable food chain.

"So I might have some of the bacon. I haven't decided yet Mum."

"Right."

"I'm not anti-meat, just not factory farming, and using up all our resources to feed cows when people are starving."

Dan helps himself to another biscuit.

"You can't really argue with that, but just don't start going on about it all the time and turning into one of those green nutters. So not cool."

Ben nods.

"I've always liked bacon Mum."

"Yes Alfie, you have."

"And next year Uncle Patrick says we can get a lady pig and have our own piglets."

"Yes, I know, and I said we'd think about it Alfie."

"Well think about it then, because me and Tom need to know."

"I'll help Mum."

"Thanks Ben."

"I might go into farming. I'm thinking about it, so it will be good practice."

"Okay love."

"Either that, or space travel. So we can live on other planets and grow food to eat when we've finally mucked up the Earth."

"Right."

"I haven't decided."

I think on balance I'd prefer him to stay here and breed pigs and grow veg. Space travel sounds a bit on the challenging side to me, particularly given he can barely remember to take his PE kit to school on the right day. He's always leaving his coat at school too, and I can't see me getting the interplanetary shuttle to retrieve his anorak for him.

Bertie is impressed.

"Good for you my boy. Space travel. Like the sound of that. Good to have a plan. What about you Dan?"

"Something in a city, with no piglets, so I can earn loads of money and not do very much work. I'm looking at my options. Or I might stay round here. I haven't decided."

Alfie nods.

"I might do farming too, or I might be a pirate. Probably a space pirate, and then I can help Ben, when he's growing stuff."

"Right. Well I hope people who are going to be pirates and astronauts or earn lots of money living in the city still know how to clear the table?"

All three of them tut.

Bertie stands up.

"Thought I might go out on patrol, before the last of the light goes."

"Alright Bertie, but don't be long, it's getting cold. Dan, help Ben clear the table. And Alfie, let's do your reading book, shall we?"

"It's not fair. I wanted to go out with Uncle Bertie."

"We need to do your reading love, and then you can watch cartoons."

"But..."

"Or you can go up and have your bath now. You need your hair washing today, so we can do that too. Whichever you prefer."

"I'll get my book."

* * *

The light is definitely starting to fade and Bertie hasn't reappeared, so I walk down to find him while the boys watch telly. I've just had an annoying conversation with Pete about the plans for Christmas. Apparently he's so exhausted they're going on a cruise, and he won't see the boys at all.

"He's so infuriating, Bertie, I can't believe I was married to him for so long."

"He knows the price of everything and the value of nothing—that's his trouble. You're well shot of him my dear."

"It seems like so much longer than a year that we've been here now, like a whole new life."

He smiles.

"It's getting cold, Bertie. We should walk back up."

"Yes, there's a real nip in the air, reminds me of last year, when Helena was still with us."

He looks a bit wobbly, and I notice the buttons on his cardigan are done up on the wrong buttonholes as I take hold of his hand.

"Sometimes I talk to her you know—in my head obviously, I'm not going round the twist completely. Unless you think that's a sign?"

"I think it's a sign that you loved her very much and she loved you. That hasn't changed, just because she's not here anymore."

"Annoyingly she still tells me off. Thought with her being in her grave she might lay off the lectures, but not a bit of it. Bit much if you ask me. Thought we could take some flowers, next weekend?"

"Of course we can."

"I'm very lucky to have found her at all, I do know that, so many happy years. Rare to find someone who you still want to spend time with, after the initial thrill of it all wears off. Do you think young Edward might have potential on that front?"

"I don't know, Bertie. He's very young."

"So are you my dear. So are you. And age has got very little to do with it—it's character that matters. Doing things that make you happy, without upsetting too many of the people around you. That's the secret. So if you did want to move on, try something new, I wouldn't want you to feel you were stuck here."

"I'm so happy here Bertie. This is our home now. We're never going to leave, not if I can help it."

He squeezes my hand.

"If you're sure."

"I'm absolutely one hundred percent sure. Shall we walk back up now?"

"Lead the way my dear, lead the way."

It's December next week, and my Christmas list is getting completely out of control. Mum and Dad have had loads of interest in their bungalow, and are busy looking at cottages. And Mum's determined to find somewhere with a really decent garden, so Celia's accompanying them on lots of the viewings. I'm not sure Dad's that pleased, but so far he hasn't said anything.

The bank has finally approved the business loan, so we've put the plans into the local council planning department, and Mr. Stebbings is talking to his friend on the committee and seems pretty confident we'll get them approved at the next meeting. So it's all systems go on the stables. I'm half-excited and half-dreading all the upheaval. I know it's the right thing to do, but it's still a lot to take on, and I keep waking up in the middle of night in a panic. I'm hoping that will stop happening when we finally get official planning permission. Either that or I'm going to have to start having afternoon naps like Bertie. I'm so tired I fell asleep in the bath yesterday.

I remember being worried when we first came here that I'd get subsumed by domestic detail and find myself turning into one of those women who lurk in the background, self-esteem shot to pieces, but it feels like almost the opposite has happened. Our new life might involve far more laundry and bed making than any sane person would choose, but it does feel like I'm part of something here, something bigger than me and the boys. The latest in a long line of women who've lived here, doing their bit to keep everything going, and there's a wonderful sense of safety in that, like you've finally managed to get home after a long and bewildering journey.

I also feel somehow younger too, like I'm not only a mum or an ex-wife, making the best of it. I've got a new life, where I'm someone who can be relied on, who can be in charge of things. Well, most of the time. So that's encouraging. And the auction is today, and I can't wait to hear what happened. I'm about to call Lola, when she rings me, sounding excited.

"Guess."

"I can't."

"Well it didn't make the reserve price."

"So I get them back?"

"No, you fool, it made more."

"Christ."

"Quite a lot more. Thirty-two thousand pounds more in fact."

"What?"

"They sold for seventy-two thousand pounds."

"Fucking hell."

"She set it up perfectly, got two of her top Russians bidding against each other."

"Oh my God."

"I know."

"That's amazing. I'm definitely getting that new boiler now."

"I give up."

"That's incredible Lola, and I can borrow less money from the bank now, which is brilliant. Oh, I wish you were here, so we could celebrate properly. Have you decided yet, about coming down next weekend?"

"Yes please. And I'd like to bring Jimmy down at some point too—not yet, too much pressure, but we'll see. I've told him all about your garden and he's dying to see it. I've got high hopes for him."

"He's the one you met at that party, isn't he?"

"Yes. We had dinner last night. He's got great shoulders—it must be all that manual labour—and he's very into modern design, sculptural stuff."

"Like those giant Perspex balls you put in the middle of your garden to sit in, so you end up looking like a hamster?"

"No, much better than that. He's won loads of awards."

"Well as long as he doesn't try to persuade Dennis we need to flatten the kitchen garden and go sculptural, he's welcome anytime."

"They'll be off soon, won't they?"

"Yes, straight after Christmas. Ivy's nearly finished her packing already. She's so excited, and May's agreed to come in and help, so Ivy's writing her lists of instructions. God, I've just thought, I can get a new vacuum cleaner now—the old one weighs a ton."

"I'm putting the phone down now, I really can't bear it."

"Thanks Lola, really, and thank Pippa too. It will make such a difference."

"*Puzhalsta,* darling—that's Russian for 'you're welcome,' at least I think it is. It might be a brand of vodka. Actually, that's a thought, let's have a vodka cocktail party when I'm down, celebrate in style. Tell Bertie, would you."

"I'll do it right now. He can make us some of his White Russians. They're lovely. Lethal, but lovely."

"I can't wait."

It's Christmas Eve, and everyone's finally in bed. I'm putting the finishing touches to the Christmas stockings, sitting by the fire and trying to stop eating satsumas. I'm even doing a stocking for Betty against my better judgement after concerted lobbying by Alfie and Ben. We had drinks at the hotel, which went well. Dad was being very jovial, and Ivy, Dennis and Bertie seemed to enjoy themselves. Even Roger was less annoying than usual. I'm wearing Lola's dark-green skirt with black woolly tights and my new black boots and a black jersey top so I look like I'm starring as Robin Hood in the local pantomime. But I really don't care.

I finished wrapping presents for the boys last night, and they helped me wrap the last few things for everyone else this afternoon. I've gone overboard this year, to thank everyone for all their help. The boys had a great time helping me choose things at the Christmas markets, and we've made up baskets with jars of jam and homemade chocolate truffles, and lots of little treats, bath things, and sweets, and mini clockwork toys which flip over, as well as books and DVDs. I've made lavender bags too, Vicky's is in the shape of a rabbit in honour of the leaping-hare wallpaper, and Sally's got a piglet shape. And we found some terrier-shaped soaps for Celia and a key ring which barks when you press it. We got one for Betty too, so she has something to dismantle on Christmas morning. I'm just getting the last batch of mince pies out of the oven, when I hear a car arriving. This better not be someone wanting B&B, or they're going to find there's definitely no room at the inn.

Bloody hell. It's Eddie.

"Hello Molly. I was hoping I could make a last-minute booking for the gatehouse. Obviously in an ideal world I'd whisk you off somewhere glamorous, but I'm not sure the boys would like that, and anyway, I haven't got a whisk."

"Right."

"So I thought if I rented the gatehouse, that would be perfect. I won't intrude or anything, I can go over to see Celia tomorrow—she's bound to invite me for Christmas lunch and—"

"I doubt it, she's coming here."

"Oh. Right. I hadn't thought of that. Actually, can I come in? It's bloody freezing out here and this bag weighs a ton."

"Oh God, yes, sorry, of course. Go into the drawing room, the fire's still on."

"I've got you a present. Damn, I didn't mean to say that, I wanted to wait until tomorrow. I've got presents for everyone, but here, this one is for you."

He opens his bag and hands me a small parcel wrapped with what feels like quite a lot of wrapping paper.

"I wrapped it myself."

"Right."

"The paper kept tearing, so there's quite a bit of sticky tape."

"It's lovely paper. Oh, Eddie, crikey, they're beautiful, thank you so much. Really beautiful. I love silver earrings, and these are gorgeous."

"Every girl should have her own emeralds. Particularly when she had to flog her last lot."

"Oh my God, are they real?"

He tuts.

"Yes they bloody are. Platinum and emeralds. I'd hardly drive all this way just to deliver cheap rubbish, would I? What do you take me for, some sort of bounder?"

"Thank you, they're beautiful, but I can't..."

"Yes you can. The record label signed me up, with an advance and everything, and I'll be on tour, in the spring, Only as a support act, but the money they've paid me is extraordinary. So please keep them, and then if I crash and burn, which I surely will, I can come back and retrieve them."

"But—"

"But nothing. Be quiet, and put them on. They match your outfit."

"I know I look like Robin Hood but—"

"I like Robin Hood."

"That's good news."

"Will you be dressed as Maid Marion tomorrow?"

"Possibly."

He smiles.

"Is there anything to eat? I'm absolutely starving."

"You're in luck, if you like mince pies. And, well, let's just say if you can wrap it in pastry, we've got it. Follow me, and take your pick."

"Sure. But first..."

"Yes?"

"Come here."

By the time Eddie walks down to the gatehouse it's half past four on Christmas morning and I'm no longer dressed as Robin Hood. The kids will be up soon to see what Father Christmas has brought, and I'm wide awake. So I think I might spend a calming half hour with a pot of tea, looking at the latest batch of catalogues from Dennis and Celia and filling in the order forms for all the plants they want me to buy. Last year was definitely a good year for the roses, but I've got a feeling next year might turn out to be even better.

If you loved
A Good Year for the Roses . . .

Check out this popular series by Gil McNeil:

About the Author

© Jerry Bauer

GIL MCNEIL is the author of *The Beach Street Knitting Society and Yarn Club*, *Needles and Pearls*, and *Knit One Pearl One*. She lives in Kent, England, with her son.